I0695324

CONTRACTED TO THE DEVIL

A DARK MAFIA ROMANCE SERIES

AGOSTINO CRIME FAMILY BOOK ONE

DAHLIA REIGN

Copyright © 2020 Dahlia Reign, LLC

This book is a work of fiction. Names and characters are the product of the author's imagination and any resemblance to actual persons, living or dead, is entirely coincidental.

All Rights Reserved. No part of this publication may be reproduced, stored in a retrieval system, or transmitted, in any form or in any means–by electronic, mechanical, photocopying, recording or otherwise–without prior written permission.

Cover Image: Rights reserved for Dahlia Reign, LLC

Editing: Pagan Proofreading and Editing

Formatting Images: Shutterstock.com Rights Reserved

Cover Creator: 3Crows Author Services

https://www.instagram.com/3crows.author.services/

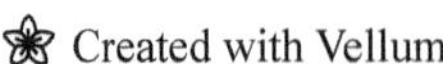 Created with Vellum

DEAR READERS,

DARK ROMANCE IS MY SPECIALTY. THEREFORE, TRIGGERS LIE WITHIN THIS BOOK. YOU HAVE BEEN WARNED. XOXO, DR.

About the Book

"My name is Lucky, but my associates know me as il Diavolo because I am the f*cking devil."

Lucifer Agostino is the eldest son of the Agostino Crime Family in New York City. Tall, dark and handsome but his blue steel eyes do little to hide the devil lurking inside. No one messes with his business, his family or something that belongs to him.

And Mirabella Moretti just so happens to be that something.

A contract between families be damned—he owns her heart and soul. But when one of Lucky's enemies sets their sights on her, they will quickly learn that the rumors of il Diavolo are true.

However, the question is.... can he save her in time?

And will Mirabella be able to survive il Diavolo without getting burned by fire and brimstone?

DEDICATION

This is for Remy...

"Tatianna and her friend are begging us to take them out. You game?" I could hear the girls' incessant giggling in the background. They were easy women and easy was boring as of late.

I needed a challenge. I preferred to work for my dinner. What primal, alpha lion wanted to have his meal cut and prepared for him? I wanted the chase before the kill. The adrenaline of that chase coursing blood through my veins. Enlivening me.

Not with Tatianna and her pack of plastic followers. They were all the same. Their daddies were rich, permitting their access to the same social circles. A false premeditation that they were my equals. They weren't. They were easy lays—a tussle between the sheets—to take the stress of business off my shoulders. Nothing more nor anything permanent. Although Tatianna was the self-imposed "boss bitch," she held no appeal. She made it desperately clear she wanted a future with me—a want I didn't share with her.

Her old man was rich and powerful because of his legitimate businesses. Mine was rich and powerful because of our illegitimate ones. And we fucking owned New York.

The girl's father was a weak man with an incomparable power, while her mother was a whore, hunting any dick to swallow that wasn't her husband's—you'd think after Tatianna walked in on me balls-deep inside the woman, she'd register my lack of feelings. Instead, she grew more desperate. More plastic surgery, more degrading sexual positions, and once even offering a threesome with her own mother. Later claiming she was drunk and only joking.

She wasn't either of those things. Merely a whore seeking a title and a powerful husband. Neither would she ever get from me.

My father, Mario Agostino, emigrated from Italy when he was just a young boy. Wanting to extend his reach to the States. He began with offering muscle and start-up funds for other immigrants to build their own lives. It amassed into an empire founded by wealth and fear. Several legitimate businesses later, and our illegal weapons distribution made us a force no one could touch.

And I was Lucifer aka "Lucky." His eldest son. The future of the Agostino family in New York. I made a name for myself, my father's hold on the city only serving to solidify my claim to the throne. My old man taught me every hard lesson. Beginning with how powerful he was and how easily it could be taken away. Never hesitating to get my hands dirty, I made sure everyone knew just who I was. Agostino or not, I was not to be fucked with.

"Yeah. I'll meet you at the club. I've got some business to attend to first." I hung up before changing my mind.

A shipment of assault rifles was unaccounted for and I needed my father's sources for intel. No one was dumb enough to steal from me— that much I was damn sure. However, this wasn't the first time a shipment had been "found" by some lesser street kid, looking for an easy payout.

It took the first one twelve hours to give me what I wanted. Twelve hours and a few less appendages. His assumption was that "finding" wasn't the same as stealing.

He wanted into my fold, wanted to become one of my foot soldiers. He was beaten, burned, and dissected for twelve hours before he confessed. His right hand losing three fingers was his undoing. I wanted to send a message that thieves weren't welcome in my crew. An eye for an eye, so to speak.

Evidently someone out there was dumb enough to test me again. They didn't call me the devil just because I looked good in red ties. No, it was the blood on my hands and the fear I instilled. They called me *il diavolo* for a reason. I was the Italian-fucking-devil.

I sent those who trespassed against me to the burning fires of hell, to suffer for their sins.

Heading down the hallway of the Agostino family compound, I searched for answers. My bedroom took up most of the second story. I had an entire wing to myself, overlooking the east end of the property. Several hundred acres stretched through rolling hills, gardens, and my mother's horse stables. In addition, I owned a penthouse in the city about forty minutes from here. It was used for business—it was also where I brought my women. No bitch was worthy of meeting my mother.

The compound offered a welcoming peace to the chaos that was our family. It was my solace away from the noise, the fast-paced streets and the danger lurking in every alleyway. Being a man in my position came with a ton of enemies. Those seeking the power and life I'd built. I was never safe. Always sleeping with one eye open, waiting for the next *puttana* who deemed themselves worthy of taking on the devil.

My four-post bed was a California king, covered in black silk sheets. All my furniture matched the shining mahogany, even my over-sized desk on the far wall. The open room worked as my bedroom, office, and dining area. Two walk-in closets were filled to the brim with suits and evening apparel. One of the many things my father instilled in me from a young age was to dress for the part you wanted in life.

I wanted to be the powerful, successful businessman people envied. Feared. I desired control in all things. My perfectly crisp suits down to my overshined shoes showed the image of a controlled man. Smart, calculated, and prepared. That was why I was Mario Agostino's protégé. The very continuance of our family legacy. Amassing power in newer and prosperous business dealings. My soldiers, my *piezans,* were the muscle under my command. Never allowing us to display a moment of weakness.

"Don't tell me you're heading out to meet Tatianna." Leaning against the doorway, my younger sister practically snarled the accusation. Had Sienna been born a boy, the girl would be giving me a run for my money.

She was too smart for her own good and just as cutthroat in her own business dealings. Her aspirations had been to get out from under the Agostino limelight and create a name for herself. She graduated top in her class and was now running a technology super company capable of more shit than my brain could understand. Surveillance, creating apps, building super computers, and insane technology that she would patent then sell to the highest bidder. A technological genius doing the dirty work for the family's background checks and pertinent intel.

If Pops wasn't so against police, she'd be working for the government.

She had beauty and brains. For as smart as she was, she was ten times more beautiful. Sharing the same Agostino blue-steel eyes the entire family possessed. The stories on the streets spoke of our cold blue-grey eyes setting men on fire with one glance. She stood tall—under my six-three height—at about five-ten and was built strong. She trained with the best of the best in the ring, precisely as I did. She worked her body and her brain just as hard as she did her business dealings. She was a powerhouse, wrapped up in a designer label, dark-chestnut hair, and an endless supply of Chanel blouses.

"If she were smart, she'd leave you alone and chase Marco. His dumbass would believe he knocked her up and marry the cunt." My sister recognized Tatianna's inner gold digger while our baby brother, Marco, was the youngest of the four Agostino children and the most likely to be killed for stupidity. He left the business to the rest of the family so he could act a fool and chase skirts.

"I fear the mere thought of that happening." I cringed, shaking my head as I adjusted my tie. Sienna chuckled and headed down the main staircase towards the marble foyer. I wasn't far behind her.

"Father wanted to see you in his office."

I nodded and kissed her forehead before she pivoted on her heel, going wherever it was that she presently spent most of her time. I could barely keep track anymore.

My father's office was in the front of the house, next to the main entrance. He always said his associates didn't need to wander his family's home when business was concluded. Especially since sometimes those meetings ended in bloodshed. It allowed his security to throw them out without much revelry. I'd seen men dragged across the white marble, red trailing behind them as they went, more times than I could count.

The foyer was left plain for that exact reason. Nothing for people to break or damage on their way out. Solid white pillars in the corners and a door opposite his office to a simple half-bath.

One of his armed guards stood outside the door as I approached. The man nodded his respect, his concentration never breaking his perusal of potential threats. Pops had a strong following of men who both feared and admired him. He ran his empire with a firm hand but treated his men well. That was why he was such a force. Those men came from nothing and could now take care of their families because of him.

The office door opened quickly, hammering into the wall with such force that both of us pulled our weapons. My senses were rattled for a second as a thin girl with silky hair as black as night ran past me, heading for the bathroom. She slammed the door behind her while two armed guards left the office to stand outside.

She was a tiny slip of a thing, looked no more than sixteen and had more hair than body. Her black locks fell to her mid-back, thick and full but appeared soft to the touch. Her sobs were muffled by the wooden barrier between us but I could hear them. Her. I could hear her.

What the hell was going on?

"This is the only deal I'm willing to make, Anthony. This is the only gift I will take to save your family." My father's voice commanded the room.

"I said you had a deal. The gift for the docks."

I recognized the answering voice. Anthony Moretti.

The Morettis were the closest ruling family in New York; though their assets were nowhere near what Pops had amassed. They often fought us for power, but they were only allotted as much as my father deemed necessary. I never understood why we didn't wipe them off the face of the earth. When I asked my old man, the response was always the same. *History.* Of which I was ignorant. If Anthony stayed in line, my father promised his family was safe to continue business.

However, the gift they just agreed on seemed to be inadequate in exchange for releasing the docks to Moretti control. Our guns and drugs all came through those ports. Handing one over to Moretti seemed like a major mistake. I would never say that to my father; his business was just that… *his.*

I was extremely confused to say the least. He had something up his sleeve—that much was certain.

Just then my phone vibrated in my pocket, alerting me to a text message. Tapping on the screen, I watched as a picture popped up: Marco, Tatianna, and her friend all cuddled up in the back of his town car. A chill went up my spine just thinking about spending the night near that cunt. No doubt she'd cling to me at the bar, begging me to take her hard and fast in the VIP lounge. She never came to the compound. I only ever fucked her in the penthouse, where my foot soldiers would remove her the moment she drained my cock.

Spinning on my heel to head to the family room, I paused in my steps when my solid body slammed into something small and fragile. The little girl had left the bathroom, her slight frame running smack-bang into me with a squeak. I grasped her elbow and tugged her upright. She was hidden by a veil of black tresses and felt even tinier in my arms. The softest pale flesh, a stark contrast to her midnight black hair. A zap of electricity flowed through our connected skin, stirring the strangest feeling in my gut.

Protection. She needed to be protected.

Her sudden gasp and erratic breathing told me she felt it too. Pulling her thick, dark hair away from her face, I watched as the tendrils fluttered through my fingers. An angel stared back at me. A small, delicate nose with a light smattering of freckles and a prominent chin, making her features both elegant and refined. She stirred the most illicit feelings inside me, both confusing and all-consuming.

My dark heart skipped a beat. The normal rush I felt when men cowered at my feet didn't compare to… this. Whatever it was.

Red-rimmed eyes brandishing fresh tears cascading over her round cherubic cheeks made me want to kill the man who put them there. She was angelic and perfect—filling me with devilish thoughts too crude for her innocence.

She was soft. She was sweet. And she was too fucking young. Barely sixteen next to my twenty-six years on this earth wreaking havoc. She was the light to my dark and soft to my hard edges. She was an innocent compared to the evil lurking under my Armani suit. But I wanted her. I wanted to protect all the good that was seeping from her delicate soul and guard it with my life. I wanted to shield her from all the evil this world had to offer, except for mine.

Our eyes locked—each equally confused and unspeaking—as we continued to hold on to each other in the foyer.

She looked back and forth between my devilish blues. I did little to hold back the desire I felt. The pulse in her elegant wrists became erratic against her deep breathing. She was just as lost in my eyes as I was in hers. While mine were often called cold and calculating, I could only imagine what people said about hers—they were breathtaking for another reason altogether. The brightest, clearest blue ocean couldn't hold a flame to her gorgeous left eye; while the other was the deepest shade of emerald green, like an exotic stone that paled in comparison to anything man-made.

Yes. She had one green and one blue eye. And it was enthralling. She was perfection. She was just too fucking young...

Before I could speak a word, her guards beckoned her to the door. A small, sad smile graced her perfect face before she turned on her heel. The two men, now holding her tightly, left without a backwards glance.

Blood boiling, I could feel the evil lurking beneath my surface, begging to be freed. The desire to rip their fucking arms from her small body and shove them down their throats became prevalent. But I remained rooted to my spot, reminding myself she was too young.

And too fucking pure for someone like me.

Anthony Moretti stepped out of my father's office, straightening his tie and nodding once before he shook hands with Pops. His smile was smug and cruel as he followed my angel, no doubt loving whatever arrangement they'd just made. There had to be more to this deal.

"The docks?" The rage burned under my skin, threatening to send me on a murderous rampage. Moretti's presence, new deals, and a little girl in tears was aggravating the devil I'd been known to become.

"We just made a deal to ensure I own that family." Slapping my shoulder, my father motioned to his office. I followed him inside the expansive room with floor-to-ceiling bookshelves, where he lowered himself into the oversized leather chair in front of his gigantic cherry-red desk. "He thinks giving me a gift will *give* him the docks. Instead, he just signed over a healthy fee and a gift to *use* our docks."

The smirk on his face matched the one I saw in the mirror every day. I was a younger version of my father, with the same brilliant mind that padded our legacy. An empire that prevailed by owning the only other family with some capacity to hurt us; a family who was now relinquishing additional fees with the promise of more to come.

"Son, let me tell you a story. Like all good stories, it starts with a girl. Thirty years ago, there was a girl who could've offered me the smallest taste, and I would have left my kingdom behind. But she was already betrothed to another."

This was interesting. My father held my mother on a pedestal, acting as if she walked on water. To hear there was another woman before her piqued my interest. But that wasn't even the most shocking part, I'd come to realize. Seeing as, thirty years ago, my old man agreed to do right by the woman he loved. He was still protecting her to this day. And this new deal would ensure he kept his word.

Story time with Mario Agostino was both enlightening and disconcerting; the tale my father spun throttled my system while anger burned my insides and begged me to unleash the devil.

It was typical for families such as ours to arrange marriages. Children garnered money, alliances, and a new sense of power. My father's past was a shock, to say the least.

Nearly an hour later, I was finally headed to meet Marco. My Mercedes pulled up to the curb outside the illustrious *Danza* nightclub. The bouncers nodded their heads in respect, opening the ropes for my immediate entrance.

The smell of sex, the heat of bodies moving, and the loud bass bombarded my senses. My manager, Nico, saw me enter and promptly stopped me in my tracks. "Boss."

Stepping into the soundproof office off the back room supply closet, I took note of Nico's expression—the man was pissed.

"I-I-I... tonight went too far."

He turned the cameras around and hit play on the video feed. And I watched the screen as Tatianna strutted her plastic ass up the stairs to the VIP lounge on the second floor with my brother and her friend in tow. The VIP waitress Natalia, who was also Nico's fiancée, was setting up my bottle service. Marco and the friend started gyrating on the leather sofa, barely paying attention to anything around them, while Natalia reached out a hand to stop Tatianna from touching my bottle of Glenfiddich. There were a few heated words exchanged between them before Natalia tucked my bottle safely behind the bar.

Natalia had worked for me for the last five years. A small thing with a tight, enticing body. Brown soulful eyes and thick brown curls overpowered that petite frame. Once a headlining dancer at another club I owned, she'd seduced my long-time friend. The guy fell hard and fast for her. To show Nico the respect he deserved, we moved Natalia to *Danza* to get her out of the strip club. She became my personal VIP waitress and acting manager. Natalia had an eye for detail, a great personality for customer service, and a good head on her shoulders.

We'd previously discussed her becoming a VIP and marketing manager for all my clubs, but she respectfully declined. She and Nico were starting a family and they'd agreed it was better for her to work less. She didn't take shit from anyone and was loyal to the core. I respected the hell out of her. She knew I hated people touching my stuff. She also knew exactly who Tatianna was. And that bitch was nothing to me.

Tatianna waited for Natalia to turn her back before she struck. The bitch snatched the waitress's ponytail; Natalia lost her footing and landed backwards onto the table. Shattered glassware and bottles be damned, she caught the slap Tatianna meant for her and quickly rose to her feet like the agile girl from the streets she was. Tatianna took a step back in fear. Only then did my idiot brother step between them.

"Is Natalia all right?" I turned to my manager.

Nico nodded, his lips curling into a proud smile.

"I know she can handle her own. My concern is for the baby."

"She's fine. She still goes to the gym and attends yoga classes, against my urging—though her pride is hurt that Marco and I wouldn't let her finish it."

My natural hard-set glare broke a little at the thought of the five-foot-nothing girl with a powerful temper and punch to match. "Remember the cartel issue at *Striscia?*"

Nico nodded, shooting a quick glance at the woman on the monitor in lustful rumination.

"He was what... three hundred and fifty? Impressive, to this day."

We had an issue with a few lone cartel men who wanted to create a fuss. Before my security could get to them to break up the fight,

Natalia had it handled. One was knocked out cold from her stripper heel, the second ran in fright, but the third was how she earned my respect. Three times her size, and yet she'd dropped his large ass on the stage and used a whip prop to choke him out. I think Nico fell in love with her that day.

"Send my apologies to Natalia. I will make this right." I pivoted on my heel, my eyes burning with anger at Tatianna's blatant disrespect. Natalia worked for *me*. In *my* club. Disrespecting my staff was a direct insult to me.

Rage boiled inside my stomach; flames threatened to seep from my pores. People in this world made assumptions that their power came from the balance in their bank account. A little girl with a rich daddy held no such privilege. The money wasn't hers, nor was the respect it had the potential to earn. This lack of consideration for everyone and everything around her further ignited the growing fire in my gut and demanded action.

"*Grazie*, boss." Nico acknowledged me with another curt nod.

Fixing my cufflinks, I headed out of the office. One of the shot girls was in the supply closet as I passed. Wobbling on a few broken boxes, she struggled to reach the top shelf.

She was a short little thing with a pear-shaped body. Sexy as fuck from the back, a small waist leading to an ass just begging to be slapped. I only employed the hottest workers in my clubs. Some—not all—I had personally tasted and held with high regard. Nico must've hired this one, though, because I hadn't seen her before.

My lean torso pinned her to the shelf, my hard cock digging into her back. With a sharp gasp of shock, she froze in panic. As I helped her off the boxes, she flipped her hair out of her face. Through the use of shy, subtle glances delivered through a pair of dark lashes, the girl tried to portray innocence. I could smell innocence, taste it on my tongue. And she was as close to being innocent as I was to being a choir boy.

No more than five-four, with a tiny midriff, thick thighs and an ass with plenty to hold. My dick was begging for reprieve from the pent-up aggression of the day. And she was the perfect target. She looked tempting in her club uniform. Images of her black thigh-high boots with diamond studded heels wrapped around my torso plagued my mind. A thin belt of diamonds looped across the narrow curve of her midsection and rested on that heart-shaped ass.

"Mr. Agostino. I'm so sorry."

As I handed her the trays, she pinned them to her delectable body. Licking my lips, I stepped closer and invaded her space. I could already feel the heat from her arousal and hear her panting in response to my sudden proximity.

"You can make it up to me."

Looking up quickly, her chocolate brown eyes did little to hide their lust.

"Do a round, then wait for my signal in VIP," I commanded. She nodded repeatedly, ducked under my arm, and practically ran for the bar.

That's right, little girl. Run. But when the devil calls, you come.

As I made my way through the crowded dance floor, clubgoers skirted past, giving me a wide berth. It was no hidden fact that I owned this club. My family may have dealt in weapons, but we had several legitimate businesses. *Danza* was a premiere nightclub in New York City. Socialites, rich kids, and the elite often partied here. For a hefty door price and the cost of expensive cocktails, you got the best DJs, the sexiest staff, and generous bartenders.

The first level housed three main bars, which were spread around the gigantic dance floor. On each side of the DJ booth, there were large roped-off areas dedicated to providing bottle service. The entire space consisted of black velvet, diamonds, and a spectacular digital light show. Elevated cages and platforms were scattered around the seating areas and dance floor for the professional dancers. The booths came with a high cost but were cheap compared to the VIP balconies.

Security stepped aside, holding the ropes open for my ascent to the second floor. Each VIP room was styled differently. Mine was black with leather furniture and a glass table in the center. Leather barstools scattered around the edges of the tinted glass, allowing the occupant to look down and yet remain hidden if someone looked up.

Several security team members roamed the stairwell, ensuring the top clients weren't disturbed. As I said, I employed not only the hottest but most obliging staff to cater to my hard-to-please clientele. Giving extras wasn't a requirement to work here; however, security ensured both anonymity for the elite customers as well as the safety of the girls willing to cater to certain requests.

As I stepped inside my room, I made note of the occupants. Marco and his plaything were making out on the sofa, ignoring everyone and everything around them. Tatianna was watching my entrance, leaning back on the plush leather sofa and sipping her cocktail. Adorned in a partially see-through black lace dress, which was two sizes too small and clearly a cheap imitation, she left nothing to the imagination.

She leered at me, sucking her straw deep into her mouth and smiling what she probably deemed seductively. Her makeup was excessive and unnecessary. Her infamous large and over-sprayed curls were pinned around her head while her pushed-up, fake breasts threatened to spill out of the dress. She'd gotten another round of lip-fillers, looking more and more like an overly tanned duck. I had no idea why women thought *this* was attractive. She had so much work done I probably wouldn't recognize her before the surgeries.

There was something sexy about a woman who owned who she was—flaws and all. Who didn't hide behind fake societal ideals. "Fake and cheap" came to mind when you looked at Tatianna. Sure, those filled lips felt great wrapped around your cock but that was it. Was it fair that I deemed her so inadequate and yet I still let her suck my dick? Probably not. But if someone was going to use her, it might as well be me. I've never given her false promises to mess with her head. The rest was on her.

"Miss me?"

She licked her lips, an eager nod her only reply.

"I heard you've been bad while you've been waiting. Now, is that true, Tatianna? Do you need to be punished?"

"Yes, sir."

Snatching her glass out of her hands, I hurled her against the wall. With a flick of my wrist, Marco and his date quickly exited the room. I paused and made myself a drink to further draw out the suspense. The room fell silent except for the ice clinking in my glass and Tatianna's labored breathing. I looked down into the crowd, the shot girl catching my eye. I nodded, and as if on cue, she started moving from the other side of the club.

Reveling in the woodsy taste and the burn of my Scotch, I swallowed, beckoning the devil before storming across the room. Tatianna cowered, trying to push herself farther into the sofa. I pointed towards the single chair and she hopped onto it at the snap of my fingers. I never lost my cool, always calm. Calculating.

As the outward manifestation of fright vibrated from her every pore, my rage boasted in merriment. She panted with need, moaning with fake gusto in a lackluster attempt to please me. The carnal desire inside me needed to purge the rage she'd elicit. Exaggerated moans, degradation, and disdain filled the room. The pungent odor of which burned my nostrils.

Shredded down the middle, her dress was discarded in tattered pieces. All that remained was her bra, her panties, and her pleas for punishment. Her body was tight and muscular from the gym. It was a shame really, since all of the plastic ruined any sex appeal she might have had. She was one of the few who enjoyed my play and could handle my dick—these were the only two reasons she was still here.

Opening the drawer, I concealed my intentions while she tried to catch a glimpse of what I was doing. The uncertainty and anticipation I could impose on her was half the fun. Moving swiftly, I had the thick leather cuffs attached to her wrists and ankles and pulled tight, before latching them to the bolts on the floor. Her arms were stretched to the sides of the chair while her legs were pulled apart, leaving her open and bare for me. Her lace panties weren't doing much to hide anything. She was pinned. With nowhere to go. Waiting to be used at my disposal. In whatever manner I saw fit.

Lust-filled eyes watched my every move, as she licked her lips expectantly. I slowly removed my suit jacket and placed it over the back of the chair. I did the same with my shirt. Standing in only black slacks, I watched her greedy eyes travel down my body. She responded with a subconscious lick of her lips at my dick. As I began tweaking her hardened nipples, she moaned—the sound irritating and nasally. I unzipped my pants to pull myself free. This action was met with yet another instinctive flick of her tongue against her moistened lips. She leaned over to take me in her mouth; however, I pulled back as the door opened and the shot girl crossed the threshold.

Tatianna's anger immediately surfaced upon realization, followed by a spluttering of profanity pelted towards the girl's entrance. I snapped my fingers, silencing her outburst and returning her attention to my throbbing cock. Her eyes followed the up-and-down motion of each stroke I self-administered. I gestured for the shot girl to take a seat on the sofa. Far enough away that my actions remained in full view but close enough to be in arm's reach at my command. I continued stroking myself in front of Tatianna, before grabbing a hold of her hair in a tight grip and tugging her head back a little harder than I needed to. I waited for her answer. She opened wide with silent approval, and I thrust inside her warm, wanton mouth.

The shot girl rose from the sofa to get a better look. Running her hands up and down her body while her gaze emitted pure desire. Tatianna gagged and choked on my thick cock which was showing no mercy to the back of her throat. There weren't many women who could withstand my size or my painful playing. It wasn't necessarily that Tatianna could handle it, but rather she had the ability to adapt to whatever I wanted. No matter how well she swallowed my cock, I wasn't interested in settling down. When the time came for an arrangement, I would do my duty; however, I had no desire to spend the rest of my life with one woman.

Without having to be asked, the shot girl placed herself on the other side of Tatianna. She reached between her thick thighs and unsnapped the black bodice she was wearing. Pulling the material over her head, she shamelessly displayed a pair of perky breasts with hardened nipples. Like a good girl, she kept on the belt and choker. She sought to entice me as she watched and traced the glistening nub between her thighs. Constricting my hold on Tatianna's throat with one hand, my assault unwavering, I used the other to pinch the shot girl's nipples.

As I removed myself completely from her blocked airway, Tatianna gasped in respite. She looked frantically between me and the naked shot girl, rattling the chains that were pinning her down. Her cheeks—once flush with passion—were now colored by outrage as the realization sunk in. She was being punished, but not pleasured. I was withholding my dick. And not actually gonna fuck her.

I snarled a grin in her direction before driving home my point. "I think this punishment fits the crime. You are nothing, Tatianna. Never come to my club again." I stepped around the recliner as Tatianna started wailing. She rattled her chains and begged me to fuck her even as I continued to increase the distance between us. Instead, I advanced on the shot girl, turned her to face the glass wall, and made quick work of dragging on a condom.

She arched her back, her thick ass jiggling in invitation. She was about a foot or so shorter than I was, forcing me to bend her in half to reach her. Gripping her wide hips, I lined up my length with her dripping-wet entrance. It was clear she didn't need any warming up. She was primed and ready for me. I took her from behind, hard and fast.

Tatianna's cries of protest mixed with the shot girl's cries of pleasure. Her big ass rippled from my repetitive assault. The echoing sound of flesh hitting flesh was so erotic my balls pulled and writhed with need. I reached around to pinch her nipples. She shook hard in reciprocation, the action sending her over the edge as she came all over my cock. With a few more hard strokes, I finished right behind her. Grunting and panting, I came hard, lost to my thoughts.

The climactic sensation lingered for what felt like eternity; however, the pleasure had nothing to do with either of these girls. The shot girl, whatever her name was, looked up at me. And yet, despite the intimacy we shared but moments ago, I didn't see her. Just the ghost of two different colored eyes staring back at me.

Bending down, the now faceless and nameless girl snapped her uniform back into place. She smiled sheepishly before leaving without a word. Still haunted, I adjusted myself and poured another Scotch, all the while Tatianna continued to snivel in the background. She hated not being the center of attention; even more so, she hated not being the center of mine. I kept telling her "no" and she kept coming back for more. And I used to let her—well, until she put her hands on Natalia. You didn't fuck with me. And you didn't fuck with what was mine. Once my suit jacket was back in place, Tatianna's pathetic whimpering turned into full-blown hysteria.

"Never come back into any of my clubs, Tatianna. We're done. You touched my employee and no one hurts what's mine. You're lucky you're a woman or you'd be dead." Without a backwards glance, I slammed the door behind me, effectively silencing her pleas. "No one is to enter this room for two more hours. My brother will be back to take her home," I ordered towards the posted security standing outside the door.

Tatianna always liked it when we played little games where I left her tied up. Well, now she would have ample time to stifle her indignation and be grateful she wasn't born with a cock between her legs. Otherwise, she wouldn't have been left breathing.

CHAPTER 1
MIRABELLA MORETTI
FIVE YEARS LATER

Manarola, on the Cinque Terre coast of Italy, was just as beautiful as the books and internet told you it would be. The streets were alive all day and night with local artists brandishing their art in various gorgeous mediums. Sitting on my balcony sipping a nice dry glass of merlot, I kept my eyes closed and listened to the water splash against the rocks. I should be happy. It should be the perfect life. Having spent the last five years in this city, I completed high school and then college with access to some of the foremost private professors and tutors.

I didn't want to sound ungrateful; however, despite all these privileges, my life was seriously lacking in culture and fun. I wasn't living. I was existing. I had a shadow looming over me 24/7, taking note of all that I did, who I interacted with, and how hard I studied. The reality of my captivity was almost startling when I discovered I was under surveillance when I visited the Church of San Lorenzo. It seemed that even the pursuit of religious solace couldn't save me from my armed guards or my overbearing brother, Gio. I was never allowed to wander the streets alone or absorb the culture Manarola had to offer. No, instead, I studied, I prayed, I spoke four different languages, and held three separate degrees.

I experienced the outside world vicariously. I would immerse myself in literary works and internally create my own images as my professors spoke of their actual travels. I was a polished young woman, about to be twenty-one, and I had amassed a ton of knowledge during my time in Italy. But I yearned for more… I needed more… I wanted to create my own experiences. I wanted to take off without my guards and wander the local villages discovering their history on my own. I wanted to meet a man who could sweep me off my feet and make me fall in love... A man who could take me away from my family obligations and was willing to create our own future—our own family.

"Let's go!" And just like that, my special moment on my private balcony was ruined. My overbearing and abrasive eldest brother started slapping the wall in annoyance.

"Keep your pants on for once, Gio. I'm ready." I drained the rest of my glass of sweet, dry, delicious nectar of the Italian gods and walked back into my private bedroom.

It was simple but perfect in my eyes. Yards of neutral-colored fabric adorned the large bed, which was centered between the glass doors of the balcony that overlooked the ocean. The shear, pale-pink curtains covering the doors flapped in the breeze, wafting the space with a pleasant aroma from the water below. It mingled with the scent of fresh flowers present on every available surface in the room. Peach, light brown, and tans everywhere. It was my own personal sanctuary that Gio was currently invading.

"You know father hates to wait," he chided, cracking his thick neck to further demonstrate his growing annoyance.

You'd think babysitting your sister in a gorgeous Italian town, inundated with beautiful women, would make him a happy man. His room was down the hall, the proximity of which allowed me to overhear each and every one of the escapades he brought home night after night. Then the following morning—like clockwork—whoever "she" was would skip into the dining room before cuddling him and eyeing me curiously while I attempted to eat my breakfast. Like it could possibly be more than a one-night stand with the handsome American-born Italian prince.

It was a new girl almost every morning at breakfast, unless they were continuing their bedroom romps while I ate and left for class. If Gio wasn't free, one of my designated shadows attended classes with me. I was never permitted to leave the compound alone or do anything other than go to class. Gio only took me out for dinner or lunch when he was tired of my whining. My newest guard wasn't around as much as I would like, and I had Gio to blame for that. I desperately tried to hide my interest in the man but my brother could read me like an open book.

"We can't have father waiting on his first visit to his only daughter in over a year," I muttered, walking past the object of my contention.

It was warmer lately and the windows were left open so that the fresh sea air could naturally cool down our two-story village home. The walls all held ornately decorated sconces and picture frames, while antique tables and light fixtures spread around to give it that expensive Old-Italian taste. The décor may've provided insight into the wealth of the individuals who owned it, but it didn't mean all of them had class. For example: my brother, who was currently grunting and scratching his balls as he followed me down the stairs.

The marble staircase descended into the living room, decorated with rich burgundy colors and dark gleaming wood accents. It really was a beautiful and amazing old home, having been in my family for decades. I just wished it wasn't also a prison for me. The sound of short heels scurrying away in the close distance drew my attention to Carmen—one of my housemaids as well as best friend. She was beyond petrified of Gio and even more so, of my father. The two men were known to degrade and talk down to the staff, so I kept her as far away from them as I could.

"There's my girl! Even more beautiful and grown than the last time I saw her." Anthony Moretti was a good-looking man for his age. Gio resembled him more than my second oldest brother, Dominic. The men all sported thick dark hair, olive skin, and heavy-lined eye lashes coated their honey brown eyes. Charming, perfectly straight, white, toothy smiles and cocky personalities wrapped up their domineering

Italian men complex. I fared more like my mother with our porcelain skin; however, she had hazel eyes.

"Daddy, it's been too long." Embracing him in an awkward hug among related strangers, I breathed in deep. He smelled just like I remembered him. When I was younger, the scent of his aftershave could keep the monsters in the closet and make the world a better place. He was my hero, my savior, the world's best daddy. But it seemed the older I got, the less like a hero he behaved. I became the property he shipped off to another country until I was of use. I was just a pawn in his business ventures.

He sent my eldest brother to lock me down in our Italian compound and refused to let my mother see her only daughter. At the ripe-old age of sixteen, a time when a girl needed her mother the most, I was sent here. Alone. If it wasn't for Carmen, who was three years my senior, I would've died of embarrassment asking my brother about periods.

I learned to be strong on my own, rely only on myself, and harbor an intensity to succeed in anything I put my mind to. I refused to be that weak and lonely girl they shunned, the one they'd expected me to be. Furthermore, I would not grow into an obedient and well-educated woman who could be sold off to a husband in exchange for power. And that's all I was to my father—his meal ticket to link a prominent family to the Moretti name. I was nothing more than a disposable pawn in their twisted game of ownership.

"How are Mother and Dominic?" I hadn't spoken to them in ages, my mother more so than my brother. Still, it wasn't nearly enough. She called me last week to warn me that my father had plans to come to Italy. I didn't believe her until I heard he was on his way. The only time he came to visit was to handle business and one could only wonder what this trip entailed.

"Your mother misses you terribly. Your brother, on the other hand, is becoming unmanageable with his lack of impulse control. I'm afraid he's stirring up some enemies and I'm running out of patience, cleaning up his messes." My father cut into his steak dinner with a less-than-pleased expression. He was getting older. The frown lines around his mouth were more prominent and his hair grayer than I remembered.

Dominic had been a loose cannon as far back as I could recall. He picked fights all through elementary school, both on and off the streets. His anger was always most palpable when he didn't get his way or, worse yet, when someone got in his business. I was about ten or eleven when boys started to pay attention to me, trying to earn my father's favor. I got cornered on my way out of school one day by three teenage boys hounding me. When I tried to leave, one of them ripped my shirt at the exact moment Dominic had come looking for me.

Dominic broke four of his bones and put the boy in a coma. The other two were lucky and had ended up with only broken noses and concussions. I became untouchable from that day forward. Oh, and as a result, Dominic got three weeks in a juvenile detention center for his actions—something my father's connections would've been able to avoid. Doing time spoke volumes about the kind of lesson my big brother needed to learn. One he failed to heed time and time again. I loved him a lot more than Gio. He'd always protected me, both from strangers and from my father, and always pushed me to want more than this family had to offer. He urged me to get out and explore the world, to fall in love and to be happy. But that didn't happen to the Moretti children.

Anthony Moretti ruled his family and his businesses with an iron fist. His children's only importance was what they could offer to help him and his empire. Dominic was a powder keg of unpredictability as well as a sadistic enforcer, used to torture those who went against the Moretti name. Gio was sent to protect me because he was too dumb and too much of a nuisance to keep back in the States. His craving for power was ill-advised and he often got himself into more trouble for it.

Then, of course, there was me—the only daughter of Anthony Moretti. For years, families craving power had attempted to pair me with their sons in an arranged marriage. To be able to suckle the power teat that was Anthony Moretti. I was kept out of his hair until he needed me. And suddenly, here he was, looking to bring me home. The Lord only knew what he could possibly want now.

"We've spared no expense for your birthday. Everyone of importance will be there to welcome you home and celebrate."

I was lost in my thoughts, awakened by the commentary on my stateside birthday celebration. Of course, the big twenty-one was coming. The day I'd dreaded for the last five years. It was time. I was being brought home and put to good use.

"I'm sure it'll be great." Attempting a convincing smile between bites of my salmon and roasted potatoes, I hid my pain. I had been living in Italy for these last five years and tomorrow I'd be heading home—to a place filled with so many childhood memories, and not all of them grand. The only thing that made me happy was the prospect of seeing my mother.

Serafina Moretti was a kind, beautiful soul. She kept the monsters back even if it meant putting herself in harm's way.

Throughout my youth, I'd overheard things about my mother's indomitable strength—a quality that allowed her to amass respect and admiration from those around her, myself included. My parents had an arranged marriage; a linking of old money from my mother's Sicilian family to the influence of the Moretti name. My father would kill for her out of both love and possessiveness. She seemed to stay only as an oath to her family. True love didn't exist for her, not towards him. I'd caught her praying one night, begging God to forgive her for hating the father of her children. She pleaded for him to return her to her one true love.

There wasn't much to love about Anthony Moretti. He earned his power and respect through sheer brute force and rash decision-making. He stole what he wanted and never apologized for it. The only person in our world with the ability to "put him in his place" was Mario Agostino. The Agostino Crime Family ruled New York and ruled the Morettis just the same. I wasn't supposed to know that my father had once challenged his biggest rival and lost. Nevertheless, I didn't know the details, nor did I care to ask.

"Well, children, I have some business to attend to." With a kiss to the top of my head, my father dropped his napkin on the table, leaving as quickly as he came.

I rubbed my temples aggressively to stave my approaching migraine, as I looked around the room. The beautiful tapestries and curtains twinkled, illuminated by the sun setting over the coast. The smell of fresh flowers hung in the air and mingled with the fragrant seasoning of my salmon dinner. A decadent meal that I no longer had the appetite for. Gio sat at the head of the table, casually tapping away at his cell phone. I had little doubt that my father's "business" was with a local girl or two. Presumably, he intended to quench his thirst before returning to the States... and his wife. Any minute now, Gio would be headed off to do just the same.

Like father, like son, I thought.

"Pack your shit, Bella. Our flight leaves tomorrow morning. *Early.* Be ready to leave by eight." Without looking up from his phone, my brother left the room. I dropped my fork on my plate, realizing the pounding in my head had increased.

"Not hungry?" A deep voice came from behind me. Alexander was one of the compound guards, and while there were many, he was defi- nitely the best looking. We'd been playing a game of "cat and mouse" for months now. The random times Gio allowed him to watch over me, there was a slight electricity in the air. Unsure what was crackling between us, I dreamed of exploring all the sensual possibilities...

"Not for food." Tossing my napkin onto the table, I slowly and seductively rose from my seat. I loved short, tight bodice dresses. My innocence may've been preserved but there were other more subtle ways of rebelling against my father. And a more scandalous dress code was just one of them. Tonight, I paired a spaghetti strap dress—short and tight to my body—with a black and purple lace robe. The sheer garment was wrapped seductively around my svelte frame. My strappy wedge heels snaked around my calf muscles, giving an arch to my back and subsequently making my perky breasts appealing in their relatively small size.

Stalking around the chair, I traced my fingertips over the ornate designs carved into the wood. As I eyed Alexander from across the room, I couldn't help but smirk at him. The wine from this afternoon had given me liquid courage and that could be dangerous. I bit into my bottom lip while his eyes watched my every move. Standing just over six feet, with a lean and muscular build, he was one of the few guards who could keep up with me on my morning runs. He was the epitome of tall, dark, and handsome and was my exact type of fantasy man.

"You're leaving tomorrow."

I nodded, disheartened by the finality of his words. We'd never had the chance to get close, and he wasn't permitted to come back to the States. Tonight seemed to be the perfect opportunity for me to shed my innocence, and he was just the man to do it. Both my father and my brother would be out enjoying their last night in Italy, so why couldn't I?

This would be the ultimate rebellion against my father. The one and only decision I'd make for myself. Consequences be damned.

He followed me down the hallway as I headed back to my room to pack. In truth, there wasn't really anything I wanted to take with me. I was certain that once I got back to New York, I'd be given an entirely new wardrobe to assert my new position. A position not much different from that of a prized horse—paraded around and auctioned off to the highest bidder. In my mind, I could leave all my belongings behind because the girl inside me now was not the girl I would be in New York. I had a job to do, and Little Miss Mirabella Moretti was heading home to fulfill her duties.

"Can you give me a hand with some of my packing?"

Alexander nodded at my request and followed me back into my room, his eyes continuously sweeping for any potential threats. Dimming the lights, to showcase the sunset peeking through the doors off my balcony, I removed the sheer cover-up to my skimpy dress and filled two glasses with a splash of merlot.

"What did you need help with?" Alexander was all business, and yet I saw the glances he gave me. I was constructed out of five-feet and six-inches of flawless porcelain skin and toned muscle. My chest— while on the smaller side—was proportional with my petite frame. In stark contrast to my pale complexion, my straight jet-black hair and mesmerizing eyes were visibly striking, or so I'd been told on more than one occasion.

I handed him the glass of wine and his eyes panicked for a moment as he realized my true intentions.

"It's our last night. I need your help making it memorable." I took a final sip of wine, before stepping closer. I placed my palms against his chest and slowly, one button at a time, began to remove his shirt.

That look in his eyes emitted a lustful foreshadowing and coated my panties with anticipation. On any other day, his expression would be locked in place, a wall of indifference. He was so controlled in all things that this mere moment made my decision that much clearer. Outside of physical attraction, I didn't feel anything for this man. But for the time being, I wanted him to take away the pain I'd likely endure at the hands of my future husband.

"Miss Moretti, please. You know the rules. I can't." Panic was radiating off him.

"You can't. But you want to. Please, Alexander. Give me this goodbye present."

Indecision flashed across his face before he made his move. His lips crashed onto mine, powerful and all-consuming. I might have been a virgin, but I had read my fair share of romance novels. A feeling of sadness took over once he caved to my demands. There was no longer an ounce of enthusiasm inside me. The gesture did nothing for me, and I felt hollow.

And, damn, was that depressing.

But, as they said, when in Rome… Or rather, in this case, in Manarola…

I was going to lose my virginity on my terms, by my own choosing. And I was choosing Alexander. I was about to be twenty-one, the legal drinking age in the States, and I was headed into the unknown. But, hell, I was going to enjoy it even if it killed me. It may not have been a romantic storybook encounter with a meet-cute. But it was something and I would make it work.

His hands roamed freely around my body, gripping my ass under my dress. Exploring, pinching, and kneading. I was desperately trying to maintain my composure and any semblance of enjoyment. His animalistic grunts were ruining the moment, and his man-handling wasn't helping. His large muscles were enticing until his movements turned aggressive. He behaved as if he owned me.

In the stories I'd read, the women described the kind of passion that bordered on pain. The whipping, the clamps, and the rough choking all sounded incredible in the heat of the moment. However, this wasn't that. This was nothing like what I'd imagined. I could only compare his clumsy, impassioned assault to that of an unskilled masseuse blindly fondling his first customer. One whose singular focus was his own enjoyment and gratification. I was quickly losing both my courage and my desire. As if on cue, and at the very moment I was about to stop him, a sound emitted from the hallway. Carmen's startled squeak could mean only one thing: my brother was home.

"Bella!" she hissed through the door in warning. Alexander jumped away as if he'd been burned.

"Fuck," he muttered in panic as he frantically looked around the room for a way out. As he suspected, there was none. "We can't be seen together. It's too early. It'll ruin everything."

Too early? His words stopped me in my tracks and I froze, unable to process his meaning. It was then that I remembered I hadn't even locked the damn door…

Shit!

I hastily took note of my surroundings. The glasses were filled with wine, my cover-up was missing, and Alexander was in my room. Alone. The outcome was obvious. He was dead—there was no question about that. And I was about to be scolded like a disobedient child. Or worse yet, my virtue would be questioned before I even had a chance to give it away. Unable to risk any further delay, I quickly combined the contents of the two wine glasses into one. Next, I flung open my suitcase and filled it to capacity with whatever I could grab in arm's reach.

There was a box of books, by the fireplace, that I was planning to donate to the local library. Pointing to it, I hoped that we could share an unspoken understanding. However, the idiot took way too long to figure out what I was trying to tell him. Finally, Alexander picked up the oversized box right as Gio swung the door open. Pretending as though I hadn't noticed his intrusion, I continued packing things into my suitcase. Alexander grabbed a few more books from the shelf and added them to the box. His face was shielded by an expressionless mask. Empty and impenetrable. Presumably not knowing what else to do, he kept dutifully adding to the box.

"What the fuck is going on here?"

I jumped at the anger in my brother's voice, even though I expected it. He should've been long gone into town already. I had no clue why he was back so soon.

"What do you mean? I'm packing?" I tried to sound innocent and confused, even though my neck burned red hot.

"Why the fuck are you in here with the door closed?" He challenged Alexander with a sneer. Something seemed *off*. It was odd, the way my bodyguard didn't appear the least bit shaken by my brother's insinuations. It was almost as though Alexander was far more concerned about Gio's inopportune timing than about the repercussions of his actions.

Strange.

"My balcony is open. A gust of wind must've knocked the bedroom door shut. And he's packing the books to take to the library for me. Honestly, Gio, you know me better than that. Besides, in case you didn't notice, the door wasn't even locked." I feigned outrage and annoyance, which seemed to calm his rage… at least momentarily.

"Better be the truth or you're six feet under, motherfucker." Leaning in closer to Alexander, he waited a moment, letting the discomfort of his proximity help make his point clear before backing off. "Father wants to get drinks. Let's go."

Gio stormed from the room as quickly and as angrily as he had entered. Alexander looked unconcerned, if not amused by the exchange. Any chance I had of him taking my V-card had just passed. Yet another moment ruined by my hulking brother. Tossing a few more last-minute items into my case, I motioned for Alexander to leave, as Carmen snuck inside.

She smiled knowingly as she watched Alexander exit the room behind her. Holding my thumb and pointer finger an inch apart, I acknowledged how close we had been. Her eyes widened in response to my wordless confession. I wasn't sure if she was more shocked or proud of the idea—or maybe even a mixture of the two. Either way, I couldn't help but giggle out the door as I went to follow Gio.

Before I could even make it halfway down the hall, Carmen's hurried steps clicked after me. She was clutching my disheveled cover-up in both hands as she rapidly approached and tossed it over my shoulders. The additional clothing was meant to conceal the exposed skin that my dress certainly did not. Winking in appreciation, I wandered out of the compound and down to the car idling at the curb.

"I figured you deserved your last night to be on the town," my father said, looking all too pleased with himself. Five years and here we were—a fake happy family—all pretending I wasn't being forced to say goodbye to a place I called home. Pulling up outside a small café, we were promptly escorted to a lonely booth in the back. Just the three of us. Our security detail remained outside, spread along the streets and around the building.

I had never been inside this one before. Although, my brother was known to frequent it because it turned into a club later in the night. The interior was modestly decorated with candlelight, life-like vines trailing numerous glass shelves that showcased their wine options. My father, obviously unconcerned about my aversion to sweet white wines, quickly ordered the most expensive option for the table.

I blocked out the conversation between my father and brother, too lost in my own thoughts of what America would offer for me to care. As expected, they were formulating their plans to expand the Moretti empire. They all but forgot I was at the table until the topic of my birthday plans arose. No expense was to be spared for the event in an effort to show me off and appease the other wealthy families. All the most influential business partners and their snobby daughters would be in attendance.

Great!

"It's imperative that it's a perfect reintroduction of you to all of New York, my dear. It's of the utmost importance that you shine. And with your mother's gorgeous looks, you will shine indeed. I need that sweet, submissive daughter of mine from earlier years. Not this outspoken woman who meets with her security detail, alone and behind closed doors."

My brother, the little prick that he was, had thrown me under the bus. No doubt they were questioning my virtue.

"Gio ignored my numerous attempts to take my books to the local library for donation. I was out of time with tomorrow's departure, therefore Alexander did it."

My brother's eyes snapped in my direction.

"You were the reason she was alone with a man? A man who clearly desires her youth, beauty, and innocence?" My father's anger spiked to an all-time high, making Gio squirm in his seat. "And how many times have you been the cause of your sister's unruly behavior?"

"I-I, Father, I protected her with my life. Alexander was vetted by me and your head of security. His intentions are good. He is her protector." Gio began to sweat, concerned about the way the conversation was being steered. Although it was true that my father bestowed a great deal of pressure on him to keep me safe, I just wanted a loving older brother. Not the cruel bastard I was stuck with.

"Her virtue will need to be confirmed intact. I assume I have nothing to worry about?"

Gio shook his head.

"Confirmed? What?"

Ignoring my question entirely, they continued their conversation about their plans back home.

"Daddy. Confirmed?" I repeated, slightly louder this time. He slammed his fist onto the table, startling me and causing me to spill my wine on the red tablecloth.

"Goddamn it, Mirabella! I am talking business with your brother! What the hell have those nuns been teaching you?" he seethed, breathing heavy pants of fire.

I hung my head, not knowing how else to respond, looked at my lap, and mumbled my apologies.

"*Mio dio*, nothing! She's learned nothing!"

Once again, their conversation started back up like I wasn't present and my question went unanswered. What the hell did that even mean? How would they *confirm* my virtue and for what reason would they have to do it? None of this was sitting right in my stomach. I knew I was headed home to be their show pony for my birthday, but to what ends would they be putting me on display? And more importantly to whom?

The existence of arranged marriages in our Italian circles was no secret; some were even orchestrated at birth. If this had been true in my case and my mother knew, she would've told me over the years. No decision had been made to my knowledge. There hadn't even been orders from higher families, such as the Agostinos, that I didn't happen to hear about—one way or the other. So, why all this talk about my virtue?

The ride back to the compound was quiet as my stomach churned in fright. Without another word, I was ushered inside by security and told to finish packing. Alexander was nowhere to be found and I was smart enough to not ask anyone about him. I spent the rest of my night crying with Carmen, distraught over the loss of our friendship. Packing up the last five years of my life burned a hole through my heart. We held each other and cried ourselves to sleep.

My tears flowed over the truth of what my future held and the alliance undoubtedly planned with another family. But, most of all, they flowed for myself. I prayed my future husband was a kind and caring man—someone who would value me at his side, unlike most Italian men in our tight circle. Typically, the women raised the children and kept the homes, denied any part of the business.

I was outspoken and unruly. A challenge to anyone seeking to tame me, my new husband included.

CHAPTER 2

MIRABELLA MORETTI

I boarded the private jet the next day. It was clean and comfortable as I sat in the back, buried in my music and reading a motorcycle romance novel. The idea of a caveman-style love those men gave to their women enthralled me. They were tough and rugged. They were territorial over their possessions, but their women were their prizes. If I could only be lucky enough to find that. To find someone powerful and daring enough to stand up to my father. To take me away from the mess my family was trying to throw me into. Someone who could make grown men cry in fright. But who also loved me so deeply and passionately he would ruin me for other men.

If only that could happen for me.

I didn't have that in my future. I had whomever my father deemed worthy enough to hand over the only Moretti daughter. I was not looking forward to this party or to watching who would win that chance. It was going to be a cattle auction—my father parading me in front of all the wealthy benefactors until he chose the best contract for himself.

I was sick to my stomach over the whole idea.

I went through the motions, lost in my head, till suddenly we entered the gates of my childhood home.

It looked exactly as I remembered it five years ago. There were so many damn *green* bushes against the *green* grass, leading up to and then encasing the large red brick house. No other colors. Nothing exciting. Just a gigantic house, meant to show the money and power Anthony Moretti had amassed. The armed guards roamed the expansive lawns with their dogs, surveying for possible threats.

Gio and my father talked amongst themselves, ignoring me as usual. I was hoping my mother would've been out front to greet me.

"Your mother will meet us for lunch in the main dining hall. Go to your room. There are a few dresses that will do for now." With a simple kiss to my forehead, I was dismissed and Gio was already out of sight.

"Welcome home, Bella, and to your newest prison," I muttered to myself, heading inside the familiar compound. It smelled of heavy cleaner and was free of clutter. The atmosphere was sterile and lonely.

All of the furniture was dark wood, uncomfortable, and pristine to the eye. Antique burgundy throw rugs lined the halls and the living room screamed old wealth with no taste. It was cold and uninviting, much like everything else. A few servants I didn't recognize wandered around cleaning, mostly keeping their eyes to the ground and remaining silent. Their only interaction was a respectful nod as I passed.

Opening the door to my room, I froze. All my girly possessions were gone. The room was stark white with black furniture and little to no décor on the walls. All the pink accents, stuffed animals, and teen heartthrobs were removed and replaced with boring white! I hated white! I loved color, natural sunlight, fresh flowers, and the feeling of being free!

What the hell was this about?

Then a terrible thought hit me. They removed all my stuff years ago because they knew I'd never come back permanently. And it was all coming true. My twenty-first birthday party was going to be my coming out party. Or, more likely, my engagement party. They removed all signs of life in this room because it was all only temporary, a holding place until I was married off.

Just the thought of it made me ill. Running to the window for air, I banged my hands against it to no avail. I was locked inside, an attempt orchestrated by my father to control me under lock and key.

My breath quickened in pace and intensity until it elevated into a labored pant. I felt like the walls were caving in and I couldn't do anything to stop it. I clawed at my throat, frantically gasping for fresh air as a panic attack took hold of me. Five years ago, my world fell apart. I learned my father had indeed planned to use me to further his position. Having been shipped away not long after, I was able to create a safe little bubble where I never thought of it again. In my mind, I envisioned a world where I married for love and happiness rather than political gain or family position. What a fantastic imagination I had.

Movement just outside the window caught my attention. It was then I saw my mother walking through her garden of biblical stone figures, the place she went to pray.

Madre!

I needed the love and support only a mother could give. I ran back down the stairs and out the back door, my stiletto heels be damned. Breathing deep so as to not startle her, I found her exactly where I had expected—kneeling in prayer in the stone gazebo. The first thing I noticed was the same calming sensation I got whenever she was close to me. The second was the weight she'd lost. And sadly, she didn't have much weight to lose to begin with.

"Please, please, Lucifer. I beg you to protect my daughter from all the evil this world has to offer. Even protection against her own flesh and blood. Keep her safe and cherish her, just as your father has always watched over and protected me. She's sweet and deserves so much more than the hand she was dealt. I beg of you. Protect her with love and surround her with happiness, Lucifer." My mother was whispering her prayers, eyes closed while rocking on her knees.

Lucifer? She was praying to the devil to keep me safe? I guess it all made sense now. Whatever plans my father had, even God couldn't stop him. My angelic mother was here, praying for the devil's protection. I guess I really was screwed and there was nothing anyone could do to help me. She may not be able to save me herself, but she would do anything she could to try. Even if it meant turning her back on her religious beliefs.

And I couldn't help but think: *if you throw it out in the universe, the devil may just appear.*

"*Madre.*" I emitted the emotional cry, as the dam finally burst.

"*Neonata!*" She called out in excitement before wrapping me in her warm, loving embrace—the kind that only a mother could give. It was like all the bad in the world could be swept away by her arms clinging to me. Even in my twenties, she still called me her baby girl and it made the world right. I loved this woman more than anything.

As she held me, I couldn't help but notice that her smile was still so radiant and ageless five years later. It was as if no time had passed in the comfort of her arms. The hint of sadness behind her eyes rattled me to my core. She was a shell of the woman I had left all those years ago —as if the time apart from her daughter had broken her beyond repair. Or was it my father who had broken her?

"You're so grown. Such a beautiful young woman. Oh, my *neonata*, so precious and home! You're back home with me!" Jumping up and down, our embrace never wavering, we cried in elation. It had been too long.

A girl needed her mother and I especially needed mine. Our separation hadn't been good for either of us. She had always been my best friend, the only person who understood me.

"We have much to discuss over lunch and shopping! But my… You just… You are so gorgeous. I did one thing right in this life, giving birth to such an exquisite creature." Tucking my hair behind my ears before holding my face with her soft hands, she gently kissed my forehead, then led me back towards the house.

"What is to become of me, *Madre*? I know I was brought back for a reason." She only *played* dumb to the business around her. My father believed that women were meant to tend to the home. However, she was inquisitive and cunning; she'd know exactly what was going on without my father being the wiser.

"*Neonata*, I have done my best over the years to protect you. There are plans I cannot divulge. But understand one thing. I have prayed for *il diavolo* to protect you himself. He will keep you safe, just as his father has kept me safe for years." She kissed my forehead with a sad smile gracing her lips. Turning on her heel, she left me in the garden. Alone, with my daunting thoughts. The fresh air allowed me a moment to think... to clear my head.

Her ominous declaration had my mind reeling with the potential hell I was being forced to endure. None of this made any sense. First her weight loss and now this recent devil talk... the combination was concerning.

I promised myself many years ago that I would survive and succeed. It wasn't in me to allow anything to break me. Come what may, I would own it!

"Bella! Father needs you." Startling me from my inner pep talk, Gio was barking at me from the door.

Inside our expansive dining room, my mother cuddled up under my father's arm. Despite my health concerns and her age, she looked young and vibrant, even on the arm of a madman. She was about my height at five-six and barely one hundred twenty pounds of perfectly shaped goddess-like form. In her long, sleek designer dress, she was sexy in a demure motherly way and she looked incredible. No one could say Serafina Moretti was anything other than the epitome of sophistication and grace.

"Shopping with your mother will have to wait. I am taking you and the boys to lunch at *Vino*." Issuing his directive, the Moretti patriarch kissed my mother passionately and released her from his embrace. She scooted out of the room in a flourish of smiles and twirls of her dress. "Fortunately, that dress will barely work for lunch. Your mother will need to get you evening attire for other occasions. Now fix your face and meet us in the car."

As I stepped into the bathroom, I took in my appearance. My eyes popped with the smoky eye shadow and perfectly placed winged liner. My complexion—effortlessly smooth and even—resembled that of an impeccably poised porcelain doll. And my hair was poker straight, falling halfway down my back in soft and lustrous locks. Today I was wearing my black stiletto heels and a designer bandage dress that hugged my slight curves like a second skin. It was a low enough cut to draw attention while maintaining my respectability.

Without a second glance in my direction, Gio and my father walked out the front door to the waiting car. Heading outside, I was met by indifference—my father talking on the phone and Gio tapping away on his own screen. The tension emanating from my father filled the limo and piqued my curiosity about our hastily timed luncheon. I'd assumed my brother must be meeting us at *Vino*, and I was beyond excited to see him after all these years.

"Dominic, be there and do not be late. End of discussion." Hanging up the phone, my father sipped his Scotch with a scowl marring his tanned face.

Vino was a gorgeous restaurant in the center of New York City. It was prestigious, expensive, and known to host mafia-linked families. In fact, it was owned and operated by the Agostino Crime Family. My hackles rose with my growing curiosity over the decision to pick this location. Dominic's reluctance to attend suggested that the reason wasn't in my best interest.

We pulled up outside the restaurant where my brother stood waiting on the sidewalk, wearing his typical dress slacks, shiny black shoes, and white button-up shirt under a black suit jacket with no tie. His refusal to wear a tie marked his attempt at rebellion and severely irritated my father. In stark contrast, Gio was in a full suit, down to the matching vest that held his tie in place.

Ever the kiss ass.

The valet stepped to my door before Dominic shoved him out of the way, reached inside, and pulled me roughly out of the car and into his massive chest. He had seriously bulked up in the last five years. And yet, he still smelled like cinnamon gum and expensive cologne... like my favorite brother. I was so excited I could cry. He was so handsome and the added muscle suited him well, as did the trimmed beard he was sporting.

"Damn. *Neonata*, you're a sight for sore eyes! Who let you out of the house in that ensemble? I'll gut them!" Smiling, he raised my arm in the air, making me do a spin. Red fire crept up my neck in embarrassment as the diners inside the restaurant stared, hidden behind the tinted floor-to-ceiling windows.

"Dominic, knock it off." My father came around the limo, scolding us. However, this did not stop Dominic from whirling me around in a final spin, then bowing with a kiss to the top of my hand. He tugged me close to his side and led me into the restaurant.

"Good afternoon, Mr. Moretti. Your attendance is required in the back private lounge. May I take your drink orders for you?" The hostess at the front desk may've been speaking to my father but her eyes were glued to Gio. Flirting with her overly made-up lashes, she took their Scotch orders and my sparkling water. I tensed the moment she said private lounge, a sense of foreboding settling deep in my bones.

Feeling my apprehension, Dominic protectively tucked me closer to his side, before pulling me through the restaurant. The main dining area was modern with sleek and sharp edges. Tables were scattered around a gorgeous elevated bar in the center of the room. The private lounge was all the way in the back, with an armed guard standing at the doorway. The moment we stepped inside the private room, I took note of how the cozy warm leather booths surrounded a large dining table. At the far end was a deep cherry-red wooden bar, loaded with top-shelf spirits and a pretty blonde bartender.

Granted, what stole my breath was the man seated at the head of the table. In front of him and arranged along the multiple place settings was a display of: charcuterie boards, cheese platters, fresh breads, and dishes of olive oil. It was the classic Italian luncheon spread in our, or should I say *my*, honor. Numerous armed guards posted throughout the room, awaiting their next orders while scanning us for any sign of a threat.

I was surprised we'd yet to be searched.

"Since I'm confident that this meeting is in both of our best interests, I have opted to not strip you of your weapons. A sign of good faith and all." Speaking with a slight Italian accent, the large man with the intimidating grey-blue steel eyes motioned for us to sit.

My father sat at the opposite head of the table whereas I sat in the corner, between him and my favorite brother—whose tense posturing only served to heighten my concern. Dominic's tight hold on me told me he didn't trust the sign of good faith that was supposedly granted.

The bartender was passing out drinks when a commotion was heard outside the room. Several men were talking amongst themselves before the door swung open, their entrance taking the air out of my lungs and stalling my heart in my chest.

I remembered him. *Oh no, this couldn't be happening. I couldn't be the guest of honor for... him.*

"Lucky, please join us." Mario Agostino gestured to the seat beside him. Lucky entered the lounge with his entourage of armed men. "Anthony, you remember my son, don't you?"

My father simply nodded, watching the newcomer without a care in the world. And Lucky didn't walk; he *stalked* to his seat. A savage beast emanating pure dominance from every pore. The same eyes as his father assessed the entire room with a harrowing intensity, while my nails dug into my brother's palm without me even realizing it.

Those eyes were haunting and yet captivating in the same breath. It was like looking the devil in the eye and knowing you'd never survive the inferno. I felt like I was going to erupt into flames at any moment.

He was pure, raw sex. I may have been a virgin, but even someone as inexperienced as I was knew the man would be incredible in bed. The confidence in his stance, the intensity in his stare, and that heaven-sent physique told me so. He had to be just shy of a foot taller than me, probably near six-five. His meticulously tailored suit molded around his muscular arms, making Dominic look small. I could feel my stomach twist at just the thought of him.

His harsh gaze continued to sweep the surroundings, staring at each of my family members as though we all threatened his existence. A look of pure disgust washed over his face when his eyes took in Gio. My arrogant brother, refusing to back down from the challenge of the stare down, snarled at him. He barely glanced at my father, who was eyeing Mario over the top of his Scotch glass. Lucky skipped over me, before looking at Dominic, whose focus was on me and only me.

Then it happened.

He looked directly into my eyes and the world stopped.

A sharp intake of breath echoed in the room—I was unsure if it was his or mine—while he continued to stare. All the disgust, hostility and anger seemed to leave him as we stared deeply into each other's eyes, his melting with molten desire. My heart racing in my chest, I squirmed in my seat under his fierce scrutiny. My body pleaded and throbbed with a need for him to satiate the burn. Just then, a look of shock crossed his chiseled, handsome face.

I was used to the shock and odd expressions when people looked me in the eye. My mother tried to tell me it wasn't noticeable, but I knew she was just saying the sorts of things mothers said. I'd been made fun of since I was a kid. No one else had eyes like mine; some called them beautiful and entrancing while others said it was like looking into the twisted eyes of an unnatural being straight from hell.

So I was used to the shock but not the hellacious fire that followed it. There was no revulsion; instead, the electricity was raw and palpable. It was the same passion, curiosity, and excitement from five years ago. He looked at me like I was the world's most prized possession. I felt honored, protected, and cherished...

Meanwhile, his enemies would have probably cowered beneath his intensity. But it only made this moment between us that much better.

The fixation of his gaze, and the coy smile that proceeded, told me he hadn't forgotten me. Not because of the ugly crying I was doing that day. And not because my beauty was so profound. Right here and now, I knew he remembered one thing. Five years ago, he looked down at me and all the bad in the world melted away in that moment. The moment his cold eyes heated with lust. And the same moment he got lost in the stark contrast of mine.

I felt special.

I felt loved.

And I felt like he couldn't decide which color he preferred. Green or blue?

CHAPTER 3
LUCIFER "LUCKY" AGOSTINO

"Why are we needed at *Vino*?" Seated in the back of my limo, my right hand lifted an eyebrow in question. Apollo and I had been best friends for the last fifteen years and he was the only person I trusted with my life.

"You know Mario Agostino. A command without any explanation." My father wasn't one who often explained himself, merely demanded. Apollo and I were out checking on a few of my local connections and gaining intel on a pallet of guns.

Someone had attempted to steal one of my shipments. It was just a matter of time before I found them and made them pay for their bold disregard. I randomly changed schedules and delivery locations to keep my men on their toes. It also presented an additional obstacle for those keeping an eye on me and who're undoubtedly harboring bad intentions. I had an inkling of someone it could potentially be, and consequently that someone had wanted to destroy me since we were kids.

"Go." Apollo answered his phone on the first ring. Listening intently, I tapped out a text message. His smirk told me all I needed to know. He had a lock on our wannabe thief. "You were right."

Not looking up from my phone, I nodded. *Of course, I was.*

We had been rivals from an early age, a conflict stemming from his constant envy of what was mine. He loathed the fact that I was always one step ahead, a million bucks richer, and that much more powerful. This time when thwarting his plan, for good measure, I made sure I was *two* steps ahead. Lesson learned. If you were going to come after a man, take what was rightfully his and earn respect in doing so, you'd better succeed.

And as always, he hadn't.

"I thought as much. It's always him. I'm officially pissed. He must be dealt with." Putting my phone back into my pocket, I grinned at Apollo.

"Ultimate punishment?" Apollo cracked his knuckles in anticipation of destroying the man with his bare hands.

"No. Not yet anyway... Besides, if anyone is going to empty a clip in him, it's going to be me. Because when that son of a bitch finally goes in the ground, he'll have no doubt who put him there. Truce be damned. Pops may head the family on paper, but he knows better than to get in my way on this." I shook my head. "No. Let the man sweat. I want it known *I know.* We'll wait him out… give him just enough rope to hang himself. After all, idle hands are the devil's playground. Let's see what he does."

Apollo laughed. We had an understanding.

My father had warned me that Gio Moretti wouldn't stop plotting my downfall. He may've been in Italy for the last few years, but he was running a crew under his father's nose. And attempting to make a name for himself with terrible decisions. I knew he wanted to kill me but that would start a war, ending the Moretti lineage. You didn't fuck with the Agostinos without facing the consequences.

We pulled up outside of *Vino* in well synchronized succession. Hopping out of our respective vehicles, Apollo and four of my men followed me inside. As we entered the building, the hostess flashed a hungry smile in acknowledgement. She been recently shared amongst my men, who were enjoying themselves with a celebratory distraction. After we had closed that contract with the Russians for some military-grade weaponry, the diversion had been well-deserved. Fluttering her eyelashes, the poor delusional girl continued to gawk at me like she had a chance.

Little did she know, unlike my men, I didn't share.

Without looking in her direction, I stormed past and headed straight for the private lounge. I had no idea what awaited me on the other side of that door; still I entered unburdened by any further thoughts of hesitation. I peered around the room, the Moretti boys appearing in my direct line of sight. Though I was snarling internally with rage, my usual shielded mask of indifference dropped over my face.

Who would have thought I'd already be getting my chance to start making the infamous Gio Moretti sweat in his stupid vest? I was somewhat surprised he was back from Italy so soon after his failed attempt at destroying me. At the thought of confrontation, cowards like him would run with their tails between their legs. Especially when cornered.

"Lucky, please join us." My father gestured to the seat beside him as my men spread throughout the room. "Anthony, you remember my son, don't you?"

Anthony Moretti barely cast a glance in my direction, his only acknowledgement a begrudging nod out of respect. Gio's spine was unnaturally straight as he perched himself on the edge of his seat, unprepared for my attendance. Deliberately maintaining eye contact, I greeted him with my most sinister smile. I let my body language deliver my unspoken message.

I knew everything and I'd make him pay in blood.

As he twitched in his seat, I knew my implication had been thoroughly received. I then switched my attention to the youngest Moretti son.

Dominic and I couldn't care less about each other. He was dealing in drugs and women. Enterprises we didn't mess with. His father hated it, not understanding how much power his offspring had amassed. If Anthony had the slightest inkling about how to grow the family business, there's no doubt that he'd be following his son. Other than crossing in similar circles of the underworld, Dominic and I had an unspoken mutual agreement to ignore each other. With a nod of respect, he continued watching his brother's discomfort in amusement.

I pulled my napkin to my lap as the bartender dropped a Scotch in front of me. Opening my mouth to engage Gio in a customary pissing match, I froze. Tucked between two Moretti men, a tiny slip of dark hair sipped on a glass of sparkling water.

Five years did her damn good.

Granted, she'd been a frail, sad little sixteen-year-old girl when I saw her last. She'd grown into the quintessential embodiment of a woman. A younger version of her mother, in fact. But out of every-thing, it was those mismatched eyes that took my breath away.

"Lucky, son. This is Mirabella Moretti, daughter of Anthony and Serafina."

I couldn't forget her no matter how many years it had been since I last saw her. Her face was still etched into the recesses of my brain. In times of loneliness, I would sit back and summon her likeness, picturing those saddened eyes. Haunting me. Driving my obsessive thoughts.

"Hello. Pleasure to meet you." She was assertive and loud with her greeting. She didn't waver and she didn't look away. Which was more than I could say for many men twice her size and holding much more authority. She had blossomed from that scared, tear-stricken girl that ran from my father's office. Witnessing her confident stature and spir-ited allure firsthand, I sensed a touch of defiance burning under that intoxicating surface. The zipper of my dress slacks tightened against my growing erection, hardening under her penetrating glare.

Apollo was looking between us knowingly. That day five years ago, I learned an interesting story from my father. I ran right to the club and let Apollo in on the sordid details. My incessant questioning regarding her whereabouts over the years convinced him I had lost my mind. Her young age notwithstanding, she was "off-limits" by surname alone. And yet, I couldn't shake the Moretti girl or the interest she stirred.

"Whispers of your beauty traveled all the way from Italy. While I see the rumors are true, the details haven't done you nearly enough justice. It's a pleasure to meet you, Mirabella." My exchange with his sister, though brief, further enraged my long-time rival—I could almost see the smoke erupting from his ears. In stark contrast, Dominic sat back in his seat, appearing quite entertained by the interaction.

"Bella. Please." She glanced back at the fucker in the vest. Noting his threatening undertone, she looked to her lap as if it held all the answers she was suddenly searching for.

"How was your day, son?" My father's attempt at levity sparked my ulterior motive.

"Ah. Now that you mention it, it was quite productive actually. I got wind of a little rat problem at the docks, but it doesn't matter. You see, the thing with rats is they always leave tracks and I just so happen to have an exterminator on the books. Drove the vermin out before they even reached the merchandise." I sliced into my chicken parmigiana, my eyes never leaving Gio. Bella shifted uncomfortably, no doubt feeling the tension.

"My son, always the strategist. Always one step ahead. Did you find the source of the… infestation?" The sound of utensils cutting across dishes echoed in the room. Gio twitched nervously, beads of sweat forming at his brow. Good. I had him right where I wanted him.

"Trailed 'em right back to the nest. And the rat did what rats do best. He squealed. Next step is to eradicate the whole colony, starting with the leader of the pack."

Gio visibly flinched, taking a sip out of his rocks glass. Nodding at the blatant double-talk, my father continued eating and drinking, none the wiser that the veritable "rat king" himself was seated across from us. Apollo was straining against his metaphorical leash, a hellhound eager to lunge on my command. We'd both always enjoyed the adrenaline of the hunt as much as the final kill shot.

"Lessons must be taught. Actions must reap repercussions," Anthony added over a sip of Scotch. Gio's face soured at the sound of his father's condemnation.

"Truer words have never been spoken, Mr. Moretti. And I am a man who believes that if someone wants to tempt their fate and throw down with the devil, they must be prepared to go through hell. And I do love the heat." Continuing my lunch, I noticed Bella finished her seasoned tilapia and was now staring daggers at her brother. Gio's responding glare was pissing me off. My urge to protect her was overwhelming.

Anthony was markedly oblivious to his eldest son's indiscretions as well as the current punishment the boy was enduring. And Dominic was too disinterested to care one way or the other. Bella, on the other hand, hadn't missed a beat. She knew exactly what was happening and what her brother had done.

She shook her head, the flush of anger clearly visible on her perfectly symmetrical face while her soft porcelain skin burned hot as the color crept up her neck. "Sometimes men forget their place or have ambitions for more beyond it. Healthy competition can't always end in blood. There is no progress if you are never challenged to begin with. After all, a champion cannot be called a champion without those he's bettered." Her voice came out strong and controlled, the polar opposite of her now cowering brother.

May God strike me where I stand, her insight rattled me to the bone. She intrigued me more with each piece of information I learned of her. She was poignant, calculated, and sexy as fuck. When words escaped those full lips, people stopped and paid attention. She was in a class by herself. She was born and bred to be the strong woman I needed at my side when I became king.

Wait, what?

My father's roar of laughter shoved those thoughts aside. Anthony was annoyed with her interruption, fixing a mocking smile on his face. He held the firm, misguided belief that women should be kept out of business, a sentiment my father didn't share. The Agostino men believed their family was only as powerful as the weakest member. I would put money on my sisters, Sienna or Octavia, being able to take on the Moretti men. We had always encouraged them to take charge of their own lives.

"Well said, Bella." My father applauded her.

I couldn't stop the thunderous laughter that left me. I'd all but forgotten that everyone else was in the room, just thankful to alleviate some of the stress. Gone were my aspirations of killing her thieving snake of a brother. For a few seconds, it was just Bella and me enjoying each other's company. She intrigued me. Outside of the intel Apollo had gathered over the years, I only knew the basics about this girl. That cunning, smart mouth of hers was a comical and yet endearing surprise.

I was still confused as to why she was present at the meeting. What ulterior motive could her father have for flaunting her in front of us?

"Now onto the docks. You've been using them for the last five years at our agreed upon price. Our contract is up and a renegotiation must be had. I want an increase of twenty-five percent." My father dropped that bomb onto their laps, without a care in the world even as the room erupted with anger.

Shouting insults at nearly every direction, Gio appeared ready to leap out of his seat. Anthony completely lost his composure, standing so quickly that his chair tumbled backwards. All the guards jumped to alert, weapons cocked in unison. Sitting back in my seat, ankle to knee, I sipped my Scotch and watched the show. Apollo stepped closer to my side and nodded at my silent command. Eyes locked, he understood my expectation without it needing to be said: *Remove Bella if shit goes bad.*

"That's not what we discussed, Mario." Anthony breathed fire; while my father, unsympathetic and impassive, continued his meal as though the blaze couldn't touch him.

Raising a hand, Pops interrupted Anthony. "We discussed this five years ago. I was to get a gift for allowing you use of my docks. The waiting period is up, as are the terms of our contract." Between each conversational pause, my father took another bite from his fork, ignorant of the steam emitting from Anthony's ears—or at least pretending to be. "I never had to give you those docks, Anthony. I did it for her. You know that. Without them, your family would've lost everything. I stopped that from happening. You've turned your business around and our initial contract is over."

Silence stretched between the two of them. Dominic continued eating with one hand while the other held on to his sister. To the untrained eye, she was calm and collected. But not to me. I noticed her shaking hands. Disgust written across his face and openly unapologetic about it, Gio looked around the room. The jackass had no idea who *she* was or what my father was talking about. His family was almost destitute before we saved them. And now we wanted a new cut.

"Ten percent and the gift," Anthony snarled back, anger rolling off him in waves. That anger was the only thing keeping Gio in his seat.

"Fifteen and the gift at the party. In front of everyone."

I had no idea what they were referencing but pretended I did. To add insult to injury, I winked in response to Gio's confusion. He nearly foamed at the mouth, thinking I knew something he didn't.

Anthony wasn't pleased but relented. "Deal. If there is nothing else, we should be on our way."

Bella rose from her seat first, causing all the gentlemen, sans Gio, to rise in respect. Dominic ushered her around the table and towards the door, before practically shoving her past the remaining Moretti sibling—who seemed to be stuck mid-tantrum. As the fuckwit continued to stare with disdain, I couldn't help but allow him to poke the devil himself.

As he started to turn his back to me, I drew his attention one last time. "There is more to discuss. And soon." His mind wandering as he considered my grave implication, he sneered at my taunting smile. Full-grown men had pissed themselves—enduring the same look with less significance—and Gio wasn't much of a man.

"Bella, dear, welcome home. I will be seeing you again. Soon. To celebrate your birthday." Accompanied by a kiss to her hand, my father's comments ignited a streak of blush along her cheeks before she tucked herself behind Dominic. Though her brother appeared increasingly indifferent and detached by the surroundings, she seemed to pray that the ground would swallow her whole. In all likelihood just beginning to connect the dots, Anthony scrutinized the flagrant hostility between his boy and me.

"What is the meaning of this?" He darted his gaze at each of us and then back again as I laughed.

"Would you like to tell Daddy, or should I?" Unable—or perhaps unwilling—to stop myself from rubbing salt in the wound, I deepened his humiliation.

"Fuck you."

"No. Fuck *you*. You insignificant son of a bitch." Storming around the table, I was in his face before he could blink. Bella squeaked in surprise while Anthony stepped closer to his son and signaled his guards to back up. "Little Gio Moretti. Nothing more than a pup begging for table scraps and hoping to snatch 'em off the counter when he thinks no one's looking. Pay attention to how the big dogs, how the alpha, conducts his business and maybe next time your rat will get the shipment schedule right."

"What? Son, is this true?" Anthony grabbed Gio's jacket and tugged him out of my face. Clearly, the Moretti patriarch had no clue what his idiot son had been up to. In truth, he didn't know much about either of his boys.

If the little bitch wanted to dance with the devil, I was ready and waiting. I had smoked men for less, emptied the entire clip—*click, click, click*—before kicking up the spilt blood to temper my boredom. That was why Bella's comments on "healthy competition" had hit so close to home. If I was complacent, it meant bad things for those who crossed me. And right now, Gio Moretti was at the top of that list.

"You fucking idiot! My apologies, Lucky. I will deal with my son."

Gio's eyes snapped to his father's, disbelief written across his face.

"Go home with Daddy, little boy. I'll deal with you another time… with far less witnesses." Shoving him towards his father, I watched as he stumbled for a second before catching himself. "A toast to your birthday, *bella ragazza*." I kissed Bella's extended hand and smiled at her bright-red neck, enjoying the fluttering pulse my touch had inspired.

Just as Anthony was hauling his wayward son towards the door, all hell broke loose. Favoring pride over self-preservation, Gio had to have the last word. If he kept this shit up, his last words would be to *il diavolo*. Before the suicidal prick could fully draw his piece, Apollo had cold steel pressed to the boy's temple while my barrel imprinted itself in his chest. He had no chance of coming out of this alive; the reckless half-wit must have had a death wish. Bella and Anthony shouted, protesting his impulsivity and demanding he stand down.

"Fuck him! Fuck this family for their disrespect! No one should speak to us like this!" Gio waved his gun in the air, not having the balls to point it directly at my face.

"You have no clue what you're talking about. Call off your son, Anthony. Or the deal is done." My father stood to my right, amused by the situation.

"Enough! You *coglione*!" Anthony seethed, his rage directed at his son, while Gio appeared ill.

"Gio." Before I knew what she was doing, Bella stepped in front of me. I dropped my pistol immediately, while the Moretti boy's hand began to waver. "This isn't how you conduct business. Please, Gio, put the gun down."

"Yes, Gio. Listen to your sister," I prompted, and having already lowered my weapon, I motioned for Apollo to do the same.

"This isn't over, bitch." Gio's fake bravado would only nudge him closer to his death. First, he tried to fuck with my shipment and now he was putting his sister in danger. He was already dangling by a short rope and that rope continued to wrap tighter and tighter around his neck. However, I was tempted to kick the chair out from under him, having grown impatient waiting for him to strangle himself.

"Please, Gio. Let's go." Bella tugged at her brother's hand, leading him towards the exit.

My amusement quickly faded at the menacing glare he turned on her. Gio stormed out of the restaurant, leaving the rest of his family following in his destructive wake. Anthony shook hands with my father, ensuring he'd get to the bottom of his son's actions. It actually wouldn't surprise me if Anthony had something to do with it.

"No need, Anthony. Lucky handles his business ruthlessly. He will find out the transgressions your son has committed. You can count on that." The elder Moretti went rigid at the comment before nodding angrily and leaving. Dominic had already escorted Bella outside.

"Apollo, I want Antonio on her from a distance and get someone next to her."

Acknowledging my instructions with a nod, Apollo whipped out his phone. Gio wouldn't hesitate to punish her for speaking out, and neither of us would accept that possibility.

"Antonio is headed to their compound to hack into their security system. May I suggest Christopher for the personal surveillance? I've yet to meet anyone as stealthy. He's able to get in and out undetected."

Following my nod of approval, my right hand started making the calls. We had many military men on our payroll, each possessing certain skills. Bella's interference would set her in Gio's sights, and she needed to be protected.

As we headed towards the front of the restaurant, it took three of my men to hold me back from the scene before me...

He was fucking dead.

CHAPTER 4

MIRABELLA MORETTI

I was a fool for interfering. *I knew that.* Lucky's look of murder brought out a sense of indomitability in me. Although I agreed that Gio needed to pay, I feared if I didn't stop it, he'd die right in front of me. Not that I blamed Lucky after learning the details of what my brother had done. Gio was many things, but smart and cunning were not two of them. His thwarted attempt didn't surprise me one bit. Gio had always wanted things handed to him; he had never worked a day in his life. He often made stupid and rash decisions, avoiding the full consequences—if any—by being blessed with the Moretti name.

Now, here he was, messing with the eldest son of Mario Agostino. Several weeks ago, I'd overheard him talking about an incoming shipment in New York. I had no clue what any of it meant until now. He knew that Lucky had a rat in his organization that spilled details to the highest bidder. Of course, Lucky was intuitive and determined, spoiling Gio's ill-fated schemes and appearing to do so effortlessly.

My brother was foolish. Rats did one thing: they ratted. And I had no doubt that said rat was quick to give up his source and save his own skin. Silence had a much different kind of price tag and only lasted as long as it took for a finger to be broken or a gun to be raised. Where

Lucky's firm hand elicited respect and built his empire, Gio's frivolity sparked resentment and left him wanting what he hadn't earned.

Much like loyalty, respect was inspired—given freely to those who achieved it rather than exchanged for a paycheck. You could buy a crew to do your bidding, but that money only went as far as their necks. And once they were on the line, your money didn't mean anything. Lucky worked in the trenches with his men and their respect for each other was mutual. No matter how much he thought it could, no number of zeroes would do the same for my brother.

Those eyes told me all I needed to know. Screw the alliance with my family, theft was theft. You didn't take from another man without paying the consequences. And Gio believed *Daddy* would get him out of everything. My father wouldn't go against the Agostino family for such a reprehensible stunt.

Lucky was a man of his word. I'd heard the stories of Mario Agostino's eldest son and his intuitive business acumen. He was smart and savvy—murderous when it came to protecting everyone and everything that belonged to him. His eyes told those stories well, hungry for the next gory shot of adrenaline. When Gio pulled his gun, it was clear that Lucky was reveling in the chaos, practically bouncing with excitement. He was ready and willing to dish out the punishment, no matter how deadly the force. My traitorous body didn't get the memo that his deadly stare had been aimed at my brother; it hummed with anticipation, imagining what that sexy confidence could do to me and my virtue.

I wanted him to destroy my innocence and explore my body in places no other man had before. Rubbing my legs together, I tried to ease the ache between my thighs that my wild thoughts had conjured there. I wanted him to be it for me, for the arrangement to be to him and only him. To wake up wrapped in his muscular, protective arms and stare into those crazed blue-steel eyes that seemed to make promises. Promises to make me feel things no man had before.

Lucky's second-in-command had the same cold, dead stare— except his was much more serious. The two men were so alike but on the other hand so very different. Lucky's jubilant personality was on full display, even in such a dangerous predicament, while Apollo looked like he needed to murder and maim just to feel the semblance of anything at all. Lucky was enjoying the moment, while Apollo was salivating at the prospect of death itself.

Growing up in this lifestyle, I knew this was how things worked. Gio's stupidity had to be punished. With that being said, knowing the rules didn't make this any easier to watch; he was still my brother at the shit end of it. The fact that Gio resorted to pulling his gun meant he knew things were about to end badly. He had already disrespected Lucky with his attempted thievery and now with the commotion in Mario's restaurant, things didn't bode well for my impetuous brother.

"Gio." Before I knew what I was doing, I attempted to shield the idiot from the potential carnage. "This isn't how you conduct business. Please, Gio, put the gun down." Lucky and Apollo dropped their weapons almost immediately. However, their momentary regard for me gave Gio the courage to finally take aim at them.

If looks could kill, I would've erupted in flames from the look my brother gave me. I knew I shouldn't interfere, was raised not to interfere. But I didn't see anyone else stepping up to stop the madness. Lucky would've killed him or ordered Apollo to do so. Mario was amused, my father was pissed and Dominic was completely indifferent. I was making him look weak but looking weak was better than *being* dead. The minute I interceded, Apollo and Lucky yielded for my sake alone—as I had hoped they would.

"Yes, Gio. Listen to your sister." Lucky's amusement was evident and if it weren't for the sheer gravity of the consequences, I'd probably melt at the playful smile on his face.

"This isn't over, bitch." It was official. My brother was a fucking idiot! He was in a no-win, no-way-out situation. He fucked up and still couldn't learn from his mistakes. Though Lucky remained in good humor, his counterpart was frothing at the mouth.

Apollo was deranged and terrifying.

"Please, Gio. Let's go." As I tugged at my brother's hand, he slowly dropped his weapon, then exited in a huff. I could hear my father and Mario speaking while Dominic ushered me outside the room as well.

"Bella. Give him a minute to cool down." Dominic steered me to the elevated bar as Gio stormed out front. My father made pleasantries with local *made men* before joining us.

"Daddy, I'm sorry for getting involved but I couldn't watch them shoot him." I was starting to panic at the disapproving look on my father's face. I may've been his only daughter but he would punish me without any hesitation.

"My *bella ragazza,* relax. You did well. That situation got out of hand quickly. Your brother may not be thankful for it but I am. *This time.* Without you stepping between them, I don't know if your brother would've survived." His gratitude was mixed with a warning to not make interruptions a consistent thing.

Breathing a sigh of relief, I sagged against the counter. At least my father knew I was right and read the situation just as I did. Dominic handed me a large glass of merlot, sipping his Scotch. We waited at the bar for a spell. They drank their liquor lost in their thoughts, and I drank my wine like a woman dying of thirst.

What the hell was Gio thinking trying to steal from an Agostino? Holding the position of eldest son, he needed to be smart and learn how to appropriately take over after my father. He wasn't going to survive long enough if this kept up. Lucifer "Lucky" Agostino, aptly called *il diavolo,* had gotten his name when he was a teenager for his proclivity for violence. Word had gotten around during a party that a grown man had inappropriately touched his younger sister, Sienna. He gutted and maimed the guy in the center of the room. Not a single person stopped to help or report it.

"Are you leaving, *neonata*? My car is outside and I have a meeting to attend." Dominic interrupted my thoughts. I nodded and followed him outside.

While my father hopped into the limo and I said goodbye to Dominic, I watched as Gio continued to pace. I waited for Dominic's car to pass before I approached my big brother. I didn't want him mad at me. I didn't plan to overstep my bounds, but I couldn't let him be hurt, no matter how much he deserved it.

"Gio. I'm sorry, I just didn't want you to get hurt." Trying to appease my brother's turbulent mood, I stepped directly in his space. "Lucky or Apollo would've killed you right there. It was all I could think of..." I stepped back as he turned around to face me. The reflective windows of *Vino* painted a sad scene: a girl standing in heels and a designer dress, pleading with her brother for forgiveness. Just then, I caught a glimpse of Lucky. Apollo and Mario remained in the foyer, watching the spectacle unfold before them. Not wanting to have this argument with an audience, I attempted to usher Gio to the limo.

"You think it's acceptable to embarrass me and stick your nose in my business?" He yelled in my face, painfully grabbing my wrist as he tugged me closer. "Listen here, you little bitch. I put five years of my life on hold to watch over you. Father wanted to protect that little golden snatch between your legs to buy us more power. That's all you're worth. Just a piece of fucking pussy to sell to the highest bidder. Well, fuck all of you because I will be *the* boss soon."

"Gio..." I didn't get the sentence out before pain bounced across my face. His slap was so fast and so harsh I cried silently. In shock, I held onto the painful cheek he had just marked. He'd never hit me before. No one had. I refused to sob outwardly; he didn't deserve the satisfaction.

Spinning quickly, he all but tossed me into the waiting limo, stepped over my lap, and sat deep inside. Directly opposite my father. The Moretti patriarch motioned for the driver to go, appearing none the wiser to the events that had occurred just outside. My brother made himself a drink as if nothing had happened. Looking out the window, I couldn't help but smile as a lone tear ran down my cheek.

Lucky was outside the restaurant, breathing fire and shouting at our moving car while Mario and Apollo held him back. They'd seen the entire thing. Lucky saw Gio hit me and the look in his eyes was ten times fiercer than what I had witnessed in the restaurant. Earlier, he had been playing with my brother... taunting him. But now... now, this look was deadly, suggesting Gio was going to die a slow, painful, torturous death.

Pulling up to the compound, the limo barely stopped before Gio was shoving me out of the way and exiting the car. He stormed around the house to his rear apartment entrance at the back. My father had remained on the phone the entire ride home and hadn't said a word to me. Or about the bruise I could feel forming on my face. I just wanted to lie down. Heading inside towards my room, I paused when my mother stopped me on the stairs.

"Did you enjoy lunch, *neonata*?" I didn't answer and kept climbing the staircase towards her. "Was there a certain handsome gentleman there that's rendered you mute?" My dear, sweet mother seemed giddy at the prospect and I could only assume she was talking about Lucky. I'd never met a more handsome man. And in this moment, all I could think about was the pain on my face and the look on Lucky's when Gio hit me.

"Yes, *Madre*. Very handsome." Though I tried to sneak past her, she stopped my movement and brushed my hair aside, gasping at my appearance. Before she could comment, I redirected her line of thinking. "Gio made some stupid mistakes tonight, *Madre*. I tried to save him from Lucky and he wasn't very appreciative."

"*Deficiente*! Such a *scemo*! How dare he touch... such perfection? Come, let's get you cleaned up. Then I am taking you out for a girls' evening." She was so happy at the prospect of us spending time together, but I was physically and emotionally drained.

"*Madre*. Please don't be upset but can we do it tomorrow? It's been such a tiresome day. Traveling... and then this." She nodded her understanding, before bringing me to my room and running a bath for me. I grabbed my robe from the closet and walked into the bathroom.

One thing I missed most about my mother was her love of lavender. If anything went wrong, lavender was the answer. If you were stressed, had cramps or a headache, then she made lavender tea. If you had a special event you were heading to, lavender perfume was the ticket. If you were having a party at the house, fresh lavender was in all the centerpieces. Now after the day I've had, she was overloading the bath with lavender bath bombs. And I couldn't be more grateful—so grateful, in fact, that I burst into tears at the smell.

"Don't cry, *neonata*. Your brother is an idiot. There isn't a nice way to say it. For years, I've worried his rash decisions and terrible temper would get him killed. He had no right to hit you when you were just trying to protect him." Nodding, I hugged her close. "Now. Was he as handsome as his father?"

We giggled and lost ourselves in tales of the gorgeous, sexy, and enthralling Lucifer Agostino. My mother told me stories of growing up with Mario. He was her first love and best friend. Even years later that friendship remained and he still kept her under his protection. When they were younger, their dream was to run away together, voiding their arranged marriages. But as an oath to their families, they stayed and made their marriages work.

Now she considered Isabella Agostino one of her closest friends while Mario continued to keep her best interests at heart and protected her. I told her about Lucky's charisma and that even though people said his eyes were those of a deadly killer—haunting blue-steel-pools—I'd seen more than that. I told her about his look of adoration, as he hung on my every word... his shining approval, as I spoke up for my brother. I even told her about seeing the look of *il diavolo* after he witnessed my brother hit me. and the fire that burned as he fought from the sidewalk to get to the limo. To Gio. To me...

"For generations, those Agostino men have been one of a kind. They all seemed to drink their own water and have different values then most powerful Italian men. You'd be lucky to have someone like Lucky looking after you."

I nodded in agreement. He made me giddy and nervous all at the same time. He made me feel shy yet overcome with a ravenous need. He made me want to forget about the integrity of my V-card and have him punch it repeatedly, demanding he kept going until I could no longer walk. I wanted him to be my first and only. Regrettably, this was all wishful thinking. My marriage, my virtue, and my life were all being arranged for me. And after the recent events, I highly doubted the Agostinos would be on my father's list.

Over the next several days, I spent as much time as possible with my mother. Shopping for a new wardrobe, picking all the details for my party, and enjoying as much quiet time as I could. Gio seemed to disappear—no doubt afraid of my father's wrath. Now that I returned to the States, my father relaxed his control a bit and allowed me out of the house with just my guards.

Back in Italy, his men had constantly patrolled the grounds and I wasn't allowed to be anywhere alone. Even in the compound, I had guards on my tail. Whether my father had such little faith in my brother's skillset or he deemed the threats greater overseas, I couldn't be sure of his reasoning. Needless to say, at this moment, I felt free. Having two guards on my detail was as close as I could ever hope.

While I was enjoying this sudden liberation, what I wasn't enjoying was the way Lucky plagued my every waking thought and dream. The dreams were cruel in the lies they told: small children... a happy marriage with a man who loved and adored me.... If only there was some chance of that reality. He consumed my mind, my body, and my pleasure in every small task I did or even attempted to do.

I did my best to stay occupied and away from the house, trying to focus on anything other than the one thing I shouldn't. Wherever Gio was hiding, he could stay there. After finally escaping from under his thumb, I was assigned new guards, who were both silent and obedient. This meant that I got the chance to go to the gym, wander a clothing store, and go to the library. My favorite of them all? I got to take a steamy romance novel to a local café—where I was left alone with caffeine and my own harem of uncomplicated, sexy, alpha men in print.

CHAPTER 5

LUCIFER "LUCKY" AGOSTINO

"Fancy meeting you here." There was something endearing about her embarrassment at the attention I paid her. She wasn't anything like the typical women I was surrounded by. She wasn't out for gratification, for title, or for money. She was quiet, educated, fierce and humble. It was an interesting combination that I was shocked to find myself intrigued by.

"Y-yes. Hello. Nice to see you, Lucky." She quickly tucked her book away and out of sight. Her face heated brighter when she realized I saw her hiding it from me. The yellowing bruise her brother left was still somewhat visible, even under her attempt to conceal it with makeup. It made my blood boil. I felt the sudden urge to unload a few rounds… with Gio Moretti being my first and only target.

"Do you mind?" I asked, motioning for the seat at her table.

"I don't. Please sit." She pointed towards the empty seat in front of me, a shy smile on her face. Apollo sipped his latte and positioned himself behind me, intently watching the door.

"An afternoon out for coffee and a good romance novel?"

I didn't think it was possible for her to glow any hotter, but I could feel the mortification rolling off her. Her armed guard was at the table next to her, smirking at my accuracy. The poor girl probably never got any privacy—her guards tasked with knowing everything about her and watching her every move. I found the fact that she was quietly sipping coffee with a pastry and reading a book alone in my coffee shop endearing. She wasn't like any other female in our world of wealth and chaos. She may have been dressed head to toe in the finest designer clothing, but she was demure and well-versed in culture. At my gesture, her guard backed off, giving us a bit of breathing room.

"A girl sometimes needs her vices to escape from her dismal reality." Motioning towards her cup, Bella nodded. "A warm mug and the sanctuary that can be found in the pages of a good book make for a much-needed reprieve... especially from the thoughts of my birthday and engagement planning."

"You're getting married?" This was news I hadn't heard. My father kept me in the loop when it came to the Morettis, however, there had been no mention that Bella was promised to someone. "I wasn't aware your father had picked a husband."

She shook her head, and I realized she must mean that Anthony was looking to negotiate an arrangement at her upcoming party. But nothing was set in stone. Yet...

"I'm sure you have heard that I'm beyond prime marriage age. So, it's time for me to do what I was born to do... further my family's name." A moment of sadness washed over her delicate features. "I escape to a world of romance and love because that will never be in my future. But it doesn't hurt to pretend a bit."

In our world, it was true. Most didn't marry for love but for organizing the alignment of powerful families. From the rumors going around, the Fiorettis were interested in conferring with the Morettis. If that happened, I sincerely felt sorry for the poor girl. The Fioretti offspring were not only some of the ugliest sons-of-bitches, but they had the manners and civility to match. And unfortunately, a connection with them may do Anthony well. With the patriarch's extensive access to quick cash and his booming export business in Sicily, they'd be a smart choice. But as an end result, Bella would suffer a terrible fate, married to a swine and producing his heirs. One could only hope the kids shared their mother's looks...

"I've heard rumors of the Fioretti clan coming over from Sicily to help you celebrate."

Her entire delectable body shivered in disgust. I couldn't stop the laughter that bubbled at her reaction. Her cold stare slowly but surely turned to molten lava. The fire in those gorgeous mismatched eyes burned right through me and into my soul. She had a vitality deep within that made her even more desirable. Mesmerizing. She didn't fall in line with the status quo, she held her own and did so gracefully.

"They came to Manarola a few times to make introductions and the word *grotesque* doesn't do them justice. They were constantly drunk, vulgar, and beyond rude with their abhorrent antics. I've lost sleep over just the idea of being arranged with one of them."

"Understandable. Enlighten me then. What interests you in a partner?"

Her eyes glazed over with excitement. The sweetest little smile graced her lips, softening her angelic features. "I'd never presume this marriage would give me a partner. The prospects are far too old-school Italian with the ideology that women should be seen and not heard. But if the choice were mine, a 'partner' would be exactly what I'd look for. Someone who understood I wanted more than to stay home and tend to the household. That I had a passion to experience the world. Share in the success of a family business or maybe create my own business and just be happy. To be loved and cared for mutually." Her smile quickly faded. "To be frank, I know how unrealistic all of that is. I'm not ignorant of my future. I'll bear children, tend to the house, and be the face of my family allegiance."

"Why do you believe that what you want is so far-fetched? My father has instilled in us the importance of family, no matter gender. Neither my mother nor my sisters are kept in the dark about anything. They know success in both the family businesses as well as creating their own. I wouldn't be interested in arm candy with no brain. Personally, I enjoy your fire and spirit. The sophistication and the vivacity that burns bright in your eyes. Don't sell yourself short, Bella. You are a catch, and any man should consider himself lucky to be your husband."

I had no idea why I was being so open and forthcoming. I had a tendency to let people make their own assumptions of what I was thinking. With Bella, it was different. She was different. The sadness behind her eyes at the prospect of a boring existence was unmistakable. I wanted her to know that she was worthy of so much more.

"You're nothing like people say." Apollo laughed and I couldn't help but smile at her light-hearted observation. "And what do people say?" I indulged.

"*Diavolo*. You're the devil. You rule your men and your businesses with an iron fist. A take-no-prisoner attitude. You're cold and emotionless. Even at *Vino*, you showed your cutthroat approach towards protecting what's yours. That blood and gore make you feel alive; it's like rejuvenation for you. Although, what I find funniest is the description of how men can see the face of death in your eyes... hollow and looking right back at them. But to me, your eyes give away the real you."

"And who exactly is the real me?"

"You have a passion for those you hold dearly. I watch the way your men admire and respect you because of how you treat them. You rule through fear but mostly with the use of a mutual respect. Your family, especially your mother and sisters, are what you hold most precious. You're smart, calculated and one hell of a businessman. You hold no remorse for what you do to those who mess with what's yours because you are a protector."

She had cut me open and bared my soul with her piercing gaze—as if I was lying there across the table, my guts removed and dripping— but instead it was her words that hung in the air.

I asked Octavia about Bella since they grew up somewhat together. She didn't know much. Only that Bella kept to herself, nose in a book and her eyes to the ground. The other kids would make fun of her different colored eyes. I loved them. The way they watched and ascertained everything around her. The way they saw through me to the person most didn't get to see. I loved those eyes. They made her that much more exceptional to me.

"Sorry if I overstepped, but you did ask." She was taking my silence as anger when it was quite the opposite. I found it refreshing that I didn't seem to scare her. When her mind was set on an objective, it worked quickly and with determination; this was evident in the way she had handled things at *Vino*. I respected that fire and would hate to see her end up with someone that sought to extinguish it.

"I did ask. And no, you didn't overstep. I find you interesting, Mirabella Moretti."

"Is that a good interesting or a bad interesting?"

I laughed, a real honest laugh at the slight insecurity in her voice. "It's to be determined, I suppose."

"Boss. Sorry to interrupt but if you don't want to be late to your meeting, we need to leave now." Apollo snapped us out of our little bubble.

"I won't keep you. It was nice chatting with you, Lucky."

Rising from the table, I smiled down at her in response before heading towards the door to leave. Until I couldn't take another step.

Something odd came over me. I froze—my heart pounding, mind racing, and lust pouring through my system. All this shit with her brother and father against my family was making this complicated. Before I could tell myself it was a bad idea, I quickly turned on my heel. "Will you have dinner with me?"

Apollo started laughing at the door, making an abrupt exit when I glared at him from over my shoulder.

"Um. Is that wise? With everything happening?"

We both knew better. Gio had to pay for his indiscretions and she might end up resenting how I'd have to handle it. Not to mention her father was scouting possible suitors to arrange a marriage. But I didn't give a fuck. I needed to spend more time with this girl.

Regardless of her answer, I'd be placing a call to my father. Anthony Moretti wanted an arrangement for power. His daughter married to the most instrumental family of New York... that was *power*. If my father was willing to give up his dock fees, hers would probably jump at the chance. Not to mention, it would protect the Moretti business with the force of the Agostino name behind it.

"I will make it okay. I promise you. I-I just... Do me the honor will you, Bella?" Her porcelain skin was coated in red heat that traveled from her neck up to her ears. Her hypnotic two-colored eyes were having a hard time meeting mine. She wanted to say 'yes' as badly as I wanted her to say it. "I will have my father handle yours. I promise you."

"I'd really like to," she admitted. Reaching inside my pocket, I pulled out my card. "This is my personal cell phone. Use it. Day or night. I will be in touch."

Her soft, delicate hand went to take it from me. Our fingers touched for the briefest of seconds, however, it was long enough to ignite the kindling of desire that had been flickering beneath the surface. I would not allow her father to arrange her marriage with someone else. Not until I got to know her better. For the second time, I said goodbye and left before I was tempted to take her away forever.

I hopped into the back of my waiting SUV, raising my hand to stop Apollo's characteristically inquisitive nature. Decisively, I dialed my father. If anyone would be able to handle this matter for me, it would be him. Apollo kept his mouth closed, surveilling me with both fascination and confusion. He knew me better than most. Which meant he knew this was completely outside the realm of my normal behavior.

"Son." He answered on the second ring.

"Pops. We need to have a conversation about Mirabella Moretti." Booming laughter echoed on the other end of the phone. Apollo could hear the outburst and attempted to cover his own with a none-too-convincing cough.

"I guess it's about time to discuss this gift Anthony Moretti has promised."

I'd heard them discussing the *gift* five years ago and again at *Vino*. I had no clue what they were referencing, but it was no doubt something that would bolster our family's stronghold in New York. I glanced at my watch. "I have a meeting with the Russians I can't miss. After that, I'm free."

He started chuckling again, inviting me to the house when I was done.

"I hope you know what you're getting yourself into," Apollo

muttered as soon as I hung up my phone. "Not only is she a Moretti but her older brother is a dead man. Do you think she'll sit idly by while you handle that? That there won't be any anger or resentment towards you after?"

"I know." He was right. I was in a precarious situation.

He started laughing again. "You know but you don't care. I saw it five years ago when you first met her. That entire night you were lost in your head about her. Now, all these years later, it took just one look… and you couldn't help yourself. You set her up to be at the café, didn't you?"

"Don't ask questions you know the answer to."

His laughter continued to bounce across the vehicle as he outwardly mocked my dilemma. He was the one who'd set up the additional bodyguards. I didn't feel Gio had her best interests at heart. When I was told she was dropped off at the coffee house with a poor excuse for a security detail, I couldn't help it. And, yes, I owned this coffee shop; it was one of my many legitimate businesses.

"I knew something was up when the pickup schedule changed." Today wasn't our normal day to be on this side of the city. "You think Mario will help you with this… *conquest*?"

"She isn't a conquest. She has all the makings to *essere mia regina*."

"Can she rule beside you in the underworld? Her family's kept her secluded. She may see and hear things she can't handle."

He wasn't wrong.

"I think she can handle it. I just don't like the danger I'll be putting her in. You know being with me will put a target on her back."

Apollo nodded, silent for several minutes. "Boss, look. I get it. But she's the only daughter of Anthony Moretti, and that's a target in itself. She may've been removed from the business but think about what we saw at *Vino*. Her loyalty to her brother didn't falter, even though it's clear she doesn't respect him. She didn't cower or even hesitate to stand in front of your weapon. She's smart and perceptive. She read you like an open book and responded appropriately. She may not be involved in their business but she's smart enough to run it."

"She does speak numerous languages and has several degrees. She could be a valued asset when it comes to our foreign partners. An ace up our sleeve."

Apollo nodded his agreement. She fit far too perfectly by my side to be wasted on some jackass her father would pick for her.

"My only concern is the repeated mention of the gift promised to my old man." I didn't want her to face her father's wrath if he disagreed with a proposal we'd sent over. Although, fuck him, because the Agostinos took what they wanted.

"Bella was there five years ago when you overheard the first mention of this gift?" Apollo asked.

"Yes, I believe so. Why?"

"She's the gift," Apollo declared boldly.

"*Fanculo!*" My jaw dropped. "Son of a bitch!"

How did I not know? Did she? How could she not hate me if she knew she was my gift all these years? Was there a chance she was playing games? Knowing full well what was planned, and trying to set me up?

I sincerely doubted it. She may have known she was the intended gift, but her body couldn't hide her visceral reaction to me. I couldn't imagine her being that underhanded; although, a second look into her didn't hurt either.

CHAPTER 6

LUCIFER "LUCKY" AGOSTINO

Our Russian business partners had been causing issues on the dock. The deal was for them to export their guns, which I purchased in bulk, an agreement that was mutually beneficial. However, more recently, their head guy had been withholding shipments if I wasn't present. I was far too busy for a tedious task like babysitting our cargo. So we were on our way to have a little chat with Yuri.

As we pulled up to the warehouse overlooking the docks, Yuri's Escalade was already waiting. He had four men standing outside and another four inside with him. Coming to a stop alongside the Russian's vehicle, our driver threw the SUV in park before we swung the back doors open in unison. I motioned for Apollo to follow my lead; together, we moved forward to shake hands with the Russian. The customary pungent smell of the Hudson River assaulted my senses, the familiar stench stinging my eyes. We made fast pleasantries before jumping right into business.

"I thought we had an understanding here, Yuri. Is this really how you handle business? Blatantly disregarding our deal? None of this nonsense is part of our terms."

The bastard reeked of heavy cigar smoke and Russian vodka. "Deal change." His heavy accent echoed in the warehouse.

My spine straightened and I kept my face passive, despite the annoyance boiling beneath.

"You not here. Yuri no deliver." He started speaking commands to his men in his native tongue. In that exact moment, I thought of Bella and how I needed her at my side as my queen. She would have been one hell of a secret weapon right about now.

She was multilingual in English, Spanish, Italian, and Russian. Having her around to discreetly translate would give us the upper hand and reduce the likelihood of unwanted surprises. Whatever they were muttering back and forth, the smirk on Yuri's face told me it was at my expense. Which was fine. He needed us a hell of a lot more than we needed him. His supply orders were a surplus for us; we weren't going to break the bank desolating this relationship.

"Okay. Deal's off then. Good luck with your next connection." Without another word, Apollo and I returned to the waiting vehicle while Yuri sputtered at my abruptness. Whatever angle he was playing, I wasn't about to bite. This meeting was a waste of my time and energy, both of which were too precious to be squandered on the Ruski's little Soviet power trip.

"Wait! I think is fair we meet. We meet face to face to do business."

His justification sounded more like a plea and I could've laughed at his dumbstruck expression. "To what purpose? Do you deliver the items yourself? Apollo said you weren't even here last time. Stick to the deal, Yuri. Or it's off and you will pay to void our contract." It was as simple as that. No love lost on my part. I was itching to figure out what the fuck he was up to. Whatever it was, it didn't seem to be going the way he'd hoped.

"Two more shipments. Then new deal. No face to face. Increase in price, *da*?"

Stepping forward, I watched as his men jumped to attention. I let my cold, dead stare show exactly what I was thinking of this new demand. People didn't make demands of me. *I made demands of them.* "Stick to the deal, Yuri, and we won't have any problems."

The thud of the SUV doors closing behind Apollo and me signaled my driver to floor it out of the warehouse and head towards my family home.

"I want to know why the bastard's trying to make waves all of a sudden. Find out why he thinks he can throw demands at me. Get Antonio to add security and snipers for the next shipment. I don't want any issues with the men's safety." Tapping away on my phone, I was getting angrier every second.

As we pulled up to my family compound, a strong feeling of happiness overcame me. Inside, my mother was standing in the foyer, canoodling with my father at his office door. As soon as the door shut behind me, they grew silent and turned to face me with mirrored expressions of amusement. Apollo stood next to me with a look to match. I'd never once shown interest in a female before... outside of the occasional fling. Hence, they were all loving this chance to torment me.

"I'll be in the kitchen, boss." Apollo said, chuckling under his breath.

"Come, Apollo, I'll make you and Octavia a little snack." Walking arm in arm like he was her long-lost son, my mother grabbed onto my counterpart and left us to our impromptu meeting. My father sat quietly in front of his desk with a smile painted across his face.

"You wanted to talk about Mirabella Moretti, son?" Smirking, he sat back in his oversized leather seat and motioned for me to speak.

"I asked her to dinner and I want you to work it out with Anthony Moretti to hold off on arranging her marriage." Point. Blank.

"Well, that will cause some problems since he plans to announce her engagement at her birthday party." My father knew exactly what buttons to push with me as he paused, using silence to bring about the *diavolo*. "Anthony Moretti has been making plans for years to further his status and it's always been through the use of Mirabella."

"I get she's his only daughter, but I'm surprised he hasn't attempted to set up one of the boys."

"Gio is a waste of space, who doesn't listen and is so bloodthirsty he can't see past his own greed. Dominic is too headfirst in his business. I doubt any woman would knowingly stay with him once they learn what he deals in. Therefore, Mirabella has always been *numero uno,* for Anthony's endeavors."

"Well, something needs to happen so I can take her out. I'm not saying I'm ready to settle down, but I don't want to cause any issues with your dealings either. Or potentially reduce our dock percentage to hold off his announcement."

"I won't reduce my increase on the dock. That's his problem, not mine. And you don't need to worry about Anthony Moretti getting in your way." Noticing my look of uncertainty, he offered me a cigar, shrugged at my refusal, and cut the end before lighting it.

"Remember five years ago when I told you I had history with Serafina?" He never gave me all the details, but my curt nod urged him to continue. "I'd always been contracted to marry your mother, but Serafina and I have been close friends all our lives. I was madly in love with her." He saw my apprehension when my eyes shifted to the open office door. "Your mother knows the story. You know I keep no secrets from her. Your mother and I were total strangers meeting on our wedding day. Our love grew in time, but we needed to get to know each other first. Anyway, Serafina was arranged to marry someone else as well. Not Anthony."

"But who? I always thought Senior Moretti arranged that marriage." I straightened my posture as I absorbed this new information.

"He did. *After* the first arrangement fell through, because Sal Ragetti died. Anthony Moretti chased her relentlessly, and with Sal in the ground, Senior Moretti jumped on it for his son."

It all started to fall into place. The reason my father didn't care about Anthony Moretti was because he had dirt on him.

The Ragettis were infamous on the west coast and Serafina's father probably wanted to go bicoastal with his family's influence. Setting up his daughter with the eldest son would ensure he'd be untouchable. I could remember the stories about the Ragettis I heard growing up. Although they usually stayed on the west coast, when they came to the east, there were a lot of battles amongst competing families. The Morettis being one of them as well as their biggest rival. Sal passed away under unusual circumstances during one of his trips to New York. It was considered a robbery gone wrong.

Call it what you want, but the Ragettis never believed it and that's why there was so much turmoil when they traveled here after that incident. They were friends of our family, always having respect for my father and grandfather. But it was no secret that Anthony Moretti and Sal Senior had a lot of issues. Now I realized it was because of his son's death, followed by Serafina's engagement to a Moretti right after.

"You let him on the dock and force him to pay you a fee without the least bit of concern. You act like you know his family can't touch you. Why?"

"Because I have evidence that Anthony was the cause of Sal's murder. And he knows that, upon my untimely death, *that* evidence will be sent directly to the Ragettis. It will start a war that won't end until there isn't a single Moretti heir left. Serafina will be married off after his passing and his boys will be dead and buried. So he keeps his distance from me and pays his dues. Then, at Mirabella's party, he will give me—well, *us*—his gift."

"What gift?"

Before answering my question, my father came around the desk and sat in the chair next to me. "You know Serafina and I are still close to this day. And she is best friends with your mother. I promised her long ago I'd do my best to look out for Mirabella. And the only way I can do that is to put her under my protection."

Then it all clicked. My father—the master manipulator and successful businessman, who may be as deadly as they come—had a heart of gold for those he cared about. "You're announcing the engagement of Mirabella to an Agostino."

Nodding his head, he puffed a few more times on his cigar. "See why I laughed so hard at your request? She is being arranged to marry *you*. And like her mother and I when we were younger, you two have already fallen for each other."

I wanted to be excited, but at the same time, I was petrified of everything he just said to me. Five years ago, he brought a sixteen-year-old Mirabella into his office to tell her she was being bartered to marry his son. Me, a man who was ten years her senior. No wonder she ran from the room crying. Then they sent her away to Italy, assuming she would be protected from her own father and potentially the Ragettis if Anthony ever stepped on my father's toes. But was I ready to be married?

"I made sure she got the best education, protection, and a chance at living a semblance of a normal life while she was in Italy. The only issue I had was Anthony demanding that idiot son of his to follow as protection. Though, after the way he struck her at *Vino*, I'm unsure just how protective he really was. But that's neither here nor there, *mio figlio*. I'm making good on my promise to Serafina and you get a perfect bride. Not to mention, it's one more way for me to control Anthony Moretti."

"So, not only will you have the evidence to hold over him, but his daughter will also be an Agostino. He will never be able to try to take you down."

Through the smoke of his cigar and with a cruel smile etched on his face, he nodded. "Furthermore, he knows that should I die from natural causes, my little evidentiary arrangement transfers to you and the circumstances surrounding your less-than-natural death. I covered all bases to ensure we were both protected. The Ragettis, even several generations later, will seek revenge for Sal. Any surviving Moretti heirs will be taken out. However, you marrying Bella protects her. Anthony is many things, but he isn't stupid enough to destroy his entire family. So, I'm supposing, with all things considered, that, yes, you may take Bella to dinner."

"Why didn't you tell me years ago that this was your plan? Why tell her but keep me in the dark?" I couldn't fathom how a girl like Bella at sixteen could learn I was her arranged husband and still seem pleased to see me.

"*Mi figlio.* That day, she only learned she was going to be part of the arrangement. She was merely informed I was the one to make future decisions when it came to Anthony's influence with the other families. She had no idea I was intending on choosing her husband and that it was always gonna be you. And neither did Anthony. When I signed over the docks, *that* was the deal I struck. He assumed I would set his daughter up with you or Marco, but I never made my intentions clear. I enjoy keeping that man guessing." My father hummed that last part with an affect I could only compare to that of a cat dangling a mouse.

Laughter echoed in the office at the expense of Anthony Moretti. Senior Moretti was a cold, powerful man but he raised an idiot for a son—the Moretti heir's lust for his wife, Serafina, had been so strong it drove him to make numerous mistakes throughout his life. The prime example being how the information pertaining to Sal Ragettis death ensured his continued submission. He had no choice but to remain hungry for power he would never obtain if my father had anything to do with it. And now that Gio was trying to fuck with me, I was pleased with this news.

I had no doubt Anthony would keep these secrets from his sons. His anger at Gio at the restaurant must've been real. Messing with me put Anthony in a bad place with my father yet again. Now in all of this, he must've assumed Bella would be the final gift and he would be free. Little did he know that his careless actions to obtain his bride would cost his entire family line such a major grievance. None of them, today or in the future, would ever be free from his misdeeds. Or from the Agostino hold.

After saying our goodbyes, I texted Apollo to tell him that we were staying at the compound and headed up to my bedroom. I was too tired to go back to the city and I had too much to strategize over.

I entered my room, hung my suit jacket over my desk chair, and began undoing my cufflinks. There was so much information swirling in my head. I was both elated with the prospect of Bella being mine and concerned of our impending engagement announcement. Gio still needed to be dealt with and I was curious on how Bella would feel about the aftermath.

"Apollo, reach out to Serafina in secret and arrange for me to meet Bella… alone."

Chewing on an apple as I spoke, he immediately reached for his phone in acknowledgement. "Another setup like today?" Receiving my confirmative nod, he started making calls and left the room.

I locked the bathroom door, stripped off all my clothes, and switched the shower to scalding hot. Pain was an incredible thing. To some it made them rash, weak, and prone to mistakes. Not me. I thrived in pain. Both inflicting and receiving. Bloodlust against my enemies made me feel alive. It made time slow down and my mind clear of anything other than the task of getting what I needed from whoever had it. Feeling pain made me realize I was still human. That someone… someday... could bring about my demise. That no one could outrun the angel of death. Not even the devil himself.

Stepping under the harsh spray—my palms flat against the glass and my head hung low under the scalding stream—I came alive. My dick grew hard at the realization that Mirabella Moretti was mine. I'd never once claimed to be interested in settling down. Tatianna and the other random women throughout the years had tried to be the one. But they did not have the appeal, nor I the intent.

Until Bella. I could smell her innocence, an aroma so crisp and delicious I would kill to take a bite. To be the first and the only man inside that temple of an Italian goddess. I had no doubt she'd break me for all other women and I'd destroy her for all other men.

Grabbing my dick in my hand, I started to stroke it aggressively. Ragged breaths escaped me at my hard up and down motion, my balls tightening at the imaginary feel of her tight pussy wrapped around my cock. I knew without having to taste test that she'd be sweet like an addictive candy. Harder and harder, I pumped. She'd take some time to get used to the way I liked to play, but I'd go easy on her. At first. Break her in right, so she'd crave it... beg me to destroy her as she writhed and moaned beneath me.

I didn't have a red room dedicated to pain. I didn't need whips and ropes to show her who owned her. The massive dick in my hands would do all of that for me. Her tiny body would bend and fold under its will. Breaking that pretty little pussy, just so it would mold my dick perfectly. When I saw something I wanted, I took it.

No second thoughts; she was mine and mine alone to break. To show her what she had been missing her entire life. Wrapping my hands around her dainty little neck and bringing her to the brink of passing out until she came hard. Then I'd revive her and do it all over again. I'd make her beg, plead, and writhe with the need for me to consume her. For me and only me to taste, to feel, to bury myself inside her. The only man to ever know what she felt like as she came on his cock.

Moaning, my hot release erupted all over the glass walls. I came hard with her name on my lips, my balls drawing up and pumping every last drop out of me. If jerking off in the shower at just the thought of her was that hot, imagining the real thing had me instantly hard again. Fuck, she was going to be the death of me. It was border-line stalking—chasing details about her and using her mother to arrange a private meeting.

Arranged to marry il diavolo.

Fuck, I was going to get married.

She deserved more. She deserved better. I would make an oath, here and now, that I would do right by her. I would protect her from her father and anyone else who wished her harm. I'd give her everything and anything she's ever desired. She'd own the throne beside me, command my men and her own—all while aiding me in building *our* empire and preparing to take over the Agostino family's reign of New York City.

Once word got out that she was mine, she'd have a target on her back. One my men and I would protect her from, even lay down our lives, if need be.

"Boss. Serafina has arranged to have a private dinner at *The Giardinos* tomorrow. She and Bella will be taking separate cars and meeting there at seven."

After acknowledging Apollo's statement, I flopped behind my desk to get some work done. I needed information on the Russians… and I needed it right-the-fuck-now. "Where are we with the Russians?"

"My contact said Yuri seems displeased with our fees. So *il pazzo* believes his family should run the docks. The Russians are tired of the Italians owning New York."

"Yuri is shortsighted, and men like him make rash calls to get what they want. He has no family stateside... besides his men. He has to have a partner." As I thought out loud, one name came to my mind immediately. Looking at Apollo, I could see the same came to his.

"He can't be that dumb... Trying to steal a small shipment is one thing, but Gio would be openly going against his father by setting up this Russian meet. You think Anthony's involved in any of this?"

I shook my head. "I've learned some details from my old man tonight. Anthony is too afraid of the consequences to be involved." Sitting back, I wanted to believe it wasn't Gio. I really did. "Get me that name, Apollo. We need to send a clear message. No one looking to go against me—no matter by word, actions, or association—is safe from my wrath."

"Got it, boss. I'll get the name and set up an introduction for *il diavolo*." An evil sneer morphed his features as he turned on his heel and left me alone with my thoughts.

Indeed. Whoever was reckless enough to work against me had no idea just how dangerous I could be. Clearly I'd let some enemies think

I'd lost my edge. Considering this recent trespass, it was time Yuri paid for his sins. The more I dwelled on it, the more I got the sneaking suspicion that this silent co-conspirator was someone close to me. And someone whose death would help me send a message detailing just how fucking scary *il diavolo* really was.

CHAPTER 7

MIRABELLA MORETTI

It had been raining nonstop for days. I needed sunlight and spring. I needed happiness. And the dark skies and torrential downpours weren't giving me that. After my guard got sick from running in the rain, I was tired of hearing his whining and agreed to go to the gym instead. The party was planned and coming up fast. Whoever was being chosen as my fiancé, it seemed everyone was being tightlipped about it. I was impatiently waiting to learn my fate.

My father hadn't said a word about dinner with Lucky. Nor had I heard from the man himself. My mother and I had plans to attend dinner this evening together, just the two of us. At least I had that to look forward to. Running on the treadmill, I noticed that the overpriced gym was packed with people. A lot of females in revealing, expensive gym clothing were gossiping off to the side of the track and not actually working out.

There was a corner buzzing with a horde of lip fillers, Botox, fake breasts, and tummy tucks. They came to the gym to keep up appearances with their girlfriends and get away from their rich husbands. The moment I walked into the gym and caught some unwanted male attention, I consequently earned theirs tenfold, snarky comments replacing the lude ones. I could feel the daggers being thrown in my direction and continued to run, in an effort to avoid making eye contact. They were the exact reason I preferred running outside.

The leering looks from the men as my chest bounced was enough to make me throw up my breakfast. Meanwhile, the female contempt could be felt across the room. Only women knew that feeling of being judged so hard it singed your skin with anger. And these women were catty as all hell. Youth and natural beauty versus polluted and stitched bodies was a wealthy woman's biggest competition in New York City. It was terrible. They didn't have a brain in their heads and married for money. Then again, at least they had a choice.

Finishing my workout, I hit the showers. Each one was like a private mini spa. It was a small piece of heaven in an overpriced, over-crowded, and over-plasticized gym. Excessive heat in the shower always made me feel better. The burn enlivened me in times when I struggled to maintain the girl I was raised to be. The girl who sat on the sidelines and let the men around her control her future. The girl who just wanted to run her own business and not be forced to marry someone because of family obligation. Sitting on the bench at the lockers and dressed in designer yoga pants with a matching jacket, I tried to smile.

"Why would he want-t-t-t to marry that? We make a much better couple, but his father wants a connection to the Morettis. It's a marriage of convenience, for power not love. Not like our marriage would be. It would just be better if someone got rid of her."

I knew that nasally voice, and it sounded exactly like the airhead she was. And that airhead was talking shit on me as she walked around the corner.

"Oh, it's you."

"It's a pleasure as always, Tatianna. And what shit are you stirring up now?" I focused on my phone, allowing my tone to further imply my boredom.

"Angelo is mine! If it wasn't for your stupid family forcing him to marry you, we'd be planning our wedding already."

Huffing out a breath, I tossed my phone into my bag and stood to face her. "What're you going on about now, Tatianna?"

"Ha! You don't even know? Clearly your family doesn't give a fuck about you! Just like Angelo doesn't give a fuck about you!" While she seemed pleased with her pathetic attempt at insulting me, I wanted to slap the look-of-stupid right off her face.

Tatianna was that girl who hid her brain behind the dumb bimbo impression and wanted so desperately to latch on to a powerful man. I just had no clue what the hell she was talking about. It was Italian mob central. I knew like fifteen Angelos.

When she didn't get the rise out of me that she expected, she continued, "Angelo Fioretti came all the way from Sicily to see me. His family is forcing him to announce your engagement at your stupid birthday party. But he doesn't want to marry you. He wants to marry me." Her hands waved in my face as her voice reached another octave —one that grated against my eardrums like nails on a chalkboard.

Angelo was the eldest son of the Fioretti family and definitely the most grotesque. He had a huge nose that was so disproportionate to the rest of him that it made you unable to look away. He was rude, a man-whore, and so dumb he made Tatianna look smart. If she wanted to marry that guy and keep him away from me, it would be a miracle in the making. The man was truly an ogre and smelled like onions all the time. Although he was on the list of potentials, I hadn't heard anything definitive from my father.

"If you and that swine wanna marry, please run away together. You'd be doing me one hell of a favor. I despise the idea of having that sweaty, malodorous, halfwit of a man even think of sharing a bed with me. But since it's you we're talking about, I'm certain he's already shared yours. And if that's what makes you happy, by all means, Tatianna, have at it." Tossing my bag over my shoulder, I plowed forward, throwing her back a few steps in my haste to get away.

I'd underestimated her bitchiness. I made it about five steps when, in stereotypical girl fight fashion, she latched on to my hair. Grunting at the sharp sting, I struggled to get her off me. My hair felt like it was going to be ripped from my scalp. I stomped hard on top of her foot, causing her to howl in pain and release her grip enough that I could pry her man-hands off my hair. I spun on my heel and my fist met her nose perfectly. The once flawlessly doctored masterpiece of reconstruction burst into a gory scene of blood and agonized cries. Having knocked her ass to the ground, I attacked.

I gripped her hair, wrapping it around my hand, and tugged her face close to mine. I bent over her pathetic prone form and forced her to look into my dichromatic eyes. The same eyes she constantly picked on for years. "Do that shit again, Tatianna, and you won't survive next time."

"You bitch!" she roared, still reeling from the trauma as blood oozed from her clearly broken nose.

I yanked on her hair harder, my hand throbbing from the punch. "Oh no. You're the bitch, dear. Now, take your little fuck-boy and run away to Sicily. I want no parts of either of you." I dropped her hair with one last shove. She landed on the floor, snarling and whimpering like a beaten animal at my departure.

My newest armed guard, whose name I'd already forgotten, eyed me suspiciously in the car as I shook out my swelling hand. My knuckles were torn up from her bony, once perfectly symmetrical nose and were turning a purple color around the deep cuts. He couldn't hide his amused expression when he noticed the ice that I'd placed in a towel from the limo bar.

I smiled back at him as we pulled up out front of my parents' home. "I'll be ready in an hour to go to *The Giardinos*."

He nodded as I headed inside. I couldn't wait for a relaxed dinner with my mother. I charged up the stairs before immediately hopping into the shower.

My black hair dried straight against my back. Adding just a touch of concealer to the faint bruise on my face and a little blush, I let the rest of my natural porcelain skin shine. A dab of smoky eye makeup, pale-pink lipstick, a few wavy curls at the end of my hair and I was ready to get dressed.

The name of the restaurant my mother picked meant "the gardens" in Italian. The roof was made of glass. There were fountains, plants, and foliage surrounding the interior. It was a fancy, eat-in establishment with a beautiful botanical feel year-round.

Opting for sex appeal after all the shit with Tatianna, I headed into my walk-in closet. Passing through all the dresses, pantsuits, rompers, and other items I received recently, I came across the perfect outfit. It was a black Chanel dress that fit me like a second skin. It hugged my curves just right and dipped low in the front, but it was seductively covered with black lace. The sides of it appeared open but had the same lace that covered my chest. It was alluring and salacious, but tasteful enough for dinner with your mother. Latching my Mary Jane style, red-soled, five-inch heels, I was finally ready.

The ride over was fast and quiet. Lost in my thoughts while nursing my throbbing hand, I tried not to think about Lucky.

I entered the restaurant several minutes later and the hostess directed me to follow her to my waiting mother. As I walked through the ornately designed interior, I fell in love with the decor. The floral fragrance that hung in the air was calming while the room invited me to stay for the evening. It made me happy. Flowers always did for some reason. We passed several rooms of tables before heading to the far end of the restaurant. A private room. And the moment I crossed the threshold, my breath was stolen from my lungs.

The space was brightly lit by chandeliers with beautiful, low-hanging diamonds. Every surface was covered in flowers, shrubbery, and gardens. The sweet, natural scent of all the flora hit you in the face immediately and it was harmonious to the senses. In Italy, I always had fresh flowers. But now that I was in the States and my father's house, he forbade it, claiming he was allergic. But here, it was a much-needed sensual overload.

While the flowers and chandeliers set the tone, the trail of candles leading to a large gazebo made that tone romantic. Unshed tears burned my eyes. My heartbeat turned rapid, and it seemed to echo in the silent room.

Standing at the step of the gazebo was Lucky in his designer suit—a black jacket and pants with a crisp, neatly tucked shirt. His tie was black and sharp while the pale blue of his shirt accentuated his smoldering steel eyes. His thick muscles flexed against the fitted sleeves of the jacket. He looked perfect, primal, dangerous, and above all…delicious. His black hair was combed back, thick, and shiny. A stark contrast to his light eyes.

Looking around the room, I noticed the empty tables behind the gazebo. Placed haphazardly as if they'd been quickly shoved out of the way, leaving the room to just us. My heart raced as I walked down the candlelit path. I was suddenly nervous as I approached the man that had been haunting my dreams. In front of me now, that very same man had a way of setting my skin on fire with just a look. I wanted to bathe in those pools of blue water, those smoldering eyes. He hadn't looked away since I'd first entered the room and we had both been holding our breaths.

Perhaps I wasn't the only one nervous? He looked as though he feared I might dart out of the room, holding his breath in anticipation. That wasn't possible. The pull between us was too strong; my legs moved forward of their own accord. The sexual tension in the air was palpable. I was drowning, with my potent desire to rip his clothes off. To let him ravage me on the ornately decorated table. I'd be his breakfast, lunch, and dinner. Anything to appease the hungry twinkle in his eyes.

His steel gaze looked me up and down appreciatively, making my body respond in a way that soaked my panties and hardened my nipples. I was ready to kneel at the altar and offer him my virginity. I was a platter of innocence begging him to destroy me. And that same all-consuming gaze told me he'd do it too. His muscular body coiled with tension at my approach.

"Bella. You look incredible."

Lost for words, I could feel my neck heat in appreciation and embarrassment at his perusal.

"Please, come sit." Stepping back, he grabbed my hand, walked me to my seat, and pulled out my chair. He was nothing like the rumors said he'd be.

If I'd listen to the tales, I'd assume he didn't have a polite bone in his body. That he took what he wanted with no questions asked or concern for who was impacted. Hell, just his choice of Tatianna told me what kind of women he shared his bed with.

A man in his position and power didn't rise in our life without spilling some blood. In Lucky's case, I heard it was a lot more than some. To be the eldest of the power family, which came second only to the mayhem you caused first, spoke volumes. He was *il diavolo,* after all.

The table was covered with several vases of freshly picked flowers and burning candles. And neatly displayed were two plates side by side, with crystal wine glasses and a bottle of a very nice merlot. My breath caught in my throat when I read the label. A vintage *Petrus Pomerol,* my absolute favorite wine.

"*Perfetto,* Lucky," I exclaimed, my eyes glued to the bottle.

"Indeed. So, you like?" he asked, but I could tell he knew the answer.

"*Si. Grazie.*" Once I was seated, I busied myself, nervously placing my napkin in my lap. My hands wouldn't stop shaking and my breathing wouldn't calm. He snapped his fingers and the lights on the chandelier dimmed, the room around us suddenly dark except for the soft flickering. The hundreds of candles everywhere danced shadows on the wall.

It was so picturesque, like something I would've read about in one of my romance novels. Although I never assumed it would happen to me. Smiling from ear to ear, I was in heaven as I sat next to a charming and handsome man who was looking at me like I was God's gift. And all of it while I enjoyed dinner in a room that was more than I could have ever dreamed.

This was perfect.

A waiter stepped into the room, depositing our platters in front of us. As the lid was lifted, my mouth watered from the heavenly aroma. Smoked salmon with herb seasoning, roasted potatoes, and asparagus assaulted my senses. Everything I would've picked for myself.

Lucky watched me intently as he filled my glass to the halfway point.

"This is so amazing. I-I-I… thank you Lucky."

As he set the bottle back on the table, I was graced with an amazing sight. He *smiled.* A true, beautiful, and happy smile. His normally hardened, professional stare relaxed into a miraculous surprise. Blushing from the sentiment, I smiled back. A stupid girly giggle escaped. I mentally slapped myself for the childish behavior and tried to cover the sound with a cough. His smirk told me it didn't work.

Clenching my thighs together, I squirmed in my seat. His smile was making the moment torturous and his knowing gaze wouldn't let me hide. Not with what he was making me feel. I wanted to crawl out of my skin with the need he elicited from my body.

Internally, I was begging him to strip me of my clothes and lay me bare. Allow him the chance to forgo the aforementioned dinner and feast on my pulsating bud. To ravage the most intimate part of me that was crying for his touch.

"I hope it is to your liking. As much as I'd love to take all of the credit, I did have some help. I wanted our first dinner to be perfect."

Smiling at his admission, I couldn't stop the giggling that bubbled out of me again.

Of course, my mother helped him. We'd talked numerous times before about the perfect date and how I prayed for a man who wanted to treat me like a queen. She knew every detail my young, naive mind had conjured. This was all of that and so much more. I had prayed for a charming man, but Lucky was beyond my wildest dreams. From his throaty, demanding voice and his perfectly sculpted body to the power he possessed to steal me from my fate.

"She's something else, that mother of mine. Regardless of the help, you still did it. No one has ever cared enough…"

He held up a palm, his lips dipping into a frown. "Forget the others. You deserve more than salmon, wine, and flowers. You deserve every dream you've ever had and so much more."

His calloused hands reached out to caress my face. I loved that even though he was powerful enough to pay men to get their hands dirty, his told me he was a man of action. Lucky fought in the trenches to continue his family's reign. He might have been born the eldest son but he didn't rest on that fact alone, opting to make a name for himself.

Holding my face gently, his own a few inches from mine, he whispered, *"Bella ragazza."*

"I didn't expect this… or you. After the dinner invitation followed by silence, I assumed my father had refused. Well, that he vetoed it."

His expression lost its soft happiness, a cloud of anger taking over. His features morphed into a blank slate of brick. Before me now was *il diavolo*. The man whose eyes alone instilled fear into men. Whose brawn and intensity could make the deadliest adversaries cower at his feet. He was dangerous. He was cold. And he was fucking sexy. I didn't fear him, even with him looking at me with the same ferocity I assumed he displayed to his enemies, right at their unpleasant and untimely deaths.

"Your father is no longer a concern. When I see something I want, I take it. Anyone or anything in my way be damned. And, my sweet Bella, lately you are all that consumes my mind and my desires." His eyes lost their anger, turning to molten blue lava pools of lust as he gently stroked my face. "Your father could object all he wants but he won't win."

My jaw was beginning to hurt from smiling so much. I wasn't used to it.

He felt the same about me. After all these years of praying and wishing a man would come into my life at the exact moment I needed him… He would be strong, powerful, and confess his true feelings for me. He would stand up to my father and refuse to cower to his demands. That man was Lucky.

"And as for being silent, there was something that required my immediate attention. Someone is trying to fuck with my business. Apollo and I have spent the last few days searching for answers. It was the only reason I was kept away."

"Did it all work out?"

"Not yet. Obviously, this doesn't leave this room. I'm trusting you, Bella." His eyes implored me to understand the gravity of this exchange. "The Russians are withholding product and are ignoring our contract. For the time being, my buyers are being patient, but I'm unsure how long that's going to be the case."

"That doesn't sound good. Also sounds a little shady." I wanted him to see how valuable I could be to him. I may've been forced to remain quiet when things happened within earshot. But I paid attention, patiently learning all I could from the mistakes my family had made. I could help if I was trusted enough to participate.

A thought occurred to me about the situation he explained. In the life we led, people didn't sit around and wait when deals went bad. Although Lucky was tackling his issues with the Russians as best he could, it still ruined his deals with others. The fact that his buyers were being so patient raised a major red flag.

"May I ask a question? If *you* had a deal with buying something and they ran into an issue, how would you handle it?" Biting my lip, I waited to see if my probing would anger him.

"I'd find another seller."

I nodded, having assumed as much. In our world, your word was all that mattered. Well, *that* and the driving force behind it.

"Exactly. Business is business. If you don't conduct it right, they'll find someone who will. Ask yourself this, why are your buyers being so patient? Because someone else is attempting to trump your deal and give them a better offer. They're waiting to see who presents the more lucrative deal. The Russians have gotten to your contacts somehow," I stated simply.

I watched the lightbulb go off in his head. Excusing himself, he pulled out his phone, rapidly typing out a message. The look of retribution on his face was borderline comical. Internally smiling to myself, I was filled with pride. For years, I'd felt the fire to do more burning inside me. No one saw the value I could provide. Until now.

He shoved his phone into his pocket before his intense glare landed on me again. "Pure, raw, angelic beauty and a set of brains to match. You're incredible, Bella." He kissed my hand delicately, heat rising on my cheeks at the sentiment.

At a moment in time when my arranged marriage was right around the corner, Lucky showed up. He stormed into my life like a hurricane of fitted suits, feared command, and unrestrained lust. He was taking what he wanted, which happened to be me, and standing up against my father's errant demands. He was *the* man I had dreamed of for as long as I could remember.

Sixteen-year-old me was told by Mario Agostino that he was to decide my future. Never did I think he'd pick a husband I could see myself with. Those eyes had haunted my dreams since the day we literally collided. As the years went on, I started to think less and less that I'd be fortunate enough to be chosen for such a man. Butterflies floated around my stomach as it all became clear to me.

"Tell me what you're thinking?" Lucky asked between bites of his medium-rare steak, cutting small pieces before placing them into his mouth. Following the trail of his fork, I watched as his succulent lips worked slowly. His powerful muscles under his suit flexed with the movement of him cutting and feeding himself. I licked my lips and my throat went dry. "Now I really want to know what you're thinking."

The combined noise from his fork dropping and his sudden throaty growl snapped me out of my impure thoughts. I scrambled to regain my composure. I was making a fool of myself. "My world was shattered when we first met five years ago. I was shipped to Italy after being told a deal have been arranged by my father, all while yours held my future in his hands. However, neither would give me the specifics. But before I left, I overheard my father say that Mario would choose my husband and announce it on my twenty-first birthday. All so he could use your family's docks." He went to speak, a look of anger and sadness washing over his face. "Let me finish, Lucky."

I sliced into my salmon, and as I placed it into my mouth, it melted like butter. A guttural, pleased moan escaped my lips while I chewed. Lucky sat back in his seat, unsuccessfully trying to hide adjusting himself in his seat. Lust and desire flashed on his handsome face while his hand moved under the table. The meal was cooked perfectly and my company was even better.

"I hated the Agostino family—your family—for making me suffer abroad, for forcing me into a state of purgatory. I was resigned to the fact that I had to do this, to ensure my family's position. And when I returned to the States, I felt the most intense urge to fight against him, to pick who I wanted even if I had to run away with nothing. Then his son barged into a meeting and changed everything."

"Bella, I promise you I had no clue."

Halting his words again with a raised hand, I watched as he sat back and waited for me to speak. "I *hated*, past tense. The more my mother tells me about the Agostinos, the more I respect Mario. She's told me about his promise to protect me. I never knew who he'd arrange for me, but his promise to my mother made it all fall into place." Taking a sip of my wine, I continued. "It was you."

"I swear to you, Bella, seeing you cry that day… it destroyed me. I remember thinking less of my father, for putting those tears in your gorgeous eyes. He never said a word until a few days ago. When I stopped in for a meeting to tell him to call off Anthony, he told me everything."

"I've spent all this time dreaming of a strong, powerful man who would step up to my father. A man who would treat me like his equal, who respected and wanted to care for me. A man who would do anything to put a smile on my face." I scanned the room and my lips curled. "And when you walked into that meeting at *Vino*, something just felt right. You make me feel cherished and safe. It was you all along. Lucky, you're the man I've been dreaming of."

CHAPTER 8

LUCIFER "LUCKY" AGOSTINO

Scaling back my shock, I was smiling inside and out. Apollo and I spent the last few days scouring the docks for information on what was going on with the Russians. Blood and guts being the cost if they didn't have the intel we needed. We were at a total loss as to what the end game was. Two simple comments to Bella and she had figured it out.

I knew she'd be the queen I needed at my side.

My inner thoughts turned devilish at the prospect of breaking her in, of giving her a throne. Her true innocence had shown in her eyes, lingering behind the fire that was ever-glowing. We continued to eat, drink wine, and entertain each other with easy conversation. Getting to know someone on a deeper level was an aspect I never once thought would interest me. Bella made me want to know every little detail about her. She was so cultured, refined, smart, and had such a passion for life. I found myself falling hard and fast.

"I see your guard dog is pacing. Don't tell me it's time to go so soon?" Pointing towards the entryway of our private dining oasis, I observed that her security detail seemed anxious.

"Cat's out of the bag... I have a feeling my father is probably to blame. He's making my guard do his dirty work. His attempt at under-mining you."

She was right. Her father was a spineless imbecile. He had more than likely been notified of who she was with and it wasn't her mother. Of this, I was certain. My heart increased its rhythm, pounding against my ribs while my anger started bubbling beneath the surface. Rising from the table to have a not-that-subtle word with her guard, I was stopped in my tracks. Her small hand rested on top of my larger one, her dichromatic eyes begging me to stay.

"Don't let them spoil this moment. It's just us." Her soft hand was so little compared to mine. The blood of my enemies soaked these hands, even if I was the only one that could see my palms drenched. That small touch of our skin connecting made it all go away. I couldn't see the blood anymore. The only thing that mattered was the way she grounded me.

"Just us." I leaned back in my seat. The aroma of the wine, the food, the flowers, and her scent was intoxicating. She took over every one of my senses, making her own mark on me. I craved it.

As we continued talking, I learned just how many languages she knew; however, French was her favorite. The passion and the love behind their words were what lit her fire.

"I've never been, but all of the books I've read make it sound like a magical place. It's more than a city with a tower. It's the culture, the people, and the scenery." Her smile wasn't lost on me; her eyes were staring into the distance wistfully. Paris. She wanted to explore Paris.

"I've been for business, but it was nothing like that. I suppose I didn't have your company, so it would pale in comparison regardless."

Her cheeks heated at the sentiment. There were two sides to this beautiful woman sitting in front of me. One was the innocent Mirabella Moretti, the girl lost in the stories of the written word because she was too sheltered to experience it herself. The other was the girl hidden behind walls and guards, all meant to preserve her purity to auction off to the highest bidder. And it just so happened that I was richer than King Midas.

And I refused to fucking lose.

I would have her, no matter the cost. I'd kill hundreds of men to win her. And I'd bathe in their blood triumphantly. I would be her first and only. I would be the only man alive to hear her moans of pleasure. To watch the euphoria of an orgasm wash over her. To watch her writhe, moan, and plead under me.

I would be the man who would shatter her innocence one finger, one lick, one stroke at a time. And she'd beg me to do it. I'd be the man to watch her fire grow and empower her to own her rightful place at my side.

The *diavolo* was itching to come out. Not to murder but to shatter that thin little membrane of virtue she still held on to. To break her down piece by piece, only to rebuild her stronger. Soft chuckles broke me from my thoughts. Bella was smiling at me sheepishly.

"What's so funny?" I asked, as she giggled a little more, sitting farther back in her seat.

"You left me. Wherever you just went, your face held a myriad of emotions. What were you thinking about?" Bella asked, taking another sip of her wine.

Leaning over the table to get closer to her, I smirked in a way that spoke of my untoward thoughts. She didn't falter, her amused expression in place while she sipped her wine as if she weren't dining on sin with the devil. I moved my eyes slowly over her trim figure to burn every detail in my brain. Her porcelain skin heated with a red flush that graced that perfect surface, when she realized what I was suggesting.

Her. Underneath me. Me. Owning every piece of her delectable little body.

Dinner progressed with her telling me about her time in Italy and reinventing herself back in the States. We discussed the arranged marriage and what it meant to each of us. She was elated by the idea that I wanted her at my side. That the Agostino men cherished their wives and withheld nothing. The concept being they'd never have the ignorance of their women work against them. She wanted to run her own business and I told her I would give her that. Just seeing that smile on her face, I'd do whatever it took to give her everything she wanted.

"Boss." Apollo stepped out of the shadows to whisper in my ear.

"Yuri wants to meet." He nodded at Bella apologetically as she smiled at him in return.

"Set it up for the warehouse again. Bella, *mia regina*, my apologies. We must cut this short. I have urgent business."

Finishing the last sip of wine, she rose elegantly from her seat. In doing so, she gave me a view of an insanely perfect body. I struggled to hide a moan. Usually I liked more meat but anything on Mirabella Moretti was perfection. Her dress clung tightly to her body, showcasing her thin build with slight curves that would make me beg to have a taste. She bent forward to place her napkin back on the table, and I continued my appraisal of the scene in full display. Perfect round globes that were just a tad big for her little body...

Again, I moaned. This time, I was forced to adjust myself as well, while Apollo covered his laugh with a cough. Shooting daggers at him only caused him to laugh harder before heading out the door in front of us.

"I'll have my guards pull the car around. This was..."

Cutting her off, I crashed my lips onto hers. She let out a slight squeak of shock before she complied and opened her mouth to me. I took full advantage. Our tongues roamed and stroked, getting to know the inner workings of each other's mouths. Her lips molded to mine perfectly, while her tiny body melted into my large embrace.

It was an almost comical pairing. A *Beauty and the Beast*, if you will. I was nearly a foot taller and a little over twice as wide. If we were ever in a position of vulnerability, I'd lay my body down to protect her. One day, she would be the mother of my children and carry on the Agostino name.

She pulled back, her chest heaving and her lips red and puffy from my assault.

"You misunderstand, *mia regina*. You're coming with me. However, for your safety, I want you hidden in the car but close enough to hear what's going on."

"I won't let you down." She was filled with excitement, her head held high and assured.

"I never presumed you would," I said with a deep sincerity.

I guided her out of the restaurant with Apollo and my men leading the way, while her guards trailed behind us. I could feel all eyes on us. Nearly hear the weight of their unspoken questions. This place was often frequented by many crime families. The workers and other patrons usually pretended to not notice, but this time they couldn't look away.

Mirabella walked with the confidence of a queen. My queen. Head held high, she morphed into a self-assured woman. Cunning and powerful. She remained at my side with pride and happiness, never shying away from my touch. Even as the whispers got loud enough to hear, she didn't falter. The patrons and lower-level families in attendance were shocked at the pairing. It was known in the mob circle that Bella was home to find a suitor. They never would've guessed an Agostino and Moretti union. They'd soon learn that the eldest son of the reigning family had found his queen.

The future of New York was in their presence. And soon, they'd learn why she had been chosen.

"Do you feel their confusion?" Bella mumbled, tucking herself farther into my body.

"I do. The Agostinos and the Morettis together without any blood-shed. How dreadfully uneventful."

"I can only assume they're in shock."

"They better get used to it. At my side is where you will remain." Kissing the top of her head, I held onto her tighter. "*Mia regina*, you are mine."

My car was idling at the curb outside the restaurant. Motioning for her to enter, I halted her guards from interfering. We were headed to a meeting that the Moretti men weren't welcome to attend. As much as their job was to protect her, my men were just as capable. If not more so, given their loyalty to me.

"Call your boss. Your presence is required back at the Moretti compound." Sliding in beside Bella, I closed the door in their confused faces.

"You are full of surprises tonight, Lucky." A coy smile broke out on her angelic face.

"It might be an arrangement, but I want you as sure of this as I am. I don't want you obligated to stay. I want you excited to be at my side."

"If the future holds as much light as I'm picturing, then my answer is simple."

"*Mia regina*, you will soon learn that you're the only light in my life. I'm shrouded in darkness, and if you aren't careful, it will consume you too."

"Everyone is a moon, and has a dark side which he never shows to anybody." Her words came out just a breath above a whisper.

"Mark Twain?" Apollo asked, turning in his seat to look at her.

She nodded with a shocked smile. It seemed Apollo had made himself a friend. The thought of my right hand and my future wife befriending each other pleased me. But her message pleased me more. She may be the light I didn't know I needed, but she also recognized a darkness inside herself. That reaffirmed everything I thought I knew about her. The bride of Lucifer Agostino wasn't intended for the weak and weary. And she was neither of those things.

"Glad to hear you say that. I look forward to basking in your darkness. Now, I promise you my men will protect you. I hope you can provide us with a little insight tonight."

She nodded, her determined expression the only outward sign of her readiness.

Pulling into the warehouse, I had no clue that bringing Bella would be the greatest decision I'd made to protect my empire. Following my intuition and my gut were the reasons I held the position I did so strongly. It never led me astray. My gut saved my ass and my men on numerous occasions.

Yuri had three SUVs full of men inside the warehouse, two more than normal. They were all armed, which wasn't anything new. Russians and Italians trusted each other about as much as you could trust a teenage boy left with a handful of cash in a whorehouse.

"My guys will be protecting you on this floor, with snipers on the loft above." Pulling Bella across the seat, I kissed her softly. I couldn't get enough of her taste. "Stay in the shadows. Move closer to my side only when the door is closed."

She nodded, and I kissed her once more before exiting the vehicle. A sense of pride and power took over me, which I quickly locked down, washing away any sign of emotion. Face blank, suit jacket buttoned, I addressed the room.

They wanted him, they got him.

The *diavolo*, in the flesh.

CHAPTER 9

MIRABELLA MORETTI

My father and Gio would never have allowed this to happen. They believed in the ideology that women should stay home while men conducted their business. Not Lucky. Without a second thought, he asked me to attend a meeting. Instead of cutting our night short, he opted for my attendance. It was true I might have been staying in the car, but this was a big deal to me. The amount of respect he gave me was astonishing.

Now seated in the back of his luxury SUV, I couldn't stop squirming. The plush leather was as soft as melted butter and the scent of Lucky's spicy cologne tickled my nose and calmed my senses. Apollo sat in the front passenger seat, ranting in Italian to someone named Roscoe. I was fortunate enough to be here, in this moment, and I didn't want to overstep my bounds. No matter how curious I was.

"Penny for your thoughts?" Even in the dimmed lighting of the passing cars, his eyes bore holes through me. "You have a little scowl, just here." Lucky tapped the crease between my brows. I loosened my facial expression and grinned up at him while he continued. "I've noticed that those little wrinkles appear when you're thinking hard."

"I think way too hard about things I shouldn't." He raised a questioning brow at me, and I cleared my throat. "You're just so different.

The Moretti men would've sent me home with an escort before heading to a meeting."

A deep laugh rumbled his chest, and Apollo joined him. "The Moretti men aren't known for their tenacity or good decision-making. We Agostinos adhere to the credence that you're only as strong as your weakest member. Unfortunately for you, that's Gio. The most powerful however... is you." He kissed me roughly to cement his meaning as my body shook with need.

That kiss. His words.

I had read about the passion, the desire, and the intensity one single person could cause, but not once had I experienced it firsthand. Until now. Until Lucky. He'd made his claim to the entire room in that restaurant. I'd seen several lower-level families mixed in with regular patrons. Undoubtedly, they would spread the gossip of their sighting.

Let them tell the world. Lucifer Agostino had found his queen.

And that was exactly who I planned to be for him. He made me feel worthy of so much more than this life had given to me. I wanted to be the strong and powerful queen the *Mafia Prince* needed at his side. I had the mind and the will to do it. I just needed to remove the bullshit my father and brothers ingrained in me since I was a little girl.

I was arranged to be married to *il diavolo*. And I would revel in the darkness with him.

I was tense the entire car ride but did my best not to show it. I didn't want him to doubt my capabilities and send me home. I wanted to uncover whatever secrets the Russians were hiding. I'd learned over the years that lower-level Russian families often went behind the backs of the *Bratva* to try to gain additional power. They were often stupid and sloppy. If they didn't manage to succeed, they'd have to pay their dues to the *Bratva* to stay alive.

"You barely know me." I couldn't stop the smile from creeping across my face. He made me so emblazoned, so fearless.

"I know enough. I've seen enough. You're smart, tactical. You have a good head for business, a soft heart when warranted, and a strong spine for the bullshit. Just surviving all these years with Gio is commendable enough."

I giggled while Apollo outright boomed with laughter from the front seat. Lucky took my hand in his, giving it a reassuring squeeze. His words against my bloodline shouldn't be funny, but sometimes the truth was hilarious. All my life, my family told me I wasn't good enough simply because I was a woman. In a matter of hours, Lucky removed that feeling and replaced it with encouragement. Empowered me to want to own my life and do with it as I pleased.

"I mean it. Every word." He kissed my hand before gently placing it back in my lap. "I need to ask something of you. If at any point you feel uncomfortable, I want you to be honest and tell me."

"I will," I said with candor, as Apollo turned in his seat to look at me.

"You speak Russian, correct?"

I nodded in response.

"Would you be able to listen from the car and report everything you hear?"

"The vehicles will pull inside the warehouse. You'll be surrounded by my men, out of sight, in the car." Lucky held my hand as he spoke.

"Can you tell me why?" I asked as he smiled in return.

"I'd expect nothing less than your inquisitive nature. They seem to be playing games and I want to know their true motive," Lucky said, his expression serious.

"And that's where I come in?" I said, straightening my spine. Apollo's mouth twitched in amusement before he faced forward again.

"Yuri, their leader, is the only one who speaks English. He addresses his men in Russian. Can you do this for me?" Lucky asked with a concerned edge to his voice.

"For you?" Looking into those icy pools of a perfect blue storm, I pretended to mull over his question. "For you and only you, I will."

The air in the car turned heated with sexual tension. I squeezed my thighs shut, squirming just enough to dull some of the ache. And he caught me—he was too perceptive to miss the movement. His stare burned through mine with a dark intensity, and his face held a knowing look as he stared at my lap. My palms were flat, my fingers spread wide on my thighs with my knees glued together.

A deep growl escaped him as he leaned over, aggressively taking my head in his hands, and tugged me towards him. His warm mouth landed on mine with a punishing and demanding pull. All thoughts of what was asked of me fled, lost in this little bubble of carnal desire. I could barely register anything else. He withdrew his touch way too quickly, his cold eyes heated with lust.

We pulled into the warehouse, and I swallowed my heart at the number of Russians in attendance. There were only four of us in Lucky's SUV, myself included, while the vehicle behind us held an additional four. The man I assumed to be Yuri stood with fifteen men behind him. The odds weren't in our favor, but Lucky didn't seem bothered as he exited the car.

The softened features he had when speaking to me were gone in a second. All emotion was removed from his face, revealing a cold, indifferent man. He was given the name of *il diavolo* for a reason, and I had a front row seat.

The Russian leader pushed to his full height, buttoned his jacket, and shook hands with Lucky. Apollo and the driver were right behind them. I slid over to the other side and glued myself to the tinted window, which was cracked just enough for me to listen.

"Yuri, Yuri, Yuri. You've broken our deal yet again. I've killed men for less." Even Lucky's—no, Lucifer's—voice was different as he spoke.

"*Da*. This time not my fault." Yuri had a very heavy Russian accent. His men were alert but seemed lost. "Our shipment stolen before get here."

"Do I look stupid to you, Yuri? Do I look like the sort of man you wanna fuck with? You've tested my patience and now you're gonna lie to my face? There's only one way this will end. *Cmeptb*." The entire room tensed at his declaration of death. The Russians turned to each other with hushed murmurs, signaling their heightened concern.

Yuri waved a dismissive arm and turned to his men. I listened intently to his pronunciation so as not to misinterpret my translation. *"The Italian pig thinks he can threaten me."* He hissed his insults in

Russian, and his men erupted with laughter while Lucky sent me the slightest glance.

"Do you really believe I'm gonna let you live? After wasting my time? After playing these bullshit, childish games with my product?"

Yuri responded to Lucky, but my attention was drawn to the small cluster of Russians laughing and talking to each other in their native tongue.

"Stupid, spoiled American."

"Why don't we kill him already?"

"Yuri wants to make his family suffer, take everything away from them."

"He's killing him today? Right? Then we go after his little girlfriend?"

My blood boiled at the conversation they were having right in front of us. They acted like Lucky was nothing. Like they were safe discussing his downfall. My stomach churned, bile rising in my throat at the disgusting things they were saying about me. The fact that they knew about me already was disconcerting. I tried to think like the queen Lucky needed me to be. But I didn't know what to do.

If I didn't warn him somehow, these men would kill him at the end of the meeting. This amazing relationship had just started and I'd already grown to care and respect Lucky. And his men. Apollo had a small place in my heart the moment he knew I quoted Mark Twain. I was falling for Lucky and I couldn't—no, *wouldn't*—let anything happen to him. Dragging in a deep breath and straightening my spine, I opened the door.

The break in silence increased the tension in the room, and all eyes turned towards me. Confident, annoyed, and powerful, I strutted past the leers. To Lucky's side. The slight tick in his jaw was the only tell-tale sign that he was upset with me for showing myself. But they already knew about me, and I refused to allow them to hurt us.

"Are your men even aware of who they are conducting business with?" I asked Yuri, head high and voice strong.

He didn't say a word to me in response. Instead, his eyes narrowed to slits, no doubt irritated by my involvement. Russian mobsters were like traditional Italian men; women held no merit when it came to business. An understanding that served to only heighten my urge to keep talking. Fuck this coward and his men threatening what was mine. Lucky was mine. His men were mine. And I would be their fucking queen.

"You're lambs being led to slaughter by this man, your coward of a leader." Pointing to Yuri, I continued addressing the room in Russian. Yuri and his men tensed at the realization I was indeed fluent in their native language. *"You've been dragged into a war with the Agostinos. The man you are so confidently threatening is called the devil. Have you heard of him?"*

The way they cursed under their breaths, ground their teeth, and paced in their spots told me all I needed to know. Yuri left them ignorant. That would be his first mistake in his plot against Lucky. His second was underestimating him. And me.

"He didn't tell his men the plan, who you are. They think you're just some spoiled American. They want to kill you and take your business." I spoke low so only Apollo and Lucky could hear me. "And they knew about me and planned to come for me when you were gone."

The snarl coming from Lucky would've made me shrink in fear… had I not known he'd never hurt me. He was frothing at the mouth. Fucking with his business earned them their deaths but threatening me added a slow torture before it.

Yuri took a step back but the angry glares from his men gave him pause. Looking from Lucky's enraged face to Yuri's, I could see fear and doubt emanating from the wannabe Russian kingpin.

He fucked up. And he knew it.

"What difference does it make? We stick with the plan and destroy them all! This is for us, for our families, and our future!" Yuri yelled and his men seemed to change tack, rejoicing with him.

"We need to go. Now!" I snapped at Lucky, who shoved me behind him and drew his gun, while Apollo shielded us both. One of Yuri's men stepped forward first, earning him a bullet aimed perfectly between his eyes. And chaos ensued.

In the movies, gunfights looked so dramatic and exciting. In real life, they went by in the blink of an adrenaline-fueled eye. Staying behind Lucky and Apollo, I held onto Lucky's suit jacket and stared at the ground. I could hear gunshots coming from all directions, with men crying out in fear and agony. I might have been confident and strong, but I wasn't going to prove anything to anyone by throwing up when I looked at the carnage.

"Fuck!" Apollo fell backwards into me, almost taking me to the ground, while blood sprayed across my face and blocked my line of sight. "Goddamn it!"

"Apollo!" I screamed and released Lucky's jacket, pivoting towards his second-in-command.

Apollo held his arm, blood pooling between his fingertips. He shoved me forward. "I'm fine. Get to the car, *mia regina!*"

"Bella, move that sexy little ass!" Jumping from the ferocity in Lucky's voice, I dove for the open SUV door. "It's bulletproof. Stay down, *mi amore.*"

Once I was safely locked inside the car by myself, I realized how fast my heart was beating. I just got him and the fear of losing him already was suffocating. Choking me where I sat. The negative thoughts weren't going to help either of us. Nestled on the floor, I was too panic-stricken to do much else. I could hear the groaning, the shots firing, the sharp pinging noises as the bullets hit the car, and screaming in Italian and Russian echoing around the warehouse.

"Get your shit together!" I took a deep breath and sat up, leaning over the front seat to get a better view of what was going on.

My reflection startled me at first. Apollo's gunshot wound had sprayed blood across my face. My eyes were hard and determined with an air of confidence even as I rippled in fright.

I could do this. Hell, I would do this. It was for Lucky and his men.

My startled scream echoed in the car as the front door opened and Apollo threw himself inside, still bleeding from his open bullet wound. "I'm okay. I'm just losing a lot of blood," he said, as if reading my thoughts. Dropping his gun in the center console, he sat back in the front seat and began removing his jacket.

I leaned over his seat and went on autopilot as I rendered aide. In another life, I'd wanted to be a nurse and did a few semesters studying human anatomy. I also thought it would come in handy, considering the family business. Thank God for small favors. Loosening his tie, I pulled it over his head. I quickly made a tourniquet on his bicep to slow the bleeding. Tugging it tight above the wound, I ripped open his sleeve to take a look.

"Oh, thank God. It went right through. Just need to maintain the pressure." I glanced out the windshield. Lucky's men were taking the lead as the Russians appeared to be retreating. "Where are you, Lucky?" I asked more to myself than anyone else.

"Fuck, fuck, fuck! He's right there." Apollo pointed to a stack of cargo directly in front of us. He was pinned down by heavy gunfire. Yuri was one row away and coming up fast. Before I could breathe, a man came from his left, and Lucky's quick moves took him down. A bloody knife to the gut—three times—and the man collapsed on the spot. Lucky was smiling a huge smile, soaked in blood and obviously enjoying the sanguine fluid pouring from his enemies. But Yuri was still close.

"Bella, no!"

I ignored Apollo's pleas, snatched his gun from the console, and rolled down my rear window. Breathing slow, my elbows slightly bent, I aimed at the man on our side. One shot and the machine gun firing ceased. With the main source of bullets down, Lucky's men continued their search for a threat. I kept shouting for them to get Lucky, but they couldn't hear me. I could see Yuri was right on him.

"He's out of bullets."

Lucky was crouched low on the ground, patting himself down. It was clear he had no extra clips on him. Rage marred his handsome face, before he glanced up at the SUV and smiled the saddest, most heart-wrenching smile at me. He wasn't going down without a fight. When he turned back to the carnage, *il diavolo* grinned at the chaos and blood-coated floor.

"Fuck this," I hissed.

Apollo tried to reach for me before yelping in pain at the odd angle on his arm.

"Pull tight with your teeth. I can't let him die, Apollo." I tugged the tie one more time and placed it in his mouth, while he stared at me with uncertainty. But having finally realized that his boss and best friend would die without help, he obliged and quickly clamped down on the material.

I opened the door and scanned the warehouse. Yuri was still gunning for Lucky. So, slinking behind Yuri's car as quietly as my stilettos in a gunfight would allow, I lined myself up perfectly. Yuri was on the other side of Lucky's makeshift cover with his gun drawn. Ready to turn and fire.

Diving around the shipping boxes, Lucky attacked like a venomous snake. All the little smiles and looks of lust were gone, allowing me to finally see him turn into the *diavolo*—his face was hardened and dangerous. As he made quick eye contact with me, I watched the anger increase tenfold. My clear disregard for my own safety enraged him. He latched on to Yuri's neck, bending the Russian backwards at an odd angle and forcing the man to lose his footing as he slowly crumbled underneath Lucky's weight.

Not Lucky. The man before me was the one and only Lucifer Agostino.

"You threaten my queen? You mock me to your men, then you're so bold as to think I'll let you live. Welcome to hell, you insolent fuck!" Lucky yanked harder as Yuri turned an odd shade of red and blue. Just as the Russian was about to let out his last breath, a bullet hit the pallet right next to my head.

I squealed and clamped a hand over my mouth, before tucking myself against Yuri's car, and watched the scene change in an instant. One second, Yuri was almost dead. The next, a large man was whaling on Lucky, who was matching him fist-for-fist despite the size differential. Yuri began breathing normally, attempting to flee as Lucky's men came charging from the other side of the room. They were too far to get to Lucky before he got really hurt.

Leaning across the hood of the car, I lined up my shot. *Breathe. Fire.* The first one was a miss, just about an inch or so off its target. *Breathe. Fire.* The second nailed its target with a confirmatory wail of pain, the bullet hitting the excessively large man's shoulder and raining blood onto Lucky's once pristine suit.

With the Russian stalled by the pain, Lucky overtook him, dropping him to the ground before driving a blade in the bastard's neck. The carotid artery was severed, pulsing large amounts of blood out of the gaping wound. He was dead in seconds. However, Yuri was still close.

Breathe. Fire.

"Gah!" He roared the moment my bullet made contact with his back. Dropping on the ground, he rolled out of sight with Lucky's men on his tail. I kept my eye on my moving target, and once he had cleared the cargo coverage, I resumed firing. I walked backwards to Lucky's hiding spot and kept firing in Yuri's direction. Once I was within arm's reach, Lucky grabbed my wrist and pinned me against him. Seconds later, splintered wood exploded where I'd just been standing.

"Apollo's in the car. I'm sorry, but I just couldn't…"

Lucky's warm, minty breath blew out before his lips crashed on mine. As I writhed against him, one hand dove for my hair and the other gripped my ass and tugged me flush against his frame. Bullets kept hitting the wooden crate shielding us but none of the chaos mattered. All that did was the two of us. The adrenaline was turning me on so much I thought I'd combust against him.

His hard cock was practically pulsing as it pressed into my stomach. The fear, the adrenaline, and the thought of losing this man before I ever really had him made me rethink the moment. Fuck our families. Fuck contracts and marriage proposals. I wanted him. No, I needed him. I needed to submit to Lucky. I wanted him to be my first and forever. Moaning as he deepened the kiss, I squirmed on top of him. Looking for that friction that would help quench this burning desire inside me.

"You are fucking incredible. I think I knew it that first time I saw you. And confirmed it at *Vino.* You are *perfezionare, mia regina.*" He tugged me closer, and I couldn't breathe as our lips locked. We assaulted each other's mouths like we were starved and ravenous.

"Please, Lucky. I need you. Be the one for me. Own my body."

Feeling sexy in my own skin, I found a new piece of confidence. I bit his ear before whispering against it. "I'm yours. If you'll have me, *mio re.*"

"Fuck me, yes, you're mine. I will take this little body and own it, sooner rather than later. Come home with me tonight, Bella. Nothing needs to happen. I just need you to be with me. I need to know you're safe."

A new rush of excitement flooded my panties, even with him tamping down the prospect of sex. I didn't care. I needed to stay close to him. To have him wrap me in his arms, to aid me once this adrenaline wore off and the reality of my actions crept in. I may have acted badass, wanting to help protect him and his men. But that didn't mean I was okay with taking lives. One thing that my father told me since I was little finally rang true today.

"Win or lose, against all odds or none, you head into battle preparing to die for your family."

I knew the situation was dangerous. That Lucky and his men were protecting me and needed my help. But Lucky wasn't my family. In fact, the exact opposite. My father might have bowed to Mario Agostino, but it wasn't out of respect. He did it because of the power Mario had over him, over all the families in New York. Yet these men threw down their lives for me, protecting me because Lucky had claimed me. And I wanted to return the favor.

Lucky and his men shielded me as we made a safe getaway to the car.

"All clear, boss. Yuri's gone but all other targets have been removed."

Lucky's death grip on my hand eased briefly. "I want him found. Now!"

Several men took off in different directions, looking for the Russian leader.

Lucky stopped to look down at me. Tucking a strand of loose hair behind my ear, he smirked. "You are a vision covered in the blood of our enemies, smelling like a freshly fired weapon." As he kissed the tip of my nose, I smiled. "What's the damage?" Lucky asked a bloody and weakened Apollo.

"That was incredible, *mia regina.* If not for your fast thinking, I fear we may've lost some of our own men." Then he turned to Lucky. "The machine guns bogged us down for a bit. But the Russian bastard underestimated her, much like we did. Once she took him down with the return fire, they didn't have a chance. She saved all our asses."

My eyes scanned the warehouse and I noticed that more men than we started with came out of the shadows. There were dozens of Italian men in suits, holding weapons and wearing matching expressions. As I locked eyes with each one of them, they dipped their heads in respect to me. Lastly, my gaze fell to Lucky. Basking in the carnage and evil hanging in the air, he was pleased with himself. And me. He kissed my hand and guided me into the car, just as a thought hit me.

If Anthony Moretti knew what I'd just done, he'd kill me. I single-handedly saved the eldest son of Mario Agostino, his sworn enemy. And I'd do it just the same, given the chance.

CHAPTER 10
LUCIFER "LUCKY" AGOSTINO

I'd had twenty-five men hidden in the shadows of that warehouse. I thought I was prepared for the war they attempted to wage on us. I was wrong. I was never fucking wrong. The moment I heard the gunfire, I knew I'd made a grave mistake. Not only had I underestimated the threat that was Yuri and his men, I'd put Bella in danger. My men signed up for this—the potential of dying tomorrow to help aid the cause. If they laid down their lives, it would be in the name of duty. Honor.

My sweet Bella was forced into this situation. By me.

Mirabella Moretti was the innocent in all of this. Even if she was the only daughter of Anthony Moretti, she was still innocent. Her family sent her away to keep her out of the mess we conducted in our daily lives. Now, it was only the first date and I was putting her in the direct line of fire. I didn't expect or want her to get out of that car.

The moment that door opened, Apollo and I both cursed under our breaths—but only for a moment—then we stood in awe at her powerful entrance. Her heels angrily stomped towards us as she fervently shouted in Russian.

She was a hell of a force to be reckoned with. And she belonged to me.

I could see their expressions turn from lust to confusion. Her words had the men seething with fury and it was directed at Yuri. The realization of my identity and Yuri's nonchalance set off a chorus of angry side conversations. Their leader had set them up, leading his men like cattle to the slaughter. And slaughtered they were.

The shining light in a room preemptively filled with blood and bedlam… my queen. She'd cemented her place at my side. My dick hardened at the sight before me. An entirely new Mirabella Moretti stood in our wake.

They threatened her. She heard it firsthand in Russian. Seen together once, and our world had spread the news like wildfire. She didn't falter or cower. And she sure as fuck surprised me. She made me proud.

Without concern for her own safety, she held her head high and faced vicious men with a ferocity unbeknownst to me. She'd been driven by her urge to warn me.

I loved it. *I loved her.*

When the Russians finally got a semblance of a backbone and attacked, she was all I could see. Underneath her calm and resolute façade, I could sense her fear as the chaos ensued. I loved the fact that she looked at me with complete trust.

She was trusting her soul to *il diavolo* and he was ready to take on such a challenge. And so much more for her. Apollo and I shielded her until she was safe within the confines of the bulletproof car.

"Spread out. I want Yuri—preferably alive. I want to send a fucking message."

Apollo nodded, motioning for our men to spread out before charging alongside me.

"That motherfucker is mine. They threatened *mia regina.* They're all fucking done."

Everyone was in motion. Doing what they did best. Destroying any threat to the Agostino syndicate. My men were precise, tactical, and lethal when it came to protecting me and what was mine. And Bella was mine. She'd earned their regard the moment she'd stepped into the dangerous spotlight. They would protect her with their lives because they'd sworn to do so. But *how* they saw her made them work that much harder.

"The fuck?" Diving behind a freight of cargo, Apollo and I grunted upon contact with the concrete floor. "These fuckers have access to machine guns?" Apollo ground out between clenched teeth.

Not once in all our business dealings had the Russians mentioned machine guns, tossing a surplus of smaller handguns and some medium military-grade weapons our way. Which they'd yet to deliver. The bastards had been playing us from the start…

"It's a fucking RPK-16, the newest edition from the Russian special forces!" Heavy gunfire was coming from the entire room. But the two RPKs were situated on opposite sides of the warehouse, meaning we were trapped. Like a pair of fucking rats.

The dead bodies surrounding us were all Russian. My reinforcements remained hidden in the shadows in order to keep the upper hand while my men on the floor were seeking shelter, waiting for the right moment to move forward.

The muzzle flashes in my direct line of sight told me that the RPKs were too far back to reach their targets. They were positioned at the wrong angle to take precise shots. Instead, the Russians had opted to rain bullets on the lower level. Aimlessly. To incite chaos.

"We don't have a chance if we don't take down the RPKs. Fuck!" Bullets continued to hit the side of the freight we were hidden behind. "Damn it!"

"Fuck! Okay, I've got this." Before I could stop him, Apollo stepped out, darting to the next closest cover as he took as many shots as he could. Even bleeding heavily from his shoulder wound, the son of a bitch was a dead shot. The groan followed by a sudden lull in gunfire told me he'd gotten to one of the RPKs.

Moving fast and low, I left the safety of my cover and headed in the direction I'd last seen Yuri. He was going to die very slowly. By my hands. More bullets flew my way. The Russians knew if they didn't take me down, I'd make them all suffer. Stepping around a corner, I saw one of Yuri's men take a bullet to the leg. Superficial. Nothing deadly. And the bastard was crying like a baby.

"Malen'kaya suka," he spat at me. I didn't know the language outside the occasional phrase, but this... this I understood.

I stepped on his leg, and he howled in pain. "Who's a little bitch now?" Without a second thought, I fired. A slug between his eyes, and I was left with a calming afterthought.

He'd died with the look of fear permanently marring his face. And I reveled in that fear. It inspired me to destroy every single one of these men. I was running out of bullets, so I drew my knife from my hip, and kept moving towards the back of the warehouse. A lion searching for his prey.

The *diavolo* looking for human souls to deposit into hell.

"Pozhaluysta, pozhaluysta."

I heard him before I saw him. "Would you have granted my *regina* a pardon? Would you have set her free from her captors if she begged?" Without waiting for a response, my curved nine-inch blade cut the Russian's throat from ear to ear. The carotid artery was always the messiest, blood spurting aggressively from the wound.

As I circled the back of the warehouse, my body count was up to seven in a span of just as many minutes. My bullets were reserved for an emergency as I thrived on the more intimate deaths with my knife. My suit was stuck to my skin, weighed down by each new splash of blood. It was both euphoric and powerful to so intimately destroy a man by your own hands. To watch their life drain from their eyes. For your face to be the last thing they see before their journey to hell.

Turning back to my car, I could see Bella was tucked between the seats tending to Apollo's wound. She'd dove into battle to protect me and now she was patching up one of my most prominent men. She was impeccable, and together we were the future of the Agostino Crime Family.

My hands dropped to my chest, searching for my spare clip while quickly realizing I was out of ammo. Bullets whizzed by my head as my eyes flicked towards Bella for a second time, a small smirk curling my lips when her gaze landed on mine.

The sound of splintering wood and crunching metal shook me from my thoughts. My position was known, forcing me to reconsider my next plan of attack. But of course my queen refused to remain hidden in the car. My dick grew harder as the rear passenger window went down. And with precision rivaling one of my best snipers, she silenced the gunfire.

It didn't take long for me to find Yuri, or for one of his men to find *me*. Then my little guardian angel saved me again. A precise shot through his chest and the oversized gym rat dropped like a brick tossed over a bridge. A second shot missed Yuri by mere inches. I was winded but filled with adrenaline as a raging hard-on pressed the limits of my pants.

Bella might've been born a Moretti, but she was ready to be an Agostino. Other women never warranted a second look, nor garnered more care than how far my dick could fit down their throats. I wanted nothing to do with the idea of settling down or creating my own family.

Until Bella.

I rushed to the car and wrapped her in my embrace. Losing Yuri was a major miss. But here, in this moment, with this woman in my arms, everything felt right.

I watched her squirming in her seat for the entirety of the ride back. Discreetly rubbing her thighs together, seeking friction to relieve the adrenaline that was surely dwindling inside her. I saw the excitement in those beautiful mismatched eyes the moment I'd invited her home, despite my gentleman's promise.

"Apollo, inform the Morettis of their daughter's whereabouts. I will have her home tomorrow morning."

He nodded as I guided Bella inside. As she looked around, I could see her confusion. The penthouse was for whores, not my future queen. I'd taken her to the Agostino family compound in the outskirts of the city.

"Come, it's late. Let's get you showered and in bed. Tomorrow, I'll show you my mother's gardens and give you a tour of the stables."

Her face lit up with such excitement and I couldn't help but smile back. "Our home is so green and bland. My father claims it has to do with his allergies, though I have a feeling it's something more absurd. I'd love to take in the gardens."

Without another word, I rushed her into the house and to my room, where she went right for the small library in my corner office. It wasn't much. Not by her standards, I was sure. Most of the books were on architectural design, business fundamentals, and minor law. The others, the ones that would probably pique her interest, didn't belong to me.

"You read Edgar Allen Poe?" Her eyes twinkled with the question.

"Those are Apollo's."

"I assumed they would be. Not many a man can quote Mark Twain. And… never mind."

"And? Come now, *mia regina*." I was toying with her, while her playful smirk told me whatever was on her tongue would be at my expense.

"I'm unsure if *il diavolo* would have time for the classics." She could barely get her sentence out with a straight face.

"*Mio angelo,* you wound me! *Oh, mio cuore!*"

Her giggles echoed in the silence of my room, and I knew her happiness would be my undoing.

"I was told the devil didn't have a heart?" she countered, gasping when I pulled her close.

"It seems someone has brought out a weakness in me."

Her eyes softened. "Lucifer."

"I'm not a good man, Bella. I've spilled more blood than you'll ever read about in those books of yours. Much more than what you witnessed tonight. And I'll destroy anyone who gets in the way of what I want. I've never claimed to be innocent with any of the women before you. Because this feeling never existed *before you.* I didn't think it possible. However, now that I know it does, I can make you a promise. I'll never do anything to intentionally hurt you. I will protect you with my life and so will my men. I want you as my queen, as the mother of my children, Bella."

"Lucifer…"

I tossed her onto the bed, and whatever she was about to say died on her tongue as I pinned her beneath my larger frame. "I know I promised I'd behave. And if you want to wait for our wedding night, I will. But tonight… tonight, I need to taste you."

Her eyes searched mine, looking for some hint of a lie. She wouldn't find it. If she wanted to wait, as much as it would kill me, I'd oblige. But I couldn't wait to taste what I knew would be the sweetest little bud of pleasure. I would devour and own her in every way possible.

Giving me a small nod and coy smile, she watched as I pulled her dress up and over her head in a flourishing swoop of material. Bared before me was pure perfection. Smooth, porcelain skin, clad in black lace that begged me to rip it to shreds.

My eyes flicked to hers and I could see the innocence and fear reflected back at me. I growled deep in my chest before my face dove between her two perfect breasts, kissing and licking them to make her writhe, while my hands tugged her core closer to me. I squeezed her ass and lifted it in the air. Her arousal was warm and wet against the fly of my slacks. And I could feel it.

The droplets of blood from our fight were peeling off her skin, turning me on all the more. Something about her perfect flesh somewhat marred with blood exhilarated me, the metallic scent in the air swirling with the sweet aroma of her arousal practically dripping from her panties. I slid them down her thighs and was met with a freshly waxed, glistening pink mound. A body that hadn't been touched by any other man. That fact alone made me crave to destroy her. To make her beg for me to take her to bed, owning her inside and out.

I continued my quest to her pink mound, lapping her peaks and curves as I went. She giggled as my stubble brushed along her stomach. The apex of her thighs was a meeting spot to heaven. One warm, wet kiss caused her to quiver with unmet need. I hadn't even touched her wet core and she was teetering on the edge of bliss. It wouldn't take long, and I was done playing.

I devoured her core like a man starved, ravaged her sensitive nub, and licked her perfect lips from top to bottom. Her head thrashed from side to side as she cried my name in a blur of mumbled adoration. Grabbing my head, her innocence forgotten, Bella held me to the place she needed the most attention. My perusal of the sensitive bundle of nerves sent her over the edge into euphoria. And I watched as she fell from heaven.

"You're breathtaking."

The red blush I loved so much crept up her skin. "Lucifer, I…"

Cutting her off with a kiss, I smiled down at her. "Come, let's get you a bath and then to bed." I grabbed a clean white t-shirt from my closet and led her into my bathroom. Floor-to-ceiling glass walls surrounded the large shower big enough to fit five people. I activated the extra nozzles on the walls, lost in thought.

Fuck me, she was perfection.

I was consumed by images of bending Bella over and pressing her against the wall, while I penetrated her aggressively from behind. I had yet to break in this shower appropriately since I didn't invite women to my family home. Stripping down, I planned to shower next to her. I *planned* to. And I really did try.

She gasped, her pupils dilating as she took me in from head to toe, her gaze stopping at my hard cock, now standing tall.

"That. Th-that." She pointed at my throbbing cock.

"Yes, *mia regina?*" I couldn't help but toy with her.

"That won't fit." Her expression remained shocked, concerned.

"It will. And you'll beg me for it." My glistening fingers entered my mouth on a moan. The sweet, sweet taste of her still on my tongue was like honey to my sensitive palate. Stepping beneath the hot water stream, I took her small hand in mine, pulled Bella to the shower's edge, and disrobed her.

Her tiny pink nipples were already hardened and begging me to suck them. Peeling a strip of dried blood from her bare chest was and oddly erotic sensation. She was still covered in the blood of my enemies. Our enemies. Because, for better or worse, what was mine was also hers.

"Shower. Then bed." I tugged her to my chest beneath the waterfall showerhead and groaned. Her mewls were challenging my restraint. I adjusted the nozzles to hit her top and bottom in perfect rhythm, eliciting a symphony of moans from her plump lips, before running a washcloth across her skin, committing her perfection to memory. I learned every curve, every freckle, every spot of transcendence. Then I went to take care of myself, turning my back on her.

"Please." A small, soft hand on my shoulder made every muscle in my body tense.

My newfound gentlemanly behaviors were being tested, and I had only so much restraint. Slowly, she replicated my movements, exploring every part of me. Once her hand dropped to my hips, she froze, looking up at me through those thick lashes. I nodded at her questioning gaze and her palm wrapped around my cock, barely able to contain it. I groaned, a guttural sound that reverberated against the bathroom walls and seemed to pique her interest. She liked the effect she was having on me. The control.

Dropping to her knees before I could protest, Bella took me fast and deep. Gagging slightly as I hit the back of her throat, she waited. It was the most arduous task to stay rooted and let her control what was happening. Her warm mouth was like perfect velvet. With the slightest provocation, I knew I'd come fast.

She cupped my balls and moaned around her full mouth. The vibration made my balls shake and tingle. I was right on the edge. She took me deeper, her movements growing more confident. I tried to pull back, but my balls tightened, causing her to suck harder. She grasped on to my thighs and kept me buried in her mouth. My queen didn't deserve to swallow my release on our first night together. But my dark angel had other things in mind. Unable to stop myself, I came hard. Spilled every last drop down her throat. And the good girl that she was swallowed without complaint.

As I swooped down to pull her to her feet, Bella wouldn't look me in the eyes. Her innocence was getting the better of her. I didn't say a word, didn't speak, afraid to discourage her. Instead, I tugged her to her feet and held her body to mine. Our heartbeats merged, beating as one. And it confirmed what I already knew. This woman was made for me. I'd been with a lot of women, all of whom paled in comparison to Mirabella.

"Finish your shower. I'll be in bed." As I kissed the tip of her nose, she giggled. A sound I'd come to crave.

I dried off and left the bathroom quickly. If I stayed any longer, my resolve would crumble and my body would pillage hers. I exited the bathroom and walked directly into my closet, pulling down a black beater and black sweatpants.

Apollo was already seated in my office area, his jacket removed and his arm freshly stitched. We had a doctor on call, but knowing him, he'd done the work himself. He waited for me behind the bookshelves, acknowledging me with a curt nod. The layout of the room would give Bella her privacy when she climbed into bed.

"He's in the wind. We have every available man on him." Apollo spilled the news I was anticipating.

"I want him found. I want him saved for me." I dropped into my leather chair, my expression solemn. "He threatened her."

Apollo dipped his chin in understanding. "That's why every man is on it. Word's already spread around the family. She's earned their respect all on her own."

"As I thought she would. Just never could've guessed she'd do it so quickly. And in such a manner."

With that matter settled, we moved on to the topic of our buyers. They were dropping like flies. The epitome of supply and demand. And I didn't have the supply. Using Bella's advice, we focused on those who hadn't cancelled their contracts—their sudden patience a waving red flag. Someone was approaching them and we would find out who.

"All right, leave me. I need to tend to *mia regina.*"

Apollo smirked at me. "After today, she isn't just yours. *Nostra regina.* She's our queen too."

I shoved him aside and stepped around the wall of bookshelves, realizing the bathroom door was open. The room empty. And a moment of sheer panic seized me.

"*Piccola ragazza,* need to feed her more." Apollo chuckled, motioning to my bed. I saw movement. She was indeed a *little girl.* So little I barely registered her under the oversized comforter.

Apollo left silently, a permanent smirk on his usually perturbed face. I slipped out of my sweatpants and climbed into bed. I moved closer, quickly noting how she smelled of my shampoo. A scent I didn't normally appreciate until this moment.

She mumbled in her sleep and rolled over, folding herself against me. "Sleep well, *mia bambina.*" I kissed her head and she sighed in response. And, before I knew it, I'd fallen into the deepest sleep I'd had in a long time.

CHAPTER 11

MIRABELLA MORETTI

"**M**y daughter is not your son's whore! She was arranged to be married! Not passed around like some cheap trophy!"

The angry voice of my father shook me awake. Confused by my surroundings, I could feel my heart racing in my chest. Mario Agostino was a man who demanded and earned respect. And I was lying like a tramp in his son's empty bed.

Hand. Slap. Forehead.

What was I thinking last night? My father was right to call me Lucky's whore. That's exactly how I'd behaved. I had let the adrenaline act as my poor decision-maker. Although my virginity remained intact, I let him taste me right before I tasted him. Who was I kidding? I liked—no, I *loved* it. With Lucky, it felt so right. Overwhelming. Intoxicating.

"*Where is she? I want my daughter!*"

I just prayed the room would swallow me whole. End my embarrassment and misery.

"I assumed you didn't want to greet your father in my brother's shirt."

I shrieked and practically jumped out of my skin, as a young woman's startled my staring contest with the ceiling. She had to be Lucky's sister. A smaller, prettier version of the man himself. I took note of her grey eyes as she smirked at my situational duress.

"My name is Sienna. Apollo told me you'd be up here and in need of a change of clothes. Come, we're about the same size."

I did my best to climb modestly out of Lucky's bed as Sienna chuckled at my struggle, consisting of me literally wrapped up in the sheet and almost falling on my face from the effort. First depositing some items on the bed—which I realized were dresses and shoes— she then waved a makeup bag at me and pointed towards the bathroom.

I'd suddenly become mute, silently following her commands. My black hair dried with a slight wave that Sienna quickly curled at the ends. Minimal makeup was applied, and in a few short minutes, I was almost presentable. She pointed towards the black Chanel dress with a silver Hermes belt. She even went out of her way to pass me a pair of brand-new, earrings, and a necklace.

I stepped out of the bathroom, quickly realizing Sienna was waiting for me on the bed. She motioned for me to spin, thoroughly appraising her work, and I laughed and froze when we came face to face again.

"Thank you. Apollo told me what you did for him and Lucky last night." A sad smile graced her inherently flawless face. She may have had a decent amount of makeup on, but the girl didn't need it.

"It was…"

Cutting me off with a wave, she pulled me towards the door. "Say nothing. You walked into danger to warn my brother and his men. You protected this family and I truly thank you."

Any semblance of a response died on my tongue as the distant shouting resumed.

"Fuck you, Lucky! Get my fucking sister!"

Oh, God. Gio was here too?

"I've killed men for less than your bullshit. If it weren't for your sister, I'd use you to paint this foyer red." Lucky's anger boomed up the staircase. The sound of *il diavolo* had me stumbling on the spot.

"Your brother's a real dickhead," Sienna commented. "My little brother is a twit, so I get it. But yours takes the cake. Anyway, we had a slumber party last night, okay?"

"Hello, dear." Isabella Agostino was the picture of perfection, even this early in the morning. She was wrapped in a cream Chanel pantsuit, open-toed heels, and diamonds that caught the light just right. "I've spoken with your mother. She's aware of the story. Just a girls' slumber party we arranged for you and Sienna."

"Th-th-thank you, both. It will help me…"

"Get her the fuck now!" Gio interrupted my train of thought. He sounded like a toddler throwing a temper tantrum.

Strutting down the stairs, my head held high and my expression stern, I approached my father and brother. "I assure you all this yelling and causing a scene isn't necessary. Mother cleared the sleepover with Isabella. Sienna and I haven't seen each other since I left for Italy. Daddy, I didn't presume it'd be an issue."

Gio was vibrating beneath his three-piece suit and my father looked like he was ready to kill everyone in the room. "That's not what I fucking heard." My brother's smug face turned to me. "I heard you had dinner with this…" Gio threw a hand in the air as if he couldn't verbalize an insult that cut deep enough. "And then attended a very interesting business meeting."

Lucky's spine went straight, my brother's access to that intel forcing his outrage to rapidly rise to the surface. Lucky and I made eye contact, each silently wondering the same thing. In the short time I'd been around the Agostino men, I knew their loyalty was to the family. Meaning Gio had to have an insider. And it wouldn't be someone on Lucky's side.

The question was: how the hell had my brother infiltrated the Russians?

Beyond the slight tick I'd caught in his jaw, Lucky's face remained impassive. We were attuned to each other on such a deep level I could practically see the gears turning in his head. Rage burned up my esophagus, threatening to scorch me from the inside out—a venom I decided to impart on my brother. "And if I believed the rumors about you, I'd assume your dick had rotted off from all the diseases you've caught.

Then I'd tattle to Daddy about how you're conducting business behind his back." All of which was true.

There was something empowering about Lucky's presence. I finally had the confidence to speak my mind after all these years. Felt that I was worth the time. That they should listen to what I had to say. And I was done with letting Gio walk all over me.

"I love this girl." Sienna was laughing behind her hand. Even his parents looked at me with a sense of admiration.

This was what I have been yearning for, for years now.

"You little!" Gio stepped in my direction before stumbling back again, Lucky's hand firmly gripping the collar of his shirt while Apollo slid in front of me.

"Watch yourself, Gio. That is my fiancée you're addressing. And if the rumors you heard were true, wouldn't you want to stay on her good side?"

My brother's face was the brightest shade of red I'd ever seen. Without a word, he went to storm out of the room. Turning in his spot, he ran directly into Apollo. Time slowed as each man glared at the other. Until Apollo smirked and let Gio pass a few moments later.

"This is final? The announcement will be made at the party?" Having previously sounded like he was frothing at the mouth, my father's tone was eerily resolute.

It took me a moment to realize everyone was staring. Lucky not only stepped forward to protect me, but I was seeking shelter in his embrace, comforted by his muscular arms wrapped around me.

"Yes." The one-word reply was directed at my father, who nodded before following Mario into his office. "You are something else, *mia regina*. I have some business I need to attend to, but my mother wanted to show you the gardens."

I couldn't help the excitement that washed over me. Grasping my arm ever so gently, Isabella led me towards the kitchen and through the open French doors.

"It's like heaven on earth." I would never grow tired of my future mother-in-law's handiwork.

Watching me smile at Lucky over my plate of fresh mussels, my mother started giggling. *Again.* "Ever since she was a little girl, Bella's been one to stop and smell the flowers."

That first morning at the Agostino compound, Isabella had given me a full tour of the gardens, before Lucky rejoined us. We shared a nice lunch and then I was escorted home.

I was fortunate that my brother was nowhere to be found and my father was out on business. It gave me time to converse with my mother and accept Lucky's invite for another date. He took me to a local greenhouse, then we went horseback riding. The evening ended with a small dinner in the barn behind his family's home, where we all sat presently, several days after the impromptu "slumber party." It was a wonder, seeing such a large man atop a horse and to do so gracefully. But I was quickly learning that Lucky didn't do anything less than one hundred percent. It was both admirable and insufferable for someone such as myself, who was barely mediocre at most things—although he never made me feel like that.

Just being close to the man was setting my skin on fire and down-right pissing me off. We'd yet to share another intimate moment together since the shower. It seemed that, besides his little touches and glances, Lucky was trying to remain ever the gentleman. Here we were, out to lunch with our mothers and Sienna, like any other day. Like I wasn't debating whether or not ripping his clothes off at the table was proper etiquette or not.

"I'm so glad you liked them! This is my favorite time of year. The drab and dreary colors of winter are taken over by the fresh colors and scents currently in bloom." Isabella and I shared the same passion. I learned she did her own planting and tending in her gardens. Their gardeners were used for the grass and maintenance, but her beloved flower beds were hers and hers alone.

"The big day is coming. Are you both excited?" Sipping her tea, my mother looked between Lucky and me expectantly.

"Beyond. As if I needed further confirmation, these last few days together have set in stone what I already knew. Your daughter is as beautiful as she is kind. Her heart is so big—it's the first thing I noticed about her. She's fierce, loyal, and unlike any woman I've ever met. Though it's her ferocity that's truly fascinating."

I could hear the way my mother swallowed and I knew the waterworks weren't far behind. "*Madre!* Please don't."

"Sorry, *bella ragazza,* it's just… I'm so grateful for his kind words. Isabella and I weren't fortunate to marry for love. We had to work for it, every day. You and Lucky are something special." She squeezed my hand under the table as I clenched my jaw to keep my own tears from falling.

"Sir." Apollo walked to Lucky's side. "My apologies, ladies." Nodding to the others, he winked playfully at me. Apollo was a conundrum that I'd yet to figure out. He read poetry and classic novels, but was equally driven to rip a man's flesh from his bones. And he had a secret, deep-seated infatuation with Sienna, who was doing her best to ignore him altogether.

"How?" Lucky hissed his reply before his eyes landed on me and immediately softened. Whatever information Apollo had whispered into his ear, it wasn't good.

"I just love that my future sister-in-law has a sharp tongue on her. I'm so thankful she isn't some daisy I have to handle with kid gloves." Sienna lightly tapped my arm while I tugged on her long hair in response, sending all the women at the table into a fit of laughter. I never would have expected for all of this to fall into place so effortlessly.

Sienna and I had become fast friends and I genuinely enjoyed her company. Apollo and a few others from Lucky's inner circle chatted with me often while Mario was becoming closer to me than my own father had ever been. Though the best part was Isabella and my mother. For women who loved the same man, they seemed to put those issues behind them and formed a sincere friendship.

"You know, Apollo is single and his eyes practically eat you alive whenever you're in the room."

Sienna's blue eyes begged me for silence, while her foot kicking me under the table reiterated the sentiment. I winked and resumed sipping my merlot.

"Tell me." The words left my mouth before I could stop them and Lucky paused mid-conversation, his attention garnered at my command.

"One of my men was murdered."

I gasped before I could stop myself. "Who?" His men protected me as much as they did Lucky and his businesses. To lose one of them was like losing a member of the family.

"Vinny." Another gasp sounded from across the table when Sienna caught wind of our conversation.

"Yuri?"

He confirmed my suspicions with a nod and I could see he was close to losing his calm façade. "He was seen on surveillance offering one shot to the back of Vinny's head. Like a coward."

"We must take care of his family."

Lucky's eyes softened. Leaning across the table, he pulled me in for a kiss. "*Mia regina*, you have a heart of gold. Yes, we will take care of everything for them." Then he turned to our mothers. "Ladies, I'm sorry but I'll have to cut the evening short. If you don't mind, I'd like to take my bride-to-be with me."

My mother swooned when Lucky kissed her cheek and whispered in her ear before he escorted me outside again, with Big Al, as I affectionately called him, at my back and Apollo at my side. It had only been a few days, but I'd grown fiercely protective over these men. They were mine, just as much as they were Lucky's. He'd mentioned his initial concern when it came to his men protecting me. They were fiercely loyal to him because it was their job. And he knew they'd protect me at his command, but ever since the warehouse their loyalty had also transferred to me. Because I'd earned it.

Curling against his muscled chest, I snuggled into his warm embrace in the back of the SUV. Big Al was driving and Apollo sat in the front seat, giving us the illusion of privacy. Lucky was busy tapping away on his cellphone between kissing the top of my head and running his fingers through my hair. My three glasses of merlot had filled me with that fuzzy sensation, as I tried to ignore all thoughts of Vinny.

"Who the fuck…? Boss, we've got company. Two cars to the rear." Apollo leaned forward in his seat, staring into the side mirror as he shouted orders over the phone.

"Seat belt, now. Quickly, *mio amore.*"

I complied just as the car bolted down the highway.

"They're coming up fast." Apollo reached under his seat, pulling out two handguns. Lucky shifted, drawing several more from the sidebar of the SUV and handing me a matte black 9mm. I slipped a round into the chamber before glancing at Lucky. His eyes were dark, lustful, as he watched me handle the gun.

"No matter what happens, you stay in this car. No matter what, you hear. My men will handle everything, but I cannot worry about you running off." His eyes were commanding yet soft, as I nodded in agreement.

"I promise."

"Take this exit and duck into the industrial park. We can loop around for the element of surprise."

I gasped as the car lurched on the turn. Big Al sped up, yanking the wheel quickly and taking the exit at a dangerous speed. Hauling ass, we plowed into a locked gate, rolling over the metal like it was nothing before he managed to tuck the car behind a metal container just as the other two vehicles approached from the front.

We now had the advantage of being behind them. The doors opened simultaneously as all of Lucky's men exited, weapons drawn and aimed straight ahead. The second SUV of men barreled into the park, effectively blocking in the offenders.

Gunfire erupted within moments, and I watched on as the chaos unfolded. I was stricken by both fear and shock. Fear at knowing men would die and shocked by the realization that I prayed it wasn't *our* men. Gone was the sheltered girl I once was. I was owning my place as their future queen.

Our attackers fled, the *diavolo and his demoni* charging through the chaos like two men on a hell-sent mission. Peeking out of the open door, I could see the two cars that had been following us, bloodied bodies hanging out the sides as Apollo and Lucky demanded answers from a man on his knees in front of them. He yelled back, I presumed in Russian, though I was too far away to know for sure.

"Get out of the car, you little bitch." A large, sweaty palm clamped over my mouth before I knew what was happening, while a thick Russian accent demanded my compliance. *"Stay quiet and you live. Speak, I make them watch you die slowly."*

"Lucky will kill you if you hurt me," I spat in response as he dragged me from my seat.

"I am already dead, bitch. Why not take the devil and his queen with me?" He thought himself clever. But I was much more so. The gun Lucky had given me was stuffed into the top of my velvet over-the-knee boots. Rising from my seated position with my hands in the air, I got a good look at my offender. His nose was clearly broken, bent at an odd angle with blood pouring from it.

"You speak the truth. You are dead," I warned in Russian, my eyes fixed on Lucky's shadow now looming behind the man. And without a word—no noise at all—a pipe flashed beneath the streetlamp as it swung. At the crunch of metal meeting skull bone, I shoved my attacker's arm to the side, making him fire into the SUV on impact.

His large frame crumbled to the ground before I kicked his gun aside. Stepping over his prone form, Lucky rushed to me, like a starving lion pouncing on his prey. Licking, sucking, and biting, his mouth attacked my entire body. He buried his face into the cleavage of my dress and pinned me to the car, my hands roaming and exploring when left to their own devices.

Apollo coughed, a subtle announcement reminding us of his presence. Lucky released me and looked down at the man bleeding out at our feet. His moans were muffled and incoherent. The blow to his head had caused some serious damage. Kicking him in the stomach, Lucky watched as the man rolled to his back, spitting up blood in heavy pools. He yelled, demanded answers, but the Russian was too far gone. Lucky dropped to his haunches and pulled a knife from the pocket of his blood-smeared suit. Apollo stepped to me, urging me to look away, but I couldn't. This was the man I'd agreed to marry. Whose children I would raise. Whose bed I would share. The partner I'd grow old with.

I wanted—no, I needed—to see it all. This was the life I was choosing. This was my choice. Both the good and the bad.

"He hurt our family," I said, gesturing for Apollo to step aside.

Looking down at Lucky, I saw the same cold, harsh blue of his eyes that men feared. I nodded my approval before his long blade thrust easily through the skin of the man's chest. Blood gushed from the wound in a torrent of dark-red liquid and his breathing increased momentarily before it stopped altogether and the man went limp.

"*Mia regina, mio amore,* Apollo will take you to my penthouse. He's not to leave your side while I handle this." Lucky's eyes flicked to the man tied up and thrown in the back of the SUV, then landed on me again. He kissed the top of my head and stalked away.

Big Al got into the driver's seat per usual, but Apollo sat in the back with me. As I looked out the side of my eye, I could see he was concerned about my mental state. Any movement, any heavier-than-usual breath and his eyes bore holes through me. He wanted to reach out and ensure I was okay but didn't want to offend me either.

"He deserved it, Apollo. As does the man who was taken. To protect what is ours. I'm okay. You can stop watching me." Grasping his warm hand, I gave a promising squeeze before looking out the window.

"I never doubted your strength for a second," he answered as my cell phone rang.

I read the name across the screen and quickly pressed accept. *"Ciao, Madre."*

Muffled voices filled the receiver. My mother was crying. Frantic. They hadn't just gone after us; they ran our mothers and Lucky's sister off the road. They were safe but shaken up. Everyone agreed that it was best for them to hole up at the Agostino compound. I sent my love and quickly disconnected the call.

"Apollo." His eyes were glued to me, having heard the entire conversation. "Take me to Lucky."

"Mia regina, please, you heard him. He will come to you when he's done."

I shook my head. My eyes told him just how serious I was. "They could've taken everything from me today. I won't allow it. Take me. To Lucky."

He stared at me with a mixture of concern and confusion, and I watched his mind tick as he considered the ramifications. No doubt Lucky would be pissed, but too bad. I was protecting my family. Finally he threw a hand in the air, as if to surrender. *"Fanculo!* Al, take us."

I watched Big Al's reflection in the rearview mirror. His features morphed into something resembling fear. "It was my demand. I assure you he will know that," I answered his questioning stare.

"And I agreed. This won't fall on you," Apollo muttered, cursing under his breath as the SUV switched directions.

"No one hurts my family and gets away with it." I let those words hang in the air as I stared out the window, the city lights racing by in a blur. Lost to my thoughts.

"I just hope Lucky lets me live after this." Apollo went back to his phone, tapping away at the screen, his face full of tension.

"Text Sienna to make sure she is okay. Let her know you're concerned."

His head snapped up at me, glaring when he noticed the smirk I was giving him, before his eyes returned to his cellular device. He acted cold and indifferent. I heard the men mutter the word 'psycho' around him. But every crazed man had an outlet. A remedy. And Sienna could be just that for Apollo.

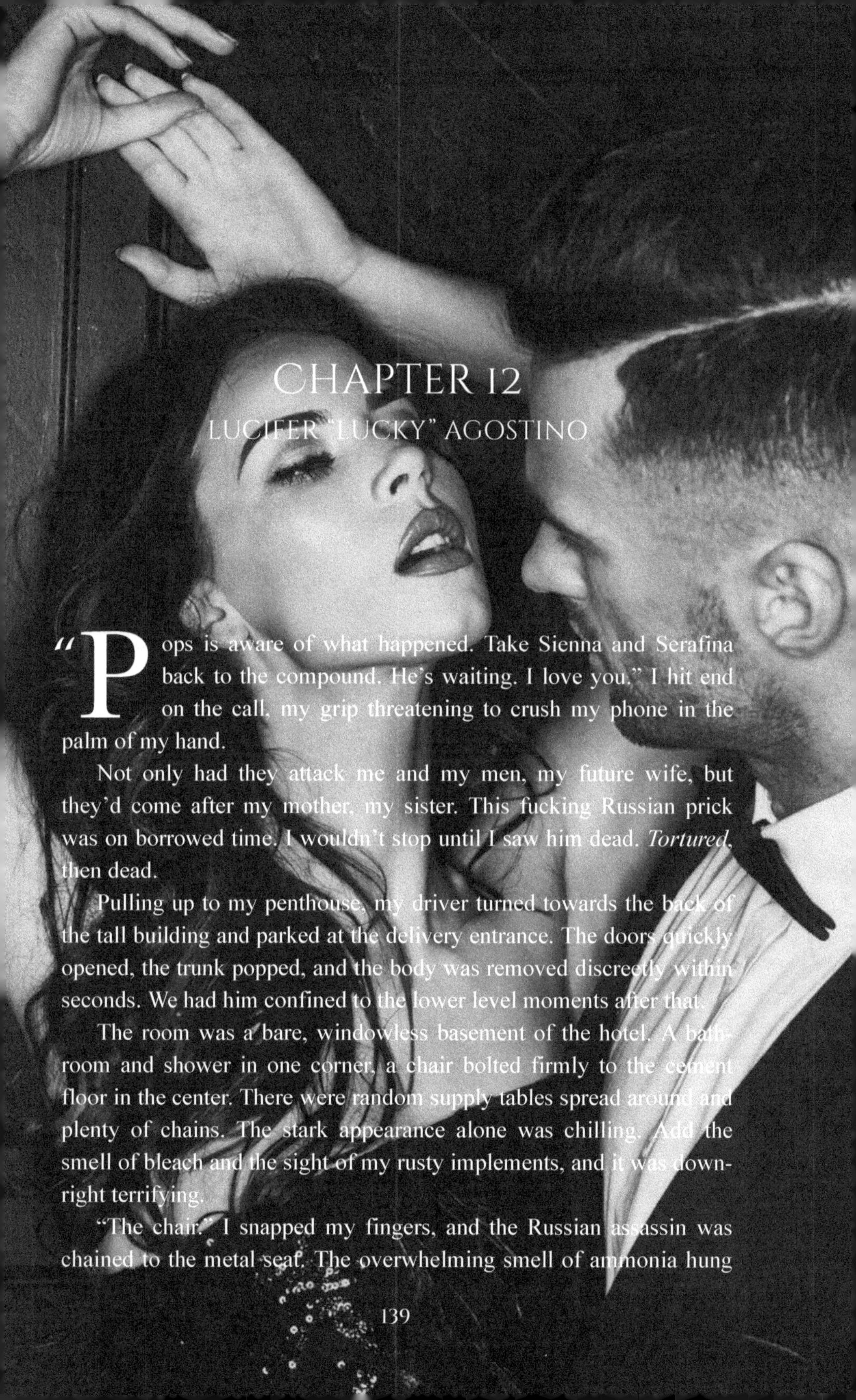

CHAPTER 12

"Pops is aware of what happened. Take Sienna and Serafina back to the compound. He's waiting. I love you." I hit end on the call, my grip threatening to crush my phone in the palm of my hand.

Not only had they attack me and my men, my future wife, but they'd come after my mother, my sister. This fucking Russian prick was on borrowed time. I wouldn't stop until I saw him dead. *Tortured*, then dead.

Pulling up to my penthouse, my driver turned towards the back of the tall building and parked at the delivery entrance. The doors quickly opened, the trunk popped, and the body was removed discreetly within seconds. We had him confined to the lower level moments after that.

The room was a bare, windowless basement of the hotel. A bathroom and shower in one corner, a chair bolted firmly to the cement floor in the center. There were random supply tables spread around and plenty of chains. The stark appearance alone was chilling. Add the smell of bleach and the sight of my rusty implements, and it was downright terrifying.

"The chair." I snapped my fingers, and the Russian assassin was chained to the metal seat. The overwhelming smell of ammonia hung in the air from our last venture down here. And it was somewhat calming to my lingering rage.

The table of devices held everything from garden shears, knives, and small household appliances. Sometimes we got bored and needed to change things up. I had a cartel member tied down here for three days before he talked; he was a record holder. Typically, once I was involved, they spilled their guts within hours of my arrival. He lasted three fucking days. Granted, he did have a hard time confessing his sins to me without his tongue. Though, in all fairness, I had warned him repeatedly to stop spitting at me or he'd regret it. After that, it was hard to tell if he was begging for God or ready to talk. I waited three days to give him a pen and some paper to finally confess all his sins.

For obvious reasons, the room was soundproof. Tested thoroughly, of course. I could tell this one was lower on the food chain in Yuri's organization. He'd barely been touched but cowered under the simplest of movement. It was going to be fun to see how quickly he would break.

"Name," I barked at the prone form, who stared back at me with terrified eyes. When he didn't answer, I smiled before slapping him across the face. Just once. Not even that hard. But he squealed like a gutted pig and caved immediately. My excitement dwindled at the realization of how easy this was going to be.

"Boris! Boris! Please," he whimpered, spitting out the slightest bit of blood.

"So stereotypical. Boris…" One of my men watching from the corner chuckled at my observation. "Do you know who I am?" When he shook his head, I could tell my stare was starting to get to him. I snarled in his direction, and he jumped in his seat. I flicked open my small pocketknife before placing it at his throat.

"Fuck! He pissed himself." One of my lower guys working his way up the organization cursed under his breath, knowing he'd be the one to clean the room.

"Well, Boris. I am your worst fucking nightmare. You came to my city. You went after my family. After my queen. Tonight, you get to dance with the devil." I folded my tall frame to lean directly in front of his face. "And it's the last fucking thing you'll do."

More cries and pleas were absorbed by the noise-reducing walls. I wanted him scared. To sweat it out. Then I'd end his miserable existence. Walking up to the table of devices, I picked my favorite: a pair of garden shears. The rust had built up over time, due to a lack of sanitation and as a result of having absorbed massive amounts of blood from cutting off the digits of my rivals. They were practically sealed closed, and once open, they barely required pressure to clamp shut again. They were dull, like a pair of children's scissors. It was on my list to sharpen them, but I was a busy man. There were always several more pressing matters requiring my immediate attention.

"Now. I want answers. The sooner you give them to me, the less painful your death."

He sealed his lips shut, like it would save him. I leveled the implement with his pinkie finger and, without a second thought, severed the digit from his hand.

"Tell me what Yuri's plans are. Why's he targeting my queen, my family, my shipments? What's he hoping to achieve?" I didn't bother with a rag to muffle his screams. There was no need, and I enjoyed the sound of them. When he didn't immediately respond, I detached his other pinky, rammed my knife into his thigh, and repeated my questions. I lifted the blade and was about to jam it into the other leg when Rocco waved to gain my attention.

My eyes flicked to where he was pointing, Boris's screams all but drowned out. Silence filled the room except for the roar inside my ears. There was so much noise in my head I hadn't heard the door open or noticed Bella standing there. Apollo looked between Boris and Bella, studying her reaction.

What the fuck was she doing here?

She wouldn't look at me. Her beautiful mismatched eyes were lost and lifeless as she glared at the man in the chair. As I motioned for Apollo to get her out of here, he shook his head. "I'm sorry, boss. She ordered us to take her or she'd find a way to come on her own."

I exhaled, attempting to stave my anger at his disregard for my order. We both knew the little minx would have found a way to be here either way. Trying to lighten my tone, I took a step closer to her. "Bella, *mio amore,* go home with Apollo."

She jumped, her startled eyes finally registering my presence. "He threatened our family." Her voice was soft, almost haunted, and so unlike her. Her eyes were sad and lost. I didn't like that he did that to her.

"*Si.* Bella, *mia regina,* I promised you I'd take care of our family. Let me do that. Go home with Apollo."

Bella's body snapped straight as if someone had shoved her, her once somber eyes now angry and fierce. My queen was stepping out of the shadows. "No. He must pay. Lucky, *mio amore,* I want to see him suffer."

The passion, the fire, and the lust in her glare set my soul aflame. If it weren't for the current crowd of onlookers among us, I'd take her here and now.

I shook my head, attempting to rid myself of those thoughts, my dick pulsing in protest. I turned my attention back to the man of the hour. He was begging Bella to save him. Not with words, but with the look in his eyes, as if her sudden appearance would somehow stop the pain I'd promised him.

"Don't look to her for help. She doesn't want you saved. She wants you pleading for your life. And *we* want the truth. Give us the truth, Boris. We know Yuri sent you. What was his plan?" My knife sliced through the undamaged skin of his other thigh, the copper aroma of blood enlivening me.

"Yuri, say you weak. Punish sister's business. Make you suffer. Take everything," he hissed through the pain.

"What was his plan with the women?" I feared the answer. It made my stomach churn, knowing what he was going to say.

"Kill parents. Sister trade. Woman, Yuri's."

I fucking knew it.

The Russians dealt guns, drugs, kids, women—whatever could earn them their next dollar. They were spineless, soulless, their actions abhorrent as they capitalized on those they deemed weaker than them.

The Italians did much of the same. But never women and kids. We drew a line in the sand when it came to those necessary evils. And we didn't cross it.

"Trade with the Trinovas?"

Boris's nod told me everything I needed to know, why Yuri was gunning for me so badly. The Trinova family was the main financiers of the skin trade that had made a home in the city. We'd taken down most of their associates and ruined their business. If Yuri was connected to them, he'd want retaliation in the form of blood and money. My family's blood and our combined money would just be the start. If he gained a foothold…

Boris was beginning to dip in and out of consciousness. As I motioned for Rocco to step forward, he pulled a metal pole from the furnace. I turned to Bella, begging her to leave, but the stubborn woman refused. Her jaw set, her eyes determined. With a flick of my wrist, Rocco stepped to Boris, cauterizing the wounds with the blunt end of the steel pole. Screams echoed off the walls as the terrible aroma of melting flesh permeated the air. A mixture that was known to make the strongest of men squeamish.

Not Bella.

She stood with a newfound confidence. The smell didn't seem to register with her. Our eyes remained locked in an embrace, just the two of us in the room. We were doing what needed to be done for our family. Once Boris's wounds were closed off, I continued my line of questioning, and he barely responded to me. The bastard was such a low-level player he didn't know what the future held with Yuri. He was just a man hired for a single-minded mission. Kill men, kidnap women.

"Yuri say bring back. When do, get paid. Paid to feed my family." The Russian was slobbering on himself now, his intel as useless as the pot he shit in.

"He didn't have an in with Yuri. He's an immigrant, working at a Russian restaurant, a man looking for a handout." Apollo was standing beside Bella, ensuring she didn't need comfort. "My informant told me he was picked up randomly. Get your fill, boss. He isn't going to give us much else."

"Bella. Please don't stay for this. I know you feel a duty to stand at my side, to show power and strength. You've done that. You don't need to stay for me. You already have too much blood on your hands," I urged her to take the out.

A coy smile erupted on her beautiful face. I knew she wasn't weak by any means. These last few weeks together had shown me everything but weakness. She barely blinked after taking the lives of our enemies. She had nothing left to prove by witnessing more carnage.

Boris started muttering in Russian behind me. Rocco was readying the bleach to clean up the scene when I was done and the odor seemed to affect our captive. He knew what was coming.

"Why don't we go home to the compound? Your *madre* is there with mine," I offered, my voice cautious. I didn't want to scare her. But her attention was focused behind me. Pointer finger to her chin, I pulled her face to mine.

Empty. Empty and soulless.

Her beautiful eyes, which were normally captivating and full of that fire I loved, were vacant. She was looking at me but she didn't see me. It was a look I had seen on so many men who'd done a lot of bad shit in their lives. I didn't want it on *mia regina.*

"Bella. Leave with Apollo." I tugged her arm towards the door and my second-in-command. Glancing up at me one more time, she nodded at both of us. I dropped her arm and Apollo motioned for her to exit first.

But, of course, she didn't.

Turning on her heel, she slid under my arm, her stride calm and confident, much like the incident at the warehouse. Although I knew he was bolted down and chained, it didn't ease my concern for her safety. I motioned for Rocco to back down; he gave her space but remained within arm's reach.

Bella leaned into the Russian's face, her tight skirt riding up her thighs and teasing me with the sight of her perfectly-toned ass. She wrapped her hands around the arms of the chair, her lips to his ear as she whispered to him in his native tongue. He was still whimpering, but whatever she was saying had the man nodding in response. Those dead eyes were concerning, but she was in control of the situation. A situation that was making Apollo pace at my side, clearly just as uncomfortable as I was.

Then she did the craziest thing. The moment she stood to her full height, she smiled at Boris, dabbing at the blood under his eye. Her expression was sweet and soft, and my inner green monster snarled at the sight. Before I could react, she bent back down, her ear turned towards his mouth. Though his lips were moving, he was speaking too low for me to hear. Nodding her understanding, Bella stood back to her full height once again.

"Please. Please."

Bella picked up a knife, and Boris's eyes widened, as if surprised. He began thrashing, sobbing, and yelling at her in Russian. An uproar of cackling laughter left her tiny body and racked her small frame.

Apollo and Rocco both stepped closer, all of us sharing the same confusion. Had she cracked? Had this been too much for my love and I hadn't noticed it? Had I not done my job of protecting her? I reached a hand forward, prepared to intervene, when Boris's shout stopped me in my tracks.

Bella's arm was raised. And in one fast, confident, and precise swoop, the knife was sliced across our captive's throat. She dug it in so forcefully I thought his head would fall from his shoulders. Bella seemed to revel in the blood that coated her hands as the man gasped and gagged his last breaths.

"Rot in hell. *Cagna,*" she growled as she watched him. She stepped back, her skirt and blouse doused in blood. And once he'd slumped in his spot, she finally turned away. When she looked at me, my heart leapt into my throat. She approached me, wrapping her arms around my torso, as I tugged her against my chest. She kissed me hard on the lips, emitting a moan the moment I deepened it.

"Come, *mio amore,* what was that about? You shouldn't have been here, let alone participated." I held her out in front of me, doing my best to not shake her.

"He was muttering to himself, saying if he didn't get to Yuri, they'd kill his family. He knew where he was all along."

"How did you get him to give up the information?"

"I told him I was the woman rumored to make you weak. Promised him I didn't want any more blood spilled, and that if he told me where the meeting spot was, I'd make sure we got his family and let them all go."

"You conniving little woman. *Cristo, mio amore.* The things you make me feel," I growled and tugged her closer.

"We will teach them. Woman or not, Lucifer Agostino isn't weak." She spoke confidently. And her words shot straight to my dick, inciting my every impulse to fuck her against the nearest surface.

My men remained at my side, seeing her in a new light. When Rocco adjusted his pants, I damn near lost my ever-loving-already-fucking-crazy mind. Roaring my demands, I told the entire room to clear out. I couldn't take this anymore. Not touching her was the purest form of torture.

"Penthouse?" Apollo asked, and I nodded my confirmation.

"I want it special."

He nodded and exited the room.

"Wait! I have the address. Yuri expects him no later than two hours from now!" Mirabella called out, tapping the information into my phone before sending it to Apollo.

"Apollo, handle it."

He glanced between the two of us and laughed as he shut the door behind him.

"Lucky, we need to go." Bella tugged at my sleeve, eager to leave all of a sudden.

"No, you need to clean this mess off you. Then I will take you upstairs. And once I know you are okay, *I'll* go destroy the threat. Alone."

She wanted to argue. With every fiber of her being, she wanted to argue with me. I could see it in her eyes. She bit her lip to keep from voicing what I could read clear as day on her face.

CHAPTER 13

LUCIFER "LUCKY" AGOSTINO

The look of malice mixed with lust was just a preemptive intuition into what I was feeling. And what I needed from her. After these last few weeks, her behavior in this room set so many emotions off inside me. And the fact that she was mine, I needed—no, wanted—to own her in every way possible. This little game we'd been playing, where I surmised there was any possibility that I would be able to stay away until our wedding night, was almost comical it was so untrue. That thought had ended, and it ended tonight.

Leading Bella by the arm to the shower, I watched as she followed willingly, though a little bashful. Her mixed eyes stared at me in such awe, a raw passion observing me as I disrobed her. The skirt and blouse went first, leaving her in those sinfully sexy, over-the-knee boots and the tiniest panties. As I licked my lips, her body quivered under my close inspection.

This strong, powerful, poised woman was mine for the taking. Any thoughts of being a gentleman were gone the moment she toted that gun into a fight with the Russians. And she was more than mine the moment she addressed that room. At my side, as my queen, I knew she was my *forever*.

I'd tried to do right and keep my distance after that evening, out of respect for her virtue. That was an option no longer valid. Tonight, I needed to bury myself deep inside her in order to forget all the chaos that was our lives.

I dropped to a knee, and her soft hands held onto my shoulders for support as I slowly unzipped her boots. Inch by inch, her breathing grew more ragged. With each movement, my heart beat faster and my slacks grew tighter. It physically pained me being this close to her. Our eyes locked as she stepped out of one boot, then the other. The depths of those eyes gave me a sharp pain in my chest. She was making me weak.

I was literally and figuratively falling to my knees for this woman. I, Lucifer Agostino, eldest son of Mario Agostino, future boss of the Agostino Crime Family in New York—the man known more proudly as *il diavolo*—had fallen in love with a sprig of a woman. An imposing figure, considered void of emotions outside of business, was willing to murder anyone who threatened his future bride. A cold, emotionless, power-hungry mobster was now falling down a bottomless well, filled with thoughts of the future hierarchy of the family he'd build with her.

She fucking owned me and fuck anyone who thought it made me weak.

"Step inside, *amore*." As I motioned her to turn around, Bella stepped out of the panties I'd yanked down her legs. Groaning as her ass swayed with each hesitant drop of her foot, I removed my clothes within seconds and followed her.

We focused on our mission at hand. Feeling her soft skin under my harsh grasp did things to me. Created immoral thoughts about my virgin bride-to-be as I barely grasped my sanity while keeping my distance.

"Bella…" I hissed her name in warning. Her back was pressed to my chest, as she wiggled her ass against me. At first, I thought it was an accident since the monster roaring between us didn't leave much space. But after the second wiggle, I knew what the little minx was up to. "I'm trying so hard to be a gentleman. Don't tempt my strength."

"Lucky. Since when has anyone called you a gentleman? I want *il diavolo*." Her dark hair soaked and hanging to one side gave me the perfect view of her long, elegant neck, her pulse beating in time with my own.

"For you, *for you* I'd tried to be a gentleman. You deserve that much until we're married."

"I'm already yours. Claim me."

The true animalistic feelings bubbling just under the surface of my skin broke loose on a roar. "Not here. Penthouse." I could barely get the words out as I smothered her with harsh kisses. I tugged her from the shower stall, water dripping down her naked form, and took in all that I owned. "Fuck, I'm a lucky man."

That red glow I loved so much crept up her neck. As confident as she was becoming, she still had her insecurities. It made her that much sexier. Her lack of realizing her own beauty astounded me. She was pure perfection in the form of a dark-haired, mixed-eyed mortal goddess. My queen. My heart. My everything.

Pulling on Nike sweatpants, I threw my white t-shirt on Bella. It was the only clothing left in the room and would have to do. The material hung just above her knees, billowing at two sizes too wide on her tiny frame. Her breasts were just visible under it, the water soaking the light material. Thankfully the penthouse was the highest floor above my unofficial torture chamber. The hotel and suites attached were the perfect cover for easy access to the basement and cleaned cash for my illegal activities. It had a private elevator to take us up, enabling me to hide what was mine. We just had to get through the lobby first.

"My clothes! I love those boots!" she insisted as I ushered her towards the locked door and pulled her through it.

"Apollo. Get her boots."

My second-in-command was waiting outside, a hand raised to his ear as he shouted orders into his phone. Spinning on his heel at the sound of my voice, he stared back and forth between Bella and me with a smirk curling his lips. Growling at the disrespectful look he was giving *mio amore,* I watched several of my men stare at him in shock.

Without a second thought, my fist launched forward, making perfect contact with his smug face. As he collapsed backwards into the wall, I tucked Bella behind me and addressed our crowd of onlookers.

"She is my queen. You look upon her as such. This is my only warn-ing." My tone forced them back a step. Only Apollo stayed in place, wiping the blood from his face. For a moment, I saw his charade drop as he offered me a glimpse of the psychopath simmering beneath the well-dressed, cultured façade in an expensive suit.

That was why Apollo was my right-hand man. Since we were kids, he had a penchant for protecting the few people he cared about, regard-less of the blood that needed to be spilled to do so. He resigned himself to reading classic literature, expressing a deep interest in the written word while amassing an extensive vocabulary. He bought the most expensive suits, demanding they remained pristine, often known for changing more than once a day if the situation called for it. He main-tained this image of control and composure to hide the beast lurking in the shadows of his mind. Apollo's past was dark and twisted. But it was also his tale to tell.

Guiding a barefooted, bare-chested Bella, we charged across the lobby towards the private elevators leading to the penthouse. Several people had stopped to stare at our state of undress, but the ones who recognized me stayed out of my way. If she'd been more appropriately covered, I would've thrown her over my shoulder with true possession before tossing her into the elevator to avoid the appreciative glares of strangers.

"Wasn't that a little harsh? Apollo would never betray you." Bella looked tiny and frail, her slight frame drowning in my oversized t-shirt.

"Behind the image of the man you see, there's a darkness. He needs to be reminded of who I am, his alpha. Every dog thinks they're on top until they're forced to the bottom." I placed a kiss to her head and tugged her closer. "You are mine and I won't let them forget it."

"I'm yours, Lucky. No one will touch me."

The elevator doors opened and all bets were off. Everything—but the two of us in this moment—was forgotten. Scooping Bella into my arms, I charged through the open layout. The master bedroom was in the back. Passing three doors, I brushed past the fourth and threw her down, watching her bounce on the oversized mattress with a four-post frame. Her dark hair fanned around her and the shirt shifted up her legs, giving me the slightest glance of the sweet apex between her thighs.

"*Perfezionare.*" I watched on as her heart-shaped mouth opened on a breathless pant as she looked me up and down, her attention lingering on my cock while her eyes begged me to own her. "Don't stare at me like that. I'm barely holding on here, Bella." My request came out harsher than I meant it.

"Let go," she urged me, and I shook my head. She had no idea what she was saying, what she was asking of me. "I've heard the stories since I was younger," she continued. The feared eldest Agostino son would replace his father one day and the city would cower. His anger knew no bounds. His cold, dead eyes could kill you with one glare. He was brutal, deadly, calculated, a true killer…"

"Yet, here you sit, offering yourself to me. Asking me to lose my control. I don't want to hurt you, Bella. But if you keep this up, I will break you."

"I want all of you, Lucifer. Break me." She knelt in front of me on the bed, and in one swoop, her shirt was removed as she bared her perfect body to me. "Break me, then rebuild me more powerful." She crawled back onto the bed, wanton and waiting. I could see her slick, glistening entrance beckoning me to ruin her.

And I couldn't stop, couldn't contain myself, couldn't restrain the beast needing to consume the woman laid out like a sweet offering. She was the perfect meal and I was a man who'd been starved for far too long. I stepped out of my sweatpants, my movements slow, measured, precise. A hunter staring at his prey. Her eyes flicked back and forth between mine, and only when they dropped to her hands did I see her indecisiveness.

"I can't promise you it won't hurt, *mia regina.*" I crawled over her naked body and dropped to my elbows, my hardened cock primed and ready at her entrance. "But I can promise I will make it up to you right after. And every day for the rest of our lives."

"*Ti amo,* Lucifer. Claim me."

My hands locked on to her thighs to spread them apart as my mouth attacked her center like a man in need. The moment I tasted her sweet flavor, I devoured her with wanton abandonment, her soft moans driving me onward. Her taste was like a drug. It fueled that primal part of me that reveled in the fact I was her first and only.

I inserted one finger and she shook with the contact, gasping before ending on a moan as pleasure replaced the initial shock. Turning that finger around, I stroked deeper. Disturbing that little bundle of nerves no one had yet to discover. Her thighs were trembling. She was close. I could hear and feel it. I rose on my elbows, my palm cupping and rubbing at her clit and my eyes locked on her face. I needed to see her come. Her head was thrown back, her breasts bouncing with each heaved breath.

"Look at me, Bella," I commanded, and her head snapped to me immediately. "*Ti amo, mia regina.* Now, don't you take your eyes off me." I crooked my finger as my mouth latched on to her clit, sucking on that perfect bundle of nerves. I maintained the eye contact, drowning in every emotion traveling across her features. Each telling me she was at that cusp. But I had to know if she was truly meant for me.

Biting down hard on her clit, so hard I could draw blood, I watched her let loose before me. That bit of pain made her lose the control she was barely holding on to. Her head fell backwards as she succumbed to the bliss I delivered her.

"Eyes!" I ordered, and she was quick to comply, offering me the perfect image of her flushed cheeks and hooded gaze. I crawled up her body and looked down on her angelic face. "You're made for me, Bella."

"Please, Lucky, please."

I lined myself up with her entrance and she nodded for me to continue. Doing my best to slow my movements, I entered her, inch by agonizing inch, until I was nearly buried to the hilt. She was tighter than I'd expected, confirming what I already knew. I couldn't lose control. She couldn't handle it.

"I'm sorry, *mia regina.*" I stroked her cheek as her soft features pinched and clenched with the pain. There was no easy way to do it. She was so little and I was… not.

Once her body relaxed, I pulled away and thrusted home. She cried out, and I froze my movements as my cock stretched and molded her core.

"I'm not going to last long," I admitted. It was all too much. The sensations. The emotions. The adrenaline. Bending down to kiss her neck, I started moving again. Keeping from slamming forward the way I liked was my biggest challenge. My balls drew up and I was ready to come. One last bite on her neck and she lost her control. I followed quickly after, spilling myself inside her.

The devil, *il diavolo*, had finally found his weakness. His queen.

CHAPTER 14

MIRABELLA MORETTI

I'd gone to school and learned about the human anatomy. And I was more than aware that the first time could and *would* be extremely painful for a young woman. Then I read romance novels, which told me that everything I thought I knew was a lie. That with the right man it would be incredible, sentimental, perfect. And he was *perfect*. The way he tried to get me primed and ready for him, it was euphoric. Then the moment he finally lost control.

Well, I realized that romance novelists were fucking liars.

It hurt. I felt like he was ripping me apart, molding my insides to fit him perfectly. Then he broke the mold, ensuring no other man would fit. Taking me with a wanton abandonment that I was unsure I'd survive. The relentless pounding burned, yet stoked a new feeling inside me. He was true to his word when he promised he'd make it better. He slowly rebuilt me. I teetered over the edge of the abyss, effervescent harmony thrumming at my core.

The harder he thrusted, the more the burning ceased. I was close to forgetting the pain as my body primed itself for a second explosion. White sparks burst behind my eyes, setting off a light show unlike anything on this earth.

I couldn't think, couldn't breathe. All I could do was feel. My muscles tensed as my body locked around my orgasm. My nerves were frenzied, lost to the mix of sensations. And my clit hummed as my body refused to come down from its high.

I barely registered his moans as he followed me into the light. We both fought to catch our breaths. I stared into his eyes and the stories of Lucifer Agostino were gone. This strong, powerful man was made for me, and I for him.

The adrenaline from the day was fading along with my consciousness. Lucky tucked my body against his, covering us with the blanket. Kissing my head, he murmured the sweetest compliments, and before I could respond, I collapsed into a deep, sated sleep.

What felt like years later, I rolled over to my side, awoken by the whispered sounds of Lucky on his phone. The sun was coming up, gorgeous yellows bursting through the pillow-soft clouds. The penthouse master suite had floor-to-ceiling windows overlooking Lucky's city. It was a new day and I was a different woman. Wrapping myself in the sheet, I looked out at my newly claimed empire with my king at my side.

"I had an outfit sent up for you." Lucky tugged me against his hard chest. Nuzzling my ear, he asked, "How do you feel?"

There was a throbbing between my thighs—not too overbearing, just sensitive to my movements. Without thinking, my hands wandered on their own accord, exploring my body before cupping between my legs. When I moaned at the sensitivity, Lucky growled, his chest rising with the sound.

I lowered the sheet, allowing the material to cascade across my frame before pooling at the floor. I could feel his hardness at my back, seeking attention, and throwing my inhibitions to the wind, I dropped to my knees, staring up at him through my lashes, and took him in my hand, relishing how soft his skin felt. The veins under his shaft seem to dance when I licked them.

Before he could protest, I brought his wide length as far into my mouth as I could. And I felt as if my jaw would break, trying to adjust to his size. Back and forth, my tongue explored every detail it could as

I took him deep, slightly gagging when he made contact with the back of my throat.

"Bella, please. Fuck, you're incredible."

Looking up at him through my lashes, I saw the normally collected man fall apart at my touch. He stiffened, alerting me to how close he was to finishing. It made me feel that much more powerful. Lucky always emboldened me, made me feel like nothing could touch me. However, in this moment, when he was the most vulnerable, I took the control he would otherwise possess.

Pulling out with a loud popping noise, he lifted me to my feet, spun me towards the window, and pressed my face against the glass. Bending just enough to pop my ass into the air, I readied myself. He was rough, animalistic, and I reveled in it. I thrived on seeing him come apart at the seams for me. While he was driving into me, all I could do was cry out my appreciation. For this man and what he did to me.

That slight discomfort was long gone as an intense orgasm snuck up on me. And all I could do was scream and ride the profound wave of ecstasy. Lucky was like a drug to me. We'd both finished moments ago but I wanted more.

I craved it. I craved him.

Finishing against the window, Lucky carried my languid body into the bathroom to freshen up. We had to meet our parents after we had breakfast. We ate waffles covered with whipped cream and fresh strawberries in bed. Naked. It was the perfect morning afterglow, making me burn brighter and more intensely than the sun.

After eating, we decided to save water and shower together. Lucky took his time exploring my entire body. Our parents could wait for us. And he took me twice more before we got out, my wrinkling skin a clear sign of the time we'd spent under the water.

"I'd always known you were a man of your word. It's just nice you held up your end of the bargain."

He looked at me confused.

"You were right about the pain but promised to make it better. Thank you."

Delivering a chaste kiss, Lucky wrapped me in a warm robe before we were interrupted by a knock on the bedroom door. My eyes flicked to Lucky, and as if reading my mind, he was quick to say, "Nothing to fear, *mia regina.* It's just time I treated you as my queen." Lucky disappeared through the door, giving me a brief respite to gather my thoughts. I could hear people talking and things moving around the room, before he reappeared, pulling me from the bathroom.

"My queen." A group of women were spread around the room to give me the royal treatment. I squealed in delight as Lucky gave me a kiss. Chuckling at my excitement, he pushed me towards the smiling women then withdrew his phone from his pocket, brought it to his ear, and slipped from the room.

Hair, makeup, and nails—every inch of me reimagined—until I was trimmed, painted, and coiffed perfectly. A stylist adorned me in a gorgeous white Chanel dress with blue Manolo Blahnik's encrusted in diamonds. Before long, I was buffered, polished and dressed. Like the queen I'd hoped to represent at Lucky's side. I took one last glance in the floor-length mirror, both shocked and pleasantly surprised with my new look. Uncertainty slowed my steps as I crossed the threshold into the penthouse living room. And any doubt I had that my polished appearance wouldn't be up to Lucky's standards dissolved the moment I approached; the anxiety disappeared into thin air when his eyes traveled up my body.

His phone was pressed to his ear, but Lucky's focus was glued to me when he spoke. "Good work, Apollo. Get me the other name. I want this handled." His eyes slowly traveled from my heeled feet, up my moisturized legs, to the designer dress before freezing on the deep V of my revealing neckline. Once he stared into my eyes, his heated expression softened ever so slightly. He hung up and quickly offered me his full attention. "Yuri is dead. The rat didn't lie. Apollo took him down easily, thanks to you, my love." Grasping my neck, Lucky tugged me to him and devoured me with his kiss.

"What of his partner?" I was quick to clarify.

He shook his head and led me towards the private elevator. "Apollo said there was no chance to ask."

We hopped inside, our proximity in the small room making the tension spark to life. Rubbing my thighs together, I tried to remain as poised as I appeared while attempting to hide my inappropriate thoughts. His soft growl told me I fooled no one. Before we could move, the elevator arrived at the lobby. Stepping out before me, Lucky surveilled the area then tugged me to his side. I could see his men spread throughout the room, their eyes scanning our surroundings.

Apollo was outside on the sidewalk waiting by the limousine. The men nodded at each other before Apollo looked at me. His glare was hidden behind his reflective shades and sullen expression. Abruptly turning as I approached, he opened my door and walked off without a word.

"Leave him," Lucky said with a sad smile at my questioning stare. I nodded my understanding.

Lucky's call lasted the entire car ride to the Agostino compound. As we pulled up to the gates, I could make out the outline of my father's SUV, which shouldn't have surprised me since my mother was here. I just didn't anticipate him to be waiting out front for me with such an endearing smile on his face. I expected his anger for spending the night with Lucky.

Lucky got out first, blocking my door as the two men exchanged words. A few seemingly angered sentiments were spoken before my father reached out a hand to me. Prior to my shoes solidly touching the ground, he tugged me to him, sweeping me off my feet into a bear hug. A hug I didn't think I'd received since I was five or six.

He transported me back to a time where the monsters under my bed were destroyed by this man. A time when Dominic was my best friend and protector. And though Gio was always distant, I still looked up to him back then.

"Mirabella. The thought of you hurt…" My father's grip loosened and he pulled back to look at me. "You get more beautiful every day. Just like your mama."

"Lucky protected me, Daddy." Smiling up at my future husband, I tried to lessen the tension between the two. I motioned at my father to snap him out of his obvious scowl. Reaching out a hand, he muttered his thanks to Lucky as they shook.

"My father is waiting," Lucky remarked dryly, pulling me from his grasp as we started towards the door. When my father held firm to me, Lucky turned with a glare. I could tell he didn't want to back down. But out of respect to my future husband and Mario's eldest son, my father finally relented.

"The queen of the Agostino family has arrived." A burning blush crept up to my ears as Lucky's younger brother approached us in greeting. Marco's appraisal of my designer-clad body told me he approved. Lucky pulled me past him, walking farther into the house towards the kitchen. At my back, a resounding slap echoed in the marble foyer, followed by Marco's breathless curse.

Lucky growled his annoyance at his brother's perusal. "On her eyes, not her ass. Fucking asshole."

"Bella!" Sienna came charging full speed ahead with my mother on her heels. After assuring each other that everyone was okay, we sat in the living room.

The lavish space was warm and inviting, soft leather sofas spread throughout the sitting area. A floor-to-ceiling stone fireplace in the center of two tall windows illuminated the room. Mario was seated in an oversized chair, a smiling Isabella positioned on the armrest. My mother was on one side of me, Sienna the other. Dominic was standing near the fireplace, holding a rocks glass and ignoring the current company while the youngest Agostino sibling, Octavia, was seated quietly across the room.

"Yesterday could've ended very badly, if not for the fast thinking of our men." Lucky addressed the room. "Apollo handled the initial threat today but we do believe there is a missing partner. Regardless, my men are on it."

"As are mine," Dominic muttered around the rim of his glass, earning himself a glare from Lucky. "She may be your future wife but she's also my sister. And I want blood."

"Where's Gio?" When no one immediately answered, I stated the obvious. "All of our family members are here except for him." Everyone looked to Lucky.

"His presence wasn't requested."

I nodded in response, ensuring him I was behind the decisions that needed to be made. My brother was a complete piece of shit. A thorn in our side, one we didn't need while we scoured the city for answers.

"Anyway, on to the good news. Our Bella's birthday is this weekend. I'd like to use that as a platform to make the announcement." Mario was smiling from ear to ear.

"Not yet." Lucky's booming voice overshadowed his father's. And the self-conscious girl inside me shouted the words I didn't want to say allowed.

He doesn't want you.

I was so stupid. Of course, he didn't want me. He owned this city. He could have any woman, every woman—hell, he practically had them all already, sowing his wild oats until the time came for him to produce an heir. An innocent naïve virgin was thrusted into his lap with a plan of marriage. Of course, he wanted to keep the engagement a secret until he could get out of it.

Swooning like a lovesick fool, I'd given myself to him entirely. I threw it all away, lost my virginity before marriage. In our world, that didn't happen. It was disgraceful to the family name. I was unwed and ruined…

Oh. My. God… we didn't even use protection! I could be pregnant with Lucky's bastard of a child. I suddenly felt sick to my stomach. My eyes scanned the room. Outside of me, no one seemed upset by his words. Sienna was grinning like the cat that ate the canary, which confused me further. As I turned to face him, I took note of how Lucky was smirking down at me. He was such a large, imposing man with the softest smile, reserved just for me.

It made my heart melt. Whatever the reason behind his refusal, that look told me he had something up his sleeve. He motioned me towards the door and led me to his mother's gardens. And my insecurities vanished.

The sun was warm, the fresh floral aroma clinging to the air as I clung to the man at my side. I was at peace. For whatever reason, in this moment, I was calm and open-minded. I trusted him.

This devil in his pristine suit.

CHAPTER 15

MIRABELLA MORETTI

"Are you all right?"

Even in stiletto heels, I had to tilt my head to look up at him. He towered over me. Doing my best to not break my ankle on the paver trail through the gardens, I decided to be honest, "Truthfully, I have my moments of insecurities. Lucky, your conquests aren't exactly shy to talk about you. I know the girls you've been with, most of whom are my polar opposites. Their affluent families raised them to be the idealistic socialites. My family kept me hidden with my nose buried in my books."

Stopping just outside of the grove of pillars, Lucky pulled me against him. I flicked my eyes up to meet his gaze again, and rage stared back at me. His normally soft expression pinched at his brows and his jaw was set tight. "Bella, you being their opposite is why I chose you. If I wanted brainless arm candy, I'd have left you alone. You're educated and cultured, refined in ways no school could ever teach them. Your family's beliefs are off base, how they see you a far different version from the woman you actually are. You were never meant to be in a man's shadow. This brain is too powerful to be wasted on a piece of shit who doesn't appreciate it."

Failing to blink back the happy tears, I was helpless to stop them from tipping over and trailing down my cheeks. Lucky wiped one away with his thumb, before putting it to his mouth and savoring the flavor on a moan. And the single action almost made my knees buckle. This man was every dream I'd had… come to life.

"I want you because I love you, Bella, *per sempre.*" Forever.

Talk about making a girl swoon for the second time in a conversation. His heartfelt words and sincere expression had my eyes burning and my chest pounding. He tugged me along until we were strolling through my favorite section of his mother's garden.

The area was closed off and to the side. At the center was a white pergola with thick topiaries blocking the view of the rest of the property, allowing for a romantic, secluded feel. Except, now, the entire area was lined with a series of red rose bushes. The stone floor was completely covered in petals and the gorgeous five-layer stone fountain was shooting water from level to level.

I didn't know what to do or say. I was frozen in place at the sight, before movement caught my attention. Lucky had dropped my hand and was walking around before kneeling in front of me. "You were a contract. A means of tying two families together in a display of ownership. But that's all changed, the deal made null and void, because it is you who now owns me, Bella. The moment I saw those tear-soaked eyes five years ago, I had this innate desire to protect you. And now that I've gotten to know you, that desire has grown tenfold. You're smart, cunning, courageous, and fiercely loyal. I've never wanted to settle down before. Not until you. You're it for me, Bella. Will you do me the honor of marrying me? *Sii mia regina?*" Be my queen.

The air was caught in my lungs, my heart pounding through my chest. I couldn't speak. This man. This man was such a conundrum. Feared by most, destined to rule the underworld, blood forever coating his hands. Yet, here he was. On his knees before me, opening his heart and offering me to take it. "Lucifer. Some would call me a fool to align myself with the devil. But I've never felt so cherished, so appreciated in my entire life. When I am with you, the world feels right. To everyone else you are *il diavolo.* But to me, *mio cuore.* Yes, my heart. Yes."

Opening his pocket, Lucky presented me with the most gorgeous princess cut diamond with a white gold band. It was simple yet elegant. As if everything he learned about me had been designed into this intricate piece. I didn't need all the bells and whistles. I didn't even need such a large stone, but the ring represented more than just me. It represented the joining of our families; therefore, while the simplicity spoke to me, the extravagant size symbolized Lucky's love for me and told the rest of the world I was his.

Standing to his full height above me, Lucky lifted me into the air, swinging my feet behind me. I couldn't believe the happiness warming my soul. His sweet, bright smile was one I would get to wake up next to every day for the rest of my life. I couldn't wait to see what the future held.

He pulled me in for a kiss, which quickly intensified into a battle of teeth and tongues. "Lucky, I need you." It was a request, an order, a plea. A need stronger than anything I'd ever felt before.

"What my queen wants, my queen gets." Without another word, he lowered me to the ground on a bed of rose petals before sliding my dress up. His immediate growl told me he'd found my surprise. I blushed when he licked his lips at the sight of me bare before him. He released his belt and unfastened his zipper, and his hardened cock was barely all the way out of his dress pants when he slammed home.

Home. That's exactly where it was. His cock buried deep inside me was where it belonged. Again, the lack of condom didn't cross either of our minds. His relentless pounding had me chasing my high within minutes. I couldn't speak. If there was a chance that I was already pregnant, there was nothing we could do about it now. Another powerful thrust forward, and I was lost to what I was thinking, consumed by the sensations he was drawing from my body. Within seconds of looking into his blue eyes while fisting my newly decorated hand in his shirt, I was falling over that blissful edge. I barely noticed he followed me as we rode out the high together.

I didn't have time to catch my breath before Lucky was helping me to my feet. He tucked himself back into his pants and straighten my clothing as we wandered along the path to the house. I was walking taller, standing straighter. Lucky stopped before opening the door. Smiling down and rubbing my neck, he gave me a simple kiss, then beckoned me inside.

"Engaged looks good on you, girl!" Sienna was the first to greet us at the door. As she pulled me in for a hug, I felt her tug at my hair before showing me a loose rose petal she'd plucked. My skin burned hot with embarrassment. "Or is it that *just fucked* looks good on you?" she whispered before handing me off to my sobbing mother.

"*Madre, madre.*" I pleaded for her to stop, as she closed me in her arms.

"Serafina. Leave the girl alone." My father stepped forward, pulling his wife to his side and offering her a small smile he reserved only for her. "Congratulations, my dear. I have no doubt you will do amazing things for this city… and our family name."

He just had to throw that in there.

It was true I was marrying an Agostino. But I'd always be a Moretti. No matter what the future held, he was trying to remind me to keep my family at the forefront. God forbid his beloved daughter had even a moment of solace. No. How dare I have the audacity to not immediately think of him above all else.

"Anthony, your daughter was made to be queen, my queen." Lucky bent down to kiss my head, holding me snug against him. "I have no doubt both our families will thrive with her at my side."

My father shook his hand, seemingly pleased with the semblance of joint power. I sincerely hoped he wasn't that much of a fool that he assumed I'd put the Moretti name first. Not when Lucky was my future. I was a Moretti first, but I'd be an Agostino last. As long as my mother was safe, I'd let the men do their best to carry on the name.

"Thank you… again. For today," my father responded with a nod and took his leave.

"Seems like he's coming around." Lucky smiled down at me.

"You mean he finally sees this marriage as a way to elevate the Moretti name?"

Lucky laughed and made his way to the fireplace, raising a champagne flute to garner everyone's attention. "Two powerful families merge as one. A born queen to rule at my side. To Bella, my future bride. This is only the beginning. With your light guiding my darkness, I may finally find my way."

Murmured cheers circled the room. I sipped the crisp champagne to hide the heat rising up my neck, while Lucky's growl of appreciation had me clenching my thighs together. The man was insatiable and making me even more so. I couldn't get enough of him. He had this way of melting me into a useless mush of a compliant woman before molding me into a stronger version of myself.

"I'd kill to know what was going on in your head."

I looked up to find him standing in front of me.

"Those thighs are clenched so hard I'd bet my entire kingdom that you could carry a penny between them."

"I want you."

Lucky made quick work of excusing us from the room. His father and mother were so immersed in their own conversation they barely paid us any attention. Dom gave me a knowing smirk, his fiery gaze directed at my newly appointed fiancé, while Sienna was grinning like a fool.

Lucky practically threw me over his shoulder to run up the stairs. To spend the rest of the afternoon and evening showing me just how bright and hot we could burn.

"How nice of you to finally join us, Bella. Hungry?"

My father ignored my mother's comments, barely acknowledging me as I entered my parents' kitchen. As she rose from the table to make me a plate, her eyes landed on the shadow looming at the threshold and she smiled.

Glancing up from the newspaper, my father scowled at my escort. "Apollo, I do believe I can take care of my own daughter."

"Of that, I have no doubt. However, I have my orders. Ms. Bella is not to leave my sight when the boss is busy," Apollo said, his voice monotone as my mother motioned for him to join us. Even after he shook his head politely, she set a steamy plate of ravioli on the snack bar in front of him.

"We go for the final fitting today. I don't know if pasta was such a good idea for lunch," I huff.

My mother made all the pasta in our house, by hand, including the present meal.

"Please, I saw the arduous run you took Apollo on around the property. Besides you're perfect, sis." Gio sat down at the table, smirking at Apollo with a challenging expression. "Thought you were going to pass out."

Lucky's second-in- command didn't take the bait, shoving the fork into his mouth while his eyes scanned the room.

"What did you do?" My mother's head snapped to my brother. "Since when are you sweet to your sister?"

"She is perfect, the only Moretti daughter. Her one flaw is the man she chose to marry." Gio continued to shovel food into his mouth, despite the rage we could all feel radiating off Apollo.

"Gio. It was my decision and I know in my heart it was the right one. Why can't you just be happy? It's a strong alliance for the family, and he is a good man." The moment those words passed my lips, he scoffed.

"Good man? He has so much blood on his hands he could bathe in it for the rest of his life."

Apollo popped up from his seat and stepped forward, his jaw tight and fists clenched. And I immediately raised a hand to stop him. "He is the eldest son of Mario Agostino. Is this not the way? He is the boss and the future king, ruling his kingdom with the firm hand required by the weight of a crown. I suppose that is too much for you to understand, seeing as you were on babysitting duty for so many years." I shouldn't poke the bear, but I had enough of his underhanded comments about my soon-to-be husband.

"Someone has surely stepped into her role at Lucifer's side." My father looked almost… *proud*. "Shame all the years learning your place seems to have evaporated into thin air." Almost but not quite…

"The Agostino men believe they are only as strong as their weakest family member. She is his queen, his confidante, and he respects her," Apollo said through clenched teeth before he stepped back behind the counter, practically vibrating with anger.

"I suppose I did forget all their teachings the moment Lucky saw the true nature within me. The one you'd hoped to break, had I been married off to someone of your choosing."

"Stupid bitch," Gio muttered under his breath, and my own temper started to boil to the surface, threatening to tip over.

My father rose from his seat so quickly it toppled backwards. My mother and I both rose from ours as well, joining in an embrace and preparing for his outburst. "Now you listen to me, you spoiled little brat!" Spittle flew from his raging mouth, as he aimed an accusatory finger at me.

Apollo charged around the counter, blocking me with his body. A movement so fast it was more of a blur. "No! You listen to me!" he roared, gesturing between my father and brother. "She is the future of the Agostino family and will not be disrespected. Before I do more than disrespect you in your home, Bella, are you ready to head to your fitting?"

I grabbed my mother's hand, and we walked out of the room, the only noise the clicking of our heels on the marble floor. Apollo stayed behind in the kitchen for another moment, likely exchanging a few more heated words, while I collected my purse by the front door. As I turned back to face her, my mother grinned. My presence was helping to steel her spine, to remind her of the woman she was before she'd fallen under my father's reign of terror.

"Ma'am." One of the Moretti enforcers walked into the foyer, setting a large arrangement of flowers on the table in front of us. Squealing in excitement, I tore off the card addressed to me.

"Uneasy lies the head that wears the crown," I read the message aloud. "That's odd." I passed the card to my mother. While I could appreciate Lucky's attempt at showing interest in literature—he knew my love for it—it was an odd quote to use.

"Shakespeare?" My mother asked, raising a brow when I nodded. "It is true. I suppose he knows your future together will be filled with trials and tribulations?"

"Shall we, ladies?" Apollo stormed into the foyer with a blank look I'd come to know all too well. He liked to hide his emotions when he was in what I called his *second mode*. The man at Lucky's side.

Nodding are agreement, we left for my fitting, the flowers all but forgotten amongst the chatter and excitement of the upcoming events.

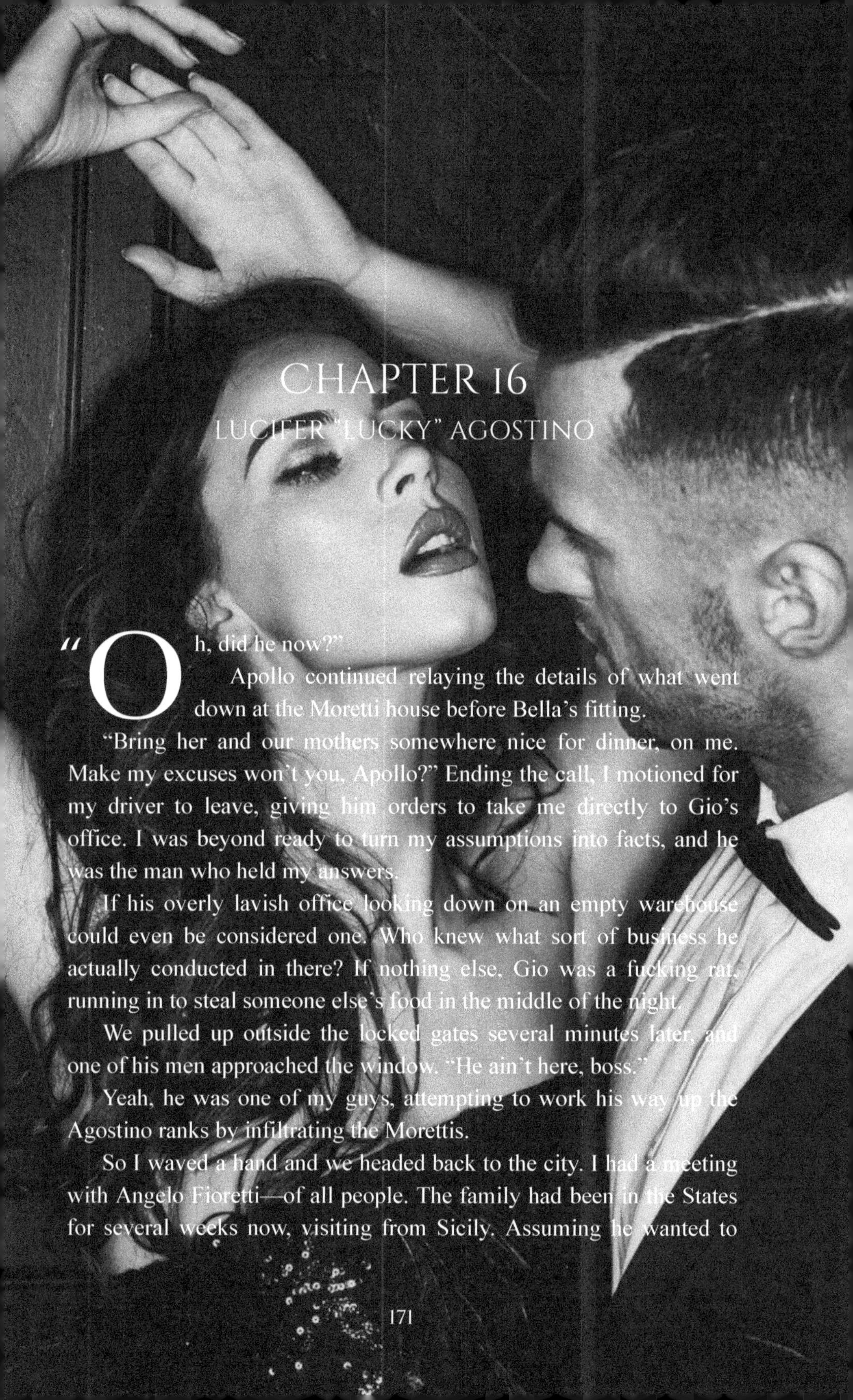

CHAPTER 16

LUCIFER "LUCKY" AGOSTINO

"**O**h, did he now?"

Apollo continued relaying the details of what went down at the Moretti house before Bella's fitting.

"Bring her and our mothers somewhere nice for dinner, on me. Make my excuses won't you, Apollo?" Ending the call, I motioned for my driver to leave, giving him orders to take me directly to Gio's office. I was beyond ready to turn my assumptions into facts, and he was the man who held my answers.

If his overly lavish office looking down on an empty warehouse could even be considered one. Who knew what sort of business he actually conducted in there? If nothing else, Gio was a fucking rat, running in to steal someone else's food in the middle of the night.

We pulled up outside the locked gates several minutes later, and one of his men approached the window. "He ain't here, boss."

Yeah, he was one of my guys, attempting to work his way up the Agostino ranks by infiltrating the Morettis.

So I waved a hand and we headed back to the city. I had a meeting with Angelo Fioretti—of all people. The family had been in the States for several weeks now, visiting from Sicily. Assuming he wanted to speak to me about the docks instead of going to my father, I extended an olive branch to strike a deal on his behalf. One that would benefit the Agostinos, of course.

"Boss. He's not alone," my driver informed me while talking into his earpiece. I lifted a brow in silent question. "A lady friend apparently." Big Al was newer to my team but rose quickly over the last few years. I respected his earnest work ethic.

"Angelo." I waltzed into my office in my penthouse like I owned the place, because *I did*, and watched Angelo scramble to his feet. The oaf was flopped back onto my leather office chair. His foot on my desk like the insolent prick he truly was. "It's been years and I see much hasn't changed." I didn't offer my hand, merely scowled at him and his untucked shirt. Doing my damn best to ignore Tatianna, who'd made herself comfortable in the chair opposite him.

"Lucky," she purred in that irritating, nasally voice of hers.

I didn't acknowledge her, unbuttoning my jacket as I took my seat. "What do you want?" I jutted my chin at Angelo.

"I came here to politely ask you to back off Mirabella Moretti."

Rubbing a finger over my top lip, I smirked at him and Tatianna. The woman was frothing at the mouth as she hissed, "Are you kidding me? What the fuck is this about, Angie?"

I cringed at his pet name, while eyeing the spectacle in front of me. Tatianna might not have aged much due to Botox, fillers, and more plastic than I could name but she still had that terrible overly artificial appearance. A living, breathing blow-up doll, if you will.

"Shut it, Tatianna. I told you my father wants me to marry her."

Her little attempt at puppy-dog eyes failed with her lack of skin movement. "But, Angie, you love me!"

To that, he scoffed. "More like I love that tight, rejuvenated pussy of yours. Now shut up."

Tatianna flopped back in her seat, scowling—or so I could only assume, seeing as her forehead didn't move.

"So… you want Mirabella Moretti as your wife? What'll you give me in return?"

He nodded towards Tatianna. Realizing the attention was on her again, she straightened in her seat. I watched her register what Angelo was offering: if I released Bella, she could finally have her shot with me.

"What do you say, Lucky?"

When I didn't immediately answer, Tatianna sauntered around my desk before pulling her shirt down to reveal the fake tits she'd increased since we last fucked.

"She's a good bloodline, tight pussy, mouth like a Hoover and is into whatever you want." He listed her assets, as though they meant anything to me.

I scowled as she trailed her fingertips along my chest, her hands fisting my shirt as she shoved my seat back so she could straddle my lap.

"All to give up a virgin so my father will be happy with me," Angelo was quick to add, then he jumped up to look at the file I'd dropped on my desk. Seeing this as her opportunity, Tatianna unbuckled my belt despite my protests.

Anger was coursing through my veins and bubbling to the surface. I was all about playing games with my opponents, forcing them to show their cards before going in for the kill. But my patience was waning. One was attempting to pry into my business while the other was trying to pry into my pants. All while slinging underhanded insults at my bride-to-be.

First of all, there was no way in hell I would give up Bella. For anything. Anyone. Second, to suggest Tatianna was on the same level as either of us was more than a slap to the face. It was sheer disrespect.

However, before I could verbalize as much, the bitch had dropped to her knees in front of me, struggling in earnest to pull my flaccid dick from my pants. Tatianna had slid under my desk, and I was doing my best to tug her out while keeping my eyes trained on the man in front of me, uncertain who was the bigger threat at the moment.

"Mirabella has a plain, pretty look to her. But what fun is a stuck-up virgin with too much mouth not being put to good use? She has little to offer aside from her name."

My lips curled at one side, partly out of irritation and partly in challenge. What was he looking to achieve with the union? What was his endgame? "Of course, it's about her name. That's all that matters. This bitch here is only good enough to suck my cock," I mocked, rising to my feet. Tatianna followed with her hand jammed in my pants. I grabbed her wrist and yanked her up. "Fucking useless…"

A cough sounded at the back of my office. Apollo had entered with an ashen-looking Bella in tow. Fuck, she definitely misunderstood where I was going with that. I meant Tatianna, not her.

"Bella, *mia regina*." I didn't know what was worse: her tear-filled eyes or her neck reddened by embarrassment…

"Lucky, baby." Tatianna dug her nails into my thigh and I shoved her off me so fast my chair rolled backward. However, she refused to release me, her hand clinging to my dick as it came to life at the sight of the one woman whose presence it couldn't ignore, no matter how hard I tried.

And I was so wrong. It wasn't the blush or her eyes filling with tears that was the worst part. It was when those same tears spilled down Bella's polished cheeks, upon seeing the position Tatianna and I were in, that utterly wrecked me. It was completely misconstrued, but it didn't matter. As quickly as the devastation came, it was gone. Her spine straightened, her eyes devoid of emotion, while her impassive tone might as well have been screaming at me from across the room.

"My apologies, Lucifer. I was unaware you had *business*." She practically snarled the last word at me, even as she somehow maintained her calm. "Apollo." She turned on her heel and exited the room as quietly as she had entered it.

"Bella!" I roared but she was already a distant blip on my radar.

Apollo glared at me from across the room, with one of the few emotions I could read on him morphing his usually impassive features. *Disgust*. My men dabbled in random pussy. It wasn't unheard of, but they respected their future queen and more than despised the woman presently clawing at my pants like she had a fighting chance.

However, I could only solve one problem at a time. And if I hoped to secure my future with the woman I loved, I first needed to handle my lingering past.

I glanced down at Tatianna, her wrist still grasped in one hand, and snapped her arm back until the familiar sound of bone breaking reached my ears. She cried out in pain as Apollo stormed out the door behind Bella.

"Well, I take it *that* is my answer. I'll go take care of Mirabella while Tatianna takes care of you," Angelo said, licking his lips at the prospect of claiming what was clearly mine.

"Take another step and you're dead," I hissed, my eyes flicking to the door. Al was blocking Angelo's only chance of escape. "I don't want your trash and you sure as fuck aren't taking Bella from me." I tossed Tatianna aside before turning my glare on her. "And you, the only reason you're still breathing is because of your father. Now, get the fuck out before I change my mind."

Tatianna was already at the door, begging Al with her eyes to let her pass. Her wrist lay limp and curled against her body, though she was lucky that was all she'd gotten, seeing as the look of betrayal on Bella's face nearly killed me.

Angelo was heaving on the spot, and I could tell he was debating his next move. But I'd had enough of his bullshit, so the moment he opened his mouth to speak, I landed one solid blow to his temple and he crumbled to the ground, unconscious. I motioned towards Al and he scooped the fucker into his arms before tugging Tatianna from the room alongside him. The moment the door closed behind them, I shoved the files from my desk in a fit of rage.

Fucking Christ!

I wasn't sure who I was angrier at. Them for upsetting her, or myself for allowing it to go that far. I grabbed my phone and called Bella. And of course, it went straight to voicemail. Opting to hang up, instead of leaving a message, I dialed Apollo next. At least he *had* to answer.

He picked up on the first ring. "What the fuck were you thinking?"

"Give her the phone," I growled into the receiver. "I can't. She left with your sister and her team."

"Fuck. No doubt Sienna will rip me a new asshole now."

Apollo started chuckling. "Nah, boss. She was tightlipped when

Sienna asked if she was okay. Kept a smile on and said you were busy."

"Jesus, she really is perfect. Fuck."

"Be there in thirty," Apollo replied, and I fixed my suit and waited.

"And nothing happened. Angelo was trying to proposition me with a trade. She walked in at the wrong time. The fuck was she doing here anyway?"

Apollo lowered himself onto the seat Angelo had recently vacated. "Your little minx had extra wine with dinner and wanted to thank you *personally* for her flowers today."

I smiled at his comment until a thought hit me. "I didn't send her flowers today." Apollo went on to tell me about the card and I sat straighter in my seat. "That wasn't me. Call Jay."

Jay was my ex-military contact. He was a computer whiz, who could hack into anything. He was my source when I didn't want my sister and her company involved. Whatever information I needed to know, he mysteriously got it to me. And quickly. He could pull files on anyone I asked, tap into any security system, and was a damn good chess player. He was also extremely standoffish, hated social situations, and only came out to meet Apollo at their "secret" location.

My phone ringing broke the silence of Apollo texting away on his. Answering on the first ring, I had to pull the device back from my ear as my sister screeched on the other end. "The fuck did you do?"

"What did she say?" I asked Sienna, loathing the situation I had put myself into.

"Nothing. Not a damn word. She was clearly upset but blew off my concern, telling me all was happy-fucking-unicorns and rainbows."

Snorting at my sister's ever-interesting commentary, I blew out a breath. "She walked into a conversation at the wrong time. What she saw, heard, it was all out of context."

"What the fuck are you doing in this building, bitch?" Sienna hissed, and I could hear her stiletto heels clicking in the marble lobby, followed by Tatianna's muffled sobs. "Lucky, please don't tell me…" Sienna huffed in exasperation, already knowing the answer to her own question.

"Like I said, sis, she walked in at the wrong time, but I never touched the bitch. I wouldn't do that to Bella."

I could hear scuffling in the background, likely Sienna chasing after Tatianna. Those two had a history, beyond me and my… *indiscretions* with the woman. This was just another excuse for my sister to sink her teeth into her rival. It was one of many altercations they had in my lobby, seeing as I held the top floor penthouse of the building I shared with Sienna, who was a floor below me, and Apollo who was a floor below her. We all had luxurious suites to ourselves when we stayed in the city to conduct business.

A moment later, Sienna was huffing into the phone again. "Well, it's now officially her birthday and you fucked up. Fix this shit and fix it now." She hung up on me, and I realized it was after midnight and officially Bella's birthday. Which also meant her party was technically tonight and I had a lot of wrongs I had to make right. She would enjoy herself. I'd make sure of it.

"Flowers were paid in cash. Shop had no cameras. He's scouting the streets for traffic cams," Apollo said.

"Fuckin' great." Add that to the list of bullshit I needed taken care of. Someone was clearly threatening Bella and I'd sent her running.

Several thoughts passed through my mind on how to fix this. But nothing seemed right. I should just give her space and make amends with her tomorrow, early, before her party and our announcement.

"Stewing women only grow angrier." Apollo smirked, knowing me all too well.

Adjusting my jacket, I stormed out of my office and stalked to the elevator. "Get me a fucking name," I called out just as the doors shut on his grin. And suddenly I felt my age, ten years older than my bride, and worlds away from where she was emotionally.

How the fuck was I supposed to man up and apologize to a woman who knew me by reputation rather than character?

CHAPTER 17

MIRABELLA MORETTI

"Shut up, Apollo. I'm talking! She called me, not you." Sienna yelled into the phone, so loudly I had to pull the device away from my ear.

"Bella, it wasn't what you think. Angelo wanted Lucky to call off your engagement," Apollo said in the background.

"The rumors appear to be true. His old man was none-too-pleased about the almost death of the call girl. To make amends, he wanted Angelo to settle down with you." Sienna laughed.

We'd spent lunch talking about the mishap with Angelo Fioretti. Apparently, he was into some rather disturbing antics in the bedroom. Long story short, he almost killed a girl with some sick bondage play.

"I'm fine. Goodnight, you two." Hanging up before Sienna could get another word in, I breathed a heavy sigh and stared into the mirror. My wariness and insecurities showed.

Was I really that naive to think that a man like Lucky would be faithful? Hell, my own father was obsessed with my mother and even he had been known to dabble in extramarital affairs. So, of course, Lucky would cheat.

Promises of ruling at his side, bearing his children, and tending to our home didn't matter. All of that made me committed to him. To the Agostinos. He didn't owe me anything. It was just how our world worked. I may have hated it but I had to accept it.

The opposing colors of my eyes burned bright from my tears. I barely escaped my parents' questions when I ran into the house to hide in my room, vowing to hold back the waterworks and only release them in the sanctity of the scalding-hot shower. Insisting to myself that once I stepped out again, I would be stronger.

I was holed up in the bathroom crying, while he was laughing about my virginity. Letting that plastic piece of shit choke on his dick. On *my* dick. Fuck that! I shouldn't have left. I was his queen and he told me he was different.

I was going to go back there and demand that he apologize. Then I'd kick both their asses for doing this to me. Throwing on my black Nike leggings and sports bra with a gray swoosh on it and straightening my spine, I charged out of the bathroom. A woman on a mission.

Practically slamming my feet into my sneakers, I realized I was talking out loud. Angry and readying myself to fight for my man, I couldn't stop my mouth from running. "…Going to rip her fucking head off for being a conniving little slut-bitch-whore…" Tatianna knew Lucky was mine. The cunt had even been crying in the gym over Angelo, only to be sucking Lucky's dick in front of him. I cursed and threw my head upside down to tuck my hair into a messy bun.

"I guess I deserve that and probably more." The baritone voice sounded from across the room, and I screamed before clamping a hand to my mouth. My chest ached as I looked him up and down. I'd fallen for this man and he ripped my heart out. And suddenly I was resolute to the fact that I was weak. I had all these plans of kicking everyone's ass, and here I was, catching my breath at the sight of him. His usually immaculate suit was reduced to a white shirt, untucked and his sleeves rolled up. Even somewhat disheveled, Lucifer Agostino was disarming. Dangerous.

"It wasn't at all what it looked…"

Raising a hand, I silenced him. "Sienna called—well, she and Apollo—after she beat Tatianna's ass for me."

He nodded, his face devoid of emotion. Taking a deep breath, I refused to cower under his penetrating stare.

"I'd never do that to you. The things he said." Remorseful eyes stared back at me as Lucky dropped to his knees in front of me.

I did my best to keep my composure. "Are you going to trade the little virgin for a piece of plastic?" I watched as his brows knitted with the accusation. This man commandeered my life, forcing me to be a reigning queen at his side, so to see him practically begging me to believe him left me at a loss for words.

"Never." He tugged me to him and I went willingly into his open arms, allowing him to kiss me after a moment of pause. His hand reaching inside my leggings had me frozen in place with the image of Tatianna running rampant in my mind.

"Don't. Not… not after." I stopped, swallowing the sob threatening to spill free. The promise I made to myself in the shower was on its way to being forgotten.

"I broke her wrist." He lifted my chin and I snapped my eyes back to him, my resolve faltering as he spoke. "And Angelo is only breathing because of his family name. However, that won't save him if he continues to disrespect you."

Even as he tugged me towards the bed and my feet followed will-ingly, my mind was in turmoil. I was pleased he taught them a lesson, but was it enough? Repeated images of the man you love with another woman swirling in your mind was a cruel form of torture.

"My dick had—*has* no interest in her, Bella." He continued as if reading my thoughts. "I was shaking her off when you walked in. And your presence was the only thing that could spring my cock to life. For you, Bella, only for you."

"You can understand my pain at what I saw though, right?" I was trying to keep my wits about me. Fighting with myself to project the strength I was capable of embodying.

"That and more. Roles reversed, I'd destroy any man who touched you. I'd wallow in self-loathing for making you turn to someone else. Then I'd take my pain out on that someone." His blue eyes stormed into thunderous clouds. "Slowly. Precisely. I'd tear them apart."

"Lucky, outside of your men and my brothers, I am not acquainted with many."

He step towards me and his sharp inhale of my hair had me quivering on the spot.

"Nor do I know a man so hungry for death he'd dare mess with *il diavolo*."

His answering growl was all I needed to hear. He came here because he wanted me. Wanted everything all right between us. Devouring me with a harsh and passionate kiss, he dominated every part of me. I tried to keep my resolve, to show him this bullshit would *not* be happening again; however, his murmurs of approval as his mouth consumed my body clouded my judgment. I could barely contain myself whenever this man was near. Add his kisses and soft-spoken words, and I was putty in his hands.

Throwing me onto the bed, he towered over me. Despite the differences between us, the obvious size differential, I knew Lucky would never hurt me. Not physically. No, it was my mental state that was in jeopardy.

"I need to taste you, Bella. I need to watch you tremble beneath me. To know you're still here. *Still mine.*"

"Show me. Show me I'm yours." I poked the devil, pleading for him to lose control. I *needed* it. I needed him.

And as if he could sense as much, he attacked, stripping me bare while his immense biceps ripped my thighs apart. He smirked down at me, tossing my legs over his shoulders as I writhed beneath him.

I couldn't speak or ask him what he was doing, only watch on as his head disappeared and his warm mouth latched on to my clit. I gasped at the contact as he sucked and stroked the sweetest of spots. In a matter of minutes, I was already on the cusp of ecstasy.

"Eyes!"

I propped myself up on my elbows and his intense gaze had me unraveling instantly. His large hands squeezing and massaging my hardened nipples forced my orgasm to blaze brighter. And just when I thought it was going to end, he bit down hard enough to draw blood, the pain adding to my intoxication. This was it. My ruin. There was no coming back from this man.

My arousal glistened on his full lips, as Lucky flicked his eyes upward and presented me with a gorgeous smile. He licked his lips on a moan. "The sweetest fruit I've ever tasted. *Mio Bella.*" I dropped onto my back, and he chuckled at my sigh. "I'm not done."

His head disappeared once again, and the next few hours were lost to the lust-induced haze of Lucky claiming and reclaiming me. Owning me. Over and over again. Until I didn't know which way was up and which was down.

Once my body had succumbed to its new liquid state, my bones pliable like jelly, Lucky climbed up the bed, pulling my back against his chest, and stroked my hair.

"Tell me about your childhood," I implored, wanting to know every detail about my future husband.

"It was murder, corruption, and deceit all from a young age. Being groomed to take over the city came early on. When my old man deemed my progress moving too slowly, he ordered me to the dungeon at the lowest level of the compound to teach me a lesson." He chuckled when I gasped in shock.

The moment I realized he was joking, I shoved at his chest. "Bastard!"

"Bastard…? You wound me!" Wrapping me against his hard chest, he continued. "I don't know. It was normal, I guess. My siblings and I were all very tightknit growing up, bonded for as long as I can remember. Were you close with your brothers?"

I scoffed at the idea, sadness quickly replacing the ridiculousness of the question. "Dominic and I were always close. He was my protector and confidante. He has such a sweet soul." Lucky made a noise behind me that I didn't quite understand. "However, Gio was always… off. I'd overhear my mother's concerns that he wasn't… right."

The conversation continued flowing into the early morning hours. Little by little, I got to know more about the man I'd agreed to share a life with. It wasn't long before my eyes grew heavy and I barely registered the kiss to my head.

"Sleep, *mio amore*. I will see you tonight. Happy birthday, Bella." The bed dipped at his exit but I was too weary to respond. My eyes closed and the sweet abyss took me over into a peaceful sleep.

Evidently, I'd forgotten to close the blinds, and the early morning sun woke me at sunrise. I stretched my limbs, my muscles tight and weak from last night's activities. *Last night.* Just thinking of the way he took me repeatedly and opened himself up to me had me smiling.

He really was the perfect man I'd been dreaming about. Today was my birthday and the party this evening would announce our engagement to all the prominent families in our midst.

Rolling out of bed to get ready for the day, I froze at the sweet scent of fresh flowers. I looked up and my breath was taken away. Vases upon vases of red roses were scattered around the room. The vibrant red overpowered every available surface, while the vase closest to the bed held a card.

Forty-two vases. Twice your age and yet not nearly as sweet. Happy birthday, Bella. I cannot wait to tell the world you're mine. Till then…

With love,

Your devil

I made it a point to smell each vase, before taking a shower and heading to my closet to throw on my workout gear. Lacing up the sneakers, I'd planned to have a quick breakfast, then take my morning run. However, Dom's angry voice had me halting in the shadows of the stairs.

"He just showed up unannounced and completely off-kilter. Something is going on."

Gio. Who else could he be talking about?

"It seems the impending announcement this evening has set him off. You know his feelings towards Lucky and that family."

That. That family? *That family* was about to be *my* family. I knew Gio hated Lucky and had a vendetta against him. But I was under the assumption my father and Dom at least saw the benefits of us binding ourselves to the Agostinos.

Clearly, I was wrong.

"I know he tried to steal Lucky's shipment. I can't believe he's still alive." Dom chuckled under his breath.

"Your sister appears to have a stronger hold on him than we expected. Apollo did pay him a visit but it was... gentle. Anyway, he won't be attending tonight."

"That's why he disappeared after the dinner at *Vino*?"

I couldn't hear my father's reply but I knew it had to be true. His disappearance after I disrespected him spoke volumes now. He was hiding, licking his wounds. I couldn't help but wonder just how *gentle* Apollo really was with him. A no-kill order for the enforcer was likely worse than death. More painful.

"I told him not to come." My mother's sudden presence at my side had me stumbling into the railing, and my frightened squeal echoed off the walls. "I'm sorry. I thought you heard me coming, my darling." Her soft voice always had this way of calming me.

"What is going on with him?"

As she stroked my face, sadness washed over hers. "Since he was little, Gio just couldn't coexist with the other boys. He always wanted what they had. To be the best and did whatever he had to do to get what he wanted."

"And he wants Lucky's throne."

She nodded. "I know you've gotten close to Sienna. Has she not told you of his proposal?"

"What? I didn't even know they'd met before me." Then again, Lucky's sister had mentioned her dislike for my brother. More than once.

"He didn't date her, barely attempted to court her. Just showed up at Lucky's club one night and demanded they marry. He believed he was the male heir their family needed. Needless to say, it didn't end well." *Sienna was known to have a killer right hook.* "Anyway, tonight is about you and about Lucky declaring his love for you. It's not about your brother and his games."

My mother took my arm and we wandered down the stairs together to have breakfast. The staff already had a gorgeous buffet setup that Dominic and my father were destroying.

"Good morning, Bella." My father rose from his chair the same time Dominic replied around a mouthful of food, "Happy birthday, baby sis."

"I have spared no expense for this evening. I've had the staff make some tweaks to the grand ballroom to propel it to the next level. Anything for my little girl's birthday."

"I'd expect no less than extravagant for anything Anthony Moretti has his hand in." I smiled because I truly meant it.

My father chuckled and offered me a seat before snapping at the kitchen girl, who quickly moved about the buffet display, depositing numerous items on a plate. My mother had already sat with her spread of various fruits and egg whites, ever the healthy woman I wished I could be. I just loved sweets a little too much to have such devotion, while my cardio routine every morning helped alleviate my guilt for indulging.

I smiled at the thin girl as she placed the plate in front of me. She must have been new. I didn't recognize her from any of our prior family meals. She shied away from my welcoming grin and quickly pivoted on her heel, only to be met by my father's glare.

"The fuck is wrong with you? Stupid, stupid girl! She has a party tonight! She gets what her mother has!" He lunged for the plate before the girl could reach for it, sending the contents flying to the floor. The delicious-looking waffles that were piled with whipped cream and strawberries now plastered the front of her uniform. "Jesus Christ! The incompetence. The fuck were you thinking, Dominic?" He snarled and exited the room, rambling down the hallway as he went.

My mother and I each dropped to the ground to help the poor girl clean up the mess. She was a tiny little thing, her hands shaking, likely in response to my father's rampage. Except she wasn't looking in his direction. Instead, her eyes were glued to my brother. The cold, dead expression on her face frightened me. I recognized the trauma there as she awaited Dominic's response.

She had to be a little under my five-six height with long, dirty blonde hair and bright-blue eyes. She was almost as pale as I was and had the body of a toned dancer, despite her thin frame. However, if you looked hard enough, you could see a hint of darkness. A light was out; something was missing. Almost like she sat on the edge, barely grasping on to her sanity.

"What did he mean, Dominic?" I looked over my shoulder at him, his eyes absent as they stared back. Whomever I was talking to, he wasn't my brother. This version was distant, closed-off.

"Nothing, Bella. She needed a job and I sent her to Father. Now, there was supposed to be a candle on that plate for you." Standing from his chair, he helped my mother and me to our feet. When he flicked his wrist at the kitchen girl, she squeaked in response.

"Sir, please. There was… it's just… *here!*" Rummaging in the mess on the floor, she lifted a single candle and placed it in his waiting hand. You could practically feel the vibrations radiating off her. The fear.

"Enough. Clean this shit up." The voice that left my beloved brother wasn't one I'd ever heard before. He wasn't normally so abrasive with the staff—that was usually Gio's pastime.

Without another word, the plate was picked up off the ground, and the blonde scampered from the room. I couldn't help but eye her uniform as she brushed by us in a blur. Our staff was always much more traditional, their outfits professional and tailored. While hers was more—well, I guess, *less* than the others. To put it bluntly, she looked like a stripper, the material tight and short.

I glanced at Dominic, taking note of how he leered at her, then I chuckled and shoved at his chest. It seemed someone had a bit of a crush. After all, it was a universal truth that little boys were always mean to the girls they liked. And more often than not, my brothers were more like boys than men. I could only pray to whomever was watching over her that a crush was all it was.

"What was it you needed to discuss with me?" I asked, unsure which pile of shit was at the top of our list at the moment.

"I've been given some insight into Dominic Moretti."

I nodded my head, urging Apollo to continue.

"It's about his transport business funneling through the Agostino docks."

"Spit it out, Apollo. We need to get to the party. I don't care about his bullshit." This verbal back and forth was tiresome.

"Would you care if said goods were actually women?"

"What?" The question came out as more of a growl than an actual word as my gaze penetrated him through the mirror I was facing.

"One of our guys watched a deal go down when we were surveilling the docks." Apollo couldn't have shocked me anymore if he tried. I knew Dominic had a growing empire, which I'd suspected could dabble in such a thing. Besides running a strip club, he was a large importer of goods from around the world. However, he'd seemed so caring towards his mother and his sister that I quickly dismissed the thought. "He pulls them off the streets from men who owe him money. He's even taken them right off the pole of his bar. He's selling them local and foreign." Apollo went on to tell me about his own investigation. He learned the wealth Dominic amassed was hidden in several dummy corporations. It appeared his family, his father included, had no idea what the bastard was up to.

"That's a conversation that's going to need to happen sooner rather than later. That shit doesn't go down in my city or on my docks." I typed a text to my father. He and I would discuss it in the very near future.

"Gio was told he isn't welcome this evening. Anthony Moretti was in agreement. The men will keep a lookout for him to ensure Miss Bella enjoys herself."

I nodded in reply, and Apollo dipped his head once before taking his leave. With one final glance at myself, I was ready to go. My black tuxedo and bowtie were perfectly fitted and the night was just beginning to look good. Bella's birthday had been moved to the top luxury hotel in the city. Beneath my penthouse.

Her father wanted it at their residence but I'd twisted his arm for her security. My men would be able to protect her much better on our home turf. Not to mention, it was the most lavish for a reason. Serafina Moretti had an eye for detail and none was spared for Bella's birthday.

I planned to spend the entire night showing Bella just how happy and thankful I was that she was born today. My future bride was proving to be more than an asset. My only present concern was how the news of her brother would implode her world. Gio was an idiot, but her beloved Dominic was selling girls off the streets, and that knowledge would ruin her.

"Apollo."

He turned in his seat the moment I entered the car.

"Bella learns nothing of Dominic tonight. We need to meet with him first before his image is forever tainted in her mind."

"Got it, boss."

The car came to a stop outside the main entrance of the hotel several minutes later. The valet opened the door and dipped his head in greeting and I made a beeline for the main ballroom.

Every table was covered with black linens and black vases filled with bright-red roses and dripping in crystals. All of the tapestries were black and showcased the sparkling chandeliers while every tabletop and open space had diamond-encrusted candles lit brightly.

The staff and attendees already present were in black attire. Serafina had made it clear in the invites: if you were in any color other than black, you would be denied entry.

My parents stood at the rear bar, my mother with her wine and my father with his rocks glass. More than likely my old man had chosen his favorite bourbon. I nodded to Apollo and he disappeared to meet with my security team as well as the hotel's to complete a final sweep before Bella arrived. Kissing my mother on the cheek, I motioned for my father to step to the side with me.

"What do you know of Dominic Moretti's import business?" I asked him right away.

"Besides it being lucrative enough to be our largest paycheck on the docks, nothing. Why?"

"How about the fact that the cash lining his pockets is the proceeds of his selling women?"

Scoffing into his glass, my father took a long sip, looking at me over the rim. "You're serious?"

My face remained stoic as I continued. "One of my men informed me."

"Jesus Christ." We each scanned the room, though neither of us could find him. "Gio isn't coming but Dominic is supposed to be here."

"I don't want to ruin Bella's night. But tomorrow this conversation will happen."

"Bet your ass it will. Then we'll shut that shit down."

As we nodded to each other, my father tapped my arm to gain my attention. It was in that moment I realized the entire room had filled to capacity with eager guests awaiting the birthday girl. There were several variations of black gowns mixed with men in black tuxedos. The lack of color made the red of the roses pop in contrast.

My eyes landed on Natalia and Nico, who were at the bar talking next to my mother, and I couldn't help but feel pleased at the turnout.

Several key players and their families mingled amongst each other, each looking to pay their respects. Granted, it was more out of respect for me than Anthony Moretti, but the only thing that mattered was Bella.

My eyes flicked up and my breath was stolen from my lungs. The music from the DJ died and the laughter of the guests ceased to exist in that moment. The only thing holding my focus was the sudden light illuminating the room. Bella had made her entrance at the top of the grand staircase overlooking the crowd. My security remained close by as she waited for her mother to descend on Dominic's arm.

My bride-to-be was dressed in a white strapless gown with a sweetheart bodice hugging her slight curves. Her neck boasted an elegant heart-shaped emerald necklace that hung low above her supple breasts. The necklace was an antique in my family, having been passed down for several generations. My mother gave it to me days ago for Bella to wear. It looked flawless against her porcelain skin. Her long black hair was swept to the side, layering silky curls I knew would be soft to the touch, with some sort of pin that kept it all in place.

Every man—hell, every woman in the room was giving her their rapt attention. As I stepped forward, our eyes connected as if nothing else existed and a coy smile graced her angelic face. A possessive feeling was overtaking me, begging me to charge the stairs and make a fast retreat with her over my shoulder, roaring and pounding on my chest to the entire room to show them she was mine. Instead, I stopped about five stairs up, holding out my hand as she approached me. Once she was halfway down, the room erupted in applause. I kissed her hand while she safely made it to the bottom of the stairs before I swept her onto the dance floor. Groups of guests cleared the space as we immediately went into our first dance of the evening.

"You made quite the entrance, *mia regina*," I whispered into her ear. "I have a sudden urge to destroy every man in this room, none of them worthy enough to watch such beauty."

"The things you say, Lucky." Her soft giggle warmed my cold-blooded heart. "I was so nervous until I saw you. You calm me, *mio re*."

"And you take my breath away. Tonight is your night, my love. I will make sure it's perfect."

"They're staring. Do you think they know yet?" she asked me, peering up at me through her lashes.

"I will make the announcement but I'm sure they've already made their assumptions."

We danced for two more songs before breaking apart and heading towards the main table.

"Bella, *sei bellissima*." My father leaned in to kiss Bella's reddening cheek. I motioned her towards her seat before dinner was served.

Things started off smoothly. Bella was laughing with Octavia and Sienna at the table. They were sharing two bottles of 2010 Petrus Pomerol merlot I'd arranged specifically for her, while Dominic and Anthony were in their own private discussion at the far end of the table. Both of our mothers were glowing from their own glasses of wine. The main course was being set in front of us as the conversation dimmed and everyone started eating.

As I looked around the room, I realized that not only was Bella the light in the darkness that was my life, but her white dress amidst the sea of black seemed to further highlight her brilliance. I reached for her hand under the table and began chatting with Marco, who was seated next to me, enjoying my bourbon until my eyes unconsciously landed on Bella again. She was frozen in her seat.

Before I could ask her what was wrong, a shrill laugh broke the silence—a recognizable sound that sent shivers down my spine. My glare shot in that direction. Tatianna and her little lover boy had arrived. I knew at least one of them wasn't on the guest list, but could only surmise that Anthony had invited Angelo and his family, seeing as they were one of his few allies.

As if her attendance wasn't an insult in itself, Tatianna was dressed head to toe... in designer white. And I was certain there had been no misunderstanding. This was a statement, a declaration of war—or might as well have been.

I kissed Bella's forehead before charging to my feet, Big Al and

Apollo already waiting at the end of the table. Walking down to Anthony Moretti, I whispered in his ear. "Your alliance with that family is done." I gestured towards Angelo, my father following my pointed gaze before rising and heading towards the Fiorettis.

"Boss?" Apollo asked, eyeing my father's conversation. "We could just hurt him... really, really badly."

Big Al nodded, his chin jutting in Tatianna's direction. "And she gets buried." When I looked at him curiously, he shook his head. "She made Miss Bella sad on her birthday."

"You can't kill him." My old man interjected as if he could read my thoughts and my eyes locked on Angelo's father. He nodded his head in understanding. We couldn't kill him... *but* he'd sure as fuck wish he were dead.

"And her?" I countered.

Stopping in his tracks, my father spun on his heel. "Her father is a fucking coward." He said no more, thus giving me my answer. He kissed my mother on her head before he walked to Bella, leaning in to whisper in her ear. Her expression softened and I knew whatever he said had eased her worries, meaning I could focus my energy on the matter at hand.

"Make a fucking scene and you'll be fucking sorry." Apollo gripped Tatianna's arm, the huge smile on his face hiding his true intentions.

"Fuck her. You can have her." Angelo flicked a dismissive hand in her direction, turning back to his conversation.

"You're mistaken. She is your date. That means *move*." Big Al shoved him around the staircase. When he started causing a commotion, Big Al's large hand cupped the fucker's mouth, his extra-wide body hiding Angelo's thrashing as he was physically carried from the room.

My men expertly hid our exit while we headed through the kitchen and into an oversized utility closet at the far end. The kitchen staff turned their backs, acting as though they were unaware of what was taking place. Four of my men stood outside the door, shutting it behind me.

Tatianna was curled up into a ball on the floor, while Al held Angelo to his chest. Fioretti was already running out of fight and stamina, though Al appeared unfazed by the struggle.

"You were warned, Tatianna." I dropped to a squat in front of her as she cried out in fright. "To leave my fiancée alone, as if you never existed. And what did you do? The very next day, you show up to her black-tie gala in white."

"You made her sad. No one makes Miss Bella sad." The angry Alvin—the one that Bella had yet to see—practically frothed at the mouth to protect her.

"Fuck her! I had you first, Lucky! She doesn't deserve you. She can't fuck you like I can! She doesn't have the same bloodline I do!" The little bitch rose to her knees, as if she'd grown a backbone all of a sudden. "You can't hurt me. My father would have your head."

Apollo, Al, and I all began chuckling at her stupidity. She really believed some politician was going to protect her from me, from my family. That her poor excuse for a father would give a shit about his daughter—one who was past her prime marrying age because he literally could not pay someone to take her. The sniveling little shit believed she was beyond my realm of torture. She'd learn she was severely mistaken.

"Tatianna, do you know who I am?" She nodded in response. "Do you know who my family is?"

"Duh! Of course I do, Lucky! They're not in politics. They don't come with the backing of the government." She scoffed as if a New York State Senator candidate held any weight in my world.

"Exactly. Which means I can do whatever the fuck I want because I am not monitored by the government." I could see her wheels turning, but the cogs weren't in place just yet.

"In other words, you dumb bitch, your Daddy can't do shit. You're ours now." Apollo grinned, pulling her off the floor and pinning her against his chest with my nod of approval. His hands roamed her plastic body as she screamed in terror. "And, Tatianna, Lucky's version of domination is child's play compared to what I like."

The girl could barely handle me; she'd beg for death after one round in the sack with Apollo. I couldn't contain the sneer on my face at just the thought.

"No one. And I mean *no one* makes *mia regina* sad, especially not a spoiled little cunt like you."

When she began struggling against his hold, Apollo slapped her once across the face. A child of wealth didn't often learn the cruel ways of adolescence. That one hit and she dropped to the ground, her eyes pooling with crocodile tears as she clutched her cheek with her bandaged wrist.

Big Al, refusing to be outdone, repeated the gesture, his open palm landing on Angelo's jawline with an audible smack. And, as I'd expected from someone not ready for the world I was running, the bastard passed out after one blow. Al took the opportunity to pull a chair from the corner, lowering himself down and tugging Tatianna across his lap.

Apollo's honey eyes lit with excitement, his chest rising and falling quickly as he removed his jacket and rolled his sleeves to his elbow, revealing the very intricate tattoos that traced his arms. I grabbed the hem of Tatianna's dress and shredded the material down the center of her body, tugging it free so she was bare to us except for her lace lingerie. While she cried and thrashed, Al held her tight, her ass in the air as she twisted to get free. I walked around to Apollo, and we both looked at the slight red marks visible under each of her ass cheeks.

"You didn't." Apollo laughed.

"Oh, she did." I laughed harder, pointing to Al, who joined in our amusement. "Tatianna, is any part of you natural?"

She continued shaking and whining, her mumbling incoherent.

"You're a spoiled little brat and you went for *mia regina*. That means you are to be punished, Tatianna. And I am going to enjoy it." Apollo let loose, his open-hand slaps landing blow after blow. As he switched from one cheek to another, her skin burned a bright-red hue.

"Fuck, I'm getting hard." Al laughed, trying to position her at a more pleasurable angle.

"Hear that, Tatianna. You're making him hard. Are you going to take care of him?" Apollo kept his hand moving back and forth as he waited for her reply. "Answer me!"

Smack. Smack. Smack.

Her spine was arched in the air as she swayed her ass to try to avoid the blows. Her skin turned a purplish shade, the top layer breaking open with the force. Pushing her down, Al gripped her tighter to his lap, matching her squirms to seek relief.

"Yes! Yes! Please, just stop," she cried out, her voice stuttering with the movement. Apollo smacked her one more time for good measure and Al released her quickly. Not able to support herself yet, Tatianna rolled onto the floor in an attempt to keep the pressure off her throbbing backside.

Grabbing her face, Apollo pulled her close. "Now, you won't fuck with Bella again. Or next time… I'll really play with you."

He waited for her wide-eyed nod before shoving her to the floor. She looked back and forth between the three of us as Al grabbed himself to show her what she'd done. And like the good little whore she was, she climbed to her knees and pawed at his zipper.

He might have been hard but I was disgusted by this little shit. Although, the really messed-up part was how Tatianna's eyes turned sensual as she pulled him free of his pants. We didn't rape the unwilling. And Tatianna was practically pleading for it. She was such a good little slut, even if she couldn't sit on her ass. As she took him into her mouth, Al sat back, grunting in ecstasy right as Angelo started to come to.

"Morning there, Angie. Have a nice nap, did you?"

Shaking his head, he took in the room from his position on the floor. "The fuck do you think you're doing? My father will kill you for this!" He rubbed a hand over his split lip, while Apollo chuckled and returned to my side.

"Real made men don't need their daddies to do the killing, Angie. No. In fact, real made men make pussies like you bleed." Arching my fist back, I swung hard and fast at his nose. Blood, bones, and his screams erupted on impact. "Daddy said I wasn't allowed to kill you and out of respect to him, I will oblige. But you will be taught a lesson, Angie."

Angelo curled up into a ball on the floor, holding his head in his hands. Lost to the rhythm of my own personal punching bag, I kept attacking. The adrenaline was coursing through me as the smell of his blood infiltrated my system. I couldn't see what I was doing, couldn't feel the skin on my fist breaking. Yes, *il diavolo* had come to play. I had men to enact this revenge on my behalf, but I reveled in taking care of business myself.

"Take it." Al was now standing in front of a squirming Tatianna. It was easy to see she was doing her best to keep her sore ass off her designer heels underneath her. "Do you like that, baby?"

Her mewling around his cock told him how much she did.

"Boss, he's out."

I'd barely registered that not only had Angelo passed out but Apollo was holding on to my arm.

"Been that way for a few now. Go back to Bella. We got this."

I nodded as he passed me a towel from the metal shelf nearby. Not wanting to scare Bella, I wiped the blood from my hands. Once clean, I rebuttoned my cufflinks and shrugged my jacket on. I shouted for my men outside the door, instructing them to enter as I motioned to the floor. "Take out the trash."

"Do we get a turn?" One of them pointed to Tatianna, who was still on her knees, her chest soaked with her spit from Al's cock buried deep in her throat.

"Apollo has next," I stated as I brushed by, taking note of how Tatianna's greedy little eyes sought him out in the room, her happy little sounds echoing around Al's cock. It seemed she enjoyed an audience. Al grunted his release, his cock buried in her throat until he grew limp and pulled back.

"But he always breaks his toys," I heard one of my men mutter as they dragged Angelo's prone form out of the room. Tatianna's smile dropped immediately, her eyes glued to Apollo as he approached and removed his belt.

"You wanted to play, didn't you? Tell me now. I only take my women willing." A look of uncertainty washed over her face before she smiled and nodded. "Now's your only chance to leave, Tatianna. This is it. Make your decision."

"I'm staying."

Apollo sneered, his honey-brown eyes turning a near black color. The psychotic side, buried under all that ink and those expensive suits, was coming to the surface. And Tatianna had no idea what she was in for. "I've got this, boss. Tell Bella happy birthday again for me."

Nodding, I buttoned my jacket and left the room with Al on my heels. The once-bloodied mess of Angelo Fioretti was just a distant memory the moment I caught sight of Bella.

CHAPTER 19

MIRABELLA MORETTI

This. Bitch.

Just showed up to my party wearing white. For the most part, I considered myself to be calm, cool, and collected.

But three strikes and you're out, bitch.

First, she made my life hell growing up. Fast-forward to the incident with Lucky at his office, and now she was wearing white. At my party. When she wasn't even invited.

My eyes narrowed in on the object of my contention. Tatianna on the arm of Angelo Fioretti. Sienna saw me staring and followed my pointed glare. The moment she noticed, anger drove her to her feet.

"Fucking cunt," she muttered around the rim of her wine, her lips rolling into a snarl. I clinked our glasses before raising mine and slamming it back in one gulp. "My father just nodded. Game. On." Sienna motioned to the waiter for refills. The situation definitely called for more alcohol.

Looking up, I saw Mario was headed our way and a calm settled over me, knowing the Agostinos were backing me to the fullest. I glanced at my mother, who appeared completely oblivious while my father watched me, his facial expression giving nothing away.

Dominic was staring—no, practically salivating with his eyes glued to a certain waitress now serving our table. Mario leaned down to speak to Sienna, blocking my view of my brother's peculiar actions. The girl headed towards me with a wine bottle in hand as Mario whispered in my ear. "Lucky will take care of them, my dear."

"And what about the Fiorettis?" I was quick to question.

He looked to Sienna with an amused grin. "Let's just say Angelo has pushed his father's patience far beyond what he should allow. Lucky has been granted approval to… correct the boy's behavior."

A small arm leaned over my shoulder to top off my glass. Sienna was already enjoying her refill, looking towards the now-empty staircase. Where had they gone so quickly? And just how far would Lucky go with his *correction*? Surely Senior Fioretti wouldn't allow him to kill his son? Would he?

A sharp gasp and a wetness coating my hand startled me from my curious thoughts.

"Damn it!" Dominic thrusted his chair back, storming to his feet. My mind barely grasped the fact that the waitress had spilled wine before my brother was already around the table, grabbing the girl's arm. Though her blonde hair was now pinned in a bun and her uniform matched that of the other staff in attendance, I recognized her as being the same server from breakfast this morning.

"Dominic!" Jumping from my chair, I grabbed the girl's other arm to stop him from dragging her away. "Take. Your Hands. Off her. Now!"

"She almost drenched your white dress, Mirabella. She's incompetent."

The girl was practically vibrating with fear. I could feel her terror beneath my grip. Her eyes were downcast and her face was twisted in agony with the pressure Dom was placing on her wrist.

"What has gotten into you? Since when do you behave like Gio?"

Dominic's head jerked as if I had slapped him, his mouth opening into a wide O-shape.

"Isn't this the kind of shit Gio would do?" I prodded.

He dropped his gaze to where his hand was still clasped around the girl's arm and immediately released her. She nodded as he whispered into her ear before she fled from the room. And I watched as two of my brother's men trailed behind her.

What was his deal with this girl?

"You're misjudging it, little sister. I merely… she needs the job and I'm trying to help. But clearly service work isn't her calling." Adjusting his tie, Dominic skirted my questions, placing a kiss to the top of my head before pivoting on his heel, none too subtle about his pursuit.

"The hell was that?" Sienna asked me. Mario had disappeared, giving her a front row seat to the odd interaction. I explained what little I knew of my brother and the girl as Sienna leaned back in her chair and sipped her wine. "Normally, I'd assume she was a stalker, after Dominic and his money. However, I don't think that's the case here. It appears as though your brother is playing some sort of game with her."

I nodded. "A game I think she knows she won't win." Before I could think more on it, Lucky came walking back into the room.

All of the noise—even the distant chatter—seemed to slip away. He smiled at me, his crystal-clear eyes sparkling with mischief, and it was like we were the only two people in the room. My breathing evened out and my racing heart thudded in time with his steps.

He was the calm to my chaos. The excitement in my boring life. My Beast and my Prince Charming. My everything.

He wrapped his arms around me, engulfing me in his spicy scent, and a shiver traveled down my spine. Clenching my thighs together, I couldn't think of anything other than needing him. Wanting him. I didn't care who was watching us, though I couldn't help but wonder…

"They're handled," he responded as if reading my thoughts before I could verbalize them. "Tonight is about you." His perfectly polished cufflinks caught the light as he reached out an arm to tug me closer to him and that's when I saw it. The blood. A droplet half the size of a dime but a stark contrast against the white of his shirt.

I grabbed his arm, lifting his hand and taking note of his split knuckles. He'd clearly beat the hell out of someone. And it didn't take a genius to guess who…

"I'm a man with a lot of blood on my hands, Bella. I make no excuses for the life I live or the decisions I've made. No one—and I mean no one—will be allowed to hurt you." He smirked and kissed me again, quickly halting my reply with the tip of a finger pressed against my lips. "Physical or emotional, I will not stand for it. You are my everything, *mia regina*."

Though part of me wanted to be horrified by all the violence I'd witnessed in the short time I'd known this man, I'd be lying if I said it bothered me. Did that make me a bad person? The fact that I would stand by his side and trust his decisions?

But I knew that answer too. Because if supporting Lucky made me a bad person, then *that* was who I was meant to be all along.

Lucky tugged me to the dance floor, and several songs later, my breaths were labored and my feet were on fire. I wanted to go back to the table, but Lucky's chaste kiss stopped me in my tracks. He looked like he wanted to say something; instead, he pulled me towards the center of the room and halfway up the staircase, where he stopped to address the crowd.

"Ladies and gentlemen, your attention please." He paused, waiting for the distant chatter to die out. "Enough of the whispers. I will answer your questions."

A loud cheer sounded from our table—no doubt from Sienna—before silence blanketed the space.

"This gorgeous, kindhearted, amazing woman at my side has bestowed upon me the greatest gift a man could ask for. You're looking at the future Mrs. Lucifer Agostino." Lucky dipped me backwards, pressing his lips to mine in a display of ownership for all to see. There was something different about this kiss, almost feral, and it solidified the feeling I'd had the second… maybe third time we'd had sex. He'd been going easy on me. My panties were soaked and I was ready to beg him to take me how he wanted.

I wanted him to own me. To not know where he ended and I began. I wanted him to consume me. To do whatever it took to please him.

My future husband.

He pulled back and the pure, undiluted happiness on his face made my neck burn with excitement. Kissing me again, but only briefly this time, he tugged me tighter to his body as we turned to face the crowd of onlookers. Their cheers increased, and my eyes landed on Sienna, who was whooping from her chair. Descending the stairs as a couple, officially announced for the first time, we made our rounds.

So many people I'd never met, whose names I'd forgotten the minute they said them, attacked me. Lucky never strayed too far from my side, always keeping me within arm's reach. My father was eating up the attention. Ever ambitious, he shook hands, smiled, and thanked everyone for coming, while offering rounds of golf and proposing future dinner plans to discuss business dealings.

Dominic reappeared at some point, his prior scowl replaced with his usual boyish charm. However, I couldn't help but notice that the girl was still missing. We would have a chat about his behavior later. Something wasn't right with their arrangement. Whatever was going on between them, I planned to find out.

"Don't you just love the overly affectionate, half-drunk women all swooning over your future husband?" Sienna whispered into my ear. Taking a sip of her wine and snickering at my expression, she nodded her head towards her brother, who was drowning in a sea of mob wives.

It was all too much. Too many overly ambitious people all wanting a piece of us. And suddenly I felt ill.

Apollo appeared at my side, his hand resting on my lower back, as if he somehow sensed the shift in my blood pressure. Lucky was trying to get his attention, to save him from the cougars I was sure. But Apollo only had eyes for me. Sidestepping a group of guests I didn't know, he ushered me out of the center of the room while Big Al stepped out of the shadows, standing in front of me to block the breakdown I was ready to have.

"Breathe. Deep." Apollo demonstrated before repeating his instructions. After several deep breaths, he leaned forward, a hand pressed to my hip to steady me. "There will always be someone who wants something from you. It is your job to deal with it. To be the queen Lucky needs at his side."

I nodded, took another deep breath, and straightened my spine. He was right after all. Lucky had chosen me. He'd saved me. God only knew what my future could've held at the hands of my father. He'd made his choice and it was fine time I started acting like the partner he needed. Instead of hiding in the corner, overwhelmed by the well-wishers, future business contacts, and fawning cougars.

"And she gets it." Apollo smirked as I nodded and threw back the rest of my wine. "Atta girl. Though I'm certain seeing us this close is probably not helping." We could feel Lucky's glare at a distance. "Do your best to not let him kill me, please." Pulling away from me, Apollo rose to his full height and adjusted his tie.

I stepped around Al, patting him on the back before pushing through the crowd to stand at Lucky's side. I didn't give the women a chance to notice me, grabbing hold of my fiancé's lapels and tugging him down for a kiss.

"You take my breath away, Bella. No more hiding out in dark corners with my men." His eyes shot lasers over my shoulder at Apollo and Al.

"They set me straight." My choice of words had his glare snapping back to me. "Calm down. I needed it."

"I thought you needed me?" he questioned, though his tone was teasing.

"Always. They just reminded me of my role. Your men are loyal, Lucky. Never forget that."

"Every history book has one thing in common. Empires have fallen, loyal men have turned, and chaos has erupted. All to gain the attention of a beautiful woman." He raised my arm and pressed his lips to my knuckles.

"What those history books fail to mention is all the times those great men refused to listen to their wives. And how much of that chaos could have been avoided if they had. I am yours, Lucky. Remember that, and the rest doesn't matter."

"Damn right you are." Lucky grinned, placing a kiss to my head before making a beeline for his men.

CHAPTER 20

LUCIFER "LUCKY" AGOSTINO

"**W**hat the fuck were you thinking?" Keeping my voice hushed, I ushered Al and Apollo away from prying eyes.

"Boss. She wasn't handling the attention well. She needed a minute. And a reminder."

"Any longer and she was passing out, boss," Al added for good measure.

It wasn't that I was pissed at them for pulling her aside or even touching her for that matter—well, that was a lie. I hated him touching her. What really pissed me off was the fact they'd noticed her distress before I did. I was so lost in the moment, telling the entire room to fuck off where Bella was concerned. Too busy practically pissing on her to realize she was stressing out.

"And your hands all over her was your way of calming her?" I raised a brow at Apollo, who coughed to hide his laugh.

"It was to snap her out of it. That's all, boss. She's good. She gets it. And she belongs to you. Heart and station."

"Fucking right she belongs to me. Next time, keep your hands to your fucking self."

"Fuck me," Al muttered at my back. I turned when he started

hollering into his earpiece. "How the fuck did he get past you? What's his position?"

My eyes immediately found Bella standing at the end of our table. Her spine was straight, her shoulders pulled back, her posture defensive. Whatever Al had just learned, she'd already seen it. Her lips parted and she called out to me. I stormed around Apollo, who peeled off into the crowd with a hand pressed to the mic in his ear as he growled out commands.

"Gio's here," Al announced, his eyes full of concern and darting out directly towards Bella. He pulled her behind him as I stepped up and wrapped her in my arms.

"I'm here to congratulate the love birds. Surely you don't-don't t-t-think I'd harm my own sister?" Gio was drunk and belligerent.

Now mind you, when it came to Bella, I held no remorse in how I handled her protection. An entire room of people be damned, I'd destroy him just to set a precedent. But those eyes... Fuck me, those eyes turned to me. And all I saw was sadness. Fear.

As much of a fuck-up as Gio was, he was still her brother. I wouldn't stand for disobedience, but at the same time, I needed to be mindful of my girl. And her feelings.

"This fucking idiot." Apollo gestured towards Gio, who was too drunk to notice my second approach from the rear.

"Enough, Gio." Dominic rose from his spot at the end of the table, slamming his hands down as he spoke.

"Fuck you, D. Our little sister got engaged... to *this*! This fucking monster, who thinks he can throw on a suit and pretend to be digni-fied." Gio flung out his arm and Dom caught him by his shoulders to keep him upright. "This... this *stronzo!* He's not g-g-good enough for her! Fuck this family."

"Gio!" Bella swung around Al to confront her brother. "Enough. Goddamn it. You think Lucifer cares for me enough to keep you alive? After all you've done! You're breathing on borrowed time, you idiot!"

Apollo hovered within arm's reach, ready to jump in if the situation called for it.

"How many times is your sister going to protect you, Gio? Better yet. How many more times do you think I will allow tears in her eyes from your actions? Answer me that." My tone was calm. Calm to the point of being eerie.

"Fuck you, you dumb fucking *wop*." Not only had he insulted me, but he shouted the one word in a room full of Italians that could get you killed. "You ain't shit, bitch." His words were slurring more with each sentence.

"Gio!" Bella gasped and slapped a hand over her mouth. "Enough. Please go." A lone tear trickled down her porcelain cheek and almost unleashed the beast inside me.

Before I could react, Gio was toppling over the table with the force of Apollo's fist. "No one makes *mia regina* cry!" His arm was pulled back ready to land another blow, when Bella stepped between them.

"Please. Enough of this. Escort him out," she begged, turning to look at me with those eyes... This girl was my undoing.

"No can do, sweet girl. He's had his chances. Plural." I wiped away a loose tear.

"Gio! Get the fuck out of here!" Anthony Moretti ordered from somewhere in the crowd, shoving towards his wayward son.

I cupped Bella's face and kissed her long and hard, while the entire room waited with bated breath to see what I would do next.

"You don't tell me what to do, you stupid bitch! You're just a whore! *Stupida cagna!* A cunt Father brought back from Italy to wrap around some Agostino cock. To make him weak! You're weak!" Gio struggled to get closer to me, a finger thrust in my direction.

I grabbed it, and before he realized what was happening, the audible snap of bone broke the silence. Gio howled out in pain, side-stepping Dom and moving quickly out of both my men's reach, and dove for me. Shoving Bella behind me, I struck. One right hook made perfect contact with his jaw and Apollo gripped his suit jacket to tug him backwards.

Now, I've had guns pointed at me, situations I shouldn't have survived, faced death on more than one occasion. And never once did time stand still. Until this moment, when it damn near came to a halt.

Because no matter what I had tried to do, how I moved or shielded her, it was still going to happen.

Apollo throttling her brother to exit the room gave Bella the incentive to get closer and Gio just enough balls for his palm to strike out and make contact with her face. The entire room filled with a collective gasp.

He was fucking dead.

Maybe not today, not in front of Bella and all these witnesses. Maybe it would be slow and painful. Maybe, or maybe not. But he was dead. Gio Moretti, eldest son of Anthony Moretti, the heir of the Moretti family was going to die at my hands. The only question was when…

"Enough!" The voice that came out of my dark angel, my beautiful queen, was one I didn't recognize. "Listen to me clearly, Gio. You are done. You're not welcome in *Lucifer's city* anymore. As an engagement present, I am asking him to spare your life this last time. If he sees you again, Gio, I guarantee you it will mean your death."

Big Al's eyes widened while Apollo looked downright tickled pink by Bella's newfound confidence. Clearly her timeout in the corner had done her wonders. She was no longer shaking, her posture tall and proud, her voice strong and commanding.

And fuck if she wasn't the sexiest thing I'd ever seen.

"Now get the fuck out of my party because, dear brother. You. Are. Dead. To. Me." Without another word, Bella turned on her heel, walking back to the table. She snatched a glass of wine on her way before flopping into her chair. Sienna and our mothers flocked to her side, checking her lip as she swatted away their concerns.

"It's an engagement party, GiGi. It'll be over soon… and then you're mine," I snarled into his face. Gio was shell-shocked, sobered all of a sudden. The realization of what he'd done compelled him to snap out of his stupor and sent him darting across the room with Dominic on his tail. "Send him a fucking message."

Nodding, Apollo disappeared into the crowd. And Al returned to the shadows of the party, never too far from Bella—who, as of now, wasn't leaving my side the rest of the night.

"Lucky…"

Raising a hand, I halted her words as those soft eyes looked up at me with fire. "I will grant you this, but only once."

She nodded her head quickly. I reached out a hand to grip her chin, twisting her head to inspect the damage he'd caused her beautiful face. My heart ached, knowing that she was touched by such darkness. My bright angel.

"Thank you," she whispered.

"Only for you, would I do this." I kissed her soft, tear-soaked lips and stared directly into her eyes. "Forget all of his other grievances, Bella. No one touches what's mine."

"I know. I meant what I said. I won't ever ask this of you again. If he comes back into your city, I won't stop you from doing what's needed."

"My city, hm? That's twice I've heard those luscious lips utter such a huge statement." I paused, taking in her coy smile. "But you were wrong. It's our city, *mio amore*. Everything I do is for you and our future family."

"Our future family? How long are you thinking until that family starts?"

I watched as a devilish grin appeared on my angel's face, the fire intensified and those mixed-colored eyes flared with lust.

"Why whatever do you mean, *mia regina?*"

Her cheeks flushed a bright shade of red.

"I want to hear you say it, Bella. Tell me. Tell me what you want."

"You." The singular word was barely a whisper as she squirmed in her seat.

"Tell me more." I needed to see that confidence again. To hear that fire in her voice.

"I want this party to be over. For you to carry me out of this room, show them all who owns me. Then take me upstairs. I want you to taste —devour every part of my body. I want you hard and fast, Lucky. I need you. I need you to *ruin me.*"

Ruin. Her.

I think I just came in my slacks. Jesus Christ. What had I done? I'd created a monster. She was throwing her inhibitions to the wind and demanding that I ruin her? Fucking right I would.

"What *mia regina* wants, she gets." Without another word, I swept her into my arms and charged across the dance floor, through the crowd, and to the elevators. Away from prying eyes.

Slowly sliding her tight little body down the length of mine, Bella was on her feet as the doors opened. Her slight panting and fidgeting was making the blood in my dick thrum with anticipation.

I stepped inside the elevator the moment it arrived, tugged her beside me and attacked her before the doors closed completely.

The keypad barely registered my code to the penthouse and I was on her. Her squeak of fright quickly morphed into mewls and moans of pleasure. Assaulting her neck, I licked and bit my way down. I hiked her dress up the best I could as I turned her to the mirrored wall. She bent at the waist, awarding me with the decadent sight of her juicy ass lifted and waiting.

"Do not. Look away." Barely maintaining control, I watched for a nod of understanding and rammed home.

And home was indeed inside her. Warm, wet, and perfect. She fit me like a glove. Like she was made for me and me alone. Lust-filled, half-lidded eyes looked back at me in the mirror.

"Lucky, please," she begged. The green one seemed to darken in anticipation of the first thrust, while the blue one twinkled with raw passion. Her back arched. I reached out, grabbing her around her throat, and squeezed. The moment I tightened my grip, her eyes closed around a throaty moan of pleasure.

"Eyes!" I reminded her on a growl and she complied. And those eyes were once again my undoing. A pinch to her swollen clit was all it took. She fell over that cliff of ecstasy, and with a few more strokes, I followed behind her.

"Lucky!" She gasped in shock.

The elevator had arrived and the doors were open to the lobby of the penthouse. My men and staff were smart enough to make themselves scarce, likely having already gotten an eye and an earful. Bella fixed her dress as I tucked myself back in my pants before leading her inside.

"Do you think they heard?" Stepping from the elevator, she glanced around the room in embarrassment.

Stroking her face with a pleased smile on mine, I placed a soft kiss on her swollen lips. "Of course, they did. You aren't exactly quiet for your man."

Her jaw dropped and her cheeks took on an even darker shade of red while I chuckled at her expense.

"You could've at least lied to make me feel better!" She slapped my arm, and I laughed harder.

"Never." Tugging her along behind me, I watched the maids in the living room scatter like ants. "I'd never lie to you. And you'd better never tone down those screams. I love to hear you shatter and come to life beneath me."

"Lucky!"

When she tried to pull back from my grip, I threw her over my shoulder. I took the stairs two at a time to get to the master suite.

"Put me down!" She struggled in my grasp, reaching out a hand to slap my ass. And I quickly returned the gesture with an open-palmed swat to hers.

"Keep teasing me, Bella, and you'll be punished. We aren't even close to being done tonight. I need to rid my mind of Gio's indiscretions by watching you fall apart beneath me." I tossed her onto the king-size bed, her giggles as she bounced tearing through my anger.

I stalked towards the bed, eyeing her like a lion approaching his prey. Her dress was gone in a matter of seconds, torn from her body, and before she knew it, I was buried deep inside her again.

The night was finally looking up...

Until I set about reprimanding her for allowing Apollo to touch her. My punishments were unhinged and out of turn for someone so innocent. But I made up for it. Over and over again.

We were lost to each other for the next few hours, only pausing when my phone broke through and burst our bubble. It was Apollo.

"Did you handle it?" I asked him.

"Yeah. But, boss, we need to meet."

I could hear the stress in his voice. Nothing rattled Apollo. So I knew whatever it was, it couldn't be good. We didn't need more bull-shit added to our plates.

"I told you after Yuri's death that I had news I needed to share. Well, Gio just confirmed my suspicions."

"And what of it?" Silence answered me. I was ready to snap when he finally responded.

"Dom is a problem we never knew we had."

"Bella's brother Dom?"

Dominic Moretti had been making a name for himself with the use of brute force and underhanded business dealings. But none of it touched me, and he'd been a financial benefactor in building up a crumbling area of downtown New York.

"Yeah. And, fuck me, you won't like it."

"Meet me in the office." An uneasy chill ran down my spine with the foreboding of what was to come. However, if I'd known what was going to happen next, I never would've left Bella in bed.

CHAPTER 21

MIRABELLA MORETTI

The night had turned into an insane whirlwind of too many emotions and it was all exhausting. As was the torment Lucky was wreaking on my body. I was falling into a heavily sedated state of euphoria from all of the arduous activities.

I was one hell of a lucky girl. *Lucky's girl.* He was commanding and cruel, yet tender and all-consuming. I was so embarrassed walking out of that elevator, realizing that the staff more than likely saw and heard our interaction.

However, when he threw me over his shoulder, I was practically dripping through my lace panties. Lucky did that to me. Never would I have thought his commanding attitude, especially after so many years under my father's thumb, would do such things to me.

Tossing me on the bed, he ravaged my body and just when I thought he couldn't take me to the peak any longer, I was crying out in ecstasy again. My body was limp and sated as I cuddled into his warm embrace, having long forgotten my brother's actions. At least for the moment.

Reaching over to stroke my once-bloodied lip, Lucky transformed, his features morphing right in front of my eyes. He was back—*il diavolo* was taking over—and a shiver traveled up my spine at the thought.

"You let another man touch you." I was confused for a second, and he continued. "Apollo. You allowed one of my men to pull you into a darkened corner without my permission."

I couldn't help it. I laughed. I'd never allow anyone to touch me, but my lighthearted response earned me a harsh glare. "Lucky he was just…" I attempted to explain.

But he shook his head and rose to his full height in all his naked glory. His chest was shaved, showing off every inch of smooth, tanned flesh. And his perfectly sculpted body rippled with each movement he made as he stalked to the end of the bed to casually stare down at my naked form. The devil may've made men run in fear, but he made my body beg and writhe with need.

"You forget who owns you, Bella. Me. And no one touches what is mine."

My thighs squeezed together, seeking relief. He had me so turned on I wanted to crawl out of my skin. "I'm sorry, sir." I was panting like a dog in heat.

"Are you really though? I don't think you are. But you will be." Snatching my ankle, he pulled me down the bed towards him. I clawed at the sheets as I tried to get away. But before I could twist my body out of reach, he was on top of me, his much larger frame pressing me into the mattress. "You wouldn't be trying to get away from your punishment, would you?" His chest rose and fell with each of his labored breaths.

"No." He raised a brow, and I rushed to correct myself, "No, sir."

"He touched you. The small of your back. The tip of your nose. He pressed his front to yours." He mimicked each motion as he spoke, and I was ready to combust with need. "Did you like it, Bella?"

"No, sir." His hand landed on first my left, then right thigh, the movement sharp and fast and the slap echoing in the room. "No, sir!" I repeated, louder this time. The tingling sensation had me bucking against him in pleasure.

"Don't lie to me. I own this body. It's mine to do as I please."

Before I could respond, cold metal was latched on to my ankles, spreading my legs wide, so I was unable to hide anything from him. Lucky rose above me, his hard erection pointed north like it was ready to pick its new victim.

Me.

And I was more than willing. I licked my lips, noting how that gleam in his eye had turned feral. He stroked himself while I watched, begging him with my eyes to let me have a taste.

"What do you want, Bella?"

My words were caught in my throat. No matter how confident this man made me feel, I still had my moments of weakness. My insecurities.

"Say it. Tell me what you want, Bella."

"I want to taste you." He raised his brow, urging me to elaborate. "I want you in my mouth, to feel you lose your control with me. I want you to fall apart at the seams from my touch and my touch alone." Sitting upright on the end of the bed, my legs spread and my hands clenched behind my back, I opened my mouth and waited.

A low, menacing growl was his answer before he stepped in front of me, allowing my lips to latch on to his cock. His hands raked through and grabbed onto my hair, holding my head as he took over, owning my mouth *and* his pleasure. But I demanded control, craning my neck to the side to take him how I wanted. He owned me. Heart, body, and soul. But right now, I was taking everything I wanted from him. Sucking like my life depended on it.

"Fuck, Bella." He was trying to slow my motions, as if he had a choice in how I pleased him.

Not right now. I could feel the swell of his balls cupped in my hands. The tightness of his shaft as he tried to hold back. But I was too much for him, and the sweetness of his release hit my taste buds before I swallowed it down on a moan. Releasing him with a pop of my lips, I smirked up at his hazy expression. I did that. I… I put *that* look on his face.

I'd turned myself into the woman who was always lurking under that timid façade. And that woman was made to stand at Lucky's side.

Or, you know, before him with my legs chained and spread eagle with his dick in my mouth—*semantics right?* Regardless, I was made for this man just as much as he was made for me.

He dropped to his knees in front of me. With a quick shove to my chest, I fell backwards, the cuffs on my ankles clattering against the steel bed posts.

"Watch." It was all he needed to say as I leaned up on my elbows and watched his mouth disappear. Warm, tingling, and sensual—he lapped away at my most private, swollen parts. I was shaking with need, right on the cusp of taking a headfirst dive over the ledge.

"Lucky!" I called out his name on a strangled moan.

And he smirked in reply. "I think this should be your punishment."

My jaw dropped at the prospect of not being able to relieve this burning desire. He'd created a monster inside me and now he was denying me the pleasure I needed to survive. I would scratch my skin wide open and bleed myself dry. Just to feel something... anything...

"This is what it felt like watching him touch what was mine." Lucky kneeled on the end of the bed, his fingers savagely attacking my clit. "Watching you look gorgeous all night. Dying to touch you, to watch you writhe underneath me. And what do I get for this lavish party? The love of my life... touching another man. Allowing him to touch her..."

"Lucky, please. Sir, Lucky, GAH!" The pressure was so intense. Right when I thought he'd let me come, he'd pull back. My mind was on emotional overload. My body was turning itself inside out. I needed it. I needed him. "You're it for me, Lucky. Apollo demanded that I be the woman at your side, the woman you deserved. It wasn't a touch of affection. It was grounding, the confidence I needed. To not let me embarrass you by being overwhelmed from all the people. Please, Lucky. Fuck, sir. Please!" I was losing it. Tears streaming down my face. From what? I was unsure. It was a heady combination, a culmination of the night's events.

"Are those tears because of the punishment? Or because of your wrongdoing?"

When I didn't immediately answer, his hands left my soaking heat before he administered two sharp slaps across each of my thighs.

"Gah! Fuck, sir, Lucky! Both! Please, please. It won't happen again."

"What won't?" the bastard asked, eyeing my red-hot skin with a morbid curiosity.

"I won't let another man touch me. I won't be weak anymore. I am yours! Yours! Fuck!" The last *yours* was rewarded with a swat to my pussy before his face plunged back down.

My orgasm tore through with the sudden contact. Writhing, screaming, and tugging his hair, I was barely back from my high when Lucky slammed inside. Hard and fast. And I tightened around him, ready for another mind-blowing orgasm that I feared would destroy me.

"Come, Bella. Fuck. Now!"

His commanding voice boomed inside my head, and I let go. Spiraling into the depths of a pleasurable abyss, suspended in time, and lost in the feelings. Coming down from the high, I was covered in perspiration and panting with Lucky's sweating body crushing me into the mattress. He rose to his feet, a sweet smile on his face as he looked down at me. As the pain settled, I watched his eyes glaze over, morphing into something resembling rage. He dropped to his knees and unlocked the cuffs, my thighs burning from his brutal assault.

I tugged against the cuffs and realized my ankles were cut open and bleeding, while his attack on my mouth had opened the laceration on my face, causing blood to drip down my chin. I felt like hell but at the same time so completely sated.

"Baby, fuck. I'm sorry," he said, scooping me up and carrying me into the bathroom. He set me on the countertop and started to draw me a bath. "I fucked up. I shouldn't have gone that far."

I flicked my eyes to the mirror and I could see why he was concerned. I looked like I'd been brutalized. The slap from my brother had split my lip and a slight black eye was forming on my pale skin. Lucky's red handprints on my thighs had cut the skin in small spots, red and angry with splotches of blood, while my thrashing against the cuffs made my ankles red and a little swollen. The left one had a dried dark ring around it.

"Lucky." When he wouldn't look at me, I climbed off the counter to force him to meet my gaze. "Hey."

"I went too far. I promised myself I wouldn't go that far with you." The look in his eyes burned a permanent hole in my heart. I hated knowing I was the reason for his despair.

"Please. Lucky, please. I enjoyed it."

He lifted me off the ground, and we settled into the oversized tub that smelled of calming lavender. My back to his front.

"I never knew there was a part of me that needed someone like you. I hated being controlled my entire life. Yet the way you control me in the bedroom is everything I never knew I needed."

"I took it too far."

I shook my head against his chest. "You didn't. If you hadn't let me come, I wouldn't have been able to handle it. I would've felt like I displeased you. But, Lucky, that was perfect. We're made for each other."

After a few more moments of tense silence, he finally spoke. "I love you, Bella. I want everything to be perfect for you. I couldn't even throw you a party without issues. Now my need to punish you for Apollo's actions left you bruised and bleeding."

Swishing the water around the gigantic tub, I rolled onto my knees to face him. "Gio has been a douchebag since I was little. He's always found a way to ruin something for me my entire life. But *you* ended that tonight. He knows not to come back here now. And, technically, he bruised and bloodied my face, my own twitching bruised my ankles, and we'll blame Apollo for the marks you left on my thighs." I smirked at him and he finally relaxed.

"How did I get so lucky, Bella?"

I rested my head on his chest and listened to his beating heart. "I could ask you the same thing."

CHAPTER 22

MIRABELLA MORETTI

After our bath, I dressed myself in comfortable yoga pants and a matching sports bra. Lucky was chatting away on his phone. I could only assume it was Apollo and neither of them sounded that pleased. I walked back into the room, my eyes landing on Lucky, and he smiled at me reassuringly.

For a moment, I had a sick feeling in the pit of my stomach, fearing Apollo had killed my brother against orders. However, Lucky's little smile set those thoughts at ease. Even though I may have been sad at the prospect of Gio dying, I wouldn't hold it against the Agostinos or their men. My brother had been warned so many times. In our line of work, anyone else would've been killed after the first indiscretion.

I'd bought Gio time to get out of the city and start somewhere new. I saved him on more occasions than he deserved and now it was up to him to save himself. The ding of the elevator broke through the continued hushed conversations. And I returned to my steamy romance novel, seeing as I wasn't expecting anyone.

"My eyes are covered and I'm not exiting the foyer until you tell me you're dressed!" Sienna's voice echoed across the marble floors and into the living area. I couldn't hide my chuckle. Climbing off the sofa, I went to greet her as she started yelling again. "Lucky, she's giggling and that isn't a good sign in the throes of passion!"

I could hear her moving around the foyer, likely bumping into the occasional odd end. Padding into the room barefoot, I crossed my arms against my chest and watched the mess that was Sienna Agostino. She was still dressed in her designer black gown from the party. Her once-gorgeous hair was somewhat disheveled, her makeup slightly smudged, and her feet sans shoes. Her hands were covering her eyes while she wandered back and forth in the entryway. When she began mumbling to herself after she bumped into a wall, I couldn't stop my laughter from announcing my presence.

"How long have you been standing there?" Lucky's hue of blue eyes on his gorgeous sister shot fire at me.

"Long enough to question your sanity and the color of the bottom of your feet."

Sienna glanced down as if only just realizing she didn't have shoes on. "Fuck!" She stumbled again, appearing a little hungover. Or maybe she was still drunk. "Where did I put them? They were brand-new… and super fucking expensive." Looking around like they might randomly appear, she stumbled once more.

Taking Sienna by the arm, I walked her into the open-concept kitchen. I grabbed her a bottle of water and placed it in front of her. She stared for a long moment, her bottom lip popping out in an obvious pout.

"What?" I prompted, worried something might really be wrong. "I'm sure you'll find them somewhere."

"Or Tatianna fucking snuck back in and took them, that treacherous cunt."

To that, we both lost it, laughing as Lucky walked into the room. Coming right to me, he pulled my body close against his, placing a kiss to the top of my head before peeking up as if just now realizing his sister was here. He paused for a moment, eyeing her appearance. "Where are your shoes?" His question sent us into another bout of hysterics. "You've both lost your minds but, my love, I need to go debrief with Apollo. I won't be long." Kissing me again, he started for Sienna, who was slightly swaying on her barstool.

"Is he alive?" I blurted out before I could stop myself.

Looking at me over his shoulder, Lucky frowned. "I promised you I'd give him this one chance. Apollo just needs to follow up with me on a few other things." Putting Sienna upright on her stool, he kissed her forehead before scowling. "They were three grand, Sienna. They better not be lost." He headed towards the elevator, halting in his steps when Sienna called out to him.

"I didn't fucking lose them!" she yelled before the doors opened and he stepped inside. Once they closed on his handsome face, she looked at me with a pointed glare. "I simply lost where I put them…"

And I just about doubled over with more laughter. Gasping for air, I realized her knuckles were torn. "Who were you fighting?" I asked.

"She shouldn't have worn white."

My jaw dropped. "I didn't see you leave the party…" I questioned, and her nostrils flared with her deep inhale.

"Because I didn't. I stayed after you and Lucky rushed off to your sex tower." She cringed in mock disgust and I shoved at her chest, having to catch her before she fell off the stool. "When Al came back to escort me home, I ran into the bitch. She taunted me. Practically begged me to beat her ass." Tears were pooling in Sienna's eyes as she spoke.

The girl never showed emotion like this. Not that I'd seen. I wanted to blame the alcohol that was wafting from her breath, but her normally composed stature was hunched as if physically pained. It was a gut-wrenching sight, to watch such a powerful woman crumble.

"She took him from me too… When is it my turn?" Sienna dropped her head into her hands on the counter and cried.

I was trying to figure out what she was talking about when the dinging of the elevator caught my attention. Big Al walked into the kitchen, his expression dark and his eyes narrowed.

"You were told to stay in your suite!" he roared at Sienna.

I stepped closer to her, the need to protect my friend driving me forward. My intuition told me Al'd never hurt her. But her emotional state was too fragile.

He charged towards her, freezing when he caught sight of her face. "Sienna… are you crying?" he asked with evident concern.

Steeling her spine, she glared back at him. "Fuck off."

"The hell happened?" I turned to Al for answers. The night really had gone to hell in a handbasket. And that handbasket had lots of liquor.

"We left the party and waited for the elevator when Tatianna walked up. The bitch made a few snide comments, and our girl here whooped her ass before yelling at me, insisting she was spending the night on her floor. I checked the cameras when the door alarm alerted me and I saw Sienna stumbling her ass here."

"Fuck you! I'm fine in the tower with the queen. You can fuck right off. I'm sure Tatianna will swallow your cock much easier now that I knocked her teeth loose."

I winced while Al appeared unaffected.

"Fucking hell, Sienna, you love Apollo. What's the deal?"

Her head snapped up, and she hobbled off the stool as she ran through me to charge at him. "Anyone! Anyone could suck your dick! Not her! You're my best friend. You know how I feel about her!"

Then it all fell into place. Sienna had a twisted affection for Apollo, which neither of them would act on out of respect for her brother. And she and Al had become close during his time assigned as her guard. Something had happened between her and Tatianna, and though she never divulged the details, the two women were sworn enemies. Meaning Al's indiscretions might as well have been an act of treason in Sienna's eyes. Her normally masked demeanor dropped to reveal the pain morphing her features, and Al flinched, rubbing at his chest as if to ease the ache.

"What happened?" I asked as Al looked at me with desperation in his eyes. "Apollo and Lucky taught Tatianna's boyfriend a lesson. We don't hurt women—you know that. She was willing. She showed how little she cared and… and..."

I raised a hand to halt his words. I didn't need (or want) to hear anymore. I shook my head at him as I helped Sienna slide off her stool, wrapping my arms around her protectively and ushering her to the elevator. I could tell her limited composure was on the verge of collapse. A woman like Sienna would hate herself for appearing weak. I needed to get her to her floor.

"You can stay here. I will escort her back."

Big Al relented, his eyes filled with a mixture of anger and concern. He agreed because we were safe—well, *he was safe* from facing off with Sienna in a closed space—not because he wanted to. And no one else could ride the elevators between the top floors without the code. He'd fucked up and he knew it. There was no point in me repeating it in Sienna's presence. But I would tuck her in and then tell the man how I really felt.

We stepped into the elevator and it started its descent. "How is she still alive?" I muttered loud enough for Sienna to hear, earning me a strangled chuckle.

"Not even officially an Agostino and so bloodthirsty already." Her hand went to her chest in feigned shock. As we laughed together, I could feel the mood in the elevator lifting and watched the toughened mask fall back over her face. And I prayed to be as strong as she was one day.

The door opened to her level and I followed Sienna into her suite, making a beeline for her bathroom, where I dropped a lavender bath bomb in her tub. As I waited for the water to warm, my eyes flicked to the corner and I started to chuckle. Makeup remover was sitting next to an open bottle of vodka and a pair of shoes were kicked off under the cabinet. Evidently, my future sister-in-law had decided that coming to see me was better than bed. I crossed the distance, plucking up and lifting her abandoned designer heels to eye level. Her surprised gasp quickly morphed into more laughter.

"I'm not getting naked for you. Perv." Sienna smirked, gesturing for me to leave.

"Don't make it easy on him to win back your favor." I offered her a sad smile. "And one day we're talking about Apollo."

She hiccupped a sob in reply. "That will never be anything. So, no, it doesn't warrant a conversation. But I love you, B."

I hugged her tight before leaving the bathroom. "I love you more!" I called out over my shoulder as I waited for the elevator in the foyer, a sudden sadness and exhaustion sweeping over me.

Women like Tatianna would never learn. She tried to fuck with me and Lucky, now Apollo and Sienna. If that wasn't enough, rubbing it in Sienna's face was the signature on her death warrant.

My future sister-in-law was right. I was yet to be an Agostino, but I'd turned bloodthirsty. And I'd make Tatianna pay for her indiscretions. If not for myself, then for Sienna. Our rival deserved another ass whooping… as soon as she shit out the teeth Sienna had made her swallow.

Laughing at the thought, I climbed into the elevator, beyond ready for bed. Hopefully Lucky was back from his brief with Apollo. I wanted him to cuddle me. To sleep in late tomorrow and to sexually sedate me for the rest of the day. My lust considered that to be a brilliant idea while my sore body ached in protest.

The elevator doors opened to chaos. Shattered glass and a knocked over table in the foyer.

Ugh, these Italian men and their fiery tempers really were something else, with little care for those left to clean up after their messes. And! And it was all because of his own poor decision-making.

Tiptoeing around the shards, I stormed into the living room. "You're cleaning that shit up, Al! Don't you dare leave it for the poor staff." I paused midstep, taking in the upturned coffee table. This man and his adult tantrum. "I'm serious! Al, you bet—oh!" My words were severed as I ran smack-bang into a hard chest before a pair of rough hands clamped around my wrists to keep me from falling backwards.

"Bella."

I looked up at the sound of my name, confusion halting my reply. *He shouldn't be here.* He wouldn't be assigned to me, not now. Not in Lucky's house. His answering smirk confirmed my fears. My fight-or-flight senses kicked in and I tried taking off. But his grip remained firm as I struggled against it.

A quick kick to his shin forced him back a step as he grunted and cursed in my direction. His hold loosened and I twisted away, slamming my palm into his neck as I rotated my body and aimed a foot at his torso. He stumbled, a hand clutched to his throat, and it was an amazing feeling... for all of a split-second. I turned to flee, making it five steps into the living room before he was on me again.

His heavy frame slammed into me from behind. Unable to catch my balance, I went down hard, my face making direct contact with the marbled flooring. He rolled me onto my back, using his weight and leverage to hold me in place. My head a hazy mess of fog and confusion, I looked up into his familiar eyes as a wave of nausea churned my gut. Flicking my gaze to the side, I saw Al's large silhouette on the ground. Unmoving, lifeless. Surrounded by a pool of his own blood. And dread replaced my panic.

Was he dead? Sienna would never survive if their last moments consisted of them arguing... Big Al was my friend too and rage prickled my skin as the need for revenge boiled my blood.

"Why fight me, Bella? You know you can't win." My attacker smirked down at me, his eyes sparkling with a darkness. And I wondered why I'd never seen it before... No, this was new. I would have noticed otherwise. I was certain of it.

"What do you want?" It was barely a whisper, more like a questioning plea.

"You. Your brother promised you to me. And I've come to collect on that promise."

My head was pounding as once again everything fell into place. Disgusted by the truth, I spit directly in his face, a loud splat resounding in the silence of the room. It was quiet, too quiet, and I could only hope no one else had been harmed. I considered calling out, and just as my mouth parted, I watched his closed fist fast-approaching my face. He was sitting on my chest. There was nothing I could do but brace for impact. Pain ricocheted in my head, and the looming fog that had been threatening to take over finally succeeded.

What was to become of me now? Would Lucky find me in enough time? If he didn't, I knew I wouldn't survive, not this and not now. Of course, this all came back to Gio. He'd arranged for me to be taken. He'd never give up. He'd do whatever it took to ruin my happiness.

I could feel my attacker moving me around, hear him talking to someone else. But I couldn't open my eyes, couldn't move my limbs. He was taking me away from my happily-ever-after, from my new family. From the man I loved more than anything. All because my brother was a selfish prick. And I knew one thing for sure… I was well and truly fucked.

Lucky, please. I love you.

Then the darkness replaced the pain…

"Wait a minute… Say that again." I had to be hearing him wrong, though Apollo knew better than to bullshit me.

"You heard me right the first time." The bastard smirked.

Fuck. Me. I was in love with the only daughter of Anthony Moretti, who fathered two sons. One was a total jackass, overloaded with testosterone and prone to poor decision-making. A jackass for thinking he could fuck with my business and my future wife. As if I'd let him live to tell the tale. His only saving grace was my promise to Bella. For the moment, Gio was beaten to a pulp and making a hasty escape from my city. And apparently the fucker's lips loosened on the way out.

Meanwhile, Dominic had slid under the radar. His strip club, local bars, restaurant, and other odds and ends were making him successful. Much to his father's dismay, the fucker had no interest in furthering the Moretti name. He was the smarter of the two sons as well as my future wife's favorite brother. She could talk for hours about their childhood together. And that same brother was apparently using all of those businesses as a front to cover his main source of income. Dominic Moretti was the leader of the second largest human trafficking syndicate in the US.

He was the competition Yuri had been discussing with me—the one that had been fucking with the *Bratva's* main income. The Russian had spoken of a man who was not only sadistic, cruel, and calculated but also head of an underground ring Yuri was looking to take over. Something my family and I didn't participate in, nor condone.

"He uses the strip club as a front. The talent on his stage, from what I can tell, is all legit. Once a month, though, he broadcasts new dancers in an online forum, where the girls are sold off to the highest bidders." Apollo's fists clenched and unclenched at his sides. It was understood that women and children did not get touched. Not in my family and not in my businesses.

"Anthony Moretti?" I asked, confused as to how the patriarch could be aware of his son's fortune and still be under my father's thumb.

"Not a clue. Gio only recently found out because of Yuri doing his own investigation." It wasn't in Anthony Moretti's nature to willingly play bitch if he had access to those funds.

Holy fucking shit. Dominic Moretti was a master manipulator. A sadistic fuck, who was somehow able to fool us all.

"I need to call Pops. Fuck, my old man is going to flip his lid. He'll kill the entire family for this grievance." Reaching for my phone, I flopped back into my office chair.

"It's all true. I did the questioning myself." Apollo's specific set of emotional disconnection made his interrogation skills one hundred percent effective. His… customers, as he called them, begged for death. No one lied about even the most minute of details for fear of dealing with him again. "He bled. He cried. He confessed his deepest, darkest secrets. Dominic was hiding it from everyone. Most of all, Bella."

The bourbon from earlier was curdling in my stomach at the thought of everything that was to come. Bella was going to be devastated. She had enough pain from her family. She loved Dom with the sort of fervor only a younger sister could possess. He'd sheltered her in a way Gio wasn't capable. But under that protective façade lurked a monster of a man. My bride-to-be would be crushed by this revelation. If my old man got word that her father was involved, she'd lose all of the men in her life in the blink of an eye. Regardless of why, that wouldn't be an easy pill to swallow.

Snatching my cell phone off the desk, I mulled over the predicament. Innocent women were being taken from their families, their homes, and coerced into a life of servitude, abuse, and extortion. It was sickening and a clear example of the sort of bastards Anthony Moretti had raised. None of them belonged in our world.

Our motto was rather simplistic: *Run your home and your business with an iron fist. Take no shit from anyone. And destroy any threat to what belongs to you.*

We dabbled in guns; some families preferred drugs. But to sell women, especially when you had a beautiful mother and incredible little sister at home, was disheartening. He had to be stopped. Though the bigger issue was, now that the secret was out, what would it mean for Bella?

She was already losing one brother. And now the other. News of Dominic's immoral activities would destroy her far worse than his death at my hands. She said she understood not to get in my way if Gio came around again. But words were much different than actions. When the time came for both of them to repent, would she stand beside me?

"This is going to destroy her." Apollo sat in the chair across from my desk, speaking my thoughts aloud as if he could read my mind at a distance. Ankle to knee while bracing his hands on the arm of the chair, he added, "She grows stronger every day. I just don't know if she can handle this."

"For now, not a word. To anyone. I'm going to get my father involved and see what we can figure out."

"Dominic isn't going to just walk away from such a lucrative business. He knows too much. You can't just quit that position. His customers will take him out if he even tries."

"Yeah, there's no winning here. Not where Bella is concerned." I quickly dialed my father. It rang twice before he answered. And my phone beeped with an incoming call—Sienna. Hitting ignore, I greeted my father. Al had already updated me on their drama and I didn't have time for one of her meltdowns.

"What has Gio done now?" my old man asked with a lighthearted chuckle. Another series of beeps and I saw Sienna's name flashing again. The girl was drunk and enraged. She needed to learn that overconsumption didn't look good on her. Nor did threatening to remove my men's balls.

"Not Gio. It's Dom this time." My father replied with a growl just as Apollo's phone started ringing. "Sienna?" I asked, and he answered with a nod before sending her to voicemail. The moment he put his phone down, it lit back up again.

Something was wrong.

I could feel it in my bones. Forget the fact that Sienna was blowing us up. Unease had settled in the pit of my stomach since I'd left Bella. Everything told me to stay with her. To hold her longer, but duty had called and I'd answered.

"We're busy, Sienna…" Apollo said in way of greeting, only to be cut off by her panicked screech.

"She's gone! Bella isn't in the apartment and Al's barely holding on! Don't die on me. Damn it, Al!"

My legs carried me out of the room, my mouth barking orders into the phone for my father to rally the troops, while my brain tried to comprehend what I was hearing. Apollo was hot on my heels as we rushed to the staircase—the fastest way to my penthouse. The three flights went by in a blur before we slammed through the door and were welcomed by chaos.

Shattered glass, broken furniture, picture frames ripped off the wall… Sienna's security detail was blocking her from my view. I could barely make out the image of her hunched on the ground next to Al's large body. Her tears and wordless sobs told us how bad it was. Blood was smeared on the tile around him, and his face was barely recognizable. Thankfully, I could hear him mumbling—though his words were incoherent.

"Lucky! Please, she's gone!"

I stormed to Sienna as she rambled on about what had transpired. Al had stayed behind while Bella took my sister back to her suite.

Sienna came back to apologize for fighting with Al, only to find him a bloody mess and the penthouse empty.

It wasn't long before my private emergency medical team rushed into the room, pushing people back and shouting commands. Once I was assured Al would make it, I set to planning, making a beeline for the security control room with Sienna close behind me. Apollo was already tapping away at the computer like a frenzied madman.

"They cut the feed to the main video source. Thankfully the halls and bedrooms are on a different server… for your privacy." Apollo was working fast to rewind the feed. It didn't have the greatest vantage point, but it showed a white male in a mask sneaking up on Al. He was quick with his knife, but Al was so large the fucker had to jump onto his back. "Here's where she comes in." Apollo tapped on the screen, gesturing to Bella.

The shadows from the elevator entranceway danced in the background as the cloaked figure waited for her to round the corner. Bella appeared to be calling out to the room, her head down and focused on the glass as she navigated around the debris. She didn't see him at first but when she did… it was evident she knew him, recognized him, but didn't understand his presence. She attempted to attack but he was too fast. A solid strike to the head and she went limp on the ground.

Rage burned from my heart to my veins, spreading throughout my entire body as I continued to watch the scene play out.

Though Al was bleeding heavily he crawled forward, smearing blood across the floor in his attempt to reach her. Noting his movement, three more men appeared from the hallway, one stopping to kick him in his side. Bella was out cold, her body motionless as she was picked up, thrown over her assailant's shoulder, and carried out.

I slammed my fist down on the console in front of me.

"The hotel feed is gone. They wiped everything clean. I can't see them anywhere, coming or going." Apollo's words were accompanied by the sound of his frenzied typing.

"Where is she?" My father flew into the room with Anthony Moretti filing in behind him.

"Where is Gio?" I roared, slamming Anthony against the wall.

"This wasn't him! You fucked him up—the boy can barely walk. He's at my compound, saying goodbye to his mother before leaving the city for good."

I balked and Apollo sneered, neither of us believing a word that came out of the man's mouth. Gio might not have taken her himself but the bastard was involved. I had no doubt in my mind. Gio was doing a lot of shit behind his father's back. The deal with Yuri—case and point.

"Maybe he didn't physically do this. But sure as fuck his actions caused it," I growled. Anthony scowled, his lip split from where my elbow landed on his face, before drawing his phone from his pocket and speaking in hushed tones.

Apollo, my father, and I worked endlessly, trying to tap into any local security cameras, to get sight of our target. Anything was better than what we had at the moment. When something was outside of my control, I didn't handle it well. I obsessed over everything that went wrong and everything I should have done to prevent it. However, all the *what ifs* wouldn't help me at the moment. They'd only hinder my ability to get her back.

Just as I was shaking myself from my morbid thoughts, shouting erupted in the main living area and Dominic barreled into the room.

"What do we have?" he growled, as though to challenge me and my capabilities. Before I could respond, his phone rang. And he turned his back, purposely lowering his voice and addressing the caller. Apollo was close enough to overhear the exchange and motioned for me to follow him, as Dom cursed and threw his fist through a wall. "Fuck! I want them both back. Right fucking now!" Dom seethed.

"Bella and another girl—his girl—were both taken." Apollo nodded towards Dominic, and I quickly spun on my heel.

"Fucking. Explain. Now." Hands twisting in his shirt, I slammed Dom into the wall repeatedly.

"Gio came to say his goodbyes. Short and sweet. I was too busy in a meeting to have him escorted out. He took… something that belongs to me." There was a look in his eyes I'd never seen before…

And it was disturbing.

"Something or *someone* you feel belongs to you?" I raised an inquisitive brow, and Dominic shook with visible rage.

"She's fucking mine."

Staring into his soulless eyes, I could see just how true he believed that statement to be. I felt the same for Bella. I'd do whatever needed to be done to get her back. And Dom would do the same, not just for the girl but *to her*. There was a darkness beneath his surface. And I didn't know how I hadn't recognized it before.

"Go on." I shoved the bastard against the wall and urged him to continue.

"My darling brother took her. To trade for Bella." Straightening his suit, Dominic fixed me with a stare. "One of my men caught them leaving on camera and followed."

"How the fuck does Gio know where to go?" I countered.

That motherfucker.

He knew exactly who took Bella and where she would be. The fuckers he was working with must have gotten wind that Gio was escaping the city. On my orders. And were none too happy about whatever promises were broken as a result. Hurt me, hurt the Morettis. Two birds, one stone. It was clever. And they'd fucking die for it.

Stepping to Dom, I took his phone from his grasp before smashing the screen against the wall, while a right hook to his chin sent him flying backwards. One of his men caught him mid-descent as two of mine blocked the exit.

"We're not done, you piece of shit. You can't hide anymore. Not from me." I snarled in his face, motioning for my men to seal the room behind us. We needed to be a step ahead of these Moretti bastards, so they didn't fuck up my plans.

"She's yours. We'll get her back," Apollo stated simply, stepping into the elevator beside me.

"Fucking Christ, this idiot!" I tapped the coordinates Dom's insider provided us into my phone and pressed send. My guys were already on their way. "Yeah." I answered my father's call on the first ring, listening intently as we strolled through the lobby to our waiting car. Then I hung up, climbed in the SUV, and updated Apollo. "They're minutes behind us. My dad disabled the elevators but I'm sure Dom already has men on the way."

"What a fucking shitshow," Apollo muttered under his breath.

"We have to—I need… Apollo." Emotions I didn't recognize thickened my voice. Consuming and crippling me. And I allowed a few moments of weakness to take hold.

"We'll get her. They don't have much of a head start…" Apollo looked down at his watch, and I saw the tightening of his jaw. "By the time we get there, it will only have been…"

"Four fucking hours."

I thought back on all of the shit I'd done in my life, and everything haunted me in this moment. Four hours was a long time to hold on to someone. Enough to do a lot of… bad things.

Had she been raped? Was she calling out for me to rescue her as she was brutalized and beaten? What was she thinking?

All I knew was that whoever had a hand in this was going to die a slow and painful death.

This, the drive there, was the only time I'd allow myself to be weak. To think all the errant thoughts I shouldn't. Once we arrived, gloves were off and guns were loaded.

I'm coming, mia regina.

CHAPTER 24

MIRABELLA MORETTI

Fear was a complex emotion that seemed to take over all of your senses until you were drowning in it. When someone was tasked with protecting you with their lives, you gave them a certain amount of faith. Faith in a safety net when situations got bad. However, when that safety net was the reason you were in danger in the first place, things changed. The fear became all-consuming and you doubted this was something you'd survive. Increased heart rate, audio hallucinations, and impending dread were just some of the side effects. Everyone you ever loved flashed in your mind. Did you tell them you loved them? What was the last thing you said to each other? Would you ever see them again?

My head was pounding with the lingering effect of whatever knocked me out. Add the cotton mouth and lightheadedness, and I wasn't doing too well, while the lurching and turning was worsening the nausea. I was in a car. My eyes blinded by some sort of silk cloth, my hands tied behind my back, and my legs pinned closed as I faded in and out of consciousness.

What happened? Where was I? What was the last thing I could remember?

Think, Bella. Think!

Lucky! Oh-my-God! The most amazing night of my life. The engagement party was remarkable, despite the minor issues. Alexander had come to pick me up from the penthouse and we left in the car. But… wait a minute… Alexander? He wasn't one of Lucky's men. My head continued to pound, the looming haze distorting my thoughts.

But we'd left Alexander behind in Italy…

"Good morning, my pet."

The sound of his voice revitalized my senses as panic rose in my throat.

"I know you're awake, Bella, so stop faking it."

Though I refused to respond, I could feel him moving around the stale-smelling room. I was placed on some sort of makeshift bed, my hands tied above my head and connected at the wrist by metal chains. The mattress swayed and creaked with his weight as he sat beside me and stroked my hair away from my face.

"Time to wake up, sleepyhead. Today is the first day of *our* new life together." When I still didn't acknowledge him, his patience grew thin. A quick pinch to the inside of my bicep had me jolting; however, my legs were tied down and pulled apart so I couldn't thrash. Alexander climbed over my body to straddle my hips before pulling my sports bra up to my chin and revealing my breasts. I could feel his eyes on me as he proceeded to knead and squeeze my chest.

He removed my blindfold and I blinked away the harsh light, my retinas burning from the bright assault. Alexander was exactly as I remembered him, blonde and handsome. But there was a newfound darkness in his eyes. And I couldn't help but wonder if it had always been there, lingering beneath the surface of his polished façade. Had I been blinded by my inherit trust for the men hired to protect me?

"There she is. Nice of you to finally join me, Bella."

My head was thrumming behind my eyes and my stomach continued to twist as I took note of his Russian accent, which hadn't been present in Italy—of this much, I was certain. While I was still trying to make sense of my current predicament, he leaned forward, inflicting a gross, wet trail of saliva from my neck down to my breasts.

"Alexander, I wasn't aware you were in the States." His only answer was a smirk. "What do you want?" I pressed, exhaustion evident in my tone as my eyes flicked from corner to corner. The paint was peeling off the walls and God only knew what stained the carpet while this overly used mattress appeared to sit on top of a cast-iron bed frame. There were no windows I could see and only one door, giving me little hope for my escape—though I wasn't going anywhere with my wrists chained.

"I already got what I want… what I was promised." It didn't take a genius to know he meant *me*. "You were never supposed to leave Italy without me. Your bastard of a father ruined our plans and I had to let you go. To wait. But my patience paid off in the long run."

"What do you mean?" I questioned, and his eyes narrowed in on me.

"We were supposed to leave for Russia the night you invited me to your room. You've been promised to me for quite some time and I'm done waiting."

"Promised by whom?"

His lips curled into a snarl. "Are you that dumb you need to ask? You're boring me, Bella. Did all those books of yours teach you nothing?" His accent was much more prominent now that his mask had dropped.

"The flowers." I wasn't asking. It was all so clear as I recalled the bouquet and the ominous card that had been attached. We all had assumed they were from Lucky… but this made much more sense.

"Did you like the quote?" He smirked down at me. "I remembered how much you liked all those storybooks of yours, and I wanted to send a message to the King of New York—a warning."

I opened my mouth to question him further and was quickly silenced. The slap across my face was so hard my neck snapped to the side, while the pounding in my head increased to a full-blown drum solo and my stomach threatened to empty its contents right on this bed. As if sensing what I was feeling, his open palm clamped over my mouth and he shouted for me to swallow. The acid burned my throat as I forced it back down.

"No more questions. Your brother got what he was promised and now I got mine. We leave for Russia shortly. Where we will be wed and you will be taught just what it means to be a wife. *My wife.* Then I'll punish you properly for murdering my father."

Murdering his father? What the hell was he talking about…?

"You may not have killed him yourself but you were the cause." Noting my confusion, he switched to Russian. *"You signed your death warrant the moment you stepped inside that warehouse. You made a mockery of an organization far greater than anything you've yet to see."*

My mind raced to put all the pieces together. The warehouse… with the Russians… and Yuri…

"Figure it out yet?" He taunted me with a twisted smirk. And my fear suddenly dissipated to rage. I refused to be some little girl at the mercy of yet another cruel man. I refused to lie back and take whatever it was he planned to do with me. And I refused to let him win… Lucky had helped me find my backbone and I wasn't about to lose it again.

Alexander allowed his hands to freely roam my body, exploring parts of me only one other man had ever known. His touch burned and bristled upon contact. I fought against my bindings, kicking out my legs and trying to buck him off me. However, my former bodyguard remained unaffected. No, not unaffected. He enjoyed it. He enjoyed my discomfort, my struggle serving to only intensify the fire—the lust—I saw in his eyes.

"The accent doesn't suit you."

He smiled, resembling the man I once knew though the moment was fleeting, and responded in rapid Russian. *"It will in time."*

Doing my best to distract him, I asked the one question left unanswered between us. "So which one was he?" He raised an eyebrow and I clarified. "Your father. Which of the Russian bastards happened to be yours? I can only hope his end was slow and painful." I had no doubt my comments were going to piss him off—not a single part of me expected less. I also knew his response would be violent. I just didn't care at the time, realizing if I let this interaction continue in the direction it was headed, the alternative was far worse. Physical wounds healed; emotional ones were long-lasting.

And I'd been right. He reached an arm out and clutched my throat beneath the force of his grip, cutting off my oxygen until I was on the brink of unconsciousness. I clawed at his hands, my only satisfaction the warmth of his blood and the knowledge I'd broken skin. When he finally released his hold, I heaved and coughed, sucking in as much fresh air as my lungs would allow. Alexander sat back on my waist, looming over me while the pungent stench of vodka seemed to soak into the lacerations on my face.

"Yuri was more of a leader than your bitch of a fiancé will ever be," he hissed, answering my question without having to answer it. "Those men—*my family* deserves to run New York. Not the Agostinos. They may think they've won, but the war has just begun. I'll destroy them, piece by piece. And watch Lucky crumble when he sees you at my side."

I wanted to scream. To yell. To tell him I'd never willingly stand by him. But I couldn't force the words out between painful rasps. Instead, a breathy laugh escaped my lips, and it sounded nearly as agonized as it felt.

"Let that settle. I have work to do before we leave. But mind my words, Bella, I will break you. Then rebuild you into the dutiful wife and mother of my children." He kissed my forehead, climbed off the bed, and slammed the door without a backwards glance.

And in that moment, I felt weak. No matter how strong I pretended to be. My limbs were shaking and my bottom lip trembled at the thought of never seeing Lucky again. Letting him down, disappointing him. Because I was too weak to endure the pain I knew was to come.

I twisted and turned on the spot, tugging at the metal, even with the knowledge it was futile. I was open and exposed. He'd left my bra rolled up, my breasts on display while my traitorous nipples hardened with the chill. My legs were spread wide—I'd never been more thankful to be wearing pants—and my feet were bare. I slammed my head back on the mattress and released a frustrated growl, yanking on my wrists again just because I felt like it.

"It won't work." A voice from the closet next to the bed startled me. "Trust me. I've tried." She sounded broken, hollow, like a shell of a human being behind a locked door.

"Who's there? Are you in the closet?"

She responded with an eerie chorus of laughter. "The closet, my home. Since you took my bed. I feel bad for you. I was just where you are… and it's not fun. Sprung from one prison and thrown into another. Such is life."

"What happened to you?" I couldn't help but ask, even while knowing the answer would likely make my skin crawl.

"I was stolen by a monster in the middle of the night—one of many. Chained to him and coerced into being his slave. A taste of freedom was the lie that brought me here. I don't know which was worse." Her voice lowered to a whisper in the end. And a scratching noise, like a fingernail on wood, accompanied her words.

"Did they…" The question lodged in my throat.

Her reply was more tortured laughter. "What didn't they do? Whatever horrific thing is bouncing around that mind of yours, the answer is… yes, they did it and more. If not them, I'm willing to bet someone else did at some point in my life."

"I will get us out of here. One way or another, there will be a chance for us to break free. Or Lucky will save us. We have to have faith and hold on a little longer." My words felt empty, hollow, but I tried to believe everything I was saying. To make her believe as well.

More laughter. "The Agostinos… the Morettis… the Russians. They're all alike. Some are worse than others. But it's all the same. They can come. Then they'll hand me back over to my master."

What the hell was she talking about? Lucky wasn't an innocent man. Hell, he was far from it. But he didn't hurt women and children. He'd never hand her over to someone looking to hurt her. And what did she mean by master?

"You're a beautiful, sweet woman. But, sadly, you're also so very delusional. Those closest to you have dark, terrible secrets. Things that will haunt you once they're made known. You'll never be the same again. I'm never going to be the same—thanks to him. Might as well send me back. I'm nothing because of that bastard." She stopped speaking, refusing to answer my questions with anything other than laughter, before she started humming old church hymns. The more I tried to pry, the louder she sang. Once I went quiet, she spoke in a hushed tone. "He'll kill me if I ever told. The truth would destroy you. He'll kill me if I tell you. I must thank you, though. For being nice to me in the midst of all the violence. You were a shiny beacon of hope amongst the bleakness."

I didn't know what more to say, so I left her to sing her songs. I needed to get us out of here. Somehow. Someway. And I needed to protect her. A sick feeling settled in my gut. She knew me and someone close to me. Someone with a secret. Whatever the truth was, I could sense that she was right. It would ruin me.

"Persephone," she muttered after a few moments of silence.

"What's that?" I asked, shifting as close to the closet door as I could. My shoulders ached and my nipples strained against the cold in the room, sending shivers down my spine.

"When you're saved and I don't make it, please remember me. Persephone. That's my name, Bella." She knew exactly who I was. "When Alex was watching his line of men sample *the new goods*, he told them to indulge. Because you were off-limits. You'll be okay."

My stomach lurched with a new wave of acid. She'd been raped. By numerous men. It was sickening. The poor woman just wanted someone to remember her name, her will to live no more than a candle slowly burning out. My promises meant nothing; they were broken before they ever hit the open air. Because everyone had already failed her.

"It's all right. It's okay. I'm gonna kill them all someday. It's all right. It's okay. I'm gonna shower in their blood someday. It's all right. It's okay. I'll take everything from them before I end them someday." She sang the cryptic song, and all I could do was listen and pray that Persephone was right.

CHAPTER 25

As hard as I tried, I was too stressed and too tired to stay conscious. I would get a few minutes of glorious sleep to escape my current hell before a noise startled me awake. Followed by a new wave of alertness coated in nausea. Persephone would be singing to herself each time I woke, while my gasping breaths elicited small giggles from the closet.

"How did you get here?" When she didn't answer, I continued to press her. "You said your first master…"

"I was a free, free little bird. Free to travel and experience the world. Until I wasn't. And the saddest part, Bella… The saddest truth of this tale is the fact that I liked it. I liked him." Her voice hardened. "The violence. The control. It shut off all the insane thoughts rampant in my mind. He took them from me. When he was commanding me, things were simple and the sex was phenomenal."

My stomach twisted at her words. She was delusional to believe the man who controlled, brutalized, and destroyed her was anything more than a monster in the night. However, the conviction in her voice told me just how much she believed what she was saying.

"You will be free again, Persephone."

She laughed, a loud cackling sound. "I will never be free again. I could walk away right now, and I can ensure you I will never be free. Not for a single second. My master will consume my thoughts. I'll spend every day looking over my shoulder to see if he's found me. Unless… *it's okay. It's all right. I'm gonna kill them all someday.*" She began to chant to herself again, leaving me to fade in and out of a restless sleep.

The more time I was strapped to this bed, forced to listen to Persephone slipping further and further into madness, the harder I prayed for a merciful death. "Please stop fucking singing." I couldn't help it. The incessant sound was driving me to the brink of insanity. "I can't fucking take it anymore." I rattled my chains against the bedrails and screamed out my frustrations.

"It's not fun falling from grace, is it? The queen, treated like a slave. I feel bad for you. Someone must've not gotten her waffles with fresh strawberries and whipped cream today."

What? How did she know my favorite breakfast? Then it clicked.

"Persephone, were you in my parents' house?"

"Congratulations on your engagement. You look glowing in white."

She was at my house and at my engagement party. She was that girl. The one Dominic seemed to obsess over. Her silence was all the confirmation I needed.

"*Bella wasn't part of the fucking deal.*" Gio's angered voice in the hallway snapped my head in that direction.

"She was always part of the deal. You promised her to me from day one. And I promised I'd remove all your competitors for you." Alexander sounded almost amused.

"When Yuri was killed, the deal changed. I gave you that other girl in place of Bella. You don't have the same power your father did."

A loud bang like something or *someone* being slammed against a wall rattled the door to my prison. Grunting and cursing, flesh pounding into flesh, and more slamming ensued. My brother may have been an idiot, but he could hold his own in a fight. I'd never seen the violent side of Alexander in Italy—though, going by his size, I could only assume he wouldn't go down easy. Our altercation at the penthouse proved as much.

"Marrying that girl gives me the upper hand. While Lucky is scrambling to find her, his businesses are suffering. Allowing me to take a stronger hold. Unlike you, I've been patient. I know what it takes to remove the king from his throne."

"He will come for her and it will be your end."

"Let him come. It will make his fall that much easier. As we speak, I have his arms delivery in possession and a master list of his clients. My men are ambushing two more large shipments that he's neglected since your sister came into the picture. Women make you weak, and I took advantage of that weakness. His head isn't clear and he will continue to make bad choices till he has nothing left."

Fuck! Everything happening… we assumed it was all Gio. And we assumed wrong. My brother had his hand in it, but the real threats were Yuri and his offspring. I was making Lucky weak, and everything and everyone around him would suffer because of it.

"I'm taking Bella with me. None of this was part of the plan. You have the other girl, who's practically trained to your liking already. This is done." Heavy footsteps bounded down the hallway in my direction, followed by another scuffle and more mumbled threats.

"He won't save you. He planned to give you away. Then when he didn't get exactly as he wanted, he tried to trade me for you." Persephone's soft lilt had been replaced by rage. She was certainly going on one emotional roller coaster in that locked closet. I couldn't blame her though. I was feeling much the same.

The door slammed open, revealing a bloodied Gio with Alexander hot on his heels. My brother dove for me, covering my breasts before releasing my legs. His eyes wouldn't meet mine as he mumbled something about helping me escape. There wasn't a sorry bone in his body. Only displeasure over not getting what he'd wanted. And resentment that his plan to destroy Lucky had been foiled.

"She isn't leaving, Gio. She's my future wife. You're outmanned and outgunned." Alexander blocked the doorway.

Free from my chains, I hopped off the little mattress, readjusting my clothing as blood flow returned to my limbs. "I'm not your anything. You fucking disgust me."

A cruel smile replaced Alexander's blank expression. "What about that afternoon in Italy? When you were begging for my dick? Closing the bedroom door to shut out this jackass. Lust-soaked eyes matching your soaked panties, craving a taste of what I could give you, only to be ruined by an Agostino instead. But it's fine... Willing or not, I own you."

Gio attempted to block his approach. The lion stalking his prey. "I said no."

Alexander's smirk vanished, and Persephone started giggling again from the closet. The darkness seemed to be rampaging her psyche. She didn't cry out or beg anyone to save her.

"You have no choice here, Gio. You signed her over to me in Italy. And I think it's time for you to leave now. Seeing my bride before me, I need a taste."

My brother and I moved at the same time. He charged at Alexander while I ran to the closet, desperately tugging at the knob to free Persephone. Tears poured down my face and I cried out to her when the knob wouldn't budge. Gio was quickly subdued by several of Alexander's men, who came running at the sounds of the commotion. My brother was on the floor, bloodied and beaten. My head connected with the closet door before a fist wrapped around my hair. The force of the repeated blows made my brain slow and hazy. My small frame was pressed into the wall, with a hard body keeping me in place, and the scent of mint mixed with vodka on Alexander's breath was enough to make me gag.

"I do love when you fight. I'm looking forward to seeing how long this spirit lasts." He emphasized that statement by grinding his erection into my spine.

"Do what you want. I will never be yours."

He pulled my head back by my hair, slamming my forehead against the door. My limbs slackened as my coordination diminished. And Alexander flicked his tongue out, licking my tears as they fell freely now. Gio was a barely conscious mess, moaning on the floor. The Russian enforcers quickly dragged him from the room with a simple snap of their master's fingers. Alexander yanked at my hair for a second time, and I had no choice but to comply. My back arched at an excruciating angle in an attempt to relieve some of the pressure on my neck, before my legs gave out from underneath me, and I crumpled to the floor.

Alexander scooped me up and tossed me onto the bed. I bounced once before he was on me again. Sitting on my hips with my arms secured above my head, he stared down at me with a look that made me want to vomit. *Possession.* It wasn't lust. No, it was ownership. And not in the way that spoke of protection. I was an object to him. To do with as he saw fit.

"Shut the fuck up in there," he hissed between clenched teeth, and Persephone stopped singing immediately. "I like this, Bella. The feel of your skin under me. Fighting me until your last breath. But I can see you growing tired. Your brain wants to shut down to protect itself. That's why I won't take you yet. I will train you, and only when you're worthy will you get my cock." He rotated his hips against me, pressing his erection into my stomach as he spoke. And I knew without a doubt that I was ready to take a beating if it meant he wouldn't touch me.

Lucky owned me. Body, heart, and soul. No one else was allowed to share that special part of me. And that realization steeled my spine as I launched a big glob of spit into Alexander's face. However, his answering smile chilled me to my core. He leaned forward, my saliva slowly dripping from his nose and landing with a splat onto my own. Before I could apologize, laugh, speak—before I could even breathe— he attacked.

His head smashed forward, leaving me in a daze as agony burst behind my eyes and my sanity bounced around with it. When he decided to climb off me, I remained motionless, my eyes staring into the ceiling but seeing nothing. I could hear the creak of the closet door, Persephone's whimper as Alexander yanked her out, and the thud of her body as it met the floor. Then he reached down and forced the girl to her feet, holding her out in front of me to give me my first real look at her. It was all the confirmation I needed. She was the waitress from my engagement party and the girl in the maid uniform.

Her gorgeous eyes appeared dead and distant as she knelt before Alexander with a blank expression on her face.

"You will beg me for a taste. To touch you. You haven't earned that yet. So, for now, you will learn how I like it. Forget everything you think you know. Today is day one, my future bride." Releasing himself from his pants, Alexander slapped Persephone across the face with an open palm. She barely flinched and her lips parted on command.

"You're fucking disgusting," I hissed, though I couldn't will my body to move, and my eyes closed as if I no longer controlled them.

I couldn't tell if seconds, minutes, or hours had passed but I could hear distant shouting. It must have been a cruel joke. A nightmare. My mind had to be playing tricks on me... Alexander was yelling in Russian but I couldn't understand it. And more voices filled the room before heavy footfalls pounded down the hallway. The sweet oblivion of darkness was taking the reins once again, and I didn't know what was a dream and what was reality. Though I could have sworn I heard Lucky's name mentioned. His voice. But there was no way. It was too late. I belonged to someone else.

"Bella, *mia regina.*" My mind was conjuring up images now, Apollo's image, as he loomed above me.

"Apollo... Persephone. Please, help her," I muttered to the apparition. Or did I? Then the lights went out and eviscerated what was left of my consciousness.

CHAPTER 26

LUCIFER "LUCKY" AGOSTINO

Four hours and counting.

That was how long my Bella had been in the hands of a man with a major vendetta against me. A man who could be doing God knows what to the love of my life. We had the coordinates and were ahead of Dominic's men by about half an hour. She was being held somewhere totally off grid. A once flourishing area outside the city that had been evacuated due to floods and left in ruin.

That's where she was. Being held against her will. In some rundown shack.

"Roger." Speaking into his phone, Apollo nodded at me. "She's there, about fifteen men in total. Gio just showed up."

"I'm going to fucking kill him." Cracking my knuckles, I thought of a million ways I planned to make him suffer. Before finally taking his life. Though I hadn't determined my method as of yet. I just knew it would be slow and painful.

"You may not have the chance. Apparently, he tried taking Bella back. No update on signs of life." Apollo continued to text away.

I stared out the window, saying a small prayer to the powers above. A power I didn't have the right to ask a single thing from. I wanted

Bella alive and unharmed. And I wanted Gio alive just long enough for me to kill him.

"Radio silence," Apollo announced into his headset.

The headlights of our four SUVs shut off in time with each other, so that the moon served as our only form of illumination as we navigated the tree line in tight formation. As we crept closer, I could smell the wood fireplace burning and make out the flickering of lights from the distant windows. Moving quickly, I issued various hand signals and my men spread out while Apollo understood his sole mission. He'd been instructed to go in first. Alone. He'd efficiently take down any threat on his way to getting Bella out safely.

The holding site was an old farmhouse in the middle of a clearing. The markings of the flood waters showed on the collapsing porch, a ring of damage marring the foundation of the home. According to the floorplan we'd unearthed, the dilapidated structure had several rooms to utilize for their base of operation. But one stood out that we could all but guarantee was Bella's location. Logistically, it made the most sense to secure her there. Buildings such as these were known for having a lot of little rooms. One in particular towards the rear left side of the house could easily fit a single bed and appeared to have a small closet and no windows. It's where I'd put her if it were me. Meaning there was no escape and only one way in. But it was closer to the rear entrance, so I could slip her out the back amidst the chaos.

"Two down. Southeast rear entrance." Apollo sounded like a stranger in my ear. He was colder. More emotionless than normal. A dog with his eye on his bone. And I knew nothing would get in his way.

I motioned for my crew to advance as several of my men scattered, awaiting Apollo's orders to breach the building. Things seemed calm and quiet, minus the conversations and bullshitting going on inside the house. Peering in the window, I could make out

Gio's motionless body on the ground, a pool of blood surrounding him.

Idiot.

"Three more. Four doors over from the rear." That left about ten armed men in the house. Movement through the window showed Alexander entering the room. He flicked his eyes to Gio before throwing the tip of his boot into the bastard's gut and spitting on him. The resounding grunt was the only sign of life.

Good.

"Fifth door, target acquired. Go, go, go." The first 'go' was barely in my ear before I was moving. Diving through the window with a shattering of glass, I reached the first fucker before he could registered the crunching of bone as my fist made direct contact with his face.

Chaos ensued, sprinkled with blurred movement, gunfire, and shouting. Out of the corner of my eye, I caught sight of two of Alexander's men. The first one went down with a knife to the carotid artery, blood spraying over my face and torso, while the second crumpled over with a bullet between his eyes.

I continued down the hallway, in the seemingly never-ending race for the fifth door. My men were easily overtaking the ill-trained Russians, which was exactly how I knew Alexander didn't have support from the *Bratva*. Their men would never have been this clumsy and unprepared. But I also knew because my father had called a meeting, demanding to know why they were looking to start a war.

They weren't.

Alexander and his late father were lone wolves, and the members of the *Bratva* were in full cooperation. If we didn't take him out, they would. And the bastard would end up wishing I'd been the one to end him. The Russian mob was a whole different level of brutality.

By the time I made it to the third door, I could feel her. I knew she was close, her heart calling to mine. Begging me to save her. And at the fourth door, I could finally hear her. My heart lurched in my chest, pushing my body harder to get to her.

"Fuck," I hissed as a sharp pain radiated up my shoulder as a bullet tore through flesh and muscle before embedding itself in the wall in front of me. Spinning around in the tight hallway, I barreled into the man with his finger on the trigger.

The Russian shoved me to my knees, causing my temple to catch the corner of the doorknob. Temporarily dazed, I refocused my vision and searched for his gun while a jab to his throat with my elbow got me the few precious seconds I needed. I grabbed the gun from his hand as I slammed the full force of my weight into his torso. He rolled to his side, already attempting to pull a backup pistol from his waistband. But the Russian bastard was moving way too slow for me to worry about him causing any more damage. One second, he was smirking at me like I was a dead man walking. And the next, two holes were drilled into his forehead. I instinctively turned towards the muzzle flare to find Gio bracing himself on the doorway.

"This changes nothing," I stated as I pushed to my feet. "You're still fucking dead."

Gio's nose was broken, both eyes swollen, and his face was marred with a grotesque mixture of blood and bruising as he stared at the floor like it held all the secrets to the world's mysteries.

He chuckled at me, with one arm clutching his abdomen, likely supporting a series of broken ribs. "I didn't do it for you. Tell Bella I'm sorry." Without another word, he limped to a chair in the other room and collapsed onto the seat.

I mentally prepared myself for a second, opening the door and schooling my expression, Before I charged inside. And my eyes immediately fell on Bella. She was a mess of blood and bruises, her skin both lighter and darker than I remembered seeing it last. Her eyes were closed but the steady rise and fall of her chest calmed my fraying nerves. Slightly… There were chains attached to the bed but she was still dressed at least. I offered a prayer for small miracles, thankful she was alive. I'd deal with the rest of whatever she needed later.

"Find him," I hissed into my radio, commanding my men to get me Alexander.

Apollo nodded in my direction, his arms wrapped around a girl on the floor, who looked worse than Bella. Her face was covered in dirt with smatterings of blood. I'd feel sorry for her if not for the fierce blue eyes staring back at me, almost in challenge. It wasn't just the shade that was intense but the way her pupils appeared soulless and dead.

I climbed onto the bed and carefully arranged Bella in my arms, preparing to aid in her escape. The sound of heavy gunfire was exploding outside the house. And I couldn't help but grin. It seemed his men thought they would just run into the night without repercussions. All of them would pay. Every. Single. One. And if they went into hiding, I'd take it out on their families. Each generation would suffer until they gave themselves up to me.

"Persephone," Bella mumbled, drifting in and out of consciousness. As I picked her up bridal-style, her eyes opened to small slits.

"We're safe now, Bella. They've got me. I'm okay," the girl on the floor replied. When Apollo tried scooping her off the floor, she pushed at his chest and hobbled towards the door.

"You came." Bella stared at me in wonder.

"Always, *mia regina*. What would I do without you at my side?"

She offered me a small smile before going limp in my arms.

"Fifth room. Exiting southeast rear for cover." Apollo called into the mic and static crackled back before we got the clear to move.

We stepped outside the room and two men immediately flanked my left, shielding our backs, while two more waited at the end of the hall. Once we were at the rear exit, an additional three added their bodies to our wall of protection as we ran to the waiting vehicles. The extended SUV had all the doors open and ready. Apollo and I were able to climb in with each girl sprawled out on a bench in the back.

"Sir? Hospital?" my driver asked, expertly navigating the broken trail back to the main road, the surrounding trees no more than a blur.

"Negative. My parents' compound is closer."

Our eyes met in the rearview mirror and I watched him nod in silent agreement.

"Al. You're… you're okay?" Bella mumbled from beside me.

Sitting in the front seat like a true-to-life version of Frankenstein's monster, Al smiled at her. "It's just a scratch," he joked before barking orders into his phone. He was organizing cleanup for the farmhouse and readying the family doctor, no doubt relaying all of the information to my father on the other end of the phone while confirming our mission was a success.

Leaning my head back against the window, I tugged Bella closer and she clung to me like her life depended on it. Apollo sat in front of us with the blonde girl. Anytime he moved to inspect her wounds, she slapped his hands without speaking to or looking at him. The tension in his ticking jaw told me he was trying to keep his shit together, likely reminding himself she was a victim. It was hard to remember that when you felt nothing.

"Boss." Pausing for my nod of acknowledgement, Al continued, "Two are in the wind."

"Don't tell me…"

His returning glare gave me my answer. Gio and Alexander were gone. Our prime targets had gotten away. Something wasn't right about that. It was just too convenient.

"Drop me off at the first gas station you see," the blonde girl announced.

"No," Apollo barked back.

"Yes," she countered with a cross of her arms. "One prison for another and another. Charming."

"You're not a prisoner any longer. You will have your own room. A private doctor to treat you and anything else you may need while we figure everything out."

She slapped his hand when he tried blotting the blood on her chin. "Rest assured the actions I've witnessed are of no concern to the police. I know who you are and how this goes. And more so, I know how to keep my mouth shut. A simple thank you to you both for saving me and a goodbye at the gas station are my only consolation prizes." She sat perfectly poised, her eyes focused straight ahead.

"It doesn't work like that. You will stay until we say you can leave." Apollo's tone was harsh and clipped. She was getting under his skin and I rather enjoyed seeing the man unravel.

"*Though those that are betray'd do feel the treason sharply, yet the traitor stands in worse case of woe.*" When she finally made eye contact with him, I could feel the burn from the back seat. "I'm not stupid. I'm not a fucking snitch and I won't be your plaything."

"A lady after my own heart. Knows her Shakespeare." Gripping her wrist tightly in his hand, Apollo tugged the girl to face him. "And you'll be whatever the fuck I want you to be. And better yet, you'll fucking beg me for it. Now, how about we start with you being thankful and quiet." He released her arm and she faced forward again.

Bella would occasionally moan and squirm with the rocking car until I held her tighter, but once we veered onto the highway, she settled easily against me. Adrenaline was still coursing through my system as I waited for any news on our missing targets, and I couldn't help but watch as the blonde's head kept dipping down in exhaustion before snapping back to life.

"You're safe. You can sleep." Apollo grinned.

She propped herself upright, crossing her arms over her chest as she continued to ignore him. She was covered in so much filth I was surprised he hadn't shifted away. The man hated dirt and disorganization, almost as much as he despised disobedience. His current behavior was both peculiar and intriguing.

When the blonde's head dipped a second later, she shook herself and sat straighter. *"Therefore was I created with a stubborn outside,"* she said, though it wasn't clear who she was addressing.

"You're more familiar with Shakespeare than I'd presume," Apollo replied with a smirk. "Hmm, let's finish that saying, shall we? *With an aspect of iron, that when I come to woo ladies, I fright them."*

She threw her head back and cackled, and Apollo's lips dropped into a scowl.

"You can be stubborn and made of iron, but you don't scare me. I have nothing left to give so I don't dare frighten anymore." The girl slid down the bench seat, putting distance between them.

The rest of the car ride to my parents' country home was accompanied by silence as I stared out the window and tried to quiet my thoughts. Bella was here and she was safe. Now, we just needed to tend to her wounds and wait. Wait until we found the two cowards who'd fled from their deaths. Wait until I learned how much I had truly lost of the love of my life. Physical wounds would heal, but mental trauma could haunt your soul for the rest of your life. And wait for the war that was to come.

CHAPTER 27

MIRABELLA MORETTI

Pain. That came first.

Then thirst. I was so thirsty. My arms and eyes felt heavy and weird, like I was floating underwater, and whispered voices blended into the background while an irritating beeping consumed my senses.

Lucky!

I could hear him but he sounded so far away. I wanted him. I needed him. I tried calling out but it didn't work. My brain wasn't communicating with the rest of my body. I was lying on soft, smooth sheets that smelled like Lucky's cologne. Heaven. If there was a way that I could bottle up his scent and carry it around with me, I would. It was more than just his cologne. It was his power and dominance that emanated from his pores.

"If there's nothing wrong, why isn't she waking up? It's been days, Doc." Lucky sounded exhausted… defeated. A sound that was so unlike him it almost took me a second to recognize it.

Wait a minute! Days…

"Mr. Agostino, the damage to her body was extensive. This is it's way of shutting down. To fix itself."

I hadn't woken up in days. I was just lying here, useless, for no reas—

Oh. My. God.

Alexander. Persephone. Oh, Big Al! I remembered. Ow! No wonder everything hurt. I was proud to say I survived one hell of a beating from a member of the *Bratva* and lived to tell the tale.

"L-ucky." Though my voice was a painful rasp—barely audible—within a second, I felt the bed dip as he surrounded me in his heavenly scent.

"Yes, baby. God, *mia regina,* you scared me."

I opened my eyes and the bright lights assaulted my retinas, making me cry out in pain.

"Close the curtains!"

Some shuffling noises filled the background and I could feel the darkness settle into the room. Slowly fluttering my lashes open again, I waited for my vision to adjust to my surroundings, taking note of the older man in a crisp white jacket with a clipboard standing behind my fiancé. The space was crowded with our mothers hovering close by, Mario off to the side, and Apollo hanging back in a corner. However, my father was noticeably absent.

"Apollo! Persephone… is she…?" I couldn't get the words out.

He nodded, one side of his mouth curling into an encouraging half grin. "She's fine. She's staying down the hall in her own suite while we work some things out." His tone was final and oddly suspicious. And I couldn't help but wonder if the crazy little girl in the closet was giving these men a run for their money.

"You, on the other hand, have been sleeping for days and I think I aged ten years." Lucky kissed the tip of my nose as I smiled back at him.

"Still as handsome as ever." I cupped his face, his normally smooth skin prickling my palm with his overgrown stubble, as I pulled him down for a kiss. "Where is my father? Dominic?"

The awkward tension in the room grew, bubbling to the surface like water boiling over the sides of the pot. Something was going down and it appeared as though no one wanted to tell me what it was. Even Mario seemed to be avoiding eye contact.

So now we were back to sugarcoating everything for the damaged little queen?

"You know, I survived a kidnapping with the *Bratva* rejects, got my ass beat, helped save a girl, and watched a hell of a lot of death and destruction—all over the last few months. I'm pretty sure I can handle whatever you need to say." I stared pointedly at Lucky, his shocked expression staring back at me. Apollo was smirking in the background, trying to cover his laughter with a cough.

"Your father is attempting to find Dominic and Gio. They've both gone off the radar." Lucky looked away as if debating his next words.

"Gio I get. I overheard what he told Alexander about the deal involving me. But where is Dom? Did he go out looking for him? Wait a minute... Gio escaped." It was a statement, not a question. "How the fuck does that happen?" I rarely cursed so Apollo's hidden laughter turned into hysterics. Even our mothers and Mario joined in. But my anger was completely warranted. My brother betrayed me, our family, my future husband in an act of greed. "Explain Dominic." That part wasn't making sense.

"Things are a little unclear right now with Dom. We're trying to determine what we know, and right now, it's not a lot." Lucky scowled as if the words tasted sour on his tongue. It was evident that the lack of knowledge and control was a tough pill for him to swallow.

I glanced at my mother and her eyes told me everything I needed to know, without ever having to say the words. Those boys were apples from the tree of my father, and she was ready to let them rot. I'd always been close to Dom. But there was something churning my stomach, and I couldn't quite place what it was. I'd overheard something but everything was still a blur.

I could tell I was at the Agostino compound but obviously not in Lucky's bedroom. The room was smaller, though large by normal standards, and bare besides the fresh floral arrangements, a large dresser, and medical equipment. They had their own hospital. I didn't know why I was surprised.

"Okay, folks. She's awake and talking, as you all can see. Now I need to examine her in private." The doctor tapped his pen on the chart and everyone quickly exited, except for Lucky who remained at my bedside. "Tell me, Bella, how're you feeling?" He was a soft-spoken man with sincere and comforting brown eyes.

"Not bad, considering. A little tender around my nose and cheeks. The headache is a dull ache that intensifies under bright lights. I can't shake this nausea though. That's the real killer, Doc." I tried to laugh off the agony settling in my bones.

Lucky was practically vibrating. He was filled with so much concern and tension. Any slight movement had him fidgeting like a mother hen.

The doctor nodded, initiating the automatic blood pressure cuff and waiting for the reading under a heavy silence. Lucky was holding his breath, those blue eyes I loved burning bright. "Well, you, my dear, are a trooper to maintain such a comical façade when I know for a fact your pain must range from 8-9 on the scale."

I shrugged in response, wincing with the added discomfort.

"Can we just load her with some solid pain medication already?" Lucky huffed.

"What exactly are the extent of my injuries?" I asked them both, needing to know the answer.

"Your ribs are bruised but thankfully not broken. However, your nose is another story. We reset it while you were unconscious and tended to the numerous lacerations on your body." The doctor flipped through my chart, reading it off like a macabre grocery list. "The second metacarpal on the right hand is broken. Your shoulder was dislocated. Again, we reset it. And lastly, a minor concussion."

I felt sick. In other words, I was beaten to hell and back again. I gasped at the same time Lucky muttered, "Jesus."

"Well, I mean... I'm here and alive, so that's something." I attempted to lighten the mood. "I don't really like heavy pain medications. They make me sick. Speaking of, when will this nausea go away?"

"For most women, it typically dissipates in the second trimester.

And as far as pain medications go, I've had to limit it to what's safe in your present condition."

My jaw dropped, my eyes drifting to Lucky and taking note of his shared confusion. Second trimester… My condition…

I opened my mouth to speak before closing it several times. I was at a loss for words as Lucky's laughter filled the room, startling the doctor and confusing me. "Really not a time to make jokes, Doc." Lucky laughed a little harder while the old man looked at him as though he had five heads.

"Oh my, I'd just assumed with the way your mothers were discussing baby names… I…" The doctor shook his head and resumed his professionalism. "Right, well, my mistake for assuming." He cleared his throat. "Lucifer. Mirabella. Congratulations, you're expecting. And despite the trauma, the fetus appears to be healthy."

"Expecting…" If I hadn't been so shocked at the news myself, I would have burst into a fit of hysterics at the look on Lucky's face.

Haphazardly running his hands through his hair, he couldn't form a sentence. Lucifer, *il diavolo,* was rattled by the mere mention of a baby. And just when I thought he was going to lose it, he broke out into a grin. Sliding off the bed before dropping to his knees, Lucky folded over my lap, placing soft kisses to my stomach while he murmured happy little thoughts to his unborn child. I was glad he was excited, but was I?

We'd just announced our engagement and I was a disgrace. A mafia princess pregnant before marriage. Yes, times were different and I was contracted to marry this man, but this wasn't what I had in mind… However, none of this was as I imagined it. It was so much better.

"If you have any questions, please call me. And congratulations again." The doctor fled the room like hell was on his heels. The poor man was probably thankful Lucky took the news so well, seeing as it could have had a much different outcome.

"He's going to be strong. Overcoming so much already and not even born yet." I couldn't help but smile at the image of Lucky as a father.

"How do you know it's a boy?" he asked, his eyes sparkling with wonder as he crawled onto the bed to lie beside me.

"I don't. It's just a feeling."

"I think he is too. Our little man is already protecting his mama, growing strong amidst the chaos." I laughed at that, and he quickly added, "You're amazing."

Lucky proceeded to tell me the story of my rescue. He glossed over the details about Dominic, while the limited information he did provide seemed off. Forced. His closed expression confirmed what my gut was already telling me. My favorite brother was in deep shit. The conversation was then steered to Gio, who appeared to have finally snapped. He used people as a means to an end and always for something in his own favor, greed his only driving motive. My father sending him to Italy had plunged him over the edge. Gio had made a connection with Yuri, a lower-level crime lord, who seemed to be just as hungry for power. Together, they hoped to take over the city in Lucky's place, the promise of my betrothal serving to unite a different set of families.

Now, Gio was missing, and we were unsure if he'd run away or if the *Bratva* had found him and Alexander.

"Men just love to sign you over in contracts, don't they?" Lucky laughed at my glare.

"Yeah, they do. I never would've believed this would be my future. Guess my brother didn't know..." Lucky raised a questioning brow, and I smiled. "That I'd been contracted to the devil himself."

Lucky flipped the covers back and eyed me with a mixture of lust and anticipation. "You're too sore for all of it but, baby, I'm going to make you feel good. Yes, *il diavolo* is going to make you feel fucking amazing." His head disappeared between my legs and all other thoughts escaped me as pleasure replaced the pain. At least for a while.

CHAPTER 28
LUCIFER "LUCKY" AGOSTINO

I was going to be a father.

Her body was put through literal physical hell and she still protected our child. All I wanted to do was cover her in bubble wrap and lock her inside a room where no one could look at or touch her. I was never one to share, but this sense of possessiveness went beyond that. Bella consumed my every waking thought, and invaded my sleep in the form of both nightmares and fantasies, depending which part of my psyche won out in that moment.

It didn't make sense. I wasn't making sense. None of this was making fucking sense. And I *always* made sense.

Wiping my mouth with the back of my hand, I couldn't help but smile as I looked down at my angel. Her hair was spread across the pillow. Her face covered in cuts and bruises, and she was still the most gorgeous woman I'd ever laid eyes on.

My dick was begging me to throw my gentleness out the window. But she was too broken. So I tugged the blanket back up to cover her and cuddled next to her. I kissed the top of her head and held her close, too afraid I'd lose her again.

"Can I see Persephone?"

"Get some rest and then you can. She'll still be here when you wake up." Persephone wasn't going anywhere. She had the information we needed to find Dominic. She'd been his secret little plaything. I recognized her from the engagement dinner, and Apollo said he remembered seeing her at the Moretti house. Dominic had been involved in each instance. It wasn't a coincidence. I didn't believe in them.

The moment Apollo had started to question the girl, she'd gone mute. Well, when it came to saying anything coherent anyway. My second-in-command was losing his mind with her nonstop singing and humming whenever he approached her. She'd been kept very close to Dom. There was no doubt she'd have insight into locations, businesses, something. If we could get them from her…

With Dominic missing, amidst a lot of unanswered questions, we weren't resting until we found him. Gio seemed to drop off the face of the earth, and I was not completely sold on the possibility that they weren't working together. Add in Anthony's sudden disappearance, and something didn't smell right.

"You men and your egos." Bella giggled as she wedged herself under my arm.

"What do you mean?" I asked.

"Clearly you need her for something, and she won't give it to you. You think banging your fists on your chest, telling her she's Jane and you're Tarzan will encourage her to spill all her secrets." She mimicked the gestures and it was hard to stifle my laughter. "Not that girl. She was mumbling and calling me the chosen one or something. I don't understand it, but with time, I'm sure she'll open up. On. Her. Own. Accord." Bella narrowed her eyes at me to emphasize her point.

The chosen one? Interesting.

Persephone's loyalty to Dominic was disconcerting, more so considering it appeared to be trauma-induced. The girl knew who Bella was and, despite the distance, she refused to speak against the Morettis. I wasn't normally a proponent for violence against women, but this was pushing even my patience.

Apollo was against that idea. He wanted to hold on to her and wait it out. All of which said way too much in itself about this woman. Her secrets held power over me, while Apollo's protection told me she held power over him too.

"Please tell me Alexander felt immense pain." Bella's eyes burned with the hopes of retribution. I was about to crush her world with the truth and I hated it. She'd lose sleep, always looking over her shoulder until we found him. I failed her the first time. I didn't want her to question if it would happen again.

"No one hurts *mia regina* and lives to talk about it." Technically it wasn't lying. Every word of it was true. The Russian bastard would meet a painful end at my hands. I couldn't answer her question, so I'd evade it until it became the truth.

"You're lying."

Scoffing at her assumption, I charged to my feet. "I'd never lie to you."

"No. No, you wouldn't, my love. But you would do everything in your power to avoid hurting me with the truth. And that, Lucifer, was pure avoidance." Her knowing smirk made me smile even as my gut was clenching in agony. The thought of destroying that smile physically pained me.

"It's being handled." Enough said.

She eyed me for a moment longer, before she finally exhaled a huff and relaxed into her pillows. "Let me see her, and I won't ask you anything that will force you to… *avoid* me again." Bella was already rising from her hospital bed, straightening the silk nightgown I'd dressed her in earlier.

"Stay in bed!" My booming voice would've had my armed men jumping to do my bidding. But, no, not this girl. She giggled as she slipped her arms through the sleeves of her robe. "Bella! Please, when you're better, I will take you."

She ignored my pleas, limping her way towards the door as she slapped my hand away. All while she muttered under her breath about *being a queen no one obeys*. She yanked the door open, slamming it behind her as she nearly stomped out. I watched her cringe from the exertion, the pain evident on her face but she was too damn stubborn.

My eyes dropped to the spot now soaking through the fabric of her robe. "Damn it! Bella, you're fucking bleeding!" Scooping her up in my arms and squeezing tightly, I charged back to the hospital room. "When will you listen! Tomorrow, okay? Tomorrow, I will take you to see her. Right now, you need rest. And let me rebandage that wound."

Once Bella was safely under the covers, I could finally breathe again. Her eyes hung heavy and tired, her smirk replaced by down-turned lips. She was in pain, but too damn stubborn to concede. Her silence only lasted for a minute.

"They both got away, didn't they?"

My rage choked my airways and all I could do was nod in response. Each of us lost in our own thoughts, I watched as she drifted off to sleep without another word. I stared down at my dark-haired beauty for another moment, observing the slow rise and fall of her chest that told me she was finally at peace.

Now that Bella was safe in bed, I had other business to tend to. Persephone had the answers we needed and with the right kind of encouragement, I was certain she'd tell us.

I headed down the hall, towards Apollo's room. For whatever reason, my second had decided to house the ball of crazy in his space. Persephone had been quiet during her initial examination. However, as soon as she stepped foot in his room, her limited grasp on her sanity all but shattered. She'd mumble and sing to herself, her distant eyes staring at nothing and no one in particular. All of which were signs of extreme trauma. Likely a mixture of physical and mental abuse.

I knocked lightly so as to not scare the poor girl, and an exhausted Apollo answered. His normally pressed suit pants were rumpled. He'd forewent a jacket and tie, and his shirt remained untucked and half-buttoned. The man was disheveled, a side of him I hadn't seen since my father took him in when we were children.

"Why are you rattled?" I asked him, though it was hard to hold back my smirk.

"I'm not fucking rattled. I'm fucking murderous."

I threw my head back with earnest laughter. "You forget, brother, I've seen you murderous. The room around you will be bathed in blood and carnage. Yet we'd find you in the center of the chaos... immaculate. *That's* not *this.*" I motioned a hand over his large frame, and he looked down, shocked by his own appearance.

"I don't hurt women."

I nodded in understanding.

"But she makes me want to."

"Okay."

Apollo was practically crawling up the walls and tugging on his hair as he stormed across the room. "I want to murder her with my bare hands. Watch the life drain from her eyes and then revive her to do it all over again. I want to bury my dick in her and wait until the light goes out in those pretty blue eyes. Only letting her breathe when I feel her orgasm beneath me."

Did I mention my brother, my best friend, my number two was one sick fuck?

He had no clue what to do with feelings—good or bad. And the lack of control was sending the man plummeting over that edge of sanity, right along with the blonde.

"You didn't do any of those things to her though, right?" You could never be too sure with him.

"No, you fucking asshole. That's probably why I'm crawling out of my skin and want to climb these fucking walls."

For the most part, Apollo was cool and detached. His mind would wander to those darker thoughts, but never once had I seen them truly consume him. He'd spent years attempting to keep those demons at bay.

Before I could say anything in reply, her mumblings caught my attention. Persephone was balled up on the floor, wrapped tight in her hospital gown with her arms hugging her knees to her chest.

"She hasn't fucking moved. Not once. Just shakes and rocks."

"Persephone. Hey!" When trying to get her attention nicely didn't work, I pointed to the seat in the corner, instructing Apollo to drag it to the middle of the room.

"Before you touch her, just be prepared." He smirked at my nonchalant huff as we both approached the small blonde on the ground.

Her eyes were dry and vacant. No one was home. She was just an empty shell of the fiery woman I witnessed on the drive here.

I glanced at him from over my shoulder, leaning down to face the girl whose hospital gown nearly swallowed her whole. "Big, bad Apollo scared of the little kitten's claws?" I asked him. I couldn't help but wonder what my friend found so intimidating. Persephone couldn't hurt a fly.

Boy, was I fucking wrong.

CHAPTER 29

LUCIFER "LUCKY" AGOSTINO

Ignoring Apollo's knowing smirk, I widened my stance on each side of Persephone before attempting to scoop her up. Though she seemed oblivious to my presence, I continued with my mission, wrapping my arms under her bony body and guiding her to the chair. And she immediately sprung to life. Thrashing, shrieking, biting, and throwing herself around.

"Calm the fuck down, wildcat!" I shouted. Apollo did nothing to help, watching my struggle with a smug look on his face. I practically threw the girl into the chair, and Apollo handed me a set of straps to hold her down. "Ow! Fucking bitch!" Ignoring the fresh set of teeth marks on my bicep, I finished securing her in place. She continued to flail and hiss, as I rubbed my arm and watched her fight against her bindings. "Let her tire herself out," I said, stepping away and taking a seat by the window. "She been like that the entire time?"

Apollo dropped his smirk and nodded. "Why do you think she was lying on the floor? The moment she woke up, she ran circles around the room. Tried getting into my fucking closet, and when I stopped her, she dropped like dead weight. Hasn't moved since."

"Jesus, they put her through the paces. Fucking disgusting." I shook my head. I couldn't imagine what the woman had been through to turn her into… this. "She had so much fire in the back of the car, quoting literature and shit. What the fuck happened to her?"

Apollo shook his head, his eyes drifting to the woman who looked like something straight out of *The Exorcist.* "Adrenaline finally wore off and she passed out. About an hour ago, she snapped awake, mumbling and rocking. Unless you touch her. Then you get *that*." He pointed in her direction.

"She needs to work with us. Her knowledge of Dom's inner workings could help us find him before he finds Alexander." I rubbed at my eyes, feeling the weight of the world on my shoulders.

"I know, boss. He won't get away with it."

Persephone's childlike nursery rhyme cut through our discussion. "That little girl had shimmering blonde hair that glinted in strokes of silver in the sun. Everyone envied those silver highlights, wanting pieces for themselves. But they'd take and take… till there was nothing left of the little girl."

"It's been nonstop stories about a little blonde girl." Apollo shrugged.

"Persephone, I need your help. You have the answers that could save so many other girls from what you went through." Gorgeous, vacant blue eyes stared back at me. "If you tell us all the places Dom held you, we can stop both of the bad men."

Silence stretched between us, her harsh eyes staring through me. "Both? Not all?" Her questions were barely above a whisper. "You want answers to help your problem. Not fix the bigger one."

"One step at a time, my dear," I said.

She cackled in reply. "You're all the same."

"We are *not* the same." Apollo slammed his palms on the table before propelling himself to his feet. He locked his hands around the arms of the chair, their noses almost touching and the lost look in her eyes replaced by an icy-blue fire. "There she is," he muttered, as his lips curled into a half smirk.

"Prove yourself different then. Tell me your plans for destroying the greater evil? Do you have one, outside of taking down those who wronged *your* family?" Noting his silence, Persephone's expression sought to match Apollo's depravity. "You only care to hurt those who hurt *you*. When there are thousands more being hurt every day."

"Do you honestly think we can stop them all?" I said, making her head snap in my direction.

"The biggest offender is related to your future wife. Will you kill him too? Will you destroy the last of her family because of their travesties against strangers? She won't be able to see their destruction as I do." Her blazing eyes were both hardened and chillingly aware. Though I opened my mouth to speak, she ignored me to address Apollo. "You heard my whispered cries. You saw the bruises on my skin. More than once, you watched and saw his anger, his wrath against me. And you did exactly what you are… *nothing*."

She blinked rapidly, and as quickly as it came, the fire was gone. The hollow girl had returned once again. Shoving back from her distant stare, Apollo resumed his pacing. His look of guilt told me all I needed to know. They'd met before, and he'd witnessed Dom's violence firsthand. He wouldn't ignore something like that, unless…

"I thought it was some sick sex game. He had her dressed like a maid at his parents' house. I figured it was a roleplay thing. I swear to you. You know I wouldn't—"

Stopping him short with a wave of my hand, I squeezed his shoulder in support. "I know, brother. I know."

A smashing sound echoed behind me, causing us both to spin with our sidearms at the ready. Persephone had tipped her chair over and was shaking off her bindings from the broken pieces. Slowly reaching behind her back, she untied her hospital gown, removing the flimsy material from her small frame and shrugging it to the floor. Not a single ounce of remorse, embarrassment, or any type of emotion crossed her face as she stood completely naked before us.

"Go get a shower." Apollo's voice was low, not menacing, more… defeated, as she marched to the bathroom without a backwards glance.

"Jesus."

She looked even smaller naked. Every bone in her body moved with the natural sway of her hips. She appeared downright starved, not to mention all the bruises, lacerations, burns… And God only knew what else she'd endured.

"It'll heal. Most of the injuries were meant to be painful, not permanent. It'll be the invisible wounds that will haunt her forever," Apollo said, motioning for me to reclaim my seat at the table. "They wanted her obedient, not damaged."

I lowered myself onto the chair just as Al rang my cell phone. I placed the call on speaker.

"Anthony Moretti is going to find his sons and help them run. There is no doubt in my mind." Pausing to yell out commands into the background, Al continued. "Dominic's hidden office above the strip club was torn apart. Several pages taken from his income sheets, and if Anthony knows how much money the kid's made, he ain't gonna let him quit."

"Not a chance in hell. Keep searching. Maybe you'll uncover one of his stash houses, somewhere he could be holed up…" I quickly disconnected the call, our conversation cut short as Persephone walked back out. Her long blonde hair was wet and braided down her back as the steam from the bathroom filled the air. Even though there were plenty of towels at her disposal, she'd chosen to remain bare. She dropped to her knees at Apollo's feet in a perfect submissive pose, her eyes cast to the floor as she awaited his commands. Apparently, she deemed my friend her new master.

As if reading my internal thoughts, Apollo huffed in response. "Persephone. Get dressed. I showed you where your clothes are."

Rising to her feet with a muttered "yes, master," Persephone was eager to comply, only to return clothed and ready to drop to her knees for a second time.

Apollo snatched her wrist mid-descent, yanking her arm up and forcing her to her toes. "I told you to stop that shit."

And the hellion was unleashed. Persephone lost her calm submissiveness the moment she was touched. She was battling with her need to submit and her fear-driven instinct to protect herself. She kicked and clawed and screamed as Apollo scooped her up and tossed her on the bed, where he straddled her waist before pinning her wrists above her head.

Grabbing a syringe the doctor had left behind, I jabbed it into her bicep, the sleep-inducing effects taking hold almost immediately. "You're safe with us, Persephone. Give us the information we need on Dominic's stash houses, and we'll take care of you for life," I said, watching as the sedative loosened her muscles and softened her features, showing just how young she actually was.

"Safe? I don't understand the meaning. He'll never let me go, not until he's dead." Her words slowly dipped, losing their threatening tone. "I-I-I-I'll never tell-l-l-l," she repeated twice on a whisper before passing out.

"That was helpful." Apollo dragged Persephone up the bed to tuck her between the crisp sheets. "That submissive bullshit is pissing me off. Normally, I find it hot. With her…" He stopped speaking, wandering back to the chairs by the window.

"She wants to talk to her. Bella won't calm down until she sees the girl with her own eyes. I can't let that happen with her like this."

"Having her like this is actually the best time." Looking back towards Persephone's prone form under the covers, Apollo's eyes softened just a fraction. "She's not ready to learn that truth."

I agreed. Gio had been a prick to Bella all her life, while that one shiny beacon of hope had always been her relationship with Dom. If she learned the truth about him, it would ruin her. She could only take so much with all I'd already thrown her way. "I'll bring Bella to visit when she's up. The dose should have her out for at least another eight hours." As my hand closed around the doorknob, something gave me pause. "What are your plans with her?"

"Get the answers we need, then send her away. Somewhere safe. Somewhere of her choosing. No cost to you. I'll set her up."

I watched him watching her. "She's not right in the head, Apollo. I don't know if she ever will be. Do you really want to deal with all that entails?" I motioned towards the mumbling under the covers and raised a questioning brow at him.

"I get it, boss."

I nodded before leaving him to his thoughts, wondering if he was trying to convince me... or himself. There was a look on Apollo's face I'd seen before. One I saw every day in the mirror since meeting Bella. He was feeling something for the girl, and for once, it wasn't a good thing. Persephone was off her rocker and not in a way that could be composed, whereas Apollo needed a partner at his side.

I could only hope that my best friend was telling the truth and actually planned to let her go. Because God save us all when that chick finally decided to enact her revenge.

CHAPTER 30

MIRABELLA MORETTI

I wanted to wake to the sweet scent of fresh flowers and Lucky's cologne every morning. The feel of the clean sheets cocooning me shoved all the negativity of the last several weeks behind me. The warmth soothed my bones and left me feeling safe and sated. Even if there were loose ends still hanging in the air, I didn't care.

"Would you like to see her? Apollo said she's been mostly sleeping."

I rolled to my side to face Lucky and nodded. He then helped me off the bed and into my robe, guiding me down the hallway to Apollo's room. The slightest physical activity was exhausting, but I was on a mission to see what they were doing with Persephone.

I'd never been inside Apollo's room. It was much like Lucky's except smaller… and cleaner. Which was a hard thing to do, considering my fiancé was a control freak. The scent of disinfectant clung to the air and Apollo's polished wood surfaces practically blinded me with their gleam. The massive bed located at the far end of the suite had the tiniest lump of a little girl tucked under the covers. Apollo was sitting on the bed, rising to greet me as I entered. We had fallen into a comfortable friendship recently, and I enjoyed the way his mind worked.

"You should be resting, *mia regina*." He smiled through his concern, and I squeezed his arm reassuringly before stepping next to the bed.

Persephone's blonde hair was clean, a little damp from a recent shower, and fanned out on the pillow like a halo reserved for a celestial being. But my gut warned me this girl was no angel. There was something beneath the surface that told me she was troubled. Beyond that, she was also *trouble*. Especially for my fiancé's second-in-command.

It didn't take a genius to see that Apollo was enamored with her. No, enamored wasn't an appropriate word for someone like Apollo. Obsessed. Crazed. Infatuated. Those were more accurate adjectives when it came to the man who didn't know what to do with emotions.

I couldn't stifle my giggle at the realization that a small girl could bring such a large man to his knees.

"What's so funny, *amore?*" Lucky placed his warm hand on my shoulder, likely assuming all the trauma had me teetering on the edge.

"Just amused by the idea that someone so little could cause so much trouble." I glanced over my shoulder. "There's a darkness to her beauty."

"How is that funny? If you think she's trouble, she's gone. We don't need more to deal with," Lucky hissed and Apollo growled in response.

"Now, now." I placed my palms on Lucky's muscular chest in a placating gesture, and he smiled down at me. "Not too much trouble for Apollo." I flicked my eyes to the man and question, and his jaw clenched.

"I'd never allow a threat to *mia regina* to live under the same roof. You know this."

"I do. And she seems taken with you. Whatever crazy is lurking behind those beautiful eyes, I have no doubt you will be able to handle it. You're capable of helping her get back to the girl she once was." Looking between Lucky and Apollo, I attempted to restrain my chuckle. Each man seemed equal parts annoyed and confused. "I'll let you men discuss your business alone. I'm in need of some comfort food. And a lot less toxic masculinity."

"I'll send someone to your room with your favorite—"

"No, no," I was quick to interrupt. "I'm sure I can manage without anyone's assistance. I already hear the family downstairs. I'll be fine, *mio amore.*" I shut the door before he could argue further and went in search of actual clothes.

Rummaging through the closet in Lucky's room, I pulled down a pair of clean sweatpants and a tank top before making my way to the bathroom to brush my teeth. I did my best to avoid my own gaze in the mirror. Until I couldn't. And that's when I finally saw it. The brutality painted across my face. It was the only way to describe it.

Yellow and purple bruises darkened most of my skin, and dried blood from my split lip was still somewhat visible. Fortunately, a lot of the swelling in my eyes and cheekbones had gone down. If Persephone had been awake, I probably would've startled the poor girl. Pushing images out of my head of how these marks came to be, I dressed and headed downstairs, one agonizing step at a time.

"You look like you went ten rounds with Mike Tyson." Sienna laughed when I walked into the kitchen. "Well, if Mike Tyson was a sniveling little bitch like the bastard who did this to you." She hugged me too tightly, causing me to gasp out in pain. She instantly let me go, wincing at my expression before apologizing.

The rest of the occupants in the room handled me a little more gently, embracing me before I was able to take a seat next to my mother as she handed me a plate of fresh mozzarella, diced tomatoes, and basil dripped in balsamic. My favorite. I practically inhaled the plate, using my thumb to scoop up the dressing from the bottom when I was done.

"I see we haven't lost our appetite. Better heal quickly so I can beat your ass back into shape in the gym," Sienna taunted me, making her little sister Octavia giggle.

"Any word yet?" I whispered to Mario across the table. A chill went down my spine at his answer. Or rather lack of one. Those responsible for hurting me were still unpunished and unaccounted for.

"Do not fret. We will find them." He didn't have to say the rest. I knew he was also telling me: *"And they will pay."*

"No one touches an Agostino and lives to talk about it." Marco didn't say much when the family was all together, but whatever little he offered was always delivered with an underlying intensity.

"I'm not an official Agostino..." I attempted to lighten the mood with a joke, and was met by a stifling silence instead.

"Official ceremony or not, Lucky claimed you a long time ago. Which means you're family. Besides, I've considered your mother family for many years now." Isabella grinned and my mother returned the gesture.

Our mothers were different and yet so similar. They were strong women, who'd take on the world to defend those they loved. One seemed so meek and mild while the other possessed a steeled backbone. Isabella had been fortunate enough to marry a man who cherished and respected her. My mother, not so much. I wasn't delusional enough to believe my father's behavior towards her was anything more than territorial. His idea of having bested Mario.

The more I learned of my father's indiscretions, the more I empathized with my mother. Though she was a woman who was noticed for her beauty, behind those sparkling eyes was an undeniable depth. She was a force to be reckoned with, though her methods were more subtle. Something I'd only just started to recognize.

And I had a hell of a lot of respect for Isabella. She'd known about her husband's past, and instead of ostracizing the woman he'd once loved, she welcomed my mother with open arms. Seeing her as more than just a friend and treating her like family. Which was rare in a world so bloodthirsty and dog-eat-dog.

Mafioso. Mobsters. Made men. Whatever you wanted to call them, they needed our strength. Because their jobs painted us all with targets. We weren't just family. We were liabilities. Meaning there was no room for weakness. We had to band together. If not out of respect than for sheer survival.

Lucky and Apollo marched into the room several minutes later, taking their seats at the table. Unlike the other enforcers, I noticed how Apollo was considered family. I needed to ask Lucky for the specifics of that story one day. I was certain there was much more to the bond they shared.

Reaching for my hand under the table, Lucky gave it a light squeeze, his way of checking in on me. For now, we had decided to keep the pregnancy to ourselves. At least until I was a bit farther along.

"Any updates on our houseguest?" Mario directed the question at Apollo, but it was Lucky who answered.

"She's got a lot of physical and mental healing to do."

"I will be moving her into my home once the doctor has cleared her. She won't be your problem much longer," Apollo added, glancing at Mario before returning to his plate. Sienna and Octavia had been chatting amongst themselves, but immediately stopped, their matching glares snapping in the enforcer's direction.

I could only imagine the pain those words had inflicted on Sienna. Her and Apollo's mutual attraction was never acted on, out of respect for Lucky. Although I knew deep down she hoped and prayed for her brother's blessing, it would never come. Apollo wouldn't ask that of his best friend. An action that told me he wasn't good enough for her. Sienna was an incredible woman; she deserved a man who would fight for her. And Apollo wasn't that man. He didn't have the emotions required to give her the life or the love she was due. Whatever sick infatuation he had with Persephone only served to drive that point home.

His unwarranted protectiveness and plans to move the girl into his private residence showed his true feelings. He hid behind his loyalty to the family, while ignoring the fact that he had plenty of other options, should he choose to act on them.

Apollo was showing his card, and I had a feeling it was a queen.

The table clattered with moving dishes as Sienna shot to her feet, her face devoid of emotions, and exited the room without another word. Apollo watched her leave with a cold, yet curious stare. He quickly returned to his plate, ignoring the inquisitive looks from everyone around him. The man was utterly oblivious to what he'd done, and that fact made me sad for Sienna. Hopefully this was the realization she needed to see he'd never feel the same for her.

Besides showering, I spent the next few weeks in bed, sleeping and reading my time away. Lucky came to me after I was asleep and was gone long before I awoke. He spent hours upon hours hunting those who needed to meet *il diavolo*. I'd never doubt his affections or his desire to protect me, but the sudden lack of physical contact was detrimental to my healing. He was here with me physically, just not intimately. And I was crawling out of my skin with need.

Weeks! It had been weeks! My lady bits were screaming for attention. And by attention, I meant Lucky needed to fuck my brains out. It wasn't the politest way to put it but the man had turned me ravenous. Yeah, it was definitely all his fault. Or maybe this had been me all along? Either way, my vagina needed special attention. The bruises were fading while my lust grew stronger by the minute.

I'd planned to seduce him but my stupid mouth had other ideas. "Without you, I'm so weak," I grumbled into the pillow, as I lay with my back to his front.

"What did you say, *mi regina?*" His warm breath tickled my ear.

"When I was taken… I felt so weak, lost. I prayed for death. I'm not proud to admit it but it's the truth. I couldn't handle the thought of living without you."

"How does that make you weak?" Tucking my hair behind my ear, Lucky pulled my shoulder to roll me onto my back. "Human beings have a natural instinct for self-preservation. Our minds are wired that way. To do whatever it takes to ensure our survival. You fought for an escape, Bella. There is nothing wrong with being confused on how to save yourself."

"There is. I knew you'd come for me. I knew it with everything I had. Yet, as soon as that knowledge was challenged, I gave up. I let him win." Tears burned trails down my cheeks, the words choking me worse than Alexander ever could.

"He didn't win. You're here. With me. With our growing family." He lowered a hand and placed it over my stomach. "Despite your injuries, you ensured we rescued Persephone. You're not weak. You're a fighter, *mio amore*. You just have to remember to fight for yourself as passionately as you fight for others." His words and eyes held so much conviction I almost believed him. "After everything that's happened in such a short time, you have done nothing but show your strength. And earned everyone's respect. On your own. You did that, not me."

"I just hate the power I gave him... allowing him to see me broken."

Lucky shook his head, his gaze narrowing in on me to emphasize his point. "Battered and broken are two different things. Alexander is a sick excuse for a man, who battered a woman half his size. *That* isn't broken. Broken would be giving up. Broken would be shutting yourself down because of what he did. Broken would be lying in this bed with none of the fire I see in your eyes. And, Bella, that fire burns bright. You are far from broken."

It was a conversation that would stick with me in the darker days, and help me enjoy the lighter ones. I might have been beaten, battered, and bruised. But I wasn't broken. I wouldn't give Alexander the satisfaction.

CHAPTER 31

MIRABELLA MORETTI

"I want to marry you."

I rolled over. Lucky was leaning against the headboard, my favorite dazzling smile on his lips. Wiggling my giant engagement ring at him, I matched his expression. "I believe that's what I said yes to."

He shook his head, sliding down the headboard to take me into his arms. "I mean today. After almost losing you, I can't bear the thought of waiting another day. I need to marry you today."

I couldn't agree more. I'd marry him in this bed if it meant we could be together forever. "But all of the planning?" I didn't really care for any of it, and he knew that. But our parents needed the pomp and circumstance.

"I won't share you with anyone anymore. Fuck our families. This is about us."

"YES!" I shouted my response much louder than I needed to and attacked him like an awkward baby horse. Until my legs were tossed over each side of his waist and I was straddling him.

Before he could deny me again, I latched my lips on to his, cutting off his protests. I knew he was being careful so as not to hurt me, but I

285

had been in this bed for weeks. I was as healed as I was going to get, besides the slow-fading bruises still darkening my skin.

"I love you. Let's get married here and now. In bed. Like this," he insisted, as I lowered myself down on his dick, moaning as if it were the first time. He grabbed my waist, thrusting his hips in a torturously measured pace.

"Lucky. I love you. But, baby, I need you to fuck me hard and fast."

His eyes blazed with unfettered lust before he quickened his movements. He pumped upwards. Over and over again. And I lost control within minutes, tossing my head back to cry out in ecstasy. Lucky wasn't far behind me, his grip tightening as he grunted his release.

I'd barely caught my breath before he was dragging me into the bathroom, informing me that a dress would be waiting and to move my "pretty little ass." I showered fast and exited the room to hair and makeup people already waiting with a gorgeous white gown. A simple wedding dress, this was not.

Instead, I was offered a gorgeous white Vivienne Westwood gown with a delicate drape corset and a Theresa skirt with silver lace. My makeup was done with a light smokey effect to make my eye colors pop. The woman did such an amazing job with the airbrushing. My face appeared almost normal, the bruising properly concealed, while my hair was left loose with slight curls at the ends. The details and this man of mine were perfect—a word that hardly seemed to do any of it justice. Regardless of the shitstorm that had engulfed our lives more recently, I was happy. And it was all because of Lucky.

The rest of the morning was a blur of tears—mostly from our mothers—light conversation, and laughter. And before I knew it, it was time to walk down the aisle.

"Mama. Will you walk me out to him?" My father still hadn't resurfaced in his 'search' for Gio and Dom. There was no word. No concern for us. Lucky knew more than he was letting on. I was sure of it. But that was a matter for another day.

"Yes, darling. I would be honored." Everyone else scurried out of the room, giving us a minute alone. "I love you more than anything. You know that, right?"

"I know, Madre. I am who I am because of you. You've always protected, loved, and supported me. We were dealt a shitty hand when it comes to the men in our family, but you've always been my rock."

"Until Lucky. He's a good man, Bella."

I smiled and nodded.

"You know I didn't willingly leave you in Italy without calls or letters. I wanted you home, but more than that I wanted you protected. Your father used our contact as a form of punishment. It was the leverage he needed to ensure I complied."

"I know. We both know what it's like to live with the Moretti men."

She sighed as she adjusted my veil. "You're about to be an Agostino. You're free."

I squealed in excitement before turning back to face her.

"Don't." She raised a hand to stop me. "Your father is done. You realize that, right? I don't know all the details but whatever mess he's gotten himself into, I have no doubt Mario will destroy him."

It was a harsh realization. The fact that I felt relief more than anything else. And I think my mother did too. "You're free, Mama."

She smiled and cupped my cheeks. "We both are." Then she looped her arm in mine and guided me towards my future husband.

The staircase was covered in floral arrangements, which seemed to thicken the air with their scent. My mother escorted me through the house and out the back door. It was a recreation of our first date that I had loved so much. Tall tables were spread around the brick-covered terrace with fresh flowers on every available surface.

The sun was just beginning to set but the walkway leading to Isabella's gardens was littered with hundreds of candles. The path weaved and wrapped around the yard until we approached the hidden pergola, where hundreds of red and white rose petals bestrewed the ground. Tears filled my eyes and I could feel my mother's body racking with quiet sobs. As we turned the corner, I couldn't contain my gasp. Large lanterns with flames dancing in the center lined the aisle on each side, while Lucky was positioned at the end in his meticulously tailored black suit. His dad and brother stood to one side with Apollo right next to him, his sisters and mother stationed opposite them.

Once we were within arm's reach, my mother paused and kissed my cheek before handing me over to the man of my dreams. "The future king of New York or not, this woman is more than you deserve. She needs to be loved and cherished like no other. She is owed the world, the moon and the stars. All of which you will deliver to her on a shiny platter. No tears, unless of joy. No sadness by your hand, and nothing more than happiness for you both." She held me a moment longer. A little tighter. "Because *il diavolo* or not, I promise you this. I will. Fucking. Destroy. You." My mother's voice was so lighthearted it somehow made her words sound that much more threatening.

Mario threw his head back in laughter while Isabella chuckled. None of us had any doubt that my mother was one hundred percent serious. No one messed with her baby girl. And it seemed with the Moretti men missing, she was able to reignite the fire they had long tried to extinguish. With a flick of her wrist, my hand landed in Lucky's as he nodded his understanding, his expression solemn.

"Your mother's threats or not, I promise you this: You will never know another day without love and happiness. I will give you a house filled with fresh flowers every day and the love and laughter of a warm and caring family to cherish you as much as I do. You're my love, my life, and my future. And fuck if I'm not the luckiest bastard alive."

The officiant spoke to our small crowd of onlookers; however, I was so lost in Lucky's eyes I barely heard a word of it. And before I knew it, we were exchanging vows.

Lucky cupped my cheek and tugged me closer. "Mirabella, it was five long years ago I got my first glimpse of you. The most gorgeous pair of mismatched eyes begged me for help. I was enamored with a girl whose tears burned into my soul. From this day forward, I will do anything and everything to never see that look on your face again. You are mine, *mio amore*."

Do. Not. Cry. Choked by emotion, I attempted to explain myself to him. "I was destined to find a man who was going to free me from the hell I was born into. I remember you that day. I was surrounded by men who didn't care about me my entire life. Until you, this stranger, stared back at me with concern. Understanding. Devotion. I think I fell in love with you that day. I just didn't know it yet. Yes, I am yours, *il diavolo.*"

If I could explain this moment in words, I would. But none would do it justice. Perfection seemed to pale in comparison. Everything I'd been praying for since that day I was told I was betrothed had come true. It was better than my dreams because he was real. And I was more than ready for our first kiss as man and wife. A kiss that would unite our families—what was left of mine—to be the powerhouse of the city. A kiss that would bind this man to me in sickness and in health. A single kiss that, in this moment, would diminish the world around us to just the two of us.

I closed my eyes and waited for the kiss that wouldn't come. Time seemed to slow until I could hear nothing but the roaring static burning holes into my ears. It wasn't the lack of contact I noticed first. It was the piercing screams that broke me from my state of marital bliss while the heavy gunfire and the bustle of movement around me had my eyes flying open. Lucky was clutching me in his arms, rage rolling off him in waves. But beneath that, I saw concern. Worry. Desperation. As my eyes drifted down to my chest, I finally saw why.

Blood. I was soaked in blood. The adrenaline coursing through my veins left me frozen in place and I couldn't process where all the blood was coming from. His shirt was splattered red and my dress was coated in it. I sucked in a deep breath, grabbing his jacket as my legs gave way beneath me and pain ripped through my rib cage.

"Bella! Goddamn it! Please, no! Please, *mio amore*! No!" The agony in his voice hurt more than the bullet in my chest. "Baby, no."

Gunfire continued to boom in the distance, our private ceremony devolving into a chaotic bloodbath. Mario came out of nowhere, shielding Lucky as he dragged me out of the line of fire. His mouth was moving but I couldn't hear him. Just the beating of my own heart.

The sound was deep, unnatural, thrumming like a pair of hummingbird wings.

Holding Lucky's face in my hands, I pulled him to me. One last kiss was all I needed. The same kiss that was supposed to unite us was now our goodbye. I knew it. I could feel death's grotesque hand slowly gripping my throat, making it near impossible to breathe, hear the bell tolling in the distance, and see the light beyond this realm.

I could only pray this loss didn't destroy him, that vengeance would be a strong enough force to drive Lucky forward. But my heart ached for my unborn child who hadn't even had the chance to take the world by storm. A child who would never know the love of his parents or feel the warmth of the sun. A child who was damned before he even took his first breath.

"I love you," I whispered, hoping he could hear my final words and cherish them as much as I did our time together.

I wanted to fight. To show him I was as strong as he claimed me to be. But I was just so tired, my eyelids so heavy. So I gave in. I let them —whoever they were—win. But the darkness didn't bring peace; it brought unrest.

CHAPTER 32

We turned over every stone in the city, searching for answers on each of the men who were deserving of more than death. I'd already lost count of the number of lives taken by my hands in an attempt to get the information I needed from those either unable or unwilling to provide it.

Bella was healing physically but her troubled sleep was carving new wounds into my heart. I'd failed her and every nightmare reminded me of that. And now I was failing her again.

Every night that I climbed into our bed with her warm body against me was slow torture. I was trying to let her mend but my body begged me for the release I knew we both needed.

This woman called to me. She was my heart, the lifeline that kept me sane. And I couldn't wait to marry her. While I was hunting down dead ends, I had our mothers and my sisters organizing an impromptu wedding. Close friends, constituents, and family would be the only attendees and I'd called in extra security.

Every detail was organized and ready to go for today. I couldn't wait to see this incredible woman walk down the aisle, to be handed off to me for the rest of our lives. I quickly bustled her into the shower, elation seeping into my soul at the look of excitement on her face.

Leaving her to her morning routine, I headed to see if my father had any updates. I found him seated behind his desk in his office. His face seemed to age before my eyes, worry adding to the lines on his forehead. We both wanted the threats against Bella neutralized; however, his expression told me there were no changes.

"How can they just disappear?" I asked, my tone harsher than I intended. The raise of his brow told me I was dancing on a very thin line. Son or not, he was the boss and demanded respect. However, I was doing my best to keep my barely contained rage from exploding every minute of the day.

We hadn't left a single stone unturned and yet all the potential threats were in the wind. With Persephone still drugged and barely lucid, we hadn't been able to find Dominic, which we hoped would lead to the other two Morettis. The more we delved into Alexander and Yuri's dealings, the more I was sure Bella's family was involved. We'd confirmed Gio had his hand in the proverbial pot, but there was no way he was the mastermind. Anthony and Dom held the answers we needed. I just knew it. So I needed to find them and introduce them to my basement. Alexander was the most prominent threat against Bella and he was like a ghost. The moment that we got word of a possible location, he was gone. And my control was hanging on by a thread.

"I know you're in pain and beyond fucking stressed but watch your goddamned tone with me. I'm fighting just as hard to get an answer. My biggest concern right now is ensuring you two make it down that aisle in one piece. With God only knows what breathing down our necks, I don't need your shit attitude added to my plate."

He was right. This wasn't his fault. His failure. It was mine. "I'm taking her away after the wedding. To the compound in Italy. She'll be safer there. No one would dare mess with her for fear of angering the *capo dei capi*."

Everyone had a boss. Even Mario Agostino. My father's boss was the head of the Italian family in Vatican City. His compound was surrounded by a high stone wall with hundreds of men scouring the area for outsiders. He even had a small number of catholic radicals protecting the Pope on his payroll. The Boss was more than willing to host Bella when I reached out to him.

"This is why you're my son. I called him earlier today, and he told me you'd already spoken. Serafina, your mother and sisters will be staying there as well. We protect what's ours, son."

"Pops… I…" I was at a loss for words. These emotions were all so new. And it was hard to admit I wasn't in control.

"It's overwhelming, isn't it? Loving a woman more than anything else in the world, wanting to protect her more than you care to protect yourself."

"It is… But it's the not knowing that's most unsettling."

"I know, son. It's troublesome to me as well. Alexander will no doubt show himself soon. But we need something to bring out the missing Morettis. A Trojan horse, if you will." His eyes glinted with a look I knew all too well.

"What do you have up your sleeve?" He had an idea, but he'd never share the details until the plan was already underfoot.

"Rest easy, son. We have something in place. We will work it out." He slapped my back as I tried to offer him some semblance of a smile. "Now, let's get you married."

"Sir?" My father's head of security was waiting at the door.

"Go, son. I'll be there shortly."

His soldier's face gave away nothing, but behind his eyes, something was there. Some sort of information. A missing piece of the puzzle. A silent discussion that seemed to have my father's spine straightening.

"Lucifer. Go."

As he shoved me through and slammed the office door, I waited a beat, on the off chance I could hear their conversation. It wasn't like me to pry into my father's business, but my hackles had risen. There was news of our situation. When I couldn't make out anything more than a few mumbled words, I turned on my heel and headed down the hall. He'd inform me the moment they had something concrete. My only job right now was to marry the love of my life.

The irony of the situation wasn't lost on me. It hadn't been all that long ago that I had stormed into that same office, demanding to know more about the girl who'd been escorted out of the house in tears. And now she was all mine.

Getting dressed took up my remaining time, and it wasn't long before I was waiting for my bride to make her appearance. I had no interest in exchanging pleasantries or entertaining guests. And if it weren't for the fact that I wanted everyone in attendance to know Bella was my wife and off-limits, no one would be here at all.

Distant movement caught my attention. It was too cliché to say she took my breath away. There was more to it than that. My future was strolling towards me, and so my breath didn't leave my body. Instead, too much air filled it up. My chest heaved with the overwhelming weight of her beauty, while my feet were cemented in place—though the rest of me was begging to charge ahead, shake her loose of her mother's grip, and finalize the ceremony here and now.

As I took my beloved's hand and we exchanged our vows, I could barely register anyone or anything else until it was too late. Until she was bleeding out in my arms, and nothing else mattered. Not my status, my money, my contacts, or my rage. None of it prevented this moment from happening.

"Bella! Open your eyes!"

Her breathing was slow and shallow, the color draining from her cheeks, and her body motionless. And I couldn't help but think that this was karma rearing its ugly head in my direction, recompense for all the lives I'd taken.

"Bella! Breathe, baby, breathe," I begged to no avail.

"*Mia bambina*! No!" Serafina crawled across the grass to reach her daughter.

"Damn it! Fina, stay down." My father attempted to grab her leg and drag her back to cover. She kicked him loose and propelled herself forward, quickly stumbling to her feet and pulling Bella to her chest.

Indecision stunted my senses as I realized I had two options. I could leave my love with her mother, trusting Serafina to get her to safety while I helped neutralize the threat. Or I could stay and hope my men could handle it on their own.

My eyes scanned the chaos as I teetered on the edge of what to do. Bodies were strewn across the yard, most of whom I didn't recognize, until I spotted Apollo behind a tree, a gun in each arm as he attempted to suppress the returning fire. We locked eyes, and I could see the pain there. He was just as worried about Bella as I was.

"Go, Lucky. The doctor has her and I will watch over them." My father shoved me aside as he helped our personal physician take Bella from my arms.

"Lucky!" Apollo called out my name as a different kind of pain traveled up and down my arm. I had been so lost to my inner turmoil, I'd put myself right in their crosshairs.

Blood sprayed across Serafina's face as a bullet tore through my barely healed shoulder. She tugged me behind a makeshift blockade of metal chairs, before tearing the hem of her dress and wrapping it around my arm to stop the bleeding. "It's fine. It went through the muscle. I can see the exit wound. You'll be all right," she assured me with a nod.

Apollo was yelling orders in the distance. He and Al were backed into a corner and taking on heavy gunfire.

"Fuck." Checking for my 9mm in the back of my pants, I felt someone tug it free. I glanced behind me to find Serafina propped up and taking aim.

"Lucky, here." My father passed me a new piece while stuffing two more into the back of my pants. "Give her a moment, then move your fucking ass. I will go with Bella to the hospital."

I nodded my gratitude and waited for Serafina to take out the machine gun, much like her daughter had done in the warehouse. I then hopped over the chairs and hauled ass to my men, shoving my thoughts aside and allowing my rage to consume me... to get the job done.

"How are they?" Al asked, once I'd slid down behind them.

"Sienna has a flesh wound from a bullet on her hip and my mother is bleeding pretty heavily from the head. Serafina was the one who took down the machine gun."

Al's eyes widened in surprise. "Guess we know where Miss Bella gets her aim." He chuckled, and I flinched at the mention of her name.

"Boss, please don't tell me..." His words trailed off as I watched his initial sadness morph into rage. Rising to his feet, Al charged around the tree with Apollo on his heels. They nodded at each other and flanked our remaining targets. I watched for a moment before catching a glimpse of the piece of shit himself.

Alexander stood far enough back to avoid the barrage of bullets, sending his men to do the dirty work for him. The apple didn't fall far from the tree. He was just as much a coward as his father. Apollo was taking out the Russians one by one, until those who remained were either dead or retreating.

Alexander turned and attempted to flee, but he didn't see the real threat looming at his back as my feet stomped pavement, and I took him down by sheer force of will. He landed with a thud, his face taking the brunt of the impact, and I rolled him over.

"Hello, you dumb motherfucker."

His eyes flicked from side to side, as if searching for someone to save him.

"You're on your own, bitch," Apollo grunted beside me, his black and white suit painted with various shades of red.

"You're ours now, you piece of shit," Al barked, holding a hand over the oozing wound in his leg.

"Fuck you all! She was mine. If I can't have her, like fuck would I let you take her," Alexander hissed, grunting as Apollo's fist smashed into his face until laughter revealed a set of broken, bloody teeth. "How is Bella anyway?" He grinned.

CHAPTER 33

APOLLO DELUCA

There was something to be said about watching someone you're close to fall apart. To have no way to help them in their despair other than to be the silent ally at their side.

The leader who ruled his world with an iron fist was a shell of the man he once was. After the massacre at the wedding, and having sent Alexander off to the basement with Al, we headed to the hospital where Bella had been taken. The car ride was eerily quiet as thoughts of death and loss hung heavy in the air.

Mrs. Moretti sat in the waiting room alongside the Agostinos, all with the same bleak expressions on their faces. Mirabella was the glue that held these two families together. She inspired us all to be better. Do better.

"What's the news?" Lucky asked as we approached the women bursting into tears at the sight of him.

"She was taken into surgery. We've heard nothing yet." Serafina Moretti was an older version of her daughter. Years spent under her husband's thumb and yet her fire still burned bright.

"Does anyone want coffee?" Sienna rose to her feet, turning her back on me. Several nods of gratitude were issued before she stomped off in a huff.

"I'll help her." Leaving Lucky to console his mother and talk business with his father, I followed the dark-haired beauty, quickly stepping into a small alcove in the lobby, where there was a coffee dispenser and several vending machines.

Twirling in her towering heels, Sienna offered me a smile as fake as her present emotionless facade. "I'm good, thanks." She turned her back on me yet again, punching the numbers into the keypad with a little too much gusto.

I was many things: murderous, psychopathic, emotionally inept. But above all else, I was determined. I didn't understand social cues or gratuitous exchanges; therefore, her current anger seemed transposed and I wasn't in the mood to deal with it. It had been a fuck of a day and this attitude wouldn't work for me.

Snatching her wrist, I spun Sienna around to face me before pushing her against the vending machine with my body. Even with the added height of her heels, I looked down at the enraged beauty before me. Fire brewing in her eyes and she was still a sight to behold.

"Get. Off. Me." I could hear her teeth grinding between each word.

Yeah, she was pissed.

"To what am I owed this misplaced irritation, pray tell?"

She liked to pretend she hated how I spoke to her. But I was so attuned to her body I could hear the spike in her breathing whenever I'd quote Shakespeare or Mark Twain.

"This isn't about you, Apollo. My sister-in-law is getting surgery on an injury that should've been prevented." Tears began filling her eyes. "The chances of her survival are slim to none and I know it will kill my brother. Right now, all I care about is getting a fucking cup of coffee." Shoving me out of her way, Sienna spun around, jabbing the dispense button several more times as small, barely visible sobs shook her shoulders. Her attempts at constantly hiding her feelings didn't surprise me. Where I had none, Sienna was plagued by a revolving door of emotions, many of which she had no control over.

"The coffee is already in the cup." Stepping around her, I took it out of the machine and started another serving.

"Thank you." It was barely audible as she held the warm Styrofoam in her hand.

"Whatever happens, we will get through it, together. Just like this family has always done." Whenever strife hit the Agostinos, they banded together, demonstrating a strength and impenetrability like nothing I'd seen before. It was peculiar to me, their inability to shut off their emotions to deal with the problem at hand.

I understood Sienna's concern. On the off chance Bella didn't survive, a piece of Lucky would die with the girl. As much as I didn't recognize that feeling myself, I could see the devastation on his face. I had read enough about the biological system and the human mind to pinpoint the neurological distress signals coursing through his body.

"We won't get through this together," Sienna mumbled, pushing me away when I attempted to draw her closer.

"The hell we won't. I'm here, Sienna. I will be the strength you need."

She shook her head and retreated to the farthest corner of the vestibule.

There were many sides to Sienna Agostino. As she stood in front of me in her ripped designer dress, with a hole at the hip revealing her fresh stitches, I wondered which one was about to attack. Hidden behind an expensive label, a female version of every Italian cliché, and a too-smart-for-her-own-good persona was a wildcat.

She was an enigma, looking to hide behind couture and familial expectations. One minute she was threatening to flay you alive, and the next she was crying over a romance novel. She was the CEO of a Fortune 500 company, while also fearing she'd be forever buried beneath the weight of her family name. She fought with men twice her size and was swift enough to avoid being taken down. During my studies on cognitive psychology, I learned Sienna had what other women wanted. Yet here she was, hiding behind her coffee cup and staring at the dark liquid like it held all the answers. She was upset about her family—true—but there was something else lancing that vulnerable heart of hers.

"Fucking spill, Sienna."

"We won't get through this or anything else *together.* Once all of this is handled, I'm leaving." Raising a brow at her outburst only fueled her rage. "I want more than mafia vendettas. More than old-school Italian facades and men attempting to gain power at the expense of others' misfortunes. I crave more, someone offering more."

Both at a loss for words, we stared deeply into each other's eyes as the silence stretched on for a few more moments. I was aware of her dislike for the parts of the mafia world that disgraced women, outside the Agostino household. But the mere mention of leaving everyone, leaving all of it behind, was something else.

"Sienna."

Raising a hand, she stopped my words and stepped into my space. "I've always used your lack of emotional capacity to justify why things between us would never work. Loyalty to Lucky and the family was the only real thing you felt. I was okay with that. With believing one day, emotions aside, you'd see we were a good fit." Setting her coffee on the counter, she peered up into my eyes. "But I was so wrong."

"Sienna…"

Cutting me off again, she spun on her heel before pausing at the threshold. "I hid behind your apathy because I thought it was hardening my heart. Making me stronger. But all that did was brutalize everything I believed in. And once I saw the emotions that you've been keeping hidden, I realized I was a fucking idiot."

The more recent events had set the woman on edge, to the point she was seeing things that weren't there. Whatever sentiments she had were totally irrelevant. I didn't feel anything outside of the loyalty I'd given to the Agostinos.

"You know my clinical diagnosis…"

Her chest rose and fell with her panted breaths, her ample breasts heaving with the motion. Further proving that loyalty and lust were the only two things I truly felt. And *neither* could technically be considered emotions.

"That's bullshit. You're bullshit," she hissed the accusation, drawing out the suspense before asking me a question that felt like a slap across the face. "Did Persephone settle into your home okay?"

That's what this was all about? She believed I harbored feelings for the damaged soul I'd helped escape Alexander? That girl had several issues, none of which stirred anything inside me, besides the rage her singing seemed to elicit.

"The fuck that have anything to do…"

Lucky's pained roar in the next room stopped our conversation.

"No!" Sienna rushed past me, running towards the sound of more inconsolable screaming. I followed behind her, watching the only family I'd ever known collapse at the surgeon's feet, his scrubs more red than green at this point.

"Fuck." I shook off my initial shock and marched towards the man I considered a brother.

Mirabella Moretti was the glue now removed from the two most prominent families in New York. She was the calm that rendered the devil tame. The loss created an odd feeling in the center of my chest. But I dismissed it as nothing more than a sense of foreboding as Lucky tore through the hospital towards the exit.

I flicked my gaze to Mario, the only real father I ever had, and recognized his mask of indifference. Though he clung to his wife and Serafina in a manner that would suggest comfort, something about his posturing bothered me. It bordered on guilt as he stood witness to the devastation the news of Bella's passing left in its wake. After working beside this man for so many years, nothing about his current expression made sense. I knew for a fact that he'd ensure his enemies would pay, but there was something else lingering beneath the surface too. The way he locked his face down told me he was plotting, and his future plans wouldn't be what everyone expected.

Shouting alerted me to a rising commotion outside, the noise sending more security charging through the doors. I was quick to follow them. Watching Lucky punch, kick, and throw the men attempting to restrain him around like rag dolls would've been comical if it weren't for the look on his face.

They'd just taken his queen, the one person who'd been able to calm his rage. Now they got what they wanted. *Il diavolo* was coming for them.

And it would rain fucking blood.

CHAPTER 34

LUCIFER "LUCKY" AGOSTINO

"I'm sorry. We did everything we could…"

It took every ounce of restraint I had within me to not grip the doctor by the throat and watch the life drain from his eyes.

He was sorry.

He did everything he could.

If that were the case, then Bella would be alive. Instead, the best thing that had ever happened to me, one of the few truly good people in this world, was gone. Dead. Snuffed out by a piece of shit with some self-imposed claim on her. Alexander might've been the asshole who ordered the hit, but Gio was the bastard who started it all. My efforts to find him and the other Moretti men just became my one and only priority. Their deaths wouldn't bring her back or take away my torment, but it would ensure they didn't have the chance to live in a world they didn't deserve.

Apollo slammed me against the hospital wall, snapping me from my thoughts of revenge and forcing me to take in the aftermath of my rage. Several members of the hospital security lay beaten and battered on the concrete by the entrance. Police sirens were fast approaching, and I knew they were coming for me.

"Apollo, get him out of here. I will deal with this." My father had always been a force, but the man before me was one I didn't recognize. He shoved me aside and we rushed towards the waiting SUV.

"Take me to him."

Apollo and Al both nodded, the car lurching forward on squealing tires as we pealed out of the parking lot. The ride to the basement went by in a blur, while dangerous thoughts plagued my subconscious. I couldn't—wouldn't—think about her in this moment. I'd wait to take my grief out on the man who caused it, on the stupid fuck I'd kill a thousand times over and it still wouldn't be enough.

As we bounded down the basement stairs, our shoes echoed off the concrete walls, the metal frame threatening to give way from the force of our steps. My men were spread throughout the room, their glares doing little to mask the mixture of sorrow and rage that permeated the air. There was no doubt that they'd heard the news and were awaiting my response.

My mind swirled as I stood in front of the chair presently bolted to the floor and holding a bound and beaten Alexander. A loud static roared through my head. The same noise that usually charged me into action now seemed to cement my feet in place as I stared down at my prey.

"Lucky. I didn't expect to see you so soon. I assumed you'd be on your honeymoon."

I didn't flinch, didn't give a fucking thing away.

"No? How is the blushing bride?" Spitting blood on the floor, Alexander smiled at me triumphantly.

"She's well, thanks. Sends her regards."

His face dropped, confusion pulling his brows together. He wanted a rise out of me, and I wasn't about to play into his hand. "Pity she didn't come herself. Why is that?" He was fishing for answers, while I was struggling to stay in the moment.

She was gone, dead, taken by his hands…

STOP! Handle what you can control.

And right now, the only control over life and death currently within my grasps was that of the man in front of me. He was dead, a corpse waiting to be buried.

Without hesitation, I attacked. Right, left, right, left. Over and over, I pounded my fists into him. Even after he was battered beyond recognition, his faculties no longer conscious, and my hands covered in open sores, I refused to relent. My chest heaving, I stepped back to stare down at the lump of ruined flesh slumped over in the chair. My eyes burned from the tears pouring down my face, tiny drops of pain fleeing my body at the realization that my heart was missing.

"Keep him on ice." Ignoring Apollo's attempts at cleaning me up, I stormed back up the stairs.

Hotel guests took in my deranged appearance, and immediately ran in the opposite direction. Blood soaked my shirt and pants, my ruined wedding attire coated in unsated vengeance. I grabbed my phone, barking orders to pull the car around before storming through the lobby. The SUV turned the corner as I reached the far door.

"Take me to my father," I ground out between clenched teeth, typing away on my phone and issuing a new list of instructions. I was far from done with Alexander. He needed some time to heal, but just enough so that he could still see what was coming for him. I'd kill him ten times over, then bring the bastard back to life just to make him suffer again.

Barreling inside the family compound, I was surprised by the silence. "They're at a hotel in the city. I didn't want them here while we fixed things." My father loomed on the threshold of his office.

"I want Gio's head on a fucking platter. Now!" I followed him to his desk and immediately went for the expensive bourbon.

"I know, son. I have things in play to handle that. Things I hope you can forgive me for. My heart is always in the right place when it comes to my family."

"What do you mean?" I tossed back the bourbon, only to refill it again.

"I love all of you, all of my kids. And I love Bella and her mother… your mother. I may not always make the best decisions, but sometimes we have to make tough choices in order to gain the upper hand. To protect what's ours."

"Well, I didn't protect what was mine," I said. Because it was the truth.

His mouth opened and closed a few times before he finally settled on silence and collapsed in his chair. "You tried, son." Filling my glass again and pouring him one, I sat in front of my father's desk, motioning for him to get on with it. "Anthony Moretti is still in the wind but there is a small chance he knew about the Russian connection." Looking pointedly at me, he continued. "I have intel suggesting that Gio was the front man but Anthony knew what was going on. He'd planned to sell Bella off, until I requested her presence in the States."

"He's fucking dead. I want them found." I squeezed the glass in my hand so tightly it threatened to shatter.

"I told you, son, I have a plan. I believe it will draw them out but there are repercussions for my actions. I hope you can forgive me, but I truly believe it's what's best for everyone."

Dismissing his concern with a shrug, I nodded. "As long as it brings them to me on a silver fucking platter, I don't care. The Agostinos always get their men and the Morettis have a lot to answer for." Throwing back the rest of the amber liquid, I let the taste settle in my mouth. I was practically salivating at the promise of more bloodshed.

"Bella's funeral has been arranged for two days from now."

I rose to my feet, choosing to ignore his comments. The last thing I wanted to do was talk about leaving my wife's body to rot in the ground. "I have someone to see." As I charged for the door, his words gave me pause.

"Take care of that hand before you go back. You have no idea what a leech like Alexander could be carrying in his blood."

I didn't respond, heading to my room, where I showered and tended to my hand. Dressing in worn jeans and an old t-shirt, I went through the motions while trying to ignore the ache in my chest. I slammed my feet into my shoes, intent on returning to the city.

Whatever my father had planned was weighing heavily on his shoulders. But I didn't care as long as I got my revenge in blood.

Alexander wasn't going anywhere anytime soon, so now I just needed the Morettis in my grasp.

I slipped into the driver's seat of my personal vehicle and immediately punched the steering wheel. Over and over and over and over and over. The pain I'd been trying to push back had finally resurfaced. I'd loved Bella from the moment I'd first laid eyes on her and every moment since wasn't nearly enough. She was loyal, smart, and so spectacularly beautiful. Each memory in my head burned an individual hole into my heart, until it hurt to breathe.

Pulling up outside the penthouse, I left my car in the street and walked through the lobby to the elevators, where I texted Al and Apollo to meet me upstairs in the penthouse. I wouldn't rest until she was avenged. The doors to the elevator were about to close when a slender arm stopped them. Not bothering to look up from my phone, I ignored whoever it was and continued to glare at my phone. Once Al and Apollo responded, I tucked the device into my pocket and stared ahead, my eyes landing on the last person I wanted to see.

"Hi." Tatianna purred in greeting, licking her lips as she eyed me from head to toe. "Want some company?"

I glanced at the button panel and realized she'd never picked a floor.

"Please, Lucky. Let me show you how sorry I am for your loss. Bella—"

Staring at her in a mixture of grief, rage, and confusion, I barely registered that the elevator had come to a stop just outside my penthouse. White noise replaced the sound of her breathing as I reached forward, and before I could stop myself, my fingers were wrapping around Tatianna's neck. I tugged her face to mine to ensure she could see the barely contained anger pulsing beneath the surface as I hissed out my words.

"Don't you ever say her name again." Then I slammed the back of her skull against the mirrored walls, repeatedly, until her fight gave out and she stopped clawing at my hands.

Apollo and Al were on me in seconds, pulling me from the elevator and into the hall. "Boss. Chill."

I shrugged off Apollo's concerns, attempting to storm forward again as Tatianna stabbed at the *close door* button.

"I fucking warned you!" I growled out, as panic widened her eyes.

"I wanted to show you I was sorry, help take your pain away…" She was a mess of blood and snot, cowering on the floor of the elevator with her hands raised in surrender.

"Sorry? *Sorry?*" I parroted her words with a sadistic laugh. "I'll show you sorry…" I lurched forward, struggling against the hold Al and Apollo sought to maintain on my shoulders.

"You were mine before her. I wanted to be yours after," Tatianna whimpered.

The noise in my ears had amplified, like a jet engine screaming at me to pull the trigger. Nothing else in the room mattered as my chest heaved and the hand holding my gun shook. I didn't even remember shaking my men loose and drawing it. I was barely aware that I was shouting, pleading for Bella to come back to me. Apollo and Al seemed to disappear into the background, as my sights zeroed in on my target.

"When will you learn, Tatianna?" That voice. God was torturing me, playing with my mind by allowing me to hear an angel speak from the heavens. *"He will never be yours."*

"Why am I being punished? It wasn't enough to lose her; now I have to hear her goddamn voice too!" I roared out in agony, cocked back the hammer, and aimed. But Tatianna was no longer looking at me, her focus drawn to my side. Behind me.

"I'm done with people trying to take what belongs to me." A small hand took the gun out of my grip and squeezed the trigger, firing until there was an audible click.

I spun on my heel and froze. I wasn't just hearing things. I was seeing them too. I held my breath, waiting for the image of Bella to disappear like a dream in my waking hours. Instead, she clutched her stomach and started to collapse.

"Bella!" I roared, catching her before she hit the floor.

"The men in my life might be an issue, but your whores are worse." She looked up at me and smiled.

I brushed her hair away from her face, breathing her in for a moment, then tugged her to my chest. I glanced behind me to Apollo and Al, who appeared just as confused as I was, as we all watched the doctor roll a wheelchair and IV stand around the corner.

"I told you I didn't want you to hate me." My father appeared a moment later. "But I saw an opening and took it. To draw them out of the shadows."

"Welcome back." Apollo stared at Bella, wide-eyed, before gesturing to the carnage in the elevator. "Boss, I got this."

The rest of us headed into my penthouse, where I placed a sleeping Bella onto the bed, holding her for a second longer than necessary.

"She needs a lot of rest, but the surgeon was able to remove the bullet from her lower chest. It missed all major organs *and* the baby. Both are stable," Doc informed us.

"Baby?" My father questioned, tightening his lips when I pinned him with a glare.

"Let me get her set up and then we can discuss it in detail." Doc proceeded to hook up the rest of the monitors as a nurse tended to Bella's vitals. My father and I stepped out of the room, allowing them to work but keeping the door open so I could still see my angel.

She was here. It wasn't a dream. Or a nightmare. Bella was alive.

"I received intel that Anthony had eyes on us. I didn't want to... I didn't want to hurt you, son. But I saw it as our only chance and I took it." I watched my father silently as he continued. "We staged the scene at the hospital. It needed to seem real. Authentic. There was no other way..."

I knew he was right. But I wasn't about to let him off the hook just yet. Not after what he put me through. Though I had to admit it was a smart play. The Morettis wouldn't be able to stay away much longer.

"Son, I'm so, so sorry..." His words were cut off by a right hook to the jaw. He stumbled back a step, holding his chin in his hand. "One, you get one. I know I deserved it."

"Her mother know?"

He nodded. "I told her when we got to the hotel and kept them under guard. I told everyone once we were away from prying eyes.

They understood—well, they *understand* now." He pointed to the gash on the left side of his face. I was so shellshocked I hadn't even noticed it. "Serafina has always had a penchant for throwing furniture."

"Lucky," Bella called out to me in her sleep.

"This isn't over."

He nodded his understanding before I rushed back to my wife. There was more to discuss, but right now Bella needed me. Climbing next to her on the bed, I did my best to cuddle closer without disturbing the machines. She smelled like sweet vanilla and my favorite scent of all. Bella. My chest ached with the familiarity.

We lay in silence for a few minutes, holding each other until she rolled over to look in my eyes. "It took me dying to get you out of a suit?" She ran a hand over my jeans. "I don't know if I like it," she muttered with a raised brow.

"Suit it is. Anything for you, my love."

"Anything?"

I nodded.

"Good. Go help Al and Apollo. She was your whore, your mess to clean up." Then she rolled back over, ignoring my chuckle.

CHAPTER 35

MIRABELLA MORETTI

It was the craziest thing to wake up in a hospital bed after the surgeons removed a bullet from your body. All to be told by your father-in-law that you're actually dead—for the time being anyway.

Mario Agostino stood over me, like something out of a nightmare, telling me of his plan to destroy my brother. But I knew there was so much more to it than that. Because what he had in mind would destroy my husband first.

Husband. *Husband.* The word felt foreign on my tongue, but it was true. Lucky was mine. Legally. On paper. After everything, my first thoughts weren't about how my body had just been stitched back together. I was too focused on the realization that we were finally married, despite the universe's attempts at keeping us apart.

"Your father's here. He's got eyes on you. I cannot risk our family's safety." Mario's eyes shone with determination but they were also burdened by guilt. The emotion was clear as day for anyone who knew where to look.

"Safety…? You know you'll destroy a piece of them—all of them."

He nodded. He understood and still felt it was worth the risk. "We need to put on a show to assure he buys the story. More details keep coming in but…” Mario stopped himself short, almost as if he were afraid to tell me the terrible truth.

“Say it. It can’t be any worse than what I’ve imagined in my head. Just tell me, Mario.” I wheezed, trying to sit upright in bed. When he hesitated again, I continued for him. “He had a Russian contact that he introduced to Gio.”

His nod confirmed my suspicions. Gio was never smart enough to start this war on his own. As much as he tried to save me in the end, something had always been amiss. The little conversations I’d overheard told me he wasn’t the ringleader. It would take a smart, conniving man, who under-stood the business specifics in our world, a man who held so much hate, so much resentment towards the Agostinos that no one was off-limits.

“What do you have on him? There must be something. My father has never been one to fall in line, just because it’s the right thing to do. He’s always looking for a way to get on top.”

“I have video evidence of him killing your mother’s first fiancé.”

I almost laughed, and would have if not for the shooting pain radi-ating through my side. “Sal Ragetti? He killed him? Oh… for my mother. You’d assume a man so hell-bent on winning a woman that he’d risk all-out war would’ve at least treated her right.”

Mario appeared shocked by my words.

Of course, I’d heard all about the mystery surrounding Sal Ragetti’s death. Everyone in our circle of the criminal underground knew about it, and the tension it caused between the east and west coasts.

“If that’s the case and the tape is still in your possession, what is my father hoping to gain?” The pain medications were taking over and my eyelids were growing heavy, but I had so many questions.

“Unless he assumes my leverage dies with Lucky, I really don’t know. He lost his Russian connections and your mother has all but declared him dead. You were his only remaining bargaining chip; however, now that my son has…” Mario stopped, his face turning bright red with the accusation on the tip of his tongue.

“Deflowered me,” I finished for him, and he nodded.

“Mr. Agostino, please. She needs medication and to be prepared for transport. Once that's all situated, I will… go break the news to your family," the surgeon choked on his words, as a middle-aged nurse buzzed around me in a flurry of activity.

"They're taking you to the penthouse once you're stable enough to travel. I'll be there as soon as I can. I'm so sorry for what you went through, Bella. And… for what I am about to do." Mario pressed a kiss to my forehead before making his way to the door. "If I weren't already destined for hell, I sure would be once I break their hearts." With those parting words, he exited.

"The baby is fine and this medicine will not affect it. Sweet dreams, Mrs. Agostino." The nurse smiled down at me.

Mrs. Agostino. It was the first time my married name had been used, and it was by the nurse currently preparing me to be swept out the back door, because everyone thought I was dead. It was borderline comical and heartbreaking all at the same time.

I was dipping in and out of consciousness, until I heard that voice. Her voice. And his. But Lucky didn't sound like himself. Not like the man I knew. He was broken. Enraged. And she was propositioning him.

"I didn't get fucking shot on my wedding day to listen to this shit." I propelled myself forward and out of my chair, much to the dismay of my nurse, who was trying to coax me back down. I pinned her with a glare until she relented, helped me to my feet, and guided me towards the elevator.

"You were mine before her. I wanted to be yours after." And that was the last straw.

"When will you learn, Tatianna?" I approached Lucky from behind and stepped to the side so she could see me. "He will never be yours."

"Why am I being punished? It wasn't enough to lose her; now I have to hear her goddamn voice too!" He sounded so pained, tormented. I needed him to snap out of it… for him to see that I was here. Alive.

Watching the man I love fall apart before my eyes was the last straw. People like Tatianna, like my father and Gio, would never learn the easy way. I'd warned her to leave my family alone. Lucky and Sienna had warned her. There was only one option left…

"I'm done with people trying to take what belongs to me." Swiping the gun from Lucky's hand, I turned it on Tatianna and pressed the trigger over and over until there was nothing left, and I was sure she was dead.

Once the latest spike of adrenaline had pillaged my body, another bout of exhaustion took over and I drifted in and out of sleep for the next few hours, always waking in a panic and calling for Lucky.

As my lashes fluttered open after my latest restless nap, I saw his face and smiled.

"When I thought I lost you, I wasn't living. I was going through the motions, spilling blood because that's what I know how to do. But all I could think about was everything I never got to tell you, to show you, our baby…" His voice thickened with unshed tears.

"It was the thought of you that pulled me out of the darkness. You call me your light. But in that moment, it was you. You were the light I needed to find my way."

Lucky tugged me to him and placed a kiss to my forehead. "Sleep, baby. We will handle everything else."

"So… I get laid to rest in two days?" I asked, almost amused. "But in truth, it will be my father's funeral."

"I'm sorry for what has to be done, Bella." Silence stretched between us. "But you're mine. Your mother is mine. And no one fucks with what's mine."

I nodded and snuggled closer to him. It felt good to have Lucky at my side again.

"I'm coming." It was the night before my funeral and obviously not everyone was on the same page. Lucky and Mario wanted me to stay behind. "You need all your men with you. And if I remember correctly, the last time you left me behind, bad shit happened. I'm coming. End. Of. Story." When Lucky glared at me from the end of the bed, I glared back harder. "It's not like I'm fucking asking to pop out of the casket and yell *surprise*." I smiled at his laughter. I was only half-joking.

"You'll be off your game without her. If she stays in the car, you'll know where she is when shit hits the fan." Apollo was the only one coming to my defense, and because of that, he was also my new bestie. "If she promises to actually *stay* in the car this time."

And then he had to go and ruin it. Asshole.

"It's settled. I'm going. Now, please leave. I need my beauty sleep to ensure I look my best in the morning." I sank down in the bed and curled into my pillows.

"Was it her near-death experience, or the fact that she's married to my brother? 'Cause something inside her has snapped, and I thoroughly enjoy the feistier version." Sienna exited the room with a laugh, while making it a point to ignore a certain enforcer.

"You're in trouble," I sang at Apollo's retreating form.

"Not as much as you are, if you don't stay in that car," he sang back at me, shutting the door quietly behind him.

"You better behave. I don't like any of this," Lucky muttered, climbing into bed with a huff.

"I know. But you love me."

He slammed his fist into his pillow, thrashing from side to side while trying to get comfortable. "Yeah, yeah."

Oddly enough, considering my funeral was tomorrow, I fell asleep almost immediately and woke without dreaming. I was tired of living on edge and wanted all this shit behind us. Alexander was on ice, waiting for me to feel better so I could say my farewells, in whatever manner I saw fit. But first we had to handle my side of the family.

"We'll get a ten-minute head start," Lucky said as I stomped my foot, winced with the action, and scowled at my husband.

"I'm aware of the plan. You've beaten it into my head. You leave before me, we meet up in the city, and Apollo exits to escort you to my casket." When he opened his mouth, I silenced him. "And under no circumstances am I to leave the car."

Lucky and his team left first, while Apollo and Al remained in the penthouse with me. I trusted them with my life and so did my husband. As we waited for the elevator to descend to the lobby, I couldn't help but worry about the future. My baby needed a father and we all needed a life away from the trauma my family had inflicted.

"Traffic is backed up. We have to go the long way around. Don't alter the plan, just go. We can arrive after your caravan. It won't draw suspicion," Apollo spoke into his earpiece before turning to me. "They're farther ahead than we expected. They'll start without us."

"Probably for the best. He'll stare at the car the whole time, instead of mourning me properly," I said, making Al chuckle from the front seat.

The traffic was clearing but we were still about twenty minutes behind Lucky and the rest of his family. By the time we pulled through the cemetery gates, the service had already started.

"Something's wrong." I could feel it in my gut. Something was awry. "Do a perimeter check," I commanded Apollo, who immediately began speaking into his earpiece.

"Eastside aerial isn't responding. Christopher, I need you to gain visuals." Apollo motioned to the rooftop, where the missing man should be stationed and wasn't.

"Fuck. Where is he?" I asked, more to myself. "Al, go check it out."

He nodded and climbed out.

"We knew this was where he'd strike. But how, Apollo?" As I surveyed the funeral, I could see my mourners huddled under a large tree while listening to the priest pray over my empty casket.

"He has to be on the roof of the mausoleum. It's the best vantage point and where we're missing a check-in." Apollo was sitting in the front seat, his eyes darting to every possible weak spot.

"No…" The word was barely audible as tears formed in my eyes and fear lodged in my throat.

My father seemed to rise from the shadows on top of the mausoleum, a rifle in hand with his scope aimed at everyone I held dear. Just as I was about to scream, Apollo jumped out of the car and a second man appeared at my father's back. I could only watch on in abject horror as the distant figures struggled for control of the gun until the weapon was sent flying over the roof's edge. The commotion drew the attention of my mourners, who quickly scattered like ants. It was then that I recognized the second man…

Gio stood to his full height, pulling a gun from his back and shooting our father point-blank in the head. Blood and brain matter erupted into the air like a grotesque volcano of carnage. A silent scream left my mouth, more out of shock than grief, as my brother fled as quickly as he'd appeared. There was so much chaos he was able to slip down the side of the wall unseen.

I waited two minutes before finally deciding to exit the car. Slowly stepping around the entourage of black vehicles, I watched my brother open the door to one, reach inside, and yank the driver out.

"Gio!" I had no idea what prompted me to call his name, and he appeared just as shocked as I felt. We stared back and forth in silence for what felt like hours, neither of us saying a word.

"I never planned to hand you over to the Russians. I was trying to fuck with Lucky's shipments to get Yuri to slip up." He looked distraught, ashamed. Emotions I'd never seen on him before. "If Yuri slipped up, I could finally expose our father for the rat he was."

"Why didn't you say anything?" Tears were pouring down my face.

"You know our world, sis. Women stay out of it. I thought I was saving us all. Except I kept getting pulled in deeper and deeper, waiting to be taken down. I never meant to hurt you, Bella. This whole thing has been so fucked." His eyes told me he meant it. He was telling the truth.

"Go, Gio. Don't come back." I wiped at my face before hardening my expression.

"He's good to you?" he asked, and I nodded without hesitation.

"Good." With that, he climbed into the car and slowly pulled out of the cemetery, mixing with the other fleeing vehicles.

"God forbid you listen! I said stay in the car, but gunshots ring out and you come running!" Apollo marched around the car, tugging me to the side. "Your brother's here."

"Not anymore," I said softly.

"What? He's gone?"

I nodded, and Apollo began barking orders into his earpiece.

"He what?" Lucky roared at my side.

I stepped into his open arms and he pulled me to his chest. Once everyone had regrouped in the parking lot, I relayed the information I'd gotten from Gio. Sienna scoffed, walking away in disbelief while Mario and Lucky seemed to consider my words. My eyes locked on my mother and she appeared to share my confusion. So much of it didn't make sense. Yet, at the same time, so much did.

"You know this changes nothing," Lucky growled in my ear.

"I know, my love. But for now, it's over." I sighed and he kissed the top of my head.

"Bella." My mother lowered a hand to my shoulder to get my attention.

"*Madre*," I answered back.

She pulled me in for a hug with tears in her eyes, clinging to my shirt as if I were a lifeline. Despite everything, she'd been married to my father for over two decades, he'd been her life partner, and she'd bore his children. And so, we both cried for the man we wished he had been, rather than the monster we lost.

"I can't believe…" She cut off her pained sob.

"I know, Mama. I can't believe he's gone either."

"No, I knew this day was coming. I just can't believe he thought he'd win, that he willingly put his only daughter in harm's way to beat Mario. I just…" She paused, straightening her spine and staring at Mario and Isabella. "I can't believe he'd do this to me."

And that's when I realized it wasn't about my father at all. Not really. She was grieving for the love she'd never have because he took that opportunity from her. It was jealousy. My mother was jealous that Isabella had the man she'd always wanted and couldn't have.

Mario stepped forward with his arms open to her. "Fina… I…" He stopped speaking when she moved back.

"Thank you, Mario. And my apologies for what my husband has done." With one last squeeze to my hand, my mother turned on her heel and continued down the path towards my father's lifeless body.

"*Madre*," I called after her, but she didn't respond.

"Give her time, Bella." Lucky inhaled my hair.

"I don't know if time will heal all her gaping wounds," I muttered before stepping around him.

"*Madre*, do you prefer to be called Grandma or *Nonna?*"

Once my meaning hit her, she spun so quickly I was surprised she managed to stay upright. Her gasps sounded at the same time as Isabella's, and she dropped her mask of indifference, crying tears of joy this time. The two women converged, their chatter swiftly changing from funeral arrangements to baby showers.

It was only once we were inside the car and I was curled up in Lucky's lap that I finally allowed myself to relax. Everything up until this point had been a whirlwind of conflicting emotions, and I was ready for peace.

"I'll be the best father and husband. I promise you, *mia regina*," Lucky muttered, kissing my neck. "I won't be perfect. I'm sure I'll fuck up. But I'll fight for us."

Humming at the physical contact, I couldn't help but smile. "I know. And when you do fuck up, I'll be there to set you straight." His chuckle reverberated through me. "I love you, *il diavolo*. I'm yours on this earth and whatever hell we find ourselves in after."

He didn't need to answer. I was content to just have him in this moment. Right now, it wasn't about me ending Alexander's life, finding out what the hell Dom was involved in, or hunting down Gio. It was just us, and nothing else mattered.

He was my devil and I was his fucking wife.

It all started with a contract and ended with a love like nothing I'd ever known or thought possible. Because despite the fire and brimstone, with the devil by my side, I'd never feel the burn.

EPILOGUE
LUCIFER "LUCKY" AGOSTINO-

Six years later, I was still a man as feared in rumor as I was by name. I would kill with my bare hands without a care for my redemption when I met the Big Guy after death. But that was why I was called the devil... *il diavolo*... the fallen angel. I was the calculated and ruthless eldest heir of Mario Agostino, bound by blood to rule New York City.

All of that and more was true. Mario Agostino had officially retired and whisked my mother off to Italy for a romantic getaway. They came back every so often for the family, then jetted off again to enjoy their retirement. It was the time away they deserved and needed. Now, things were different with the family.

Our legitimate and illegitimate businesses were thriving. Marco was at my side through it all and was extremely committed for once. It seemed the moment Bella had almost died, his interests changed. Sienna started another technology company and Octavia was a book publisher; both were off living their lives. All three of my siblings had their own shit going on over the years. But, hey, those were their stories to tell. Not mine.

Apollo was still my second and at my side for most things, even with the chaos that surrounded him. But he too had his own tale that needed telling.

And let me tell you, it was beyond fucked up.

Peering out the window from my office that overlooked my back-yard, I felt at peace. Mirabella not only chose this property but also decorated the entire inside. It was down the street from my parents' compound and we'd bought a new penthouse. Free of "whores and blood" as my wife would say. Bella's gardens were expansive and beautiful, and that was where I found her most days, weather permitting.

I'd built her stables, and she decided that instead of raising her own horses, she wanted to take in abused ones. Ones that had retired from the track after their owners surrendered them. We had several she'd saved from a slaughterhouse while rescuers reached out from across the globe, asking for her help. She was beyond happy with her decision to work from home.

There were hundreds of souls lost by my hands, and it didn't bother me for a second. Yet one tear from my wife was torturous. I had no clue that one day a small slip of a girl would destroy me for all others. How that same girl would go to the ends of the earth for her family, which included my men.

They opened their arms and were willing to lay down their lives for their *regina*. She earned their respect not just from the Russian meet but with how she'd taken a beating from Alexander. A man who managed a more-than-merciful ending at the hands of my beautiful wife.

"Help, help!"

The windows were opened when the terrified screams ripped through the yard, the same yard where I'd just seen my wife. I stormed from the office and was there in seconds.

"Daddy!" Nico—our eldest son at five and a half—barreled through the gardens when he saw me coming.

Racing into my arms, he almost knocked me over. For his age, he was huge. The doctors said he'd be even taller than I am if his growth continued at this rate. Bella wanted to name him after Dominic, but she didn't know the truth about him. Instead of telling her, I opted for a shortened version and we settled on the name Nico.

"What is the screaming about?" I waited for my son to answer between panting breaths.

"It wasn't me. It was Mario! He sounded like he was shouting from the stables! It's where Mama took him and Mia!" The little boy in my arms was a spitting image of his father at his age. The spitting image of me.

However, his blue eyes looked joyous and playful, instead of cold and stern. He took his job as the eldest extremely serious and watched his siblings like a hawk. Panicked squeals from Mario echoed from the stables in the distance. As we approached, we could hear Mia crying.

"Let's go see what all the fuss is about."

Mia was our third and at only three years old, she already had my men eating out of the palm of her hand.

I walked to the open doors of the stable, and Nico squirmed until I put him down. He charged to his sister, quickly shoving Mario out of the way. Bella stood to the side, smirking at me while absently running her hand over her swollen belly. My heart instantly calmed, realizing it was typical Mia theatrics.

Our little one had a flare for the dramatics and cried at the drop of a hat. It was hard to be mad at her when she looked up at you with those pouty lips and mixed eyes, mirror images of her mother's. She had me wrapped around her little finger and everyone knew it. This family was what kept me going and what made me surge for more success. I'd never let the blood that I bathed in touch them.

"What did you do?" Nico glared at his brother.

Mario rolled his eyes in response before heading out of the stables, skipping as if he didn't have a care in the world. The boy showed early signs of Apollo's affliction, a prognosis that worried us slightly. He flocked to his adoptive uncle and they seemed like kindred spirits. But my right hand's unease told me our feelings were mutual.

"Dramatic," Bella mouthed, her lips curled into a smile meant only for me. This woman, after all these years, still turned me on, especially with the swollen bump of our third son growing inside her. She was mine. And she was the best fucking contract I'd ever signed.

EPILOGUE

MIRABELLA AGOSTINO

This man was something else. The moment Mia turned on the hysterics, I knew he'd come running. He was never too far from us when he was home. When he was conducting business, Apollo was at his side and Big Al was here lurking over my shoulder. Regardless of his increasing power in the city, my husband knew I ruled this house.

He wanted his *regina* and that's what he got. I ruled at his side and was just as feared in the streets. But this house was my castle, a domain that I commanded. The power felt amazing and it took a little bit of time for me to own it, but it was what I was born to do. Though sometimes it seemed my ferocity could scare him…

Watching little Mario storm off had my heart skipping a beat. Nico was just like his father. *Overprotective.* He took his duties as the eldest son seriously. Mia enjoyed the attention and the cajoling from him— hell, from everyone around her. To say my little girl was overly histrionic was an understatement. There were numerous times I caught her faking tears, peeking out from her thick lashes to make sure she had our rapt attention.

However, Mario, my handsome little boy and the middle child, was our largest concern. Watching the calculated and shared looks Apollo gave him heightened our apprehension over his lack of empathy. He protected to the fullest of his abilities, but tears and sadness seemed to be confusing concepts. In time, we would see what that meant. Until then, I loved him just as much as his siblings.

"What happened, Mia?" Nico whispered to his sniffling sister. She'd fallen off the ladder leaning against the stall; the same one she knew she wasn't supposed to climb. The tears and screaming were because she knew she was in trouble. My little headstrong daredevil jumped off much higher things, so I knew she wasn't hurt. We'd made eye contact when I entered the stables, and she "fell" only after she'd been caught.

Nico dusted off her dress and took his sister out to play. Mia's giggles echoed as they ran across the yard. I turned to my handsome husband and I couldn't hide my grin. Even with all the issues from our families, his businesses, and the insanity that was our lives, I loved this man just as much as when I married him, if not more.

"You going to yell at her for climbing the ladder?" he asked, smirking at me. He knew she wasn't going to get away with it. I ruled my house—and that included my children—with an iron fist. This life wasn't for the meek and mild. And I'd be damned if I let my kids grow up to be entitled little shits. Like my father had allowed his sons.

Dominic and Gio, my idiot brothers, were a story of their own. Gio let me down most of my life but Dominic's was the worst kind of betrayal. The crap that went down with them after my kidnapping was an insane never-ending turn of events. However, in the end, all was made right. It sounded simple, though it was anything but.

"Of course. She thinks she's got it all figured out. But Mom is one step ahead."

"God help us when she becomes a sullen teenager. Add those incredible looks she got from her smokin' hot mama and we're in serious trouble." Tugging me close, he squeezed my ass, careful not to press hard into my swollen belly.

"You mean her mama that currently looks like an exhausted cow?"

He growled at me while his sensual lips ravaged mine. The contact sent a spark surging through my body—one that hadn't dulled in the slightest over the years. "Beautiful, *mia regina*."

Leaning into him, I whispered in his ear, "Call Al to come watch the kids. This queen needs her king to perform his duties."

I spun on my heel and headed back towards the house. I could make out the sound of Lucky barking orders into his phone. Halfway up the path, I heard the kids squeal in excitement when Uncle Al charged them, growling like an angry bear. I smiled to myself and increased my pace, knowing my husband was right behind me.

In our world, marriage was for life. In every sense of the word. I may have been a teenager when my hand was offered to a stranger, but my name had truly been written in blood. Because as long as it pumped through my veins, this man was mine.

I was contracted to the devil himself. My own personal *il diavolo*. He was my love and my light in life and he doted on me in ways I'd never known a man capable. But he was also the answer to the savage darkness that lurked under my skin—my need for pain and torture in the bedroom that only he could provide.

The king and queen had found each other in a time of turmoil and chaos. Much like the ancient rulers, whose marriages had been predestined by their parents. However, when our contract was signed, I had willingly handed myself over to this man.

And it was the best fucking decision of my life.

Turn the page for a sneak peek of "Clever as the Devil: Agostino Crime Family Series Book II."

AGOSTINO CRIME FAMILY - BOOK TWO
A DARK ROMANCE MAFIA SERIES
Clever
AS THE
DEVIL
DAHLIA REIGN

SNEAK PEEK: CLEVER AS THE DEVIL CHAPTER ONE

APOLLO DELUCA

"Who would be stupid enough to steal from Lucifer Agostino?" asked Al, one of the loyal *soldati* to the *famiglia*.

Lucifer "Lucky" Agostino was the future King of New York in the mafia world. He was Mario's eldest son, and I was raised alongside him as an enforcer and his number two. Over the years, I had learned to harness my embittered soul as well as contain my compulsory rage to wreak havoc. Now when someone muttered *il mietitore,* there was no mistaking the pain and terror that would be inflicted on those unfortunate enough to find themselves on my list. That was me, *The Reaper.*

Mario had grown to be like a father to me, an idea I couldn't fathom previous to meeting him all those years ago. I was merely a broken and battered migrant that had fled certain death and trauma while living on the streets with my foster sister Cara. One fateful day, I just so happened to come across a particular corner store, one in which I thought to rob. I took note of all the usual vulnerabilities—*the place was practically asking for it.* However, I had no clue that it was a storefront protected by Mario Agostino—fuck, I didn't even know who he was back then—an oversight that could have gotten me killed. But he saw my potential and offered me mercy.

Mario Agostino was the kind of authority figure you didn't fuck with, not if it could be avoided and not if you valued your oxygen intake. Nowadays, he focused on his legitimate dealings, opting to let Lucky and I take over the relationships he'd built over the years. Guns, drugs, loan sharks and enforcers made up the majority of the income in our entrepreneurship. Lucky was creating an empire for himself out from under the name of his father—earning his own following and respect. And as his enforcer, I acted as his muscle and reassurance that his dealings were handled.

"I have my assumptions, but I am confident I will find answers shortly." The clicking of the phone filled the silence after my verbal confirmation.

The Agostino namesake controlled the docks on the Hudson River. Anyone who wanted to import or export through the docks had to pay homage to the Agostino's—top dollar homage.

Our base of operations, a warehouse on the waterfront, acted as a convenient place to conduct business away from prying eyes. As we waited for our security to unlock the gates, commotion across the street at the abandoned building caught my attention. A male realtor, a blonde woman and Dominic Moretti were standing outside talking.

"The fuck is he doing here?" Al muttered, rolling down the driver's side window.

"No fucking clue." Picking up my cell phone, I snapped a couple of pictures.

Dominic Moretti was the middle child of Anthony and Serafina Moretti. When it came to hierarchy in the mob-controlled city, that family was the closest competition against the Agostino's. Furthermore, Dominic's older brother, Gio Moretti, was who I assumed was fucking with our shipment. Lucky garnered his power and success from hard work and perseverance. Whereas Gio lied, stole and cheated his way to mediocrity.

My assiduity with which I used to monitor that family added this observation to our list of potential complications. When one parasite was able to make its way into your home, many more would try to follow through the cracks, which were inevitably left in its wake. And I planned to exterminate the stragglers long before there was an all-out infestation.

"Bad location for a titty bar." Al pulled through the gates, laughing, before parking the car outside our warehouse.

I rose from my seat, and standing to my full height, I watched the trio wander the sidewalk. Dominic Moretti owned a couple of restaurants and strip clubs around the city, crossing into New Jersey. There'd been rumors that his club was the front for a lucrative trafficking operation. That was a depravity *we* didn't mess with and wouldn't harbor in our city.

The realtor stood next to Dominic, and animatedly talking with his hands, he pointed to the building. The blonde at his side was tall and extremely thin with a sensuous sway to her slight hips. Her clothing was tight and revealing and she shifted on the high stilettos, as if she was forcing herself to stand still. The girl appeared lost in her own world as she stared up at the sky.

The portly realtor would send her appreciative glances—bordering on inappropriate—each time Dominic turned his back. As the men wandered further down the premises, I followed along our fence line in clandestine form. I visually examined the blonde and took note from the tense hunch of her shoulders that the constraint Dominic held on her arm was likely not affable; he was practically dragging her down the sidewalk behind him.

The more I watched, the more my internal nervous system was flashing red with warning. Dominic and I had graced the same social circles for years, and usually he was the portrait of platitude and impassivity. However, in this moment, he seemed to be losing patience and was vehemently angered by the small girl. I trailed further down the sidewalk, maintaining my obscurity from the assessment of their glares.

"Let me think about it and I will be in touch tomorrow." Dominic shook his hand and they went their separate ways.

The couple walked to the waiting car, his grip still wrapped around her slim arm. He continued to aggressively drag her in his wake, his contentious tone echoing in his stead. As they drew near, I could see that the girl was holding a fist at her side—her jaw closed tight—as she stared at the concrete in front of her. He pulled her onto the sidewalk, and closer to the fence, when his anger got the better of him.

"What the fuck did I tell you?" he yelled. "I took you out of your cage to test your training. And you, my little pet, you failed… pathetically."

The fuck? Dominic's words grated my skin; it was like an ice bucket of water was dumped over me. I knew what cages were like, cramped and demeaning. And meant to break you. My knuckles cracked as I continuously flexed my hands—in an attempt to absorb my natural reaction for *fucking* violence.

"I didn't do anything wrong." The girl's voice was strong with an undertone of annoyance. But each word was like a slap to Dominic's face. He growled in displeasure before throwing her against the car. Her svelte frame bounced off the unrelenting metal, flying forward. Dominic grabbed her by the neck and pinned her to the car.

"Nothing wrong?" he snarled in her face. "Try, you didn't do a-fucking-thing right." He slapped her across her profile with enough force to snap her hyoid bone and potentially cause irreparable damage to her retromandibular vein. To my surprise, the girl didn't make a single sound, instead merely holding her cheek and looking away from him.

"I'm sorry," she muttered. However, from my position, I could tell there was no sincerity in her voice.

"Get in the fucking car," Dominic growled, shoving her away from him as he straightened his tie in the vehicle's reflection. The girl stood extremely close to the fence—so close, I could hear her labored breath.

"Did you enjoy the show, lover?" She stared in my general direction, somehow attuned to my presence. "Come to the club, and I'll give you a real show." Her blue eyes lit up in amusement.

There was a depth, showcasing what lurked beneath the surface—a woman full of fire and a rancorous soul. There was no life or spark of sanity left in them, just a captivating shade of blue that wrapped up her stereotypical blonde hair supermodel appearance. Her mention of the club didn't surprise me. She was, no doubt, one of the best dancers Dominic employed.

"Now, Perse," Dominic ordered from inside the car.

My thoughts were rattled, inundated by the savage rage threatening to release the beast inside me. As far back as I could remember, there was a part of me that was detached from other human beings. Their actions were peculiar and unfamiliar to me, their emotions consuming them and hindering their ability to think rationally.

I'd learned to harness my rage and confusion over normal social interactions in order to perform methodical decision-making; while others appeared hell-bent on self-sabotage, allowing themselves to become collateral damage in the games played out by their betters.

As I stood in the shadows and watched the car drive away, I was unnerved by my unanswered questions. I didn't get as far as I had as a *made man* by being unprepared for potential attacks. I was inclined to decipher the threat, untangling whatever intricate web that sought to threaten the family, *before* it caused an impairment to our business. I assumed that a large warehouse with access to the water—free of the Agostino's fees—would be extremely lucrative for Dominic.

I stepped out from the darkness and headed back towards the warehouse, murderous thoughts exhausting my mind. Inside, there was a rat; one whose untimely torture at my hands would reduce some of my pent-up frustration. He would be my catalyst, telling me all I needed to know about the *stronzo* messing with our shipments. A few steps from the entrance, I pulled my phone from my pocket.

It rang twice before *she* picked up.

"Oh my, Apollo. To what do I owe the pleasure of you calling me in the middle of a workday? Something the *Almighty* wants from little ole me?" Sienna Agostino was as cavalier as she was intelligent. She was one of Lucky's younger sisters and also the biggest pain in my ass.

Previously, when I was trying to work my way up the ranks, I was tasked with watching Lucky's sisters, Sienna and Octavia. It seemed an easy stint to show my value, but the two girls couldn't have been more opposite from each other. For as quiet and demure as Octavia was—her nose forever stuck in a book while she was locked away in her room—Sienna was a fucking lunatic. She loved to challenge my patience and add to my confusion; the perplexing emotions in women seeming to only further befuddle my already limited grasp on humanity.

She was just as calculated and savage as her father and older brother. She sat back with a silent intensity as she watched and acquired knowledge from those around her, much akin to myself. She could smell weakness, detect lies and plot your death—all from one meeting. She learned your likes and dislikes, watched your social cues to uncover all your secrets and didn't hesitate to use them against you. She was also one of the most impassioned women I'd ever met.

And she practically drowned in her own overconsuming emotions.

She was a cunning little bitch with soft brown hair, intense blue eyes and a tight body wrapped in tailored designer wear. People on the outside, looking in, saw a vivacious and gorgeous woman whose intellectual prowess was intimidating. She put on a sweet and endearing facade until she had the ammunition that she needed to take your legs out from under you. She learned all the grating mannerisms and quirks she could; the kind meant just to piss me off. And she fucking used them often.

She was too smart for her own good and just as cutthroat in her own business dealings. Her aspirations had been to get out from under the Agostino limelight, and to create a name for herself. She graduated at the top of her class in college and was now running a technological super company specializing in surveillance, creating apps and building supercomputers. The type of intricate and borderline ingenious industrial science that she would patent then sell to the highest bidder. She was a technological prodigy doing the dirty work for the family's background checks and pertinent Intel.

"I need information," I clipped.

"Of course you do, or else, why would you be calling?" she asked; the sound of her hands flying across keys echoed in the background.

Grinding my teeth, my voice dripped with agitation. "Fucking

Christ, Sienna." I took a deep breath and counted to five, opting to ignore her loathsome giggle. "You're undeniably the most abhorrent female on the planet."

"I highly doubt that. We both know Tatianna takes that cake." She practically snarled the name of her high school nemesis.

"Dominic Moretti was just meeting a realtor across the street from the warehouse," I deadpanned.

"What in the world would possess him to buy such a large, dilapidated building near the wharf?" I could practically envision her tapping her lip as her mouth contorted into a snarl.

"It's why. The fuck. I am calling you," I grunted; the stones under my feet scraped across the broken concrete.

"Calm down, you crazy bastard," she muttered, the clicks on her keyboard resuming. "I'll sniff around his finances and see what I find."

Before she hung up, I halted her. "I need another favor," I said, breathing out my agitation as she chuckled once more. "He was with a girl." Her sharp intake of breath stalled my line of speech.

"And?" Sienna's voice was clipped, an undertone of anger boiling beneath the surface.

"My intuition is telling me she's a possible connection to the trafficking rumors in his club," I ground out; my jaw popped from the harsh movement. "Ten minutes ago, east side camera, aerial view two."

Silence stretched between us; the only indication that she hadn't disconnected was the sound of her rapid breathing. Sienna excelled in many things but her poker face—and often, the misguided actions that followed—was the poorest I had ever seen. She was intuitive, and could eloquently assess situations for risk. She operated her business with ruthless tactics in order to destroy all her competition, and she could drop a powerful shield to mask the crazy lurking inside her head.

But... when Sienna's feelings were hurt, she screamed it from the rooftops.

"Sienna." I waited a beat before hearing her huff, and then continued. "She showed signs of abuse and trauma. The probability of her being an asset and confirming our suspicions is extremely high," I added, softening my voice a degree.

"Right…" She gnarled into the phone before hanging up.

"Fucking little bitch." I looked to the sky, taking a deep breath before turning to Al. "What the fuck are you looking at?"

Al threw me a knowing grin. Sienna was one of his best friends and they both reveled in their shared ability to piss me off. The games each liked to play were sheer asinine. But put the two of them together, and they became a fucking nuisance, nothing more than pests tromping about—their sole intent to irritate me. It was hard to adhere to a code, that focused on concealing your weaknesses from your foes, when it was those closest to you that sought to make you suffer.

"Nothing, man. Nothing." He chuckled, holding the door open for me.

We had two prime locations where we conducted business, depending on the exact type of *business* we were handling. Lucky's penthouse sat above a secured basement that was an enforcer's heaven —a dungeon of torturous delight. The Agostino family compound outside the city was for more legitimate dealings. But this warehouse was used for all of the above and just so happened to be housing a conspirator I planned to dismantle—piece by piece—until I got a resolution. Subsequently, I'd make it known—a reminder, if you will—that we didn't tolerate operatives working in our midst; foes would not go unpunished.

I opened the locked room and Rocco, another of Lucky's men, stepped aside to allow me entrance. The rat—fuck, he was practically a kid—was chained to the chair in the center of the room; it was bolted to the floor to keep our victims in place. His fear permeated the air, like a thick repugnant cologne, and mixed with the odor of his soiled pants.

It sent a chill of excitement down my spine.

I walked towards the closet, ignoring the kid's pleas for mercy. I took off my suit jacket, neatly placing it on the hanger with my tie, and unbuttoned my shirt. Rolling my sleeves up, I turned back towards the *deficiente* in the chair; eyes wide with fear, he regarded my tattoo-covered body. I could practically outline the confusion on his face as he took in my biblical tattoos.

I wasn't religious nor did I believe in God. There was no way a

God could exist if he created a creature such as me. I was born to rule as the gatekeeper for Lucifer, to punish those deemed guilty and sent to the fiery pits of hell. Not a single emotion or wave of remorse—for any of the turmoil I had inflicted—had presented itself to me in my entire life. God didn't prevail, but the Devil… he was my savior.

"Were you, or were you not, previously warned to stay away from Agostino property?" I motioned towards his missing fifth digit. "And yet, here you are, caught with a team of perpetual schmucks, armed to the gills as if they are about to start a war. Waiting for a shipment perhaps? One that never came?" I paced around him in a circle; his whimpering cries were music to my ears.

Once again, the Devil was dancing on my shoulder, urging me to douse my soul in blood.

Lucky and I avoided pilfering by switching schedules and locations frequently. This could mean only one thing—there was no other cogent argument—we were dealing with a traitor. I had too many open-ended questions and I refused to accept surprises. I'd get my answers from him… just like all the rest. One way or another, he'd fold. They all did.

"From past meetings, you know who I am and what I do for Lucky. Make this easy for yourself and answer my questions," I chortled, watching the front of his jeans soak with urine from a mere utterance of words.

"Wh-what do you mean? I didn't do *nothing*!" the jackass cried, his lies echoing off the concrete walls.

"That's a double negative." I frowned at him, his brows pinching in uncertainty. "Never mind."

There were no windows in the room, the only light from the small bulb above our heads—which flickered on occasion. Being locked inside a dark confined space, trapped with only your thoughts as you awaited your death, was a very fine form of torture. And one I'd learned to endure from an early age. My interesting childhood never dulled my mental predicaments; although, it was partly at fault for who I became.

"Cut the bullshit. You were there to steal a shipment. Who told you where to go?" I asked, leaning into his face so he could see the menace swirling behind my irises. "Two words, that's it. The name of the mole and the man you're working for."

When he didn't immediately respond, my barely-composed patience shattered. Putting my dress shoe between his legs, I pulled the knife from my ankle holster. I engaged the switchblade in one motion, and in the next, it was embedded into his thigh. My eyes were wide with excitement—I watched as his internal nervous system tried to comprehend what I'd just done.

The human body was an interesting thing. The brain had many key components that controlled one's anatomy; it tried to protect all of its organs as best it could. The injury I'd administered to his thigh took several seconds to register, before sending unpleasant impulses throughout the rest of his body. His screams were heightened as his automatic distress signals recognized the pain, eliciting a satisfied smile from me.

"Tell me!" I roared, leaning further into his face. I removed the knife from one thigh and sliced through the flesh of the other—all in the same seasoned motion.

The unsolicited ring of my cell phone forced *il demoni,* lurking in the recesses of my brain, back to its cage. Stepping away from the pained cries, I wiped my blood-soaked hands down the front of his shirt. Once they met some semblance of clean, I grabbed my phone from my suit jacket.

It was Lucky.

"Boss." I spoke over the *cagna's* whimpers.

"Did you get an answer?" Lucky's voice was tranquil, and yet, it bore a vibration of anger.

"Just started." I affixed my prey with a stare of malevolence.

"Pops called a meeting. I want you there," Lucky commanded.

"Would you like me to leave him on ice until I get back?" My mind flashed with the prospect of a painful, and quite literal, ice bath.

"Al can take over. I'll be there in fifteen." Lucky hung up.

I put the phone back into my pocket before turning to my victim. "Sadly, my time is almost up. Bigger things to do and all. Do you want to save me from missing the fun and just tell me what I want to know?" I asked, watching the kid mutely stare at his bloody thighs.

"Am I taking over?" Al asked, cracking his knuckles and motioning forward.

"Indeed. I do, however, have fifteen minutes." I grabbed a rusted pair of pruning shears from the wall of decaying devices. "Last chance." He continued to ignore me as I stepped closer.

Without a word, I tugged his remaining fifth digit into the shears and squeezed. His agony was like a classical melody strumming softly in my head—I could visualize each and every note as it danced along with the blood-curdling screams. The chaos was a soothing symphony that overtook my senses. Clipping the ring finger on the opposite hand, I was lost to the torment I was inflicting. The room around me disappeared as I closed my eyes and listened to his misery. I was no longer capable of calming myself, of drawing out his suffering, instead opting to revel in the grotesque imagery I had just created.

"Boss is at the gate," Al announced, bringing me back to reality.

"Fuck. Last chance to please me." I pushed his foot with mine, only to be ignored, as he once again whimpered.

I washed my hands at the metal sink in the corner of the room, inspecting my appearance in the reflection of the rusted mirror above it. Buttoning the collar of my shirt, I unrolled my sleeves and retrieved my tie. Tightening it in place, I left the room with a nod to Al as I threw my jacket on and headed for the door.

Mario Agostino instilled many things since he took me under his wing; one of which was my attire. I dressed to paint the image of a wealthy and controlled man. Not a single one of my suits cost less than five grand and they were in constant pristine condition or I required a change of apparel. Though ink marred my skin, winding up my neck and almost to my face, my hair was cut weekly and my face neatly shaved or my beard cleanly trimmed. On the outside, I had smooth flawless lines. On the inside, I was a combination of chaos and unethical thoughts—attempting to navigate a world that was overrun with what I saw as melodramatic absurdities.

"Update," Lucky clipped as I climbed into the car.

"Nothing," I said, raising a brow at his mocking smile. "What?"

"You're losing your touch," he snickered, while texting on his phone.

"Hardly, I had just started. Your interruption was intrusive and ill-placed," I huffed, anger seeping back into my system.

"To *Vino*," Lucky ordered his driver. "*Had* just started… then I gave you an additional twenty minutes." Lucky put his phone down, his smirk growing into a large contemptuous grin.

"Fuck you," I murmured, the urge to beat the shit out of him encroaching upon my sanity; switching tactics, I focused on the meeting. "Why are we needed at *Vino*?"

"You know Mario Agostino. A command without any explanation," he muttered, turning back to his phone.

It was true. Mario was a man who didn't explain himself, the sort of man who demanded respect. If he was calling us for a meeting, something was going on. *Vino* was a restaurant in the center of New York City. It was prestigious, expensive and known to host mafia-linked families. In fact, it was owned and operated by the Agostino's themselves.

"Go," I answered my cell phone.

"Little bitch only took one more finger before he cracked." Al snickered as the rat begged to have his missing appendages put on ice. "Gio Moretti orchestrated the attack. He wanted the shipment. The kid doesn't know who the mole is. I'm starting to clean up now."

I hung up; my grin directed towards Lucky.

"You were right," I said, watching Lucky grimace; though he did not falter, as his attention remained on his cellular device.

Lucifer Agostino and Gio Moretti had been rivals from an early age. Gio wanted what Lucky had, and everyone knew that conniving little shit would stoop to the bottom of the barrel to try to take what wasn't rightfully his. He loathed the fact that Lucky was always one step ahead, a million bucks richer, and in turn, had that much more control in the city. This time when thwarting his plan, and for good measure, Lucky made sure he was *two* steps ahead. Lesson learned.

If you were going to come after a man, take what didn't belong to you and earn respect in doing so—you'd better succeed. And as always, Gio hadn't.

"I thought as much. It's always him. I'm officially fucking pissed. He must be dealt with." Putting his phone back into his pocket, Lucky grinned at me.

"Ultimate punishment?" I asked, cracking my knuckles in anticipation.

"No. Not yet anyway... Besides, if anyone is going to empty a clip in him, it's going to be me. Because when that son of a bitch finally goes in the ground, he'll have no doubt who put him there. Truce be damned. My father may head the family on paper, but he knows better than to get in my way on this..." He paused. "No... Let the man sweat. I want it known, *I know.* We'll wait him out... give him just enough rope to hang himself. After all, idle hands are the Devil's playground. Let's see what he does." Lucky laughed as I sneered, a formidable union of power.

We pulled up to the front of *Vino* in well synchronized succession. Hopping out of our respective vehicles, I followed Lucky and another four of his men inside. As we entered the building, the hostess flashed a hungry smile in acknowledgement. I attempted to hide my physical quiver of disgust at this salivating *puttana.* She was the type of woman with little self-respect. She happily gave herself to the bottom of the food chain, assuming that made her *something.*

But she was nothing.

Without looking in her direction, we stormed past and headed straight for the private lounge. I had no idea what awaited us on the other side of that door, and still we entered unburdened by any further thoughts or hesitation. I peered around the room, the Moretti boys appearing in my direct line of sight. Though I was snarling internally, my usual shielded mask of indifference dropped over my face.

With the confirmation of Gio's attack, the tension was palpable; and the metallic sting of vengeance lingered on my tongue. I was surprised that Gio was not only back from Italy, but that he willingly dined in an Agostino establishment so soon after his failed attempt at thievery. At the thought of immediate confrontation, cowards like him ran with their tails between their legs, especially when cornered.

"Lucky, please join us." Mario gestured to the seat beside him as I motioned for Lucky's men to spread throughout the room. "Anthony, you remember my son Lucky, don't you?"

Blood was in the air—thick and fervent—and I could fucking taste it. Mario Agostino was a puppeteer and the Moretti men were his puppets… And I couldn't wait to see how he made them dance.

SNEAK PEEK: CLEVER AS THE DEVIL CHAPTER TWO.

SIENNA AGOSTINO

I couldn't help the devious smile that pulled tight on my face as I hung up the phone. It tickled me with delight to do everything within my power to rattle *il mietitore*. For all of his self-proclaimed control, in no capacity was he able to stay true to himself when I decided to play with him.

"Let me guess!" Octavia whispered from the other side of my desk. "That call must've been Apollo."

"Correct, per usual." I smiled at her.

My little sister was gorgeous both inside and out. She held the same Agostino steel-blue eyes as myself, and all the other Agostino children in fact, thanks to our father. We each had our own niche within the family and we played our parts well. Octavia just hadn't figured out exactly what hers was yet.

She was the third child and the sweetest human being you'd ever meet, though a bit of a recluse, often opting for a book rather than choosing to participate in family events. She came with a softness that the rest of the family vowed to keep intact.

Marco was the baby and the most useless member of our entire organization… and family. He was more akin to a gutter whore than resembling anything close to a viable Agostino male. He enjoyed women, women and more women—*but never the same woman*. One day, his world would come crashing down around him; and it would be the same day his actions had repercussions which his namesake couldn't save him from.

Lucky was the oldest and the future leader of the family, much to my dismay. Had I been born first—and, well, born a man—I'd have conquered the city by now, but whatever. He was in preparations to take over after our father stepped down; and at one point, that fact had filled me with such animosity, I was practically drowning in disdain for him. Like most things, I'd overcame that *phase* in my life.

After all, I was an Italian woman raised within this powerful patriarchy. I was to stand tall and proud of the men's accomplishments. A woman's worth was the shape of her body and the beauty of her face— not the brain in her head or the fire in her heart. I was fortunate that unlike most other girls in our circle, my father didn't allow us to feel inferior. Lucky had to take over by birthright as eldest son. But the Agostino's had a saying they held firm and true.

We are only as strong as our weakest family member.

A motto that bothered Octavia—she assumed she was the weakest —and that was of no concern to Marco. Whereas, Lucky and I took it to heart and demanded we prepared ourselves for war. I trained with renowned coaches in the boxing ring and graduated at the top of my class in college. It wasn't within me to bow down to the masses and accept anything other than perfection in all aspects of my achievements. And much to Apollo's disdain, I regarded him with shrewd psychological savagery.

For fun.

"What did he want?" Octavia asked, pulling her messenger bag onto the seat beside her.

"Four." She stopped, regarding me with suspicious eyes as I pointed to the bag. "Four books in there today, aren't there?" Her cheeks burning bright in embarrassment gave me my answer.

"Five." She chuckled, flicking her long brown curls over her shoulder and adjusting her glasses. "I couldn't decide! Now spill!"

"Book nerd." I smirked, rising to my feet and standing in front of the floor-to-ceiling windows in my office. "Dominic Moretti is shopping for water access."

It had taken me months to get my office styled just the way I had envisioned. I was going for powerful and sophisticated with the hint of femininity. When you walked into the room, you felt warm and fuzzy, but there was an undertone of the cutthroat businesswoman I truly was. There were a lot of white and soft cream colors, the elongated windows keeping things bright. Then I added splashes of *blood-red* accents— *perhaps a subconscious forewarning...*

I explained to Octavia what Apollo had observed and needed me to research. None of us would sit idly by and allow the Moretti's any attempt to gain a stronger foothold. I crossed my arms over my chest and stared at the cityscape below, the sun slowly setting. The symbolism was not lost on me. Just as the moon began to take over the sky and eclipse the pink hues, it was understood that this advantage was momentary—the sun would always rise again the next morning.

No matter what they pulled, we'd always burn brighter.

"What girl?" Octavia asked, shattering my silent contemplations.

"Some Moretti whore, no doubt," I muttered, walking back to my computer and accessing the cameras around the warehouse. A few clicks of a button and we watched together as Apollo stalked around in the shadows to follow the little blonde tramp.

"She's pretty," Octavia noted, much to my disagreement.

"What's your story?" I questioned, staring at the blonde on the screen; though this was directed more to myself than Octavia.

Everyone had a story. Everyone had a weakness. And I loved extorting all of the above from those in my way. Whatever interest Apollo was showing in the little bitch, I'd stomp on her like she was goddamn on fire. A few more clicks and I uploaded a clear image of her face into my software, allowing my system to do the job I built it for.

The program could learn anything about a person with but one simple image. Birth records, family information, crime jackets—hell, even your dental records if I wanted them. Then it was able to take medical records, fingerprint database information, and anything else possible to link potential genetic matches. Everyone was one click away from their entire life flashing before my eyes.

"Miss Agostino." My secretary's voice came from the intercom. "Your appointment is in the conference room when you're ready."

"Thank you." I disconnected the call. "I just need to set up a few more schematics into the software to advance my search and then I get to deal with the men of Alias Marks Corp." I muttered.

"What is the meeting about?" Octavia started packing her things onto her shoulder.

"They want me to sell the patent for the criminal genealogy software." I laughed, as if my pride and joy had a price tag on it. "Alias Marks assumes his pompous son offering me a date would be the nail in the coffin." I shuddered at the thought of the gross man-child.

I rose from the desk and locked everything up as my computer continued its analysis. Alias Marks had built his technology company by muscling computer software engineers into working for him. He also had very little dignity when he strong-armed those opposed to selling their patents, such as myself. I did very little for other businesses like his. I only worked with individuals who needed the leg up in life or those whose practices were above reproach.

I opened my closet door and checked my reflection in the full-length mirror. My chestnut brown hair was wrapped in a sophisticated bun that added to my polished attire. My cream *Chanel* pantsuit was fitted perfectly, accented by the fine silk shirt underneath. The only real glimpse into the true me was my red-soled stilettos with a modest diamond design on the buckle.

"I'll walk you out?" I motioned for Octavia to follow. "Peiro is here today, correct?"

She rolled her eyes at me but I ignored it. Though I often opted—or rather, demanded—that I be left alone when it came to security measures, the entire family required Octavia to be monitored at all times. Usually, I was either in my security-coded office or at home, so only the time between required extra attention. Octavia was the light to the dark of our family and needed the added protection, much to her dismay.

"I love you." I pulled her in for a hug before she left with Peiro in the elevator. "Ready?" My secretary and Chief of Operations both nodded, following me to the conference room.

It was a ploy, a female show of force, against two simple-minded men who assumed women were incapable of running a man's corporate world. Little did they know, I was in the process of buying out their three largest engineers and two of the companies they *thought* they were under negotiations with. I had little time and patience for men such as these and planned to leave a very strong message in my wake as I ushered towards total corporate domination.

"Hello, Alias. Thomas." I nodded, ignoring their extended hands. I took a seat at the head of the opposite end of the table with both women, one on each side. Another power play… it made them uncomfortable.

"Sienna." Thomas nodded in return, stopping when I interrupted him.

"Miss Agostino. Please," I corrected dryly.

I would have to replay this tape for myself later to further enjoy his shocked expression. His brows shot to his hairline, before morphing into uncontrolled rage. I, on the other hand, wore my poker face as I queued up their presentation on the large flat screen behind them.

"Continue," I stated, glancing at my watch.

"We've come prepared to make you an offer. One, we doubt you'd want to refuse," Alias started with a confident smirk, motioning for his son to begin.

"Miss Agostino." He practically snarled my name. I half-expected him to be frothing at the mouth. "As my father said, our offer is well above the standard rate for the genealogy software, and we've prepared a presentation to show you how we can drive it to the next level."

"Yes, so you've said. Your contract is under attorney review with Engineer Farewell, correct?" I lifted my head, waiting for a response, and I was met by their stunned silence. "No need to answer. It was rhetorical."

I rose from my seat, approaching their end of the long conference table. Marissa, my Chief of Operations, followed behind me and handed each of them several papers. Both men refused to acknowledge what she had placed before them, staring me down instead. Alias was giving me a look of agitation mixed with intrigue. But his son, Thomas, was openly glaring at me and his expression was that of pure loathing.

"You see, I had absolutely no intention of selling this patent or any of my other patents to your organization." I clasped my hands in front of me as I stared back at them. "I do not conduct business with men who will steal someone else's hard work and claim it as their own."

"Purchasing a patent is hardly stealing," Alias commented, his forehead scowling.

"Of course not. But underbidding its worth and using the threat of violence to get what you want is indeed… stealing." I motioned for them to sit in their seats and open their packets. "As you can tell by my extensive research, there is no stone that has gone unturned. Note the examples, showing the depravity of your negotiations throughout the years."

"This is bullshit," Thomas barked, shoving the documents aside. A further display of incompetence as he couldn't even understand the data before him. "Enough." Alias grunted at his son.

"Engineer Farewell is now with *Energia* Holdings." I smiled at Alias' scowl. "As are Telepark, Roam USA and West Coast Telecom. *Energia* is my baby and I won't allow you to touch what is rightfully mine." *No Agostino would.*

"You… you, can't. They weren't up for sale," Alias stated in disbelief, flipping through the packet with a sudden renewed enthusiasm.

"Money talks." I wandered back down the table, my fingers trailing along the veneer, and sat with my ladies.

"You're just a fucking whore! You can't do this! I won't allow it!" Thomas shouted, rising so quickly his chair rolled into the wall and rattled the TV behind him.

"It's already done. And I suggest you mind your tongue before I completely destroy you." My tone was clipped and direct—it was a challenge.

"Thomas…" Alias warned, knowing he'd met his match and didn't stand a chance against the fucking *whore*.

"No! It's all empty threats. I won't allow some dumb bitch to come and take what *we've* worked so hard for," Thomas sputtered; clearly now grasping at straws, he started ripping up the packets.

"You've built nothing. You're no more significant than an ant under my *Louboutin's*, Thomas. Your father built the company. Although it was off the backs of individuals who didn't know any better or couldn't fight back, I respected that he did it by his own hand, at least." I sat back in my seat.

"You *fucking* bitch." Thomas growled as his father slapped his arm. "Thomas, shut up."

"This is your last warning, Thomas. Heed your father's advice," I commanded, but he'd already lost his control and began aiming some creative slurs in my direction.

I'd heard it all before; he wasn't original in the slightest. *Agostino whore. Dirty money. Stupid bitch using her daddy*—pot, meet kettle. It didn't matter that I built this company from the ground up, first selling a video game before expanding into a large corporation. Those initial funds enabled me to start *Energia* Holdings without a single thing from my father. Well, except his unending support and love.

"That's it." As I stood again, Farrah, my secretary, handed me a manila folder. "Just remember I did warn you."

Instead of walking towards them this time, I slid the folder to the end of the table. Alias pulled it from Thomas' grasp; his face blanched as he began flipping through the photos. When it came to something I wanted, I was nothing short of thorough and methodical. And Thomas had plenty to be worried about; especially if it were to come to the light of day.

"June first, two years ago. Thomas went to a frat party at his old brotherhood and got himself into some trouble. Evelyn Campbell was a freshman from a small country town in the Midwest. She was drinking soda and preparing to leave when Thomas approached her." I clicked the TV on, and it paused on a close-up image of Thomas.

"Thomas… you said." Alias stopped, his mouth agape, silently begging his son to spew more lies.

"He said she was a liar that was looking for a payout. There were no charges because there was no proof. For having access to some pretty powerful computer geniuses, you'd think you would've protected your little secret better." I hit play.

Marissa and Farrah averted their gazes and I turned my back, not needing to see the depravity once more. It would show Alias that his son was a sick son of a bitch. He carried an unconscious Evelyn into the room and dropped her on the bed. He repeatedly raped her over and over, before electing to save the video for later. He then forced her into a shower to clean the evidence and abandoned her—naked—in a frat house bedroom.

"Shut it off!" Thomas roared. I spun on my heels, preparing myself, in case he charged forward. When I made no move to do as he commanded, he smashed his chair into the screen. "Lies! Sh-she photoshopped this, dad!"

"Enough!" Alias warned, remorse filling his face.

"Fucking whore." *Apparently, his vocabulary was as limited as his intellect.* He started around the table towards Farrah, who hit the alarm before hopping out of his reach.

When he turned to charge at me, I smiled, waiting for his next move. He was sloppy and sluggish—evidently, the man required sedatives to try to elicit any real authority. I stepped away from his punch and answered with two fingers jammed into his throat. His gasps and sputtering were audibly gratifying. I caught his arm, twisting it behind his back and slamming him face first into the table. He was larger than me, but I was more able-bodied. My hold was painful and his incapacitated breaths worked in my favor.

"I fucking warned you. I have more gifts for you when you get to prison. *Sei morta, cagna.*" The door to the conference room opened and three police officers entered. They began shouting, citing their warrant for Thomas' arrest for the rape of Evelyn Campbell.

The NYPD made quick work of escorting him out, while Alias

remained rooted to his seat. He stared at the door for several minutes after it closed before speaking. I had a feeling underneath the lies and manipulations, he had always suspected that his son was full of shit. What father wants to believe their children are capable of being monsters?

Oh, mine. Ha!

"I paid an investigator to look into that story. Thomas has always been a little off, but I couldn't find anything. I only allowed him to join the company so that I could keep an eye on him, but apparently that wasn't enough." A light knock landed on the door and Farrah moved to open it.

Evelyn Campbell was a frail, tear-soaked little girl; one who would be haunted by the actions of that piece of shit for the rest of her life. Her father and Amy, my attorney, stood beside her in silent strength. Alias' eyes went large as he recognized her.

"Not only will we be seeking to have your son charged to the full extent of the law, we are also requesting that you pay punitive damages to Miss Campbell," Amy stated.

"I-I." Alias stopped, his head hanging low. "I thought I had monitored him close enough to avoid something like this. My dear, I will give you the apology that will never come from my son."

"Your son is a monster," Evelyn said, her voice strong and loud.

"I am sorry for what he has done to you." His face and words held nothing but regret and sincerity. "Send me a proposal. I won't fight you." And then he was gone, the door shutting briskly behind him.

"Miss Agostino, I can't thank..." I raised my hand to halt her.

"You do not need to thank me. I am happy I could help you and I will continue to do so. Now, and any way possible in the future," I said with a slight smile, wiping a tear drop from her cheek. "You're back in school, right? Getting your degree?"

"Yes. You were right. He tried to ruin my life and it was up to me to fight him. My parents moved into the city to help me." Evelyn smiled at her father.

"Farrah." I extended my hand, gesturing for the next file I needed.

"Take as much time as you need to go over these numbers, Mr. Campbell. I am sure you will find it adequate enough, should you choose to join us as an accountant at *Energia* Holdings."

Her father's eyes went round in surprise, as he took in the very hefty number I'd offered for his salary. I'd done my research on her father, Jacob Campbell, who was an esteemed accountant in their small town in Idaho. No doubt moving here to support his daughter hurt their finances and I wanted to make amends. The money that came from Alias would just be a bonus, so they could live comfortably.

"Why?" her father asked, unshed tears filling his eyes.

"I need a solid accountant and you came considerably recommended. Now, as for you." I turned my attention to Evelyn. "I expect nothing but the highest mentions from your professors, and as long as that stays consistent, you will be allowed to intern with my law department."

Evelyn burst into tears, the loud sobs wracking her small frame. I squeezed her shoulder, silently instructing Farrah to take care of them, and slipped from the room. I waited until I was in my office—the door locked and secured—before I broke down. This world was cruel, fucked up at best; but to women, it had a propensity to be far more vicious.

Evelyn came from a low to middle income family, working her ass off to get a partial ride to NYU Law School. I refused to allow an insignificant prick like Thomas Marks to destroy something she'd worked so hard for. When I found the information that I needed on him, I learned she'd left school after the incident and moved back home, losing her scholarship. I worked it out with the school, ensuring that she would be back and the tuition would be paid in full by the Alias Marks Corporation.

I sat at my desk and took a deep breath, wiping the tears away with a tissue. I was many things but being overly emotional was my least favorite attribute. I could go toe-to-toe with the best in the ring or at a conference table, during negotiations. But even I had my moments of weakness, moments my heart couldn't take the travesties against the innocent. I wanted to be a resource for people like Evelyn.

"Let's see what we've got," I muttered to myself as I unlocked my computer screen. The software had continued its search and had already come up with a huge arsenal of information for me to scour through.

The building in question, the one that Dominic Moretti was looking to purchase, was more expensive than I thought. There were several dummy corporations registered under his name and they were funneling different funds from one to the other—out then back again—in an attempt to keep up the appearance of legitimacy. But my program was smarter than that. Most of his funding seemed to come from a man named John Hardwicke.

With two clicks of a button, the file my software created came up with a plethora of unanswered questions. I read the findings from top to bottom before switching to the *Moretti whore,* the blonde that Apollo had asked about. She was caught on several street-angled cameras and I'd already uploaded several different images of her.

"A ghost?" I asked myself, flopping back into my seat with disbelief. This software had a ninety-nine percent accuracy rating, and as of today, I had uncovered over ten thousand identities using it. It has only been unsuccessful in five ID's... now six. "Who the fuck are you?" I asked, staring down at my screen.

I tapped away for a few more minutes, pissed off that her identity remained ambiguous. I picked up my glass paperweight and chucked it across the room; the fine crystal burst into hundreds of shards on impact. I was *always* able to get answers. And Apollo's interest in this *ghost* only made me angrier.

I took a breath and grabbed my cell phone, prepared to tell Apollo to go fuck himself. He thought she could be helpful in uncovering Dom's alleged trafficking ring, but I had strong doubts. As shown on this video feed, she was clearly not that imperative to the deal, considering he toted her around like his own personal ragdoll.

Instead of dialing out, the phone started ringing in my hand, a picture of Apollo and me flashing across the screen. I couldn't help but take a deep breath and laugh at it. It was a still shot from a random trip to New Jersey I'd tagged along on with him and Lucky. They had business with a motorcycle club in the country and I played the tourist. I was smiling like an idiot in a cowboy hat, and he was scowling trying to take his off.

Ah! Memories!

Acknowledgments

There is so much to say and not nearly enough words for me to express my gratitude to everyone involved in this launch. This was a journey I started so many years ago, alone. And now… I am surrounded by incredible talent and amazing friends that pushed me forward. To each of you, I cannot express enough love. To each of you, you're fucking amazing.

Kitty Kat.
Finn O'Malley.
Sissy.
Mama.
Hubby.
Frankie Page.
Brittany Putzer.
My amazing readers.

You're all so incredible and I am so thankful for each of you.

Also by Dahlia Reign

<u>Agostino Crime Family Series</u>

Contracted to the Devil: Book One

Clever as the Devil: Book Two

Beautiful Deception: Book Three

And Twice as Twisted: Book Four

<u>La Reina de Escorpiones Duet</u>

Infinite Sorrow: Book One

Endless Deceit: Book Two

www.TheDahliaReign.com

ABOUT THE AUTHOR

Corporate sales by day, closet romance novelist at night—Dahlia Reign has always had an unparalleled taste for dreamy alpha-men. In her youth, Dahlia had journals by the stacks that she used to jot down her innermost thoughts; subsequently, turning them into romantic stories. Now, years later and with her picturesque alpha-man at her side, she's taken the literary world by storm. Her man, her pittie and an overactive imagination mixed with her bleeding heart—she's set off to tell the world her stories. Buck up and grab a bandaid, shit's about to get heavy.

www.TheDahliaReign.com

www.ingramcontent.com/pod-product-compliance
Lightning Source LLC
Chambersburg PA
CBHW070602300726

48975CB00006B/1691